Praise for

QUANTUM SURGE

"New military sf with both the physics and the history meticulously worked out in interesting ways"

--- David Drake
**Best-selling author of
Hammer's Slammers and the RCN Series**

~~*

"First book in a new series by Philip Nolen, an epic tour de force that will draw, hold, and envelope you in a tale of Earth's first star colony; the coming of age of a people."

--- Steve Alten,
**NY Times & International best-selling author of
The MEG series.**

A Word from
Philip Nolen

Quantum Zero is a short but exciting novel introducing the people and universe of the **Jankin Decatur Series**.

The novel you are now reading,

Quantum Surge

is the first full-length novel of the series. It incorporates many unique concepts in Sci-Fi. You will find it different from other novels you may have read but, you will see the concepts are strongly anchored in plausible physics.

This **second version** contains improvements in story flow, readability as well as expanded and added scenes.

My first and foremost objective in this series is to provide a good, exciting story that will not bore you with science. For those interested in greater detail, I direct you to the appendix at the end of the novel.

If you like the universe within which Decatur lives, it is the same cosmos in which the novels of my **Crucible Series** but, unlike the Crucible, these stories exist in our future timeframe.

You can read considerably more detail on the stories and their universe on my website at:

http://PhilipNolen.com

SCAN ME

Please feel free to drop me a note when you visit. Authors live for those who read their stories. …. And die when those who like their stories do not rate them.

Thank you and I hope you love the story as much as I do.

Philip Nolen

Edited by: Tim Schulte

Published by: Variance Author Services

First Printing: November 10, 2020

Second Version: April 2021

> Corrections, expansions, and text smoothing.

> Inclusion of excerpt from upcoming novel.

Printed in the United States of America

Fiction -- Science Fiction, Military Sci-Fi, Military Fiction

ISBN-13: **978 1935142065**

DEDICATION & ACKNOWLEDGMENTS

For *Donna*, my wife of more than fifty years now. The greatest and most beloved supporter of all my efforts to capture the stars of my dreams and the crazy idea of wanting to become an author of fiction.

―――――――――――――――――

I am indebted to my editor, **Tim Schulte** for his support and editing. Tim's wisdom and suggestions provided inspiration and encouragement as he unselfishly imparted his great knowledge of the publishing industry and the true composition of what an author should be.

The transition from an author of scientific publications and magazine articles to popular fiction is not an easy one. I want to thank **Steve Alten** -- author of the New York Times bestselling "MEG" and the motion picture of the same name. Steve helped me take the first steps in this evolution when he agreed to become my writing coach those many years ago. Steve is a hard taskmaster but well worth every minute.

THE CRUCIBLE SERIES
(Authored as Terrence E. Zavecz)

The Screams of the Hypes
- 2061 CE (2019 Novelette – Series Introduction)
*"An error in judgment has no place in the void between the stars.
At best, it will kill you. At worst ..."*
~~*

Crucible of a Species
– 2036 CE (2015)
"Colonel Drake led our first interstellar flight,
they launch only to land on a violent world occupied by strange
animals his people insist are dinosaurs."
~~*

Forge of a Species
– 2056 CE (2016)
"The Endeavor Expedition; a Colony and a Starport among the
dinosaurs. Men, women, and children face the challenge,
unexpected beauty, and pure terror of a savage world ruled by
Tyrannosaurus Rex."
~~*

NullBots
– 2058 CE (2018)
"A hurried flight, fleeing on a starship to new friends,
amazing science and dinosaurs."
~~*

THE JANKIN DECATUR SERIES

(Authored as Philip Nolen)

Quantum Zero

2170 CE (2020 Novelette – Series Introduction)
*A new ship, a new design, an old merchant captain
who finds himself in a new war.*

_   *~*~*

Quantum Surge

2170 CE (2021)
*Earth's fabled first colony gave sanctuary to Decatur as a merchant captain,
years later they called in their debt. A first in a new series of the 'Crucible
Universe'.*

~~*

Quantum Uncertainty

2180 CE (TBA)
*War lingers on. Hostile acts by both sides against the colony are rising.
Kraken citizens are split in their loyalty. Jankin Decatur takes a desperate
mission to Earth to appeal to the NAU Senate –
their final hope for survival.*

~~*

Philip Nolen

QUANTUM

SURGE

The Jankin Decatur Series

"I wish to have no connection with any ship that does not sail fast; for I intend to go in harm's way."

— Captain John Paul Jones, 1778 C.E

Contents

Slipdrive Starships, Spindizzy Fields

'First Steps to the Stars' Series – Homo Sapiens
History of the Kraken Revolution

It was the time of the fabled First Colonies. It was humanity's first faltering steps beyond the stars of our origin. It was the beginning of a period of great galactic expansion brought on by the discovery of the most minuscule particle in the universe.

It was an age that so tried the soul of humankind, as to have nearly brought Homo sapiens to an end.

Before that time, the abyss surrounding Earth appeared vast. A seemingly empty chasm separating us from the distant stars, hostile and impossible to cross. But then too, there was an even earlier day, hundreds of years before we achieved interstellar flight when our people were confronted by impossibly vast oceans. It was a time well before even the invention of electronics during which our ancestor's ships of commerce crossed the hopelessly wide and uncharted, deadly seas of Earth to visit distant ports in a great golden age of expansion. Driven solely by the wind, ancient ships of wood led the way; plying the vast, wave-capped waters of the planet, guided only by the stars and a crude optical instrument for measurements of relative position, a simple implement called a sextant.

Come the years just prior to 2032 CE, using Earth's ancient Gregorian Calendar, it became common knowledge that every element of the universe was composed of atoms which themselves were constructed of tiny particles called electrons, neutrons, and protons. However, in that year, Phillip Nolen revealed the existence of an even smaller sub-electron particle called the graviton; the fundamental building block of the universe. The discovery of the quantum gravity particle ushered in humanity's second golden age of expansion and our entry into galactic society.

As in the great release of energy in neutron or proton particles observed when an atom is riven, the split-electron releases tremendous energy and particles we now call 'Gravitons'.

Graviton particles are quantum packets of gravity which, like photons, conform to the wave-particle duality concept of quantum mechanics. Often likened to electrons that physically move opposite the flow of electricity, gravitons fly out from their source even as gravity pulls the mass inward.

Although gravity ripples through the fabric of the universe at the speed of light, free graviton particles pulse out at supralight velocities. The discovery of this strange minutia, this graviton particle, made possible the development of today's superluminal slipdrive engine as well as localized gravity control and many other applications we now take for granted.

The slipdrive field of a starship saturates the vessel, penetrating every atom and electron of every element within its field to excite sub-electron graviton particles to higher energy states, allowing them to link to the huge graviton waves of the universe. The greater the phase-aligned linkage to the wave, the faster the energized graviton particles which compose vessel, cargo, and crew travel.

Every slipdrive has two field components, a link-drive that binds the electron's high energy gravitons to the quantum gravity particles of the universe and a much more difficult to tune and maintain external repellant field, called the 'spindizzy', which is used to accelerate matter from the path ahead -- a critical component even in deep space where a mass plunging at many times lightspeed suddenly discovers that the universe ahead is not as empty as once thought and encountering even a pin-sized particle can be deadly.

The name 'spindizzy' derives from the external field's designed function of throwing anything out of the ship's path that is encountered; this is done on a molecule-by-molecule basis. This field will entrap and hold anything lying flush on the skin of the ship at slipdrive initiation. This is necessary since problems can occur when any free-floating or unsecured, elongated object is present at field initiation. These objects tend to remain as parasites in the field, draining energy as they spin because of the attempted ejection of one end of the object nearest the outer edge of the field, even as the opposite edge is drawn to the ship's surface.

Particles excited by a slipdrive field are immune to barriers postulated in classic Einsteinian relativity, allowing vessels and contents to race far above lightspeed-limiting changes of mass-expansion and momentum just as raw gravitons themselves inherently travel far in excess of lightspeed.

A slipdrive ship rides the crest of a long-wave in deep space between the stars or glides across its face to slow, shift to another wave, or simply tack or warp out to a different course. Every atom within a slipdrive field is linked to the wave whether the particle is part of a solid, gas, or biological molecule. This feature allows instant changes, or even reversals of direction at any speed to occur with no perceived change in motion or momentum and therefore no experience of matter-damaging acceleration. Slipdrive technology thus gave humanity the fabled reactionless drive since sub-particles of all electrons within the drive-field become a part of the graviton wave flow, rather than being physically pushed forward by crude reaction thrusts.

So, only a few hundred years beyond the age of wind and sail, human transportation once again finds itself subject to the whims of wind and wave but, rather than those of an ocean, today's vessels sail from star-to-star on great cosmic waves of gravitons.

You may wish to recall that all objects, down to the smallest particles in our universe, are a source of gravitic waves. Wave-strength varies in proportion to an object's mass, no matter how huge or ever so minute the body might be. As a result, travel within the planetary confines of a star system involves passing through a volume of space filled with a rough chop, as the surging waves of the star's gravity well collide with those originating in other sources of high mass, such as nearby planets.

However, the mass of a physical object is not the sole criterion for a great wave.

Gravitonic waves also depend upon an object's density. For example, a microscopic black hole radiates massive waves to distant regions of the cosmos. Expanses of dark-matter lay in the deadly gas-filled nurseries of stars called nebulae, emitting great waves capable of rolling across parsecs of space. 'Cosmic strings' create even deadlier threats emanating from these massively dense creases in the dimensional fabric of the universe. Never thicker than two sub-atomic protons, these strings extend across parsecs of space as a focused, directional current of huge, pulsed waves.

Today's starships hold many similarities to the ancient wind-powered navies of our ancestral world and we now voyage between the stars with the same relative ease our forefathers first ventured across their planet's oceans.

However, rapid cultural expansions always bring growth. Distance and growth instill self-reliance which in turn begets a love of freedom ... which brings us to our story.

MUTINY

2173 C.E.
Two Parsecs inbound to Earth
Kraken to NAU Run

A shudder slithered along the edge of consciousness as it ripped through the *S.S. Regilis.*

Crewed by sixty-seven spacers and four officers, only the engineer and executive officer (XO), Lieutenant Tyron Barry, felt the tremor as he surveyed the bridge from the Captain's chair. Only Tyron viewed this as a problem.

At twenty-one standard years, Tyron was the youngest executive officer in the North American Union's (NAU) merchant fleet. He'd been in the fleet since running away from home in Gloucester, located in the NAU state of Massachusetts, to join the merchant service four hard years ago, entering as an ordinary spacer landsman. Barry appeared even younger than his age, perhaps the result of light chestnut hair framing soft hazel-green eyes over a cleft chin. First impressions of a mild-mannered lad quickly faded before the onslaught of an aggressive persona and shoulders broad enough to carry the chip that never fell from them.

Denied the formal education he so desired by NAU caste rules, young spacer Tyron applied himself to master ship's duties. Which he did as effortlessly as he conquered the forbidden grounds of the ship's AI learning center; an accomplishment that would have resulted in a doctorate in Graviton Physics if an accredited Earth school had sanctioned the courses or even permitted them, given his class status. Tyron's heart and laser-like focus lay always upon life in the Slipdrive Service (SS) and he would not abide anyone or anything that might be a distraction from his tasks. Promotions came quickly as his reputation grew despite the jealousies of some. He'd been an officer and XO on the **Regilis** for less than a year when it happened.

"Lieutenant Aldiss," Tyron hailed engineering. "What the hell just happened? The whole ship just shook and don't tell me you didn't feel it."

The old engineer replied with disdain, "I felt it, just a hiccup or she tacked over to a new wavefront, nothing to be concerned about."

Resentment of the young XO's progress had always been a problem for the older engineer. Barry ignored the insolence, "Slipdrives don't hiccup. Check the event logs, run a deep scan, and find out why I'm no longer receiving engine status updates."

Tyron linked into the captain's push, "I have engineering ..."

Before he could finish, the bridge's airtight doors slammed open and a blue-suited spacer waltzed in, ignoring protocol as he casually sauntered to the center of the bridge, insolently waving a pulsar handgun, "Won't do any good Lieutenant. We control both the captain and engineering." He called over his shoulder to three other crewmen who entered brandishing heavy zerograv wrenches and a pipe.

"I know you can access the weapons locker. So, get up. Move nice and easy over this way and don't try anything stupid, there's more of us outside and …"

The third spacer to enter made the mistake of underestimating diminutive Navigations Specialist Simmons and learned just how serious an error it was when he exposed his back to her. In less than a heartbeat, she sent him flying across the bridge with a deadly two-handed chop to the neck using the edge of her station tablet.

The spacer's pipe scuttled forward, bouncing off the skull of the mutineer in front of him, leaving the fellow momentarily stunned. The diversion was all that Communications Officer Height needed. He kicked at the side of the mutineer's knee, ripped the wrench from his hands and, in one smooth motion, continued the long arc of its swing.

Shocked by the sudden violence, their leader brought his pistol around only to lean into the roundhouse blow of the officer's wrench. There was little force in the swing, but it was enough to throw the villain into the remaining two mutineers. Tyron dove in, ripping the pistol from the leader's grip then continued his roll across the deck while smoothly taking aim at the nearest charging man and fired.

The pistol's hypervelocity blast was enough to stun and deafen those inside the bridge. Its siliceram slug could not penetrate the hull but was extremely deadly against human flesh. The ceramic-alloy projectile struck the charging spacer and shattered, ripping a broad hole through both soft meat and bone, the mutineer folded in a spray of blood and the stink of bile.

Ears ringing, Tyron dropped the other two, giving them no chance to surrender. The fourth, cold-cocked by Simmons, lay on the deck alive but unmoving.

"Inside the bridge!" A shout rang in from the passageway startling those within, "Slide the pistol out and drop everything if ya wanna live."

Tyron rushed the door, scooped up Simmon's metal tablet with his left hand, whipped it around the bulkhead frame and down the passageway. He didn't hesitate but instead followed in a low dive across the threshold, blindly firing down the passageway in the opposite direction. A short length of pipe flashed past, glancing off his chest but the pistol's discharge had already done its worst to the spacer who'd been shouting out commands. Ignoring the pain in his chest, the XO continued his roll, twisting and firing blindly in the opposite direction.

Seeing the passageway clear of all threats, Simmons gave Tyron a dirty look as she offered her hand, "You know you'd be dead if they'd been properly armed."

Tyron didn't immediately answer but lay back against the bulkhead trying to push back the dizziness that always came after the red waves of pure anger had consumed him. He didn't have time for this self-pity, something had to be done and quickly, "I knew they were bluffing otherwise they would have charged in as soon as the commotion started. But they were right about one thing, I can open the weapons locker. Come on, we need to move quickly."

As Tyron approached the locker a pencil width of barely visible light scanned his face, reading the patterned interior of his eyes as it fluorescence-sampled his DNA to confirm he had access to its contents. Locking molecules dissolved their bonds and the cabinet opened in a quick, fluid motion.

His hand automatically reached for the heavy munitions code but pulled back after a moment's consideration and shifted to the hand-pulsars, "Here, take one. Check your clip and confirm you have ship-rated riot load, I don't want to see anyone blowing out a bulkhead, particularly if it's an external compartment."

"Simmons, with me to engineering. Height, you take the others but send someone to help the captain. Hafler, stay on the bridge. Secure it behind us and do not respond to any hale but mine. Lockout engineering's off-bridge controls and do it first."

The spartan interior of **Regilis** contained none of the niceties of a passenger vessel. Bare pipes lined overheads above hard ceramasteel decks. Life-sustainable quarters composed less than a fifth of the ship with the remainder held for cargo in vacuum stowage or stasis. Most passageways sported dead decks that must be crossed on foot except for the central glideway spine traversing the entire length of the ship.

The long strip glideway started slowly, matching their pace as they approached then immediately sped up, carrying them aft towards engineering, giving Tyron time to think and cope with his body's reaction to the abrupt violence, which was only now just setting in. He noticed his gun-hand shaking and quickly pulled it to his chest. After all, it wouldn't be proper to let Simmons see his weakness.

"It's my hope they haven't sealed off engineering. If so, we're in deep trouble. Remember we don't know who is taking part in this mutiny so be on your toes. Also, we don't know where he got that pistol. So, let's hope they have no real firepower."

Storage compartment airlocks flitted by then slowed as Tyron edged to the side of the glideway. They entered engineering's territory and the track slowed further to let them exit onto a composite deck, which was as tough as ceramasteel but as soft as a rubber mat. It was a floor that could take a dropped spanner or equipment load without damage, and would not spark, for the air down here was high in oxygen. Engineering lay ahead, marked by broad air-tight safety doors with a smaller, human-sized airlock at its bottom center. Tyron and Simmons approached the entrance but didn't key in. The XO's eyes defocused as he scanned circuitry status and atmospherics on the other side. Everything seemed normal. He began to wonder if charging down here was the right decision.

Tyron whispered without turning, "Appears normal inside. No sign of forced entry. I'm gonna key in."

"Hold on, Sir." Simmons interrupted, "Anyone in there must know something isn't right and are wondering why they've lost contact with the others. I bet they're ready and waiting for you to come charging in."

"Ship says there's no one in the control center. We're wasting time."

Tyron activated the airlock. It cycled, immediately opening the inner door since passageway atmospherics matched those inside the room. He sided against the bulkhead, cautiously moving until he could stick his head around the corner. Two blue-suited spacers lay unmoving in a still-expanding pool of blood. One so chewed up; she obviously wouldn't be getting up.

He charged in, swerving behind a control console for cover. Two doors led from the room. One he knew was an entry to the capsule of the slipdrive itself and the other was engineering's bridge, a backup for the primary ship's bridge. Tyron could hear voices inside. He was about to call out when a big spacer emerged, saw the weapons they carried, and took a half-step back. A smile crossed the big spacer's face as he slowly raised his hands and, worked his way to the side a bit, and said, "What's with the pistol, Lieutenant? I ain't done nothin' wrong?"

"I see two bodies that say otherwise."

A look of resignation came across the spacer's face, "Look, you can join us. Bucker's paying a split, enough to retire on …."

A pipe section launched out of the doorframe behind the spacer like a thrown spear. It wasn't a well-controlled toss but enough to catch Tyron's arm and hand. The spacer leaped for the pistol. A second pipe section flew past towards Simmons, missed, and went on to bounce and clang noisily against the bulkhead, its flight covered the charge of two blue-suits. Simmons fired blindly. One round struck the wall, shattering into pieces that ricocheted deep into a mutineer's arm. The big mutineer was on Simmons in an instant, brought up his fist, and launched a full jab towards her. Another blast rocked the room and the spacer collapsed on top of the smaller officer.

Tyron reached down and pulled the body off his navigator, "He's dead; only one survivor, the one that caught the ricochet. Unfortunately, it's nothing more serious than a few hours in an autodoc."

They found the engineers in the drive capsule, their arms bound with wire and skulls bashed in, "Guess they couldn't get the entry code from Chief Sandle. Pity, she was a good spacer"

A shout rang out from the passageway behind us, "We know you're in there. Come out or we're gonna gas ya."

Tyron replied, his voice cold as ice, "I'd know your voice anywhere, Ensign Tooley. Don't get over-anxious Ensign, Simmons and I are coming out."

"Situation, Mr. Tooley?"

"We have control, I left three of the crew with Midshipman Jeffreys on the bridge. The Captain's dead."

Tyron visibly stiffened; the captain had been both a mentor and a friend, one of the few in life to ever treat him like family.

Ensign Tooley seemed not to notice as he continued, "Eight more of these scumbags managed to blockade themselves inside a long-range shuttle. They want the release code with a promise to cause no more problems. My guess is they want to get to a European Union State and claim asylum."

Tyron's head was spinning a bit from the physical and emotional blows.

Let them go? They lost, now they just want to live. If we force entry, there will be more lives lost.

No, it doesn't stop here. Not yet.

"We have a dead captain and shipmates because of these hijackers. No, tell them no compromise." Simmon's barked.

But he had made his decision, "Go back, negotiate. Get them to surrender. Stall for at least fifteen minutes. If you can't convince them then release the code."

Tooley cut in, "What? I'm not giving …"

Tyrone knew what he had to do. He didn't like it or the problems it would bring afterward but now was not the time for hesitation, "Easy Tooley. Trust me, it's on my head." Tyron's glare drilled into the ensign's soul, "You need to follow orders. Remember, I need fifteen minutes!"

"Simmons, stay with me."

Simmons followed down the glideway to bay B17, directly below the shuttle dock. Lt. Barry charged in and ripped open the hard-vacuum maintenance suit locker, "Suit up."

They vac-suited in a rush, bypassing most of the safety checks in their haste, "Cycle the airlock, I'll be right back. For God's sake, Simmons, use the time to double-check your suit's seals."

Going to the other side of the bay, he returned pulling a wheeled cart, in it was an ancient portable power generator.

Simmons foolishly chuckled, "You gonna electrocute them, Lieutenant?"

"Shut up and help me align this with the bulkhead port."

Pushing the cart across the chamber and into the outer airlock, Tyron punched the button activating the sublimation pump. It chugged away converting the chamber's air into a recoverable compact solid, a passage tube extruded far enough out for them to exit beyond the spindizzy zone of the ship's slipdrive field. Passing outwards, the generator suddenly became weightless, but its mass carried them forward with the momentum of their initial push. Any slip and this weightless mass of dense metal could crush them against a bulkhead or easily sever a limb. Face drawn dark and serious, Tyrone showed no elation as they muscled the generator around and secured its magnetic clamps to the outer skin of the mutineer's shuttle.

Billions of stars from the surrounding firmament jigged their crazy dance, seen by human eyes when at supraluminal velocities, Tyron put his helmet in contact with the navigator's, "Hustle now, but no transmissions under any circumstances. We don't want them to know we're out here, they might catch on."

"Well, that's a first. You just attempted to make a joke. Didn't you Lieutenant?"

"Not now, Simmons, we need to get back inside immediately. I want to be deep in our ship's core in a minute and we have a long way to go to get there."

The airlock went through its slow thirty-second cycle. Once closed, Simmons began removing her suit but Tyron grabbed her arm and flung her inside as the inner hatch opened. He picked up a small valise as they crossed the room and called over the intercom, "Ensign Tooley, a sitrep if you please."

"Just gave them the release code but let me tell you I didn't like …"

"Shut up and listen. Hard seal the door as you exit the bridge. Instruct all crew to make for the core tunnel. I want everyone inside yesterday and you don't have time to ask why."

Inside the ship's core tunnel, he slapped the valise on the edge of the glideway railing and flipped open its lid. His eyes defocused a moment as he linked into ship's sensors, "Little further, little further. They just initiated the drive startup sequence. Now a bit more and …."

Simmon's eyes went wide when she saw the controller link to the power generator they'd strapped to the shuttle. The XO was going through the checklist as calmly as if he were running a simulation. His coldness left her shaking, "No sir, don't. We're too close."

"Pipe down. In a moment they will have an active slipdrive field established on their shuttle and they'll be off. They won't get far but should be distant enough when I fire up the wavedrive field of that old power generator. Now, grab onto something. There, it's done!"

Already distant from the merchant ship, a crude and rather dirty generator's wavedrive field bloomed on the shuttle. In the first millionth of a second, its gravitic field formed, raising every electron within its tuned ether to a higher energy level. Electron shells within every atom of the attached vehicle, cargo, and passengers were energized, releasing gravitons formed from ejected waves of gravitic energy much like the splitting of atoms releasing radiation in the crude atomic weapons of the previous century. However, this was a controlled release of considerably more energy than any atomic weapon; energy enough to capture and link their bound electron gravitons to the gravitic radiation of the cosmos.

However, the shuttle was already accelerating and approaching lightspeed with every sub-electron particle inside every atomic nucleus in the boat spinning in a highly energized state. The shuttle's drive had just stabilized when the coil inside the old wavedrive power generator came to life. The generator's field reached out and encountered the shuttle's free-ranging sub-electron particles.

It didn't care that the shuttle's electrons were already in higher energy shells as it pumped even more energy into them until they burst the bonds of every atom's electron particle, ripping out raw protons, neutrons, and gamma rays from every bit of matter previously constrained in the mass of the shuttle and its contents.

Including the mutineers.

The reaction flash-converted all it encountered from energized solid matter into pure energy expanding for a radius of one and a half light-seconds. Its high energy wave rolled outward, striking **Regilis**, scorching all it touched, instantly welding the casement ceramasteel doors of the cargo lockers that were facing the shuttle. as the resulting blow picked up the two-million-ton vessel like a leaf in a tornado.

The *Regilis* survived, but just barely.

RETURN TO BASE

"*SS Regilis*, NAU 8783 under the command of acting Captain Tyron Barry, requesting permission to dock and unload cargo in zero-grav facilities per communication 'i3490'. Request medical transport and a security detail to manage survivors of attempted mutiny."

"*Regilis*, we are waiting and ready. Enter using corridor Aries Alpha seven-zero-one."

The shocked communications officer forgot herself, "They've assigned us to an Aries sector inbound corridor, Sir. That's a thirty-minute delay using in-system transit speeds."

Tyrone was about to admonish the ensign for the unnecessary comment when an N-Crypt109 priority-one encoded personal message alert interrupted. He automatically consented to a cortical ID scan to obtain access to the secure missive. It didn't identify the sender and went so far as to present an obviously invalid traceback sequence. Whoever sent the coded message had high-tech support, but Tyron knew from the first few words of the voice-only missive it was from Tom Harrington, CFO of the company and a friend.

"You did it again. Only this time, you really screwed the pooch, so listen. I'm sure you took note of the inbound route assigned for your approach. You have less than fifteen minutes to grab what you need and shuttle out of the ship."

"Don't bother with personal information or credit links, you need to disappear."

"I'm serious. Tyron must be dead and gone as soon as possible."

"Your ship's course swings out past a major asteroid before down-cresting back into Earth's orbit. You'll be passing the rock soon after your shuttle launches, you've been there before so you'll recognize it. Forget about the shuttle, too easily traced and it has too short of a travel range."

"There's a high-speed courier on the asteroid. The courier will take you wherever you want. Tell no one your destination, and for God's sake don't tell me. In fact, don't even attempt to contact me again. You are dead and gone either way."

"One of the mutineers you put down was the son of Senator Lorry McClain. She's not about to listen to reason and has already issued a contract for your head and do not even think of fighting this in the courts. A Senate security detail's already waiting, you won't even make it to the dock. You need to disappear."

"Leave now. Goodbye and good luck."

The message vanished from his display, storage, and all logs. He checked, there wasn't even a record of its arrival. Inner turmoil churned inside Tyron.

The decisions were mine to make as acting captain. I should be here to defend my decisions, protect my crew. What do I care for myself? Once again, I've lost. Now my existence endangers my closest friend and my captain, a man who was more a father to me than my own, is now dead. All is lost.

But, if I stay, they win. This was not a spontaneous mutiny but one orchestrated elsewhere. More will follow and to give up now is just suicide, the coward's way out.

Tyron looked over his people on the bridge one last time before addressing them, "Mr. Height, take the con. I'll be in my quarters and am not to be disturbed."

However, the young officer didn't go to his quarters. Instead, he went directly to the shuttle and was surprised to find it prepped for launch. There wasn't anything in his quarters that was worth risking the possibility of picking up a tracer and if a friend could contact him and have a shuttle prepped remotely then an enemy, bold enough to pluck him directly off an incoming freighter, might also be covering all their bases.

The shuttle was clean except for a cheap spacer's bag containing a nondescript set of blue BDUs. He changed as his personal AI slipped the craft out of the dock. Beneath the garment lay a secure disposal bag for his merchant officer's dress and papers. The hastily stuffed bag ejected from the shuttle, releasing chemical reagents that dissolved the contents before directing the container aft of the shuttle. With a silent 'pop', it ejected the remnants and the cold vacuum of space instantly ablated the liquid to a rapidly dispersing cloud of rarified gas.

Ship and shuttle silently drifted apart then its slipdrive came to life and the little craft pushed onward.

Spacer habits die hard or people die too soon. He went through a final review of shuttle status then clawed his way into a hard-vacuum suit. A random realization crossed his mind, he'd finally made captain. Like everything else in his life, even that was now ripped from him along with the only people he'd allowed to be called 'friend'. No longer was he 'Captain'. Captain Tyrone Barry was dead, Captain Tyrone Barry was now gone.

A hunk of rock, visible only by the faint glimmer of a distant star reflected on its grey surface, lay ahead. It grew as he watched.

Obviously, this was his destination. Barely large enough to have a measurable gravitational field, the dust and debris-covered rock didn't look familiar. The shuttle swung around to the other side and, in the near horizon ahead, there appeared a smooth and vaguely familiar crater with smooth, glassy walls. Nestled at the bottom of the crater was a small, sleek ship, shaped rather like a compressed egg colored flat black.

Common dogma of past generations said it was not possible to cloak the presence of a vessel in space because a ship's heat signature is always present for anything that expends energy, even if it's only for support life.

The advent of the wavedrive, and the more advanced slipdrive that soon followed, put this belief to bed since the force field of the drive was pure energy itself and quite capable of recycling thermal energy as a very minor component to the energization of the slipdrive field.

Tyron knew there would be no thermal signature escaping this tight little ship and the simple sophistication of its skin texture promised more high-tech systems inside marking it to be a vessel built for speed and stealth.

He'd received a rare and very, very expensive parting-gift from Tom.

As he boarded the ship, he hoped his friend would not pay too dearly for his kindness.

Kraken Approach

2178 C.E.
Approach B28.2.33
Astral Service Lagrange-2 Port
Colony World Kraken

Kraken and its heavy-metal moon form a natural gravitic lens directing the chaotic waves of their stellar-system into a small channel where the bedlam of universe, planet, and satellite cancel. Here lies a region of calm gravitational flow and an interstellar military port known as Lagrange-2 or more simply 'L2', the colony's largest harbor. A major military and commercial port as well as a ship-building center housing over twenty-three thousand workers and their families.

On this day, all eyes within the port focused on the arrival of the commercial containership limping into port. Some expressed amazement, wondering under what laws of physics it managed to link, much less navigate home through the great gravitic chaos of the surrounding universe.

Slipdrive Ships are known for beautiful, gracefully flowing lines, loveliness derived not from artistic expression but demanded by the need to minimize link-wave turbulence and simplify field uniformity calculations during flight.

Those in the port watched the apparition-like ship limp into the close confines of the port. It risked spreading its repellant-field far ahead in a bid to stabilize the craft and reach dock without discredit. The resulting iridescence flared beautifully to the casual observer but what a pitiful show their effort made to experienced spacer's eyes.

The ship's outer shell had been savaged. A three-deck section of her rim gone with a great tear rending it so badly that even now it vented a faint stream of air, its particles fluorescing within its spindizzy field as they swirled about a jagged framing girder, ripped out and projecting from her wound into raw vacuum like a defiant, uplifted finger.

The gravitic forces of the universe transformed the normally soft-blue iridescence of a healthy slipdrive field into a churning maelstrom of colors, sparkling as they swirled about the wound, draining life-giving atmosphere and power into the interstellar vacuum. Many a professional eye wondered what magic enabled the pitiful, ravaged ship to approach the docks and maneuver, safely avoiding the crowded outer docks and automated ion cannons designed to defend against meteor threat to the installation.

An archaic Identification Friend or Foe (IFF), pulse burst out from the damaged vessel on an even more ancient, sliding frequency photon-laser packet. The station's automatics didn't blink an electron but accepted the archaic ID and shunted the freighter to an off-station dock, safely distant from the busy port traffic. The ship pulled in with a rugged smoothness, nestling into the docking bay, and no sooner had it settled in than a captain's gig emerged, taking a direct path to commercial fleet offices as Astral Service arrival protocol demanded.

Captain Jankin Decatur sat in the outer lounge of the Astral Service Fleet Offices, vainly attempting to suppress tensions brought on by the attack on his ship and bringing an injured vessel to dock at homeport. A welcome cup of strong, black coffee ready at one hand and a draft of highland single malt scotch at the other, neat of course, as he waited for the Chief Operating Officer's call. A summons that might not arrive for hours. Decatur spent these precious free moments reviewing ship's logs and refamiliarizing himself with the critical segments of documentation highlighted by his AI logistician. Anything to keep his mind occupied and push-back the torrent of self-recrimination for those who lost their lives. They were his responsibility, he'd failed them, just as he'd failed so many others in life. A fitting end for a man who, try as hard as he could, seemed to still fail at every task given him, for once again people, his own crewmates, had lost their freedom and some had even lost their lives all because of his incompetence.

The call came early, directly into his HiveTab, a device he'd grown to love and hate since his arrival on Kraken when it was first installed as a small patch behind his ear, linking him instantly to the resources of Kraken society, the service, and his ship. A device that incessantly threatened the user's peace of mind even as it brought social solidarity.

Personal isolation was a concept forever relegated to the history books.

A meeting notice flipped onto his calendar, tagged with an unheard of seventeen-minute window during which the COO was available. He'd received a priority slot and this reeked of bad news. In Seventeen minutes, he would most likely see a court subpoena leading to an end to his career. This was his life, the only he'd ever known. As captain, Decatur was responsible for ship, crew, and cargo. His cargo was mostly gone or destroyed, along with three-quarters of his crew. He'd nearly lost the entire ship.

His soul withered under the knowledge that most of his crewed spacers, those now on the NAU ship and still alive, had been forced into signing papers that would forevermore seal their fate as spacers bound to the NAU. Those more stubborn and able to resist the brutal coercion of an NAU boarding party would be shipped to detention facilities retaining little hope of ever returning.

To make matters worse, his ship was damaged when he managed to break the NAU tractor beam and blow the physical tie-downs. Miraculously, he avoided the torpedoes they'd let fly.

Avoided most of them, he thought with a shudder, *one more strike and I would not be here to enjoy what comes next.*

Jankin Decatur went directly to the nearest lift and took it up a hundred and fifty-seven floors to the Astral Administrative Offices, gave one last longing look at the beauty of the blue-green world they orbited, and the elusive freedom promised by Kraken. All gone.

He knew all hope was lost the moment he entered the COO's darkened suite.

Jack Bastian launched a quick but thankfully brief glare as he entered. Deep annoyance bordering on disgust shrouded the old man's scarred face. Decatur knew where he got the scars, everyone did. The early days of interstellar flight were not the cushy jaunts of today and the 'Miner's Uprising of 2122' had seen the fires of hell released into the cold vacuum of space. Decatur hesitated, ready to receive Bastian's barrage but instead was greeted by a nondescript handwave motioning him to an ornately carved, hard-wood chair set before the desk. The man obviously couldn't bear to gaze at the abomination standing before him. Decatur couldn't see the documents and recordings Bastian studied but knew they wouldn't be good. Bastian mumbled to himself as he reviewed the data, slowly shaking his head as he moved from item to item while letting fly sporadic low growling sounds without lifting eyes from the reports, until the corporate officer exploded into a sharp query, "Captain Decatur, do you realize how much we've lost in just this past quarter?"

"No, don't answer. You don't know. Few do."

"Nearly five-trillion thalers worth of assets. Multiply that by six to get cargo value," he ended with a flip of his hand, his eyes never leaving the desk.

"Insurance still pays for cargo and ships but we are losing ground rapidly and it's not from rising insurance costs, we can pass those on to our customers. We cannot, however, replace experienced spacers."

"Your log here says they took most of your crew and ..."

Decatur refused to let him continue, "Sir, I had little choice ..."

Cold grey eyes of the COO lifted, drilling directly into his for the first time, "Captain Decatur, I'm a busy man. You will hear me out. No more interruptions unless I request a reply."

"Sez here, you were boarded by marines yet, somehow managed to recover your command and survive to make it back to sit here before me." Suddenly shuffling past a few folders, he continued, "I understand they took most of your crew leaving you to return with .... with barely a third of your people ... in a ship horribly disfigured."

"I read your log so don't waste my time. Tell me what isn't in this report, what in God's Universe were you thinking?"

Decatur took a moment to calm himself even as he wondered why the old man was playing him. Still, he owed it to his people to deliver the story properly, placing blame where it was due.

"We were on an approach vector to Earth docking orbit, having just dropped below supralight for entry. There was an exceptional level of gravitic wave chop along the inbound course I'd taken. That was intentional. I selected that vector with a hope the sector would be empty of any military pickets on-station. Even mil-spec ships don't enjoy slow patrol in a region of high gravitic chop."

"Less than an hour into final-phase entry, we received a query ping from a fleet destroyer. I was relieved to discover it was an NAU registry, the *Franklin*, rather than Chinese, but I was immediately surprised to see our identification reply invoking a command to drop down to relative-stationary and await boarding."

"They refused to give a reason for the order. I had no choice but to match vector and speed."

"They boarded armed. Didn't even go through the farce of an inspection. Their marines produced enlistment forms, already personalized for each of my crew, and began shuffling my people off, under armed guard, onto their destroyer."

"A scuffle on board the destroyer broke out as our men were passing a second party that I now suspect was a prize crew heading for my ship. Harsh words were exchanged and blows quickly followed. In the confusion, six of my people managed to make it back on board, sealing the airlock behind them."

"At that point, I realized the NAU captain intended to take more than a few spacers, he saw my entire vessel as a prize."

"Determination rested heavily in my crew's eyes; they weren't about to be impressed into an NAU enlistment. I used the distraction to jump the marine's lieutenant before most of them could bring weapons to bear."

"The NAU marines that remained onboard fought hard, they weren't about to surrender."

"I regret to say, no NAU survivors remain on my command."

"I used a remote to blow the hard-lines holding our ship, a lucky swell jostled us, and the resulting collision shut down their tractor. They'd already offloaded most of our cargo so when I hit the drive, she quickly went into supralight, being lite-weighted and agile although a bit imbalanced at this point from the cargo transfer."

Bastian growled, "A 'lucky swell', huh?"

Decatur knew he was committed to course, "Aye, sir. It was pure luck."

"I regret to report that I struck and damaged their targeting and navigational sensor array during the initial maneuver. Still, they managed the release of a smart-torp. Must have been pure reaction on their part since it impacted before its AI was able to boot, arm, and direct the missile to a vulnerable point. Still, our damage was … well, you can see the result."

"They would have run us down in short order had we not intentionally disabled their communications and remote navigation centers. Physically, the trip back was a bit challenging. We managed only because I have a good crew."

Decatur's eyes went to Bastian to see if the COO was listening and slammed full force into the old man's intense, focused stare. The old man's lips moved, releasing a barely heard grumble that might have been, "…criminal act of war."

The captain wasn't about to accept the subject of such an incrimination. He knew his career was over but there were others to consider. His words were strong as he rose to attention, clearly ringing out to insure the office AI would record them as he braced himself against the waves of anger pounding through his body, "Sir, I want to commend the actions of my crew, both those waiting in my ship and those who couldn't make it back but gave up their freedom and some gave their lives, just to give us a chance. The damage to my ship and the loss of my crew are my responsibility and mine alone."

Unexpectedly, the COO didn't say a word, simply stared at the captain for a few moments. Returning attention to his desktop, his lips pursed into a half-snarl as his hand directed the captain to sit. He ignored Decatur as he shuffled through folders, a damning scowl riveted on Bastian's face as he grumbled into the desk-top., "Ah-Hummph."

Beyond the low growl, Bastian didn't reply much less turn his head to address Decatur. After digging through his folders some more, the words emerged cold, hard, and as sharp as a saber's edge directed at the still standing captain, "Sit, sit! Cool down young man and listen."

"Your people will be on half-pay until repairs are completed. You need not concern yourself on breaking the news to them."

"Captain Decatur, you are ordered to Pallentau City, there's a reception at the Capitol Grounds Museum. You don't have much time, pick up a change of uniform on the way, you'll need formal dress. Be there by nine, local time this evening."

"Detailed instructions are now in your Assignment Portfolio. They won't open until you're on the down leg of the trip. You'll need to agree to and sign the confidentiality wrapper before accessing the details. Ensure you read it thoroughly, young man, and understand what you are signing."

"You are dismissed. Hurry and you may just make the shuttle."

Old man Bastian's concentration returned to his desktop before the captain hastily left the office. Decatur was halfway down the corridor before he realized, *Well I'll be …. the old coot dismissed me as 'Captain Decatur'. This might not be so bad after all.*

A NEW SHIP

"*Always loved the mountains,*" the words of Captain Jankin Decatur emerged quietly, almost reverently, fearing they might break the mood. Boxdown wood fragrances drifted on the cooling breeze, carried up from ancient light-blue and the newer, green-leafed lowland forests transplanted by the original colonists. Distant woodlands moved, alive with flocks of colorful flyers leaping from limb to vine, mingling their songs with a menagerie of other forms of crooning wildlife that were scurrying across the plains below. Flocks lifted high into the air, so many feathered and leather-winged creatures flying in unison they darkened whole portions of the sky, so even the bright rays of the nearby blue-white star fell to shadow.

Many called Kraken a 'garden world', it was lush and pristine with an ecology that closely paralleled Earth, but one in which the age of saurian dominance was never interrupted. Kraken's highly evolved 'dinosaurs' never allowed the planet's mammal equivalents to rise to dominance nor had the planet undergone the ravages that passed over Earth during eons of deadly glacial scouring.

Decatur felt strangely at ease alongside the tall, grey-suited man standing silently next to him. He was a host easy to talk with, "The air is clear and crisp. Every shift in the breeze seems to bring a new scent. It's a joy to be able to see across the lowlands all the way to the green sea. This is a treat for someone who spends most of his life inside a plastisteel shell."

"Sounds like my captain needs a vacation." Commissioner Alexander Hollen said as he handed an ornate crystal flute, half-filled with red Flavian Wine, to the captain. "Unfortunately, that's not why you are here. My goal is quite the opposite."

Below, in the distant valley, a platoon of Fleet Rangers jogged up a steep hill in cadence at an easy pace he would have termed a slow run, as their voices echoed in ancient song across the valley.

> *Oh, the Zerkeys get no tail in Jasperango,*
> *Oh, the Zerkeys get no tail in Jasperango,*
> *Oh, the Zerkeys get no tail,*
> *They practice on the Zails,*
> *Oh, the Zerkeys get no tail in Jasperango.*

> *Oh, we won't go back to Zubic anymore,*
> *Oh, we won't go back to Zubic anymore,*
> *Oh, we won't go back to Zubic*
> *Where they mix our hooch with tubric,*
> *Oh, we won't go back to Zubic anymore.*

Decatur had heard it before. He wondered about its origins but suspected they lay somewhere deep in Jasper colonial history. Jasper, the home of a small monkey-like animal called a Zerkey and the pig-like rodent pests called Zails. Zubic, of course, referred to a port of questionable repute he'd been to many times but what the words implied was still a bit of a mystery to the young captain.

The low, melodious voice interrupted his reverie, "Decatur, Bastian directed you here for a reason."

"By the way, do they still call him 'Stone' Bastian as they did when I was commanding a ship? Ah, your face tells all."

"Anyway, you've had a trying time of it, but I intend to make all the suffering worth your while. We are offering you a military commission. Please, wait before you say anything and no, it's not an NAU Colonial Services appointment. Great change is on our horizon. You'll be leaving the Commercial Service and the peaceable life of a merchant vessel captain."

Decatur nearly choked on his wine.

"Ah, I thought that would bring a chuckle. Here. Use my napkin."

"You're aware of the pressures we've had to endure since war broke out between China and our NAU motherland? Legally, hostilities shouldn't involve Kraken, combatant actions are restricted by treaty to Sol system colonies where ...."

"I'm a ship's captain, I know these things." Decatur wasn't sure where this was going but he had no intention of accepting another Earth run of any form even if it was the only thing that would put him back in the command chair.

"I know all about merchant ships waylaid not only by vessels from the China Trans-Asia Coalition or CTAC but now even our own NAU. They grow bolder by the day to the point that now they strike here in Kraken's own stellar system. Both sides must be running low on qualified spacers, war is expensive. Perhaps you aren't aware of just how bad it's gotten, let me give you a little firsthand knowledge. Something I'm sure you've never heard."

"The NAU assumes any spacer, who can't prove they are born and bred a Kraken citizen must be an NAU citizen and they are inducted into their fleet. Recently, even this has changed. They are now ignoring Kraken citizenship tokens and entire crews are taken openly."

"The Chinese are even worse. They take the crew and 'space' all the officers. I imagine life on one of their death-traps is a fate worse than death, so I don't know who's better off. No, you needn't tell me and I'm not about to take any runs Earthward."

Alexander smiled in the ensuing silence, took in the bouquet of his wine, and followed with a measured sip that mixed liquid and air. As usual, the wine was excellent. Their region was famous for its fine, glowing wines, celebrated enough to make it a profitable export. A product in demand even in the distant ports of Earth. A second thoughtful sip provided a good excuse to stand back and ponder what might be the torch points for this captain. In truth, he knew the captain's sensitivities and the trick was to push him to the edge without pissing him off. But how?

He touched Decatur's elbow, skillfully directing him over to a corner away from curious eyes and ears, then whispered, "Captain Decatur, if your fears lie in the troubles involving a Mr. Tyron Barry, you need not worry. We've known all about your 'other' life from the day your sorry, emaciated body appeared on our bridge."

Captain Jankin Decatur stumbled a half step back, firing a glare towards Alexander that would have melted plastisteel. The commissioner simply smiled, undaunted by the raw threat in his eyes.

"Nothing to say? Do you honestly believe we would have taken you on as an officer and then captain without researching your background? I doubt it was a coincidence that you chose to rename yourself after your great-great-grandfather Stephen Decatur, early American patriot and naval sea captain."

"I must admit your credentials were quite nicely forged."

Jankin stiffened even more, unconsciously pulling away from the commissioner, a man he thought he knew. Alexander simply smiled and waited while taking another sip before continuing, "Oh, don't look so surprised. Didn't you ever wonder why you never received an invitation to bid on a direct Kraken–Earth run? Good thing too since the one time that you decided to chance a run back to the homeland nearly put your neck into a noose."

"Decatur come down a few notches and listen to me. First, you need to realize I'm on your side."

"Forget the past, problems enough lay ahead."

"Your information on the order of things is correct but incomplete. Uh, I must remind you of the signed confidentiality agreement, but I also want your personal word that what I'm about to tell you stays here. You don't repeat it to anyone no matter what else you may hear or see this evening. Agreed?"

Jankin flung a dark, questioning look at his sponsor, came to a characteristically quick decision conveyed by a small, silent nod. He wasn't happy about the direction this was taking and wondered just what he might be getting himself into.

Alexander continued, "Good."

"You already know a bit of the picture, let me open it to a panorama. Your recent misfortune isn't the first of such incidents. This long off-planet war has taken a toll on everyone. Besides the financial burden Earth is experiencing, now both sides have a shortage of experienced spacers. As you stated, even the NAU has gone from shanghaiing spacers to the confiscation of our ships along with cargo and crew."

"Did you know, it's an ancient practice once called 'impressment'."

"They induct those spacers who sign an NAU oath of allegiance into service with an 'as needed' enlistment term that really means, they will never get out. At least they get paid, even if the wages are poor."

"What you don't know is those who do not sign on, end up working on an NAU warbird but without pay or they find themselves in a penal colony on the far side of Earth's moon. No charges. No trial. No calls home."

"They simply disappear."

"So much for the Constitution and the laws that once made the NAU great."

Jankin Decatur knew the law. He also had direct experience with the NAU legal system's bias. Some citizens apparently were more equal than others. It wasn't right and shouldn't exist, "I thought the extremity of my encounter was an exception. They've gone too far. We have rights. We're NAU citizens in a self-governing colony with …"

Alexander waved his hand to cut short the captain's rant.

"That too is changing. We've learned the NAU is preparing to enact heavy tariffs on the goods that Kraken exports both to Earth or to any other colony. On top of that, they are raising our taxes and trade licenses. Our representatives in Washington claim the increase is there to defray the expense of defending Kraken and our merchant fleet from CTAC aggression. A strange excuse when you consider our shipping suffers more from NAU inspections and crew impressment than Chinese aggression."

"Kraken is working on a response through back channels in the government. We filed a formal complaint to the senate citing our grievances, demanding they rescind the tax and cease-and-desist harassment of our shipping."

"This is a futile but politically necessary action on our part. We simply do not have a strong enough presence in government."

"They will, of course, ignore our petitions."

Hollen paused to take another sip of wine as he examined his quarry for reaction.

"We realize there is an ongoing war between CTAC China and the NAU. All of us follow it with growing concern and our sympathies lie, of course, with our mother country. Until recently, the belligerents restricted most of the action to off-world conflicts surrounding the nearer planets of the solar system without any serious clashes occurring on Earth itself. Raids on lunar colonies or a base on Mars are far off from daily life to the average citizen. And when they do occur, their attacks focus on known, fixed points such as a military base or an orbiting satellite."

"Unfortunately, the conflict escalates and both sides now target our merchant fleets. So far, we believe it's not a deliberate, planned campaign against us. We aren't that important. They are simply taking needed resources and there are times when that includes spacers."

"Initial attacks began within the confines of the Solar System with them searching for deserters who might have joined our fleet to avoid the conflict. Since then, harassment of our shipping has grown. Now they are taking entire crews, impressing them into service or incarcerating them on off-Earth bases. They even prowl the space surrounding both Kraken and Jasper colonies. In their view, this is a small change in tactics but, the consequences will be catastrophic for our economy."

Alex paused, drawing in even closer to look deep into his friend's eyes, "Decatur, we have but one remaining course of action. We plan to break from the NAU and Earth."

"We are drafting our own Declaration of Independence."

Jankin Decatur backed off a half step in disbelief, "You speak treason ... we can't do that. We're nothing, the NAU is a superpower. We don't have a standing army much less a single battlegroup of warbirds. They'll send one task force and forcibly dissolve our congress. You'll find yourself disappearing into that lunar prison you were telling me about and that's if you are lucky and they don't simply hang you from the nearest jidder tree."

Alexander nearly bellowed with delight. He knew he had the quick-tempered captain's attention. Now to hold it without getting burnt and set the snare.

"Yes, that may happen, but they've pushed us into a bad spot. We can't go on as we are. The new taxes combined with increased confiscation of our shipping and incarceration of our people without trial will ruin us. These are not conditions under which a free citizenry can survive. Our world will not survive submission. People will starve if they remain or they will have to return to Earth, and that's assuming the NAU will even let Krakens return to their already crowded planet."

"On Kraken, we have responded by secretly expanding our manufacturing infrastructure to meet the coming crisis. Clandestine universities now offer courses to train our most promising in fields formerly forbidden to us including research in nuclear and gravitonic sciences. Our infrastructure is awash with the growth of advanced materials programming research, metallurgical industries, and shipbuilding spurred on by the removal of restrictions and regulations of Earth-based research. We have all the elements critical for an advanced citizenry and the resources needed to survive independent of Mother Earth."

"All of these are economic advantages currently forbidden by the NAU."

Jankin wasn't sold on the idea, "They will not tolerate sedition. This will mean all-out war and it will be a short, bloody one that we will lose."

"Perhaps not. We've learned that NAU resources are already stretched in their funding of the conflict. Opening another front against us will put them in an impossible position financially and physically. It's one thing to conduct a war within the confines of the Solar System. We are far from Earth. Conflict here will not be an easy task, even for a superpower, especially if we eliminate the NAU governmental structure currently on Kraken."

Decatur stiffened, hazel eyes razor sharp as he searched for lies in the politician's soul, "You are serious? What makes you think this is even possible? We haven't the strength."

"Do you think so? Good, it means I'm doing my job. Let me bring you up to speed. Please, follow me across the courtyard."

The building appeared as little more than offices from the outside. Inside he discovered a central communications center for the merchant fleet. Decatur trailed Alexander down a long corridor and into a conference room.

"Have a seat." Alexander said as he motioned Decatur into silence. The politician's eyes defocused for a moment before a smile appeared, "Okay, we're secure. We can speak freely with this running. It's one of our new developments, rather like the faraday cage they use for blocking electromagnetic waves but this baby shields even gravitonic sideband eavesdropping."

As the commissioner spoke, an image solidified above the table, quickly filling the center of the conference room. Decatur's mind wandered, thinking more of the technology capable of creating such a vivid, free-floating full-immersion experience in midair than what it actually portrayed. He'd seen many three-dimensional displays but this one was a richly colored window to another world blocking even the reality of the granite tabletop beneath the lifelike essence of the display. Something moved within and, for the first time, he focused on the ethereal world itself. He recognized the location. They were approaching the Farrier Construction and Shipping docks located at the third Lagrangian point of Kraken. He'd spent many days there with his ship undergoing maintenance and inspection as they set up for his last run.

"This is real-time. I suspect you recognize Farrier Port but you most certainly don't know the project that I'm about to show you."

The scene shifted and swung about, carrying them to the far side of the dockage and down into the half-constructed belly of a huge cargo carrier in the first stages of framing. Small wavedrive powerplants illuminated the interior as they also provided localized gravity needed for construction. On the far side of the work area, there was a large geodesic dome with woven pulse-channels for broadband telemetry spectrum adsorption. No signals or scans would be getting in or out of that dome. Their travel followed a set of narrow-band ultraviolet navigational transponders, the type that remained passive and invisible without the query of special instruments tuned to a preset-cipher ping or programmed response code.

A jitter of the visuals, a shift in the scene and the view stabilized inside another dome. No workers were visible to provide scale but it was obviously huge and at its center was a ship that looked as if it was in the process of disassembly. Jankin Decatur's interest suddenly peaked, "That's Jeremy Alfred's new barque. Why are you ripping it apart?"

"Ripping it apart? Oh, we're doing nothing of the sort." The commissioner chuckled before continuing. "You are right, though. It is Jeremy's barque. We brought her in last month after finding her derelict and adrift with only one spacer aboard, the third mate. The petty officer managed to set a distress beacon. Unfortunately, we didn't arrive in time. The ship was otherwise abandoned, must have been adrift for weeks giving the mate plenty of time to log all that happened before she too passed."

"Jeremy's ship was taken deep within our territory by the NAU Frigate *Mejico*. An unarmed barque stood no chance of escaping a military frigate so Jeremy hove to when commanded. There was no pretense of a search for contraband, CTAC spacers, or NAU deserters. They pulled aside, took what they wanted, and gave the crew the choice of signing on to an NAU navy hitch or waiting in an airlock."

"The mate was outside the airlock on an inspection when they arrived. She was also nearby when they blew the airlock to vacuum and watched her shipmates sucked out into raw vacuum, exploding like overinflated, flash-frozen meat balloons.

"They left her with barely enough power in the ship to cycle the airlock one last time. It might have been better for her if it had ended there and then. Fortunately for us, she used her time wisely recording the ship's registry and log-copy as well as personal notes that included a rather cryptic mention about overheard discussions concerning a black-market project called 'Bucker' which is some form of planned regular program of confiscation of state-of-the-art military goods."

"That's a topic you need not be concerned with. We'll be looking into this further."

Jankin Decatur's face turned dark, "It's not a project. 'Bucker' is an individual. He's the one who underwrote the mutiny on that ship I lost in my other life. I'd certainly like to get my hands on him."

Hollen continued, "Well, we must learn a good deal more about him if this is true. However, it is not your concern."

"We plan to rechristen the ship *'Alfred'*. She will be our first warbird, a man of war. Essentially a frigate class starship with some upgrades."

Decatur chuckled, "A rather innocuous but perhaps appropriate name for a tiny warbird, I think Jeremy would have appreciated the thought."

Alex smiled, "He'd have a much deeper appreciation for what she is becoming. Some upgrades are obvious. Drone blisters, graviton torpedo shafts, and enhanced sensor arrays, both passive and active, that will find any vessel in an excited graviton state at extreme military sensor ranges."

"What's not obvious is the ship's AI enhancements including multiple target tracking with autonomous weapons release and NanoBot swarm technology. We also managed to cram in a second slipdrive giving *Alfred* the wave coupling capability of a full frigate but in a frame three-quarters the size. She will be a very fast, agile, and most deadly vessel."

"Her mission is to put a damper on the liberties taken by the powers of Earth responsible for the harassment and impressment of our astral fleet. Her captain will carry letters authorizing the attack and permitting the taking as prize any Earth vessel found in our inter-colony shipping lanes taking part in or known to have taken part in waylaying Astral Fleet assets."

"Funding for the venture is always a concern. We can't afford commercial pay scales, but captain, officers, and crew will all receive portions of prize money."

Decatur couldn't believe his ears, "Whoa, whoa, whoa. What do you mean, 'prize money'?".

A twinkle formed in Hollen's eye, "It's an incentive for taking the risks you will be subjected to. Anything you capture, be it ship or cargo, and return here will be either purchased by the Astral Fleet or auctioned on the open market. Your orders allow you to repatriate our lost ships, NAU, and CTAC military vessels as well as any of their commercial shipping. We intend to give them a strong dose of the hostilities they've inflicted upon us."

"Officers and crewmembers will all share in the success or failure of your venture. They will receive a fraction of the proceeds based on rank and time in grade."

Hollen leaned in a little closer. A twinkle dancing in his eye, "A captain's share will amount to two-eighths of the proceeds of sale."

"The **Alfred** is yours should you want her, Captain."

Jankin Decatur sat back in surprise and didn't immediately respond. He wondered, W*hy me? I'm not first on the captain's list. I just lost my last command. Do they have some ulterior motive I'm missing?*

Alex knew he had to keep his quarry moving so, "I realize the immensity of such an assignment. You'll oversee the completion of

Alfred's conversion and will be directly responsible for provisioning and crewing the vessel. We can't afford more than a modest sign-on bonus but there is always the draw of prize money to attract experienced spacers."

Decatur was not to be distracted, "Why me?"

Tim's eye's widened, "What? Well, I didn't expect that to arise. Why indeed?"

"We are rolling the dice on this venture. If we lose then most likely we will pay with our lives, all of us. Furthermore, finding people with experience in conducting a military venture is not readily available to us here on Kraken. The successful captain of a warbird must embody talents and traits differing from a commercial captaincy. In truth, you are not first on our captain's list, but you have other attributes in your favor."

"*Alfred* is an experiment of sorts. We need to expand our military arm on a budget that barely allows us to commission a shuttle. If we are to succeed, we must have rapid initial success with a sizable payback to reinvest in our growth and attract new talent."

"You are our only captain with experience involving armed conflict and you have shown yourself to be a most capable, quick thinking, determined, and ruthless commander. Those are the qualities our fleet must imbibe if we are to survive as an independent planet. Spacers will flock to your flag if you are successful, if not then our hopes of survival are poor."

"One abiding directive. There will be no impressment of civilians or spacers onto any ship registered to Kraken, that is one vice we will not tolerate. Pressgangs are a carryover from Earth we are going to leave behind. Your crew must all be volunteers and it will be up to you to separate the chaff from the wheat."

STAFFING

A thousand dingy bars like it existed in the shadows of Kraken's port, each just another hole tucked deep inside the bowels of the starport. It had none of the uptown party-joint trappings, bright lights or floating servers spewing ion-enhanced air streams designed to drive a patron's high a bit higher for a few extra credits. High society magnets for rich patrons willing to exchange

a trivial sum for a bright space full of false cheer, corporate expats longing for the taste of Earth as they flocked in after-hours to feel a little less lonely, a bit closer to home.

This tiny oasis was little more than a darkened hole-in-the-wall smelling of workman's honest sweat and beer mixed with hard spirits. It appeared centuries-old and hard-used, but a spacer could sit quietly inside and get a drink at an affordable price between runs, safely ensconced far from unwelcome eyes and legal warrants. Gruff but free, unassuming voices wafted over a dirt and jidder dust covered floor riding the faint smooth overtones of oil and biozene lubricant.

Immersed in the shadows of an even darker corner sat Jankin Decatur, back to the wall, warily eyeing the entry of each new customer, waiting for a man in a place where faces and conversations would remain private.

An ancient door crafted of the iron-hard wood of a Jenkin's tree groaned as it slid open releasing a stabbing shaft of yellow-green, early morning light that cut the pervading gloom, then just as quickly vanished behind a pair of broad shoulders filling the entryway jack stud to jack stud. The backlit apparition slipped to the side, blending into deep shadow and froze until his shaded eyes adjusted to the dark interior. Chief of Boat Rendall Gleason knew better than to barge thoughtlessly into the darkened innards of a place such as this.

The door clamped shut, seating itself with a solid chunk, returning dark, blessed anonymity to the patrons. Gleason barely twitched a muscle for nearly a minute until he identified the dark figure that was Jankin Decatur nestled in the far corner, his back put safely to the wall. Objective in sight, the chief strode across the room, grabbing an outstretched mug of ale in passing, leaving nothing but a grateful nod for the barkeep.

"Startin' early today, Chief?" The greeting went out low and soft, just loud enough for the intended spacer's ears.

Uninvited, the bear-like form settled into a chair across from Decatur, "Naw, endin' da evening late. What you doing here, Decatur? Thought you'd be on Thursday's run."

"New venture. I need talent. Special talent. Interested?"

"Ain't a miner, Captain. Told ya before. Not one to be stuck in orbit pushing rocks through vacuum no matter how much she pays."

Decatur couldn't restrain the chuckle, "Well, it seemed like a good idea at the time."

The Chief released a quite grunt that may have been a chuckle, "We survived … barely. Anyway, I just signed on for a nice bunk.

My very own private quarters in one of the new Nichol's Transports. Startin' soon as Captain Alfred returns."

"Yeah, well that's kinda what I wanted to speak about. Not gonna happen, Chief. They were run down by a craft gone privateer. Jeremy's not coming back ... ever."

"Aw, no. He was a good man. I warned him it could happen. Who took him, the NAU or the Chinks?"

"The NAU and they didn't take him. He and the other officers were airlocked. They did take most everyone else, disabled the ship. Jerry and the others left behind were okay until they split the airlock wide open to vacuum. The third officer managed to escape detection and she lasted long enough to register a statement before power and life support went."

"Ah, poor Wendy. She could be a coarse pain in the butt but she didn't deserve that."

Decatur leaned in closer, "Listen, that private birth is still yours if you want it and the job comes with a chance to make some real money. I've been offered Jerry's ship. It's up in Lagrange undergoing repairs and redesign."

"Redesign? Why redesign it. She's a sweet new roomy transport with great cargo space. Latest design. I'm surprised they didn't take the whole ship along with the crew."

"They didn't take the whole crew, just those willing to sign on to service. The others they vacuumed along with the officers. I have no idea why they scuttled the ship but it's soon to be mine."

"It could be ours."

The CPO sat back, squinted an eye to allow the other to drill into the form sitting across from him, "Y'ain't tellin' me everything, are ya, Captain? Where's the catch?"

"For that, my friend, you have to give me your bond you won't speak a word of this to anyone. That's whether you sign on or not."

"I mean anyone, Chief Gleason. Agreed?"

"Cheez, yer serious about this, ain't ya? How could I do anything else with you dangling all these nothins before me? Okay, let's say I agree."

"Not good enough. I need ...." He stopped as he looked into the chief's eyes, "Ah, okay."

"Rendall, foul weather's coming. The NAU, CTAC, everyone's gone unhinged with this in-system war of theirs. Stopping of our transports, pressing of crews and goods are growing as their manpower demands for the war drain both country's resources. They're also about to impose trade tariffs and raise taxes on Kraken and the other colonies."

Decatur looked around pushing his mug out of the way to edge in closer. His voice lowered even more, "Kraken is going to declare independence. Soon. Bloody revolution is afoot and we're going to need a defense force that goes beyond crowd control."

Decatur paused to sip from his mug, "That's where you and I come in."

Gleason set his own mug down and started to get up. Decatur took a chance and laid hand on the chief's shoulder, "Just listen and try not to be so damn thick-skulled. Sit!"

"They're converting Jerry's ship into a new class of frigate, adding expanded smart munitions and the latest AI. Advanced systems beyond anything you can find even on a NAU cruiser. All we need is a good crew, one willing to risk all for their homes and maybe their pocket."

The scowl on the chief's face carried his grumbled reply, "Bright, shiny new things get ya killed, don't work when you need 'em most."

Decatur stiffened, taken aback by the CPO's reaction. The old spacer didn't give a damn about fancy new ideas, he should have known better. He had but one arrow left in the quiver, "Drop the scowl. Look, it pays next to nothing but ... they are offering prize money. We get a cut of anything we capture and as Master Chief, you'll make a pretty penny."

"Common spacers get a cut of what they take? Who ever heard of such a thing unless yer turnin' pirate? Sounds like a good way to get killed."

Decatur hid a smile inside his beer mug, all the while keeping an eye on the big spacer. He hadn't lost him yet, "You take your chances no matter what decision you make. Ship out on merchant and get pressed into their war at landsman's pay or take the fight back to them in a warbird with a chance at prize money and it's all above-board legal as far as Kraken's concerned. To cap it, you join me now and you get a say in selecting the crew and can even put your two cents into redesign."

"Yer kidden. I pick the hands?"

"What's my cut on the deal?"

Decatur slid a doc file into the chief's public folder and sat back for a long, silent sip of warm beer washed down with an Irish-whiskey chaser. Rendall's eyes glazed over for a few seconds then opened wide, "Shoot, they must be hard up to offer that much share."

"Yeah, good people are hard to find but you also have me on your side, Chief. So, we gonna team up again?"

Rendell sat back, ran a hand through his thinning hair then spent a few moments wetting his whistle, all the time his eyes never left the captain's. His reply came low and sure as the soft rumble of an ion cannon transported across siliceram decking into its cradle.

"Well, I was slated fer dat ship. Just cause she's changin' skirts ain't no reason to back out."

"On the other hand ... Awww, makes no difference. I'm yer man, Captain."

Jankin Decatur's muscles visibly relaxed. A smile flickered in his eyes.

"Great, here's the plan. Keep in mind you can't trust anyone. Even here on Kraken, there's bound to be those who don't want to break off from the NAU. Take care and pick your people carefully. One last thing, you can't press anyone into service. They have to come on their own."

Jankin Decatur sat back and took a deep swig of beer chased down by three more fingers of the spirits, scotch this round, as he watched emotions storm across the Chief's face. When he thought the time right, he added, "… of course, a little friendly persuasion never hurt anyone."

Three big spacers materialized behind the chief from out of the dark shadows. Surprised, he looked at their faces then turned back to Decatur with a hurt look on his face, "Aw, come on Jankin. You had three guys at the ready?"

"Wasn't sure how you'd take the offer, Chief. Between you and me, I was worried three wouldn't be enough."

A twinkle filled the Chief's eyes. At a nod, two dark figures materialized from the dark nooks across the bar followed by deep laughter from all as they scraped chairs over and sat in for the day's next hard round of drinks.

OF NECESSITY

The evening started dirty then slid downhill.

Jankin Decatur fumed at the night and the man responsible for his being out in it for he was the one remaining obstacle to completing the ship. A man who bore the same hated name as that encountered in another life, when a young executive officer's career was ruined by mutiny and whose name he'd first learned on that long-past day, Bucker.

Same man or not, they were losing time and Decatur would not tolerate any obstacle.

It'd been a long, frustrating thirty-hour wait. He was sore, wet, soaked to the skin from the mist injecting the evening's chill into every pore of his body despite the poncho. Miserable hours passed slowly beneath the dripping, blue-green leaves of the Jenkin trees, each drop chipping away at his hope the damn bureaucrat would return before they all drowned or froze to death.

They'd formed along the outskirts of a walled compound surrounding a large storage and distribution center. The buildings were surrounded by gardens filled with native Kraken hybrids, mixed with more expensive greenery and whole orchards imported from Earth. A mansion blended cleverly into the center of the estate. Their objective was to affect an unnoticed and unannounced meeting with the owner of the subtly defended piece of property.

The surrounding countryside was wild and isolated from most of the colonists, a location central to four major cities whose distant lights contaminated the star-filled heavens. Occasionally, Decatur turned. Hearing nothing but the rain's incessant patter, he glanced back just for the small comfort of confirming the others were still there.

They were and this time the rugged face of that damned Major of Fleet Rangers even had the audacity to smile back at him and wink. Decatur silently returned to his vigil. Waiting didn't seem to bother rangers in the least, at times they seemed to be more machine than flesh and blood.

A hammer-like tap on his shoulder followed by the grip from a hand as strong as a construction drone, closed around his arm, pulling him back for a whisper, "They're coming. We'll take them at gate seven."

John Bucker … the very name set him on edge. The same cretin responsible for a containership mutiny those many years ago as well as the sacking of Jeremey Alfred's ship. They'd finally tracked him down and were immensely surprised to discover he had ties within their own organization. The man was a mid-level bureaucrat for Kraken Colony with close links to Earth. That described a lot of people on Kraken these days but this rotten piece of … colonial citizen was also the money-grubbing, selfish CEO of Blackfire Slipdrive Distributors. A middle company for trading high technology.

Bucker carelessly cooked his books and skimmed every transaction while shuffling funds and supplies to all of his favored contacts, all the while shunting goods into the black market for personal gain and he didn't seem to give a damn who knew it.

Decatur first met Bucker nearly a year ago, immediately disliking him. It wasn't the fact that the little worm wouldn't look you in the eyes, nor was it the pale face, flabby arms, and repulsive gelatinous handshake. The captain's dislike was from Bucker's infatuation with money above any other pursuit in life. The man had no ideals and even fewer morals.

The biggest rub was, he was also the biggest impediment to their launching of *Alfred*.

Bucker's customized Congress Corvair was still out of sight when they picked up its flight signature. A unique vehicle, the Corvair employed a miniature antigrav powerplant adapted for civilian use from first-generation wavedrive designs. Just the style of transportation for a pompous nobody who thought such things put him a step above everyone else. The Corvair moved silently, was completely safe even in a crash since its wavedrive field provided protection from any penetration.

Unless you happened to be a Fleet Ranger Special Operations team.

The vehicle slowed as it approached the entrance to Bucker's estate, they could see confusion then surprise race across his features when the gates didn't open. A moment of indecision and the Corvair's powerplant shut down and the vehicle dropped to the ground in a jaw-wrenching thud that popped the driver's door wide open. With less notice than a black shadow passing in the night, the rangers roughly extracted and hooded the scratching, kicking, screaming bureaucrat from his vehicle, bridled him with memtape and whisked their package off to a waiting covert operations container.

Decatur watched from the shadows. Waiting a few more soaking minutes didn't seem to matter anymore. Shortly a transport appeared above the container but was gone before the ranger lieutenant had even reactivated the gate's security systems.

Bodyless words drifted dully beneath mist-saturated air, "Ain't never felt anything like it. He ain't fat or nothing but lifting the guy's like lifting a sausage skin stuffed with pudd'n. Zero muscle tone and …"

"Trooper, I heard that. You're breaking protocol, can it." Sergeant Jaeger's directionless whisper cut the saturated air like a slap in the face, "Were you two playin' with yourselves during briefing? You will forget tonight. It never ever happened. Now I'm sure you have something constructive to do …."

Captain Decatur ignored the discussion at the gate. fleet rangers take care of their own and right now he had a bigger fish to skin inside a small chamber set to the side of Bucker's own launch bay. The transport circled back over their heads after an extended, jostling ride designed to further confuse its cargo. Earlier the rangers discovered a chamber in Bucker's own bay to be secure and nearly soundproof, they didn't care why he went to the expense of creating such isolation, but it certainly suited their needs.

Despite past familiarities with the man, Captain Decatur found no real joy in what was about to transpire. It was just a job, the elimination of another impediment to launching the *Alfred*.

Well, maybe there'd be some joy….

Jankin Decatur entered the chamber, closing the door so the screams and curses would not disturb others on the outside.

They removed the gag with a bit more vigor than needed and the bureaucrat began with a panicked screech, "Whoever you are, I'll find you, all of you behind this. Don't try and hide. Kidnapping is a death sentence and I'm going to enjoy every second watching you squirm and hang."

Jankin Decatur smiled at the major standing in silence behind the hooded captive. He leaned closer to address the blubbering fool's left ear, the unexpectedly soft voice silenced their guest immediately, "You seem a bit nervous, Mr. Bucker."

"Ah, perhaps it's because you lost your pants. A bit drafty. No?"

Bucker was enraged, "I'll sue you and everyone you know. I'll ..."

"This is unnecessary. Simply open access to your warehouse and you'll be back, safe and sound in your comfy manor."

"You son of a jiker, you're never gonna ..."

Decatur leaned in from the other side, "Well, I imagine you must have pretty big ones to fling threats at us while we are discussing business so politely. Perhaps we need make an adjustment. Agent One, have your people remove one of those things he cherishes so deeply."

Decatur was surprised at the genuine delight appearing in the major's smile and thought a few words might help, "Agent One, you seem to be enjoying this a bit more than I anticipated. Would you happen to be a past acquaintance of Mr. Bucker?"

"No but growing to love him more every minute, sir, that I am. Ah, but you may have misunderstood. I smile only because I enjoy business discussions. Ah, have you a preference for which one?" As he waited for a reply, the obvious scraping of the major sharpening an old-fashioned fighting blade quite noisily filled the chamber.

"Heavens no, simply remove the nearest, but must you make that annoying noise. I'm sure it's sufficiently sharp."

"Ah, now look." Major Walters commented as he poked the victim's lower abdomen with the tip of the blade, leaving a tiny dribble of blood to mark the spot, "This presents a bit of a problem, Sir. He seems to have drawn them up, tucked 'em quite neatly into his belly skin. I didn't realize a man could do that without immersion in ice-cold water."

"Never fear, not a big problem although I may have to dig around a bit."

Decatur attempted to feign exasperation in his voice, "Very good, I'd like to finish this soon but I'll not rush you. I'm anxious to return to our negotiations so ..."

The squeal came from the hooded captive as he sensed the major's approach, "Noooo. No, wait. Please, please wait."

The major hesitated, "Oh, would you like a sip of water first?"

Decatur spoke up, "Tch, tch. I wouldn't if I were you. Not a good idea right now. You'll most likely regret it later. Bound to sting for a bit, ya know."

Somehow their victim managed to descend to an even paler level of skin tone, "Let's negotiate. Negotiate, please."

The major returned a loud whisper intended for more than the captain's ear, "No need to rush into negotiations, Sir. We can get a better deal by ..."

"No, no, no, please. I'll give you whatever you want just don't ..."

"Don't what?" Decatur replied innocently.

"I'll release it."

"Hmm, well I hate to disappoint my companion but, did you bring the remote, Agent One?"

"Not sure I can find it right now. I was so looking forward to ...."

Captain Decatur gave the major a stare that said quite clearly, *Time to stop'*.

"... ah. Yessir. Have it right here. Shall I free his hand or simply remove the finger and ...."

Decatur launched an unspoken command at the major that would have melted plastisteel but got only a friendly grin in return.

Unbinding the prisoner's hand, they brought the controller to where their guest could feel it. Bucker fumbled with his free left hand until he felt the sensor then moved his index finger over it and ...

Swift as a viper's strike, the flat of the major's blade slid under the finger, drawing another drop of blood as it lifted the digit from the sensor. Words as cold as the ranger's heart followed, "I swear the turd has no sense a'tall. Put your index finger to it and the alarm sounds. We know your tricks. I'd really like to know just what you thought would happen after you sent out an alarm?"

"Perhaps you'd like me to simplify the choice of fingers, I can reduce it to one if you wish."

Shaking, Bucker extended the correct finger and pressed it to the pad.

The frown of disappointment was evident in the major's reply, "Oh, much, much better. Thank you, Mr. Bucker."

"Having been so cooperative, you are of no further use to us. No use at all."

Bucker was left sitting in his chair with ear and mouth muffles reapplied and the hood draped over his head and only his imagination to keep him company. Obtaining their needed items, they silently departed after securing the door behind them. Decatur waited in the swirling mist for it to seal before turning to Major Walters, "No further use to us? You just had to leave him with the uncertainty of those last few words. You've a nasty streak in you Major."

"I'm Fleet Rangers, captain. Prerequisite of the job."

"Couldn't happen to a nicer guy, as far as I'm concerned. You sure you want him left there safe and sound? Not good leaving a live enemy in your rear."

"We're through with him, major. They will eventually find him in the morning although it'll be a while since I understand he's habitually late for the office. Let him return to his little kingdom carrying the casual reminder that we can easily conduct a second visit along with the uncertainty of who we were."

"Aye aye, Sir. As you wish."

"I just received confirmation, the slipdrive is on its way along with a few other needed items."

"Major, we are only here for the slipdrive."

"Had to do it, Sir. Liberating only the slipdrive would have directed the finger right at us. Besides, you know this clown's been selling our supplies on the black market. Things we requisition always seem to be unavailable, yet there they sit in his warehouse. Might as well take advantage of the situation."

"I'd prefer to not know the details, major. Thank you."

"Let's get back to the ship. I'm anxious to review the status of the torpedo loads and we can slip the drive into its socket immediately. I've targeted later this week to finally take her out for trials."

~~*~*~*~*

Chief Rendall Gleason barely squeezed out from a hatch obviously ill-designed for a spacer his size. Ladders below the hatch led to the skin tunnels used for maintenance within the narrow confines that isolated the living quarters of the ship from the outer shell. They were rarely used and very claustrophobic even for the smaller, hardened spacers they called 'tunnel rats'.

Captain Jankin Decatur, a wide grin on his face, watched his chief emerge, "Last time I saw you squirm like that, you were trying to squeeze out of a vacuum pressure sock that had leaked itself nearly dry. Big guys like you shouldn't be in those tunnels. Get some scrawny tunnel rat to do the duty."

Gleason didn't see the humor in his captain's sudden appearance, "You're apt to shorten a guy's life coming up on a fellow quiet like that. You know better. Shouldn't startle me, it ain't healthy."

Decatur wondered if the 'shortened life' crack was meant to apply to him or the chief himself, "Didn't mean to surprise you but the statement's a serious one. Suppose you slipped and got stuck between the hulls. Our only option would be to cut you out and I'd have to make a bad decision on whether to do so or leave you there until you slimmed down enough to squirm out."

CPO Gleason was inspecting a rip in his uniform's elbow, "I did have a skinny spacer down there. Simmons was tracing lines when she found him. Apparently, the NAU pirates missed more than one spacer. Can't ID who it was yet, but he managed to crawl deep into the tunnels and never made it back out. Must have wanted to avoid the NAU press-gang really bad. Don't see how they missed the body during refit but now it's a pretty mess."

"I'm giving Simmons extra leave for doing clean-up, she barely groused when I gave her the job."

Decatur nodded then motioned his friend, "Chief, walk with me a bit."

"Aye aye, Sir. Lead on."

Alfred had been eighty-seven percent gutted in the redesign. Decatur and Rendell traversed newly created passageways and bulkheads upgraded for internal safe transport of munitions and storage. Passing crew's quarters into a small flight deck that had been converted from the huge storage bays of the one-time freighter. A merchant such as this typically supported a crew of thirty to fifty spacers but a fully staffed frigate warbird required three hundred seventy-seven, even with the support of advanced AI and robotics.

Decatur had not expected the gift but they were assigned a flight wing of single-pilot multi-purpose fighters with support elements. This was an unheard-of configuration but then the mission of this ship was to discover how to do the impossible while standing up to long-established space fleets, meet their objective, and come back alive. Desperate needs demand extraordinary measures and, in *Alfred's* case, that meant the presence of a fighter wing on board in addition to the Fleet Ranger contingent. Requiring an organizational discussion with his chief of the boat.

WARBIRD

2180 C.E.
Travis Shipyard and Skunkworks Perimeter
Military Orbital Station- L2, Kraken

The sleek two-passenger autonomous swiftboat threaded its way much too quickly through the civilian shipyard on a course that led to a winding defensive channel brimming with AI Sentinel safeguards. One mistake of the swiftboat's AI, and their atoms would be wildly spread across space and left to the mercy of the stellar winds. This swiftboat however, made no mistakes, for it had traveled the intentionally complex path many times and soon would arrive at Kraken's most secret of destinations.

The ship's slipdrive field masked any perceived changes in momentum caused by the sudden twists and radical turns of their vessel. Not a single wall display or port was present to convey a sense of travel; a radiation-active shell blocked any transmission from coming into or attempting to leave the vessel, whether it be from sophisticated neutrino wavelets up to quantum entanglement hyper-photon swaps. Stealth and isolation were intentional, for this course wove them through the inner sanctum of Kraken's military defenses to a remote site restricted to only those with the highest security clearance.

The thought of 'high security' had originally instilled a touch of excitement to its passengers but the novelty had quickly faded to boredom. Margo Stoudt shifted in her seat wishing for a distraction, any distraction, "I'd give a year's salary to be able to see where we're going."

Lieutenant Mark Mason of the Kraken Home Rangers (Retired) snapped out of his own personal thoughts. For the hundredth time, his eyes shifted to the short, gruff-voiced dark-haired girl that somehow managed to come across as very sexy. An attribute even greater in its effect because she never played the angle. He liked working with professionals and took her address as an excuse to don a broad grin while gazing into her green eyes, "They didn't bother to give us anything to snack on, so it can't be a long ride."

Recently retired from active service, this new career was suggested at his retirement party by a commander who thought he would enjoy the challenges of something different … a combat recorder. He was the first of a new breed that hadn't existed until recently. Kraken had no military arm, nor had they needed one since they were protected by the NAU military machine. Of course, they had received little in the way of protection services from their homeland for quite some time now.

Mason had never thought his duties would include babysitting a female journalist on assignment. The thought occasioned a glance over to the shapely, deep-voiced brunette sitting across from him, *Well, I guess I've been on assignments a lot worse than this. How bad can the mission be if they're letting this pretty thing come along?*

Margo's head snapped around to look at him. He would have sworn she had just read his mind.

"Mason! Are you listening or do you always drift off into La La Land like this?"

Mason's only reply was his habitual grin as he spitefully intensified his stare. Heck, but it was something to do and, with her, it was fun.

Being the first in his profession left Mason with the honor of deciding what to call it. In past years they had been called combat photographers. But that title didn't do his work justice, he was no mere recorder of images. Sights, smells, fear pheromones and sometimes even jubilation all went into his recordings. All the human sensory input that immersed a viewer into the world of the recorder. Even the onset of death … if he could believe the stories he'd heard Earthside, such scenes were never released to the public.

"I know a place, it's not exactly in La La Land, Margo, but if you want to go there someday just let me know. It's a sweet place over on Jasper …"

"Not interested, big boy. Look, let's pool our information, maybe we …"

The hatch slid open, revealing a broad-shouldered spacer backlit by the glare of the starport. A melodious base voice cut through the whines, sharp clanging, and distant shouts gushing in from outside, "Good evening people. Welcome to Travis Shipyard and Skunkworks. Please leave anything you carried on board, right there at your seats. They'll be waiting for you in quarters. Watch yer step as ya exit, this ain't no plush passenger terminal."

"I'm Master Chief Rendall Gleason. Please hold off on questions. You have a meeting in ten minutes with Captain Jankin Decatur and his Executive Officer, Commander Harriette Hopewell. Follow me and don't stray."

The chief led them briskly across a broad siliceram landing field. Mason made the mistake of looking up and a queasy feeling washed over him. No sky was visible above, only more buildings and construction … but they were inverted. Busy fabrication and construction bays surrounded them. As a first-time visitor he expected to see some sky or maybe even a patch of black space overhead peeking through the cavernous buildings but not here.

Looking straight up, the view presented a view of the heavens packed with upside-down buildings, streets, and distant people scurrying about their business. It was as though they were flying inverted in a shuttle looking upwards into the bowels of a great city with unnatural clarity, for the atmosphere was tightly controlled and cleansed.

There was not a hint of walls, much less a horizon. Not even a tiny flicker of blue sky or coal-black space, managed to get through the intermingled layers of industry. A glance to the side was even more disturbing for the streets crept upwards in the far distance as though they stood on the inner skin of some great tennis ball, for any side street continued off into the distance, eventually climbed up the steep 'mountainside' but with the far-off buildings slanting inward towards the ball's center until the distant street could be followed to eventually hover, inverted quite unnervingly directly over their heads.

Margo tapped Mason's shoulder, pointing upwards, "It's like being on the streets of New York City except there's an upside-down reflection of the city over our heads."

Mark grinned at the journalist, "Yeah, I was thinking the same thing. I suspect we're inside a globe composed entirely of buildings with the construction docks connecting them. The things one can accomplish when you control gravity are mind-boggling. You can use it to constrain atmosphere to an area without binding it in with walls. Heck, you can even bend photons and cosmic rays around the whole facility to hide it from an unwanted gaze and the sensors of others. You know, we might be situated out in space, but we could just as easily be deep beneath Kraken's ocean or inside the clouds of one of our gas giants. Any guesses?"

"Naw, I thought for sure I'd be able to at least make a guess of where we are, but I'm lost."

The big spacer leading them must have been listening since he glanced back with a wide grin on his face and said without losing a step, "Put yer questions to the captain. Who knows, maybe he'll help ya."

"Here we go, into this building and up the first lift on the right to the twenty-third floor."

The human eye requires a thirtieth of a second to register an image, so Mark felt, rather than saw, the security flash of light as they approached the door and knew he'd been scanned. The doors opened and Chief Gleason motioned them down a second corridor. It was a wide thoroughfare, more like a small city street than a hallway and the ex-ranger in him wondered why they needed such wide corridors with ceilings at least three times their height.

Gleason pointed them to a cordoned-off enclosure that he called a 'Lift'. The lift appeared to be little more than an empty tube, a hole in the floor below with a corresponding aperture above that was wide enough for more than a few individuals to pass simultaneously.

"No need to hesitate, people. Step on out, ya ain't gonna fall and if you don't look down but keeps yer eyes up, ya'd swear ya were walking on a solid floor. It's all synced to your HiveTab implant ..." The chief's eyes defocused for a moment as he obviously checked on their status, "Ah, well, ya'll get upgrades soon enough but until then don't try it on yer own."

A faint breath of air passed over them with their upwards travel. Then, in less than a minute, the levels stopped passing by, "Okay, step out, twenty-third floor. Kinda fun what some innovative eggheads can do with a constrained slipdrive field, ain't it?"

They walked down a broad hallway and then through a door. Margo expected an office but the broad space inside was a hive of high-top tables and manufacturing activity. Sounds of heavy construction filled their ears but were muted enough for the chief to speak without projecting his voice, "Noise mufflers are operational or ya wouldn't be able to hear yer own thoughts. Follow closely now, the captain's reviewing the project map with Josh Humphrey, he's the ship's primary architect."

Margo noticed two men standing at a planning workbench and with their backs turned. One was a tall but obviously well-built figure standing ramrod straight but the other, a shorter man with noticeably wide shoulders and close-cropped chestnut hair seemed to be doing all the talking. As the chief approached, she was surprised to see him address the shorter man first, "Captain Decatur, Mister Humphrey. I'd like to introduce Ms. Margo Stoudt. She's a journalist, and Mr. Mark Mason, he's a …. what'd you call yerself?"

"I'm a Combat Recorder."

Jankin Decatur's mind flashed through half a dozen reasons why it was a bad idea having civilians on station. The situation was about as dirty as it could get politically, and the last thing his command wanted was to have this intended poke in the motherland's eye erupt into all-out conflict and maybe even revolution. Well, for now, these two were a minor problem compared to the boatload of other serious worries surrounding him. He turned to the newcomers, any hint of a welcoming smile absent from his glare, "I objected to your presence on the mission but was overruled. This isn't going to be a pleasure cruise."

"You will be isolated from all outside contacts and restricted from any reporting until later in our mission. I'll let you know when you can submit reports for our review. If approved, then we will transmit them for you."

"Please bear with me if you've heard this before but our people are being crushed under a burden laid upon us by the warring nations of Earth. Even our own North American Union has opened hostilities against our commerce fleets by stopping our shipping mid-transit and pressing our crews into service or sending them into incarceration without trial. These infractions have increased in frequency and severity to the point that they now confiscate both ship and cargo, as well as pressing the crews. Kraken's pleas for protection and our attempts at negotiation have been ignored. Colonials are ignored and preyed upon by all and the situation just becomes worse as time passes."

"*Alfred's* launch and mission will be our initial response. We will be the first to deliver payback to both the NAU and to the CTAC atrocities. We will force them into a position of negotiation."

"You will most likely find yourselves declared as pirates or even traitors. Don't expect your journalist's credentials to protect you. Make no mistake. In joining us, you risk your personal future, your fortune and even your life."

A man approached without salute, apparently a Major of Fleet Rangers by his insignia, "Good afternoon, Captain. You requested my presence."

Decatur noticed the major staring at the newcomers, paying particular attention to Mr. Mason but decided not to comment, "These journalists will be our guests for the cruise, Major. Allow me to introduce Ms. Margo Stoudt and Mr. Mason."

"Mister? Why, I know this fellow, Captain. Lieutenant Mason, how the heck have you been and what the hell are you doing out of uniform?"

He suddenly stopped as though he'd stepped on a half-thaler chip and looked at the captain, "Ah, I apologize for the colorful bit of Chinese in there. I just didn't expect to see this guy ...."

"Wait one."

"Captain, did you say they're coming with us?"

Decatur's expression didn't vary, he was busy and had little time for such niceties, "Mr. Mason has retired from Homeland Rangers and now freelances as a journalist. He and Ms. Stoudt today begin an embed with us. They will be quartered with your people. You'll treat them as guests but beyond normal courtesies, there will be no favored accommodations."

"Ms. Stoudt, this is Major Stephen Walters of the Kraken Astral Rangers."

"We are preparing for departure so things are a bit hectic. I have copies of the nondisclosure and confidentiality agreements signed by each of you. Should you manage to initiate contact with anyone who is not a member of this crew or persons not privy to discussions of our work and mission, you could be arrested, tried, and face incarceration or even execution at my discretion."

The captain's abruptness startled Margo then she noticed the look of amusement on the major's face and felt annoyance welling up inside, "Thank you, Captain Decatur. We'll try not to be a bother. Could you at least tell us about our mission, or should I turn to the major for that bit of information?"

Decatur ignored the frost in her reply, "Please join me at the wall display, Ms. Stoudt. Do you see the hull down there going through final fitting? That merchant hull is the framework for our ship, the **KS Alfred**."

"After launch, she will be classified a light frigate and will be Kraken's first vessel designed as a warbird. In case you wonder, a frigate is a ship that is a bit smaller than an NAU destroyer. **Alfred** started life as a merchant, captained by an old friend of mine. They were waylaid by an NAU destroyer in Kraken space and her crew pressed into the NAU Starfleet. The great defenders of our motherland then murdered my friend and his officers in addition to any of the spacers who refused to sign on the NAU roster."

"We found the ship and learned this only because they were sloppy and allowed one officer to survive long enough to launch a beacon, she was valiant enough to log what happened despite knowing death was imminent. **Alfred's** name is a bit unconventional for a frigate, the council named the ship after her owner-captain."

"**Alfred's** conversion is nearly complete, thanks to efforts of Mr. Humphrey and others. We will leave shortly on a shakedown cruise to weed out design and construction bugs. After that, you will learn the objectives of our first mission, even as I discover them."

"Major Walters, they're all yours. Josh, you're free to take a break if you care to go with them. I'm sure Miss Stoudt and her companion have a thousand questions about the ship's design." Without even a goodbye, he returned to his office.

~~*~*~*~*

Somehow, the day seemed a bit brighter as they exited the building. Major Walters led the way, reviewing his schedule as they walked, "I'm clear for the rest of the evening and your personals are waiting in your quarters on **Alfred**. How about dinner and a beer? I'm buying."

Margo had been looking skyward, feeling a bit nervous at all the dangerous-looking activity going on overhead but still managed to reply quite casually, "I can see you two are just itching to trade old war stories. I'm an excellent listener, but I also have a thousand questions so I'm game. Lead the way."

The hard, weather-beaten lines of the major's transformed into a broad, rather engaging smile, "There are a dozen cafeterias nearby but when you've been here a while, you discover places that are relaxing with food that's a little more than processed cellulite."

Mason's eyes took in everything as they walked. He was impressed by the well-organized, massive shipyard. Worker's needs were always at hand or somehow managed to be nearby when required. A stroll down a narrow side street brought them to a darkened doorway with an honest-to-goodness wooden plaque hung out above the portal with the words *'The Charging Batha'* playing across its surface. A waiter recognized and warmly greeted the major as he led them to a corner table at the far end of a crudely carved bar. Soft music filled the air along with a few sports vids comfortably off in a far corner.

Mason entered a drink order then turned to his host, "I assume we need to be circumspect with regards to our discussion topics. This place can't be secure."

"Those here have all been security screened. We're also at a relatively safe table location but we will avoid touching on anything too sensitive. I'll warn you if things move in that direction."

"As you heard the captain state, Josh Humphrey here is ship's upgrade architect so take advantage of him. You're the journalist here Margo, any questions about *Alfred* itself?"

A thousand questions screamed across the journalist's mind, the problem always was how to get the most critical information out into the open and do so early in the conversation. Yet, she couldn't hold the smile from her face as she asked, "Let's start with a simple question. Mister Humphrey, Captain Decatur briefed us on the history of the ship. We get the point of the tragedy involved and the atrocities committed, but why invest the time and energy into converting a civilian shipping vessel into a military ship and why does it take a ship designer to install a few torpedo launchers on the *Alfred*? Why not simply arm your freighters?"

Humphrey took a sip of his beer, wondering just how far up 'simplicity street' he had to start, *she's either good at what she does or just lucky. Didn't waste a second asking what the upgrades are but went right to obvious fundamental.*

"As simple as it sounds, the addition of armament to a civilian ship does little more than give a feeling of security to the crew since even a small military courier would have the specialized equipment to overcome any torp we can install on a commercial frame. Ah, that's 'Ion Torpedo' to the uninitiated."

"Keep in mind, it takes more than munitions to defend, much less defeat a warbird, you need intelligence gathering, long-range sensor arrays, and combat analytical AI."

"*Alfred's* design class of interstellar freighters is our most advanced. We believe they are the best frames in the known universe surpassing even Earth's 'Great White Fleet' for speed and accuracy in navigation. Lucky for us, the NAU pirates left minimal damage to the ship itself other than wiping its core, murdering the AI, and crudely ripping through some interior bulkheads."

"Captain Decatur has direct experience with their boarding methods, which we have used to our advantage in configuring *Alfred's* new bulkheads and armament, some of which are quite innovative. Her slipdrives incorporate a new Kraken-confidential design and we've solved the problem of mounting two drives in the same drive core which are capable of working independently should one fail or as a complementary phased system with an ability to link deeper into the Gravitonic Ether than any other drive. We expect they will deliver a significant improvement in both speed and agility."

"From all outward appearances, she'll carry the sensor signature of a freighter, but this will be a compact warbird with a bite many times worse than its bark."

A puzzled expression came across Margo's face but before she could ask, the major continued, "Sorry, it's an old Earth expression gathered from watching too much of the old cinema. The expression means she's going to have a lot of power, much more than outward appearances would suggest."

Ex-lieutenant Mason had other concerns, "I'm more concerned about the legality of the venture. This seems a bit more than self-defense and the NAU is not going to take kindly to anyone attacking their ships."

Major Walters sat back in his seat and sighed, "I guess you haven't been fully informed of this but I believe it qualifies as a justifiable topic of discussion at this point."

"Before we begin our first mission, or very soon thereafter, Kraken will take a major step in demanding a stop to NAU depredations. Should they refuse, we will move to declare independence from the NAU. We will not be conducting war but justifiably protecting our livelihood and sovereignty as an independent world."

"There's significant probability the NAU will view us as rebels, maybe even pirates. You know the fate of pirates from days past. There is also the possibility of conflict with Asian CTAC assets although I suspect this is a small probability at this early point in our venture."

"If you cannot live with this, then there is still time to back out from the assignment."Jasper Convoy

2180 C.E., three months later
Travis Shipyard and Skunkworks Perimeter
Military Orbital Station- L2, Kraken

She doesn't feel right. Captain Jankin Decatur let the course calculation flow unimpeded into the new HiveTab interface located behind his left ear, where it released a flood of information directly into the command and control center of his brain, his cerebral cortex.

The ship's responding much too quickly. Rapid fuzzy calculation results such as these aren't normal for a ship's AI. Rather than our course being a simple packet matrix analysis of cold numbers, the AI anticipates and includes course-node uncertainties right up front in the initial plot. The course isn't a fixed path. It's actively linked into the ship's AI as though it's a thought sequence with decisions yet to be selected as we reach each correction point.

Very much like the approach a human would unconsciously apply to any situation.

God forbid if this creates uncertainty or hesitation during combat maneuvers.

"Problem, Decatur?" Captain Decatur's musing shattered beneath the crisp, harsh tones of his XO, Commander Harriet Hopewell.

Decatur looked up at the interruption but the expected blistering response to such a blatant intrusion never surfaced. Harriet was a faithful companion from many past voyages and had earned the right of familiarity. They had grown close over the years, but she wasn't his type. Too much like himself to tolerate anything deeper than a professional relationship.

"Ship's plot of our port exit course doesn't feel right." Decatur replied with an unconscious shaking of his head, "The results came back too fast and the course itself is more of a dynamic envelope of options than a single exit vector matrix."

"Well, the shakedown cruise will give us a chance to discover any major design problems. I only hope this isn't one of them. Everyone be on your toes. Have navigation keep a close eye on helm response until we're in deep space. Shakedown or not, we can kiss our careers goodbye if we smash into a docked vessel or structure."

Harry smiled at her captain, she knew his distrust of AI systems, "**Alfred's** simply accounting for the uncertainty of all potential interactions. The results show up as an active probabilities envelope of anticipated corrections. The potential course vectors packet's a bit noisier here in dock because of wave filtering and all the graviton-photon interactions existing inside a multiple quantum well system, coexisting inside convergent microcavity arrays."

Decatur turned to her, one eyebrow lifted in question, "Really XO? You think I don't know about Thompson Tubes?"

"Enough, let's get this tin-can moving. Put me on …."

"Captain Decatur." A crisp, clear woman's voice, one that easily would carry though the thickest confusion of battle rang inside his brain, *"I respectfully request the 'tin can' be addressed as 'Alfred' or simply 'Ship'."*

"I will open the 'all-decks' audio link for you."

Decatur bolted upright in his chair, "No, no, no, and no. Just when did this start. How in the world do you expect us to associate a ship named 'Alfred' with a sexy voice like that? What…. What?"

The XO quietly replied, "As you requested, *Alfred* put you into the general audio push. Everyone on board is privy to your words."

Decatur slammed the communications system to off, "*Alfred* is a mil-spec Artificial Intelligence Entity and now he's telling me how to address it … uh, her … whatever is this thing supposed to be, anyway? There will be no levity in the program. A ship of war cannot indulge in practical jokes … and should not be anticipating my commands."

Alfred's soft voice flashed directly into his brain, "I apologize, Captain, but there was no joke intended. Surely, you saw my 'general push' notification sent out in response to your request for the service."

Checking again to confirm the general push status to be on local, Decatur replied, "No backtalk. I don't care how advanced you are. When you address me, you will dispense with any hint of practical joke or levity and I will address you as I choose."

"Aye aye, Sir. Would you like to continue with your announcement? Or shall I command the crew to stand down?"

"I'll address them. Reopen the general push, full-spectrum vid directly across HiveNet, general push this time."

Decatur waited as *Alfred* announced him to the ship's complement then,

"Crewmembers of the *Alfred*."

"This is a day you will tell your grandchildren about and they will look up to you in awe. From this day forward, you hold the honor of being plank owner crewmembers of the first warbird of our new and independent world. Every man, woman, and child in Kraken and Jasper will remember your name."

"Our sister colony on Jasper has stood at our side from the day of their founding. Today they join our effort to protect our spacers and commerce from the atrocities of both CTAC and NAU aggression."

"You may have heard others describe our first mission as a ship's shakedown cruise. They are wrong. This first flight will be a test of not only *Alfred,* but each of us. We have been assigned to provide a convoy escort for eight merchants traveling directly to Jasper. We will shield them from the harassment and abduction of personnel. A crime that has grown so commonplace, it threatens to strangle our livelihood. Make no mistake, we are setting a historic precedent. Whether history calls us a success or abject failure, patriots or traitor will be all up to you. Make our memory shine. Thank you."

Switching Hive-com over to the ship's channel, "*Alfred,* give the thirty-second warning after port authority clearance. Run through the checklist once more then proceed at best safe speed to rendezvous."

A departure alarm sounded. Local port gravity zeroed out and the ship's slipdrive spun up an elliptically rotating magnetic field about the vessel that pulsed bursts of energy into every electron of every atom within it. Electron's subparticle orbital shells expanded, exposing their gravitons to the universe, pulsing bursts of gravitic packets into the cosmos. In a billionth of a second, the drive synchronized the graviton particle spin of every electron in the ship, aligning the high-energy chaos into partial phase with the local swells of the surrounding gravity waves. *Alfred* lifted a hair's breadth and hesitated for three-point-two milliseconds as it completed an all-systems check under load.

Alfred's graviton field phase-shifted ever so slightly into closer alignment and she pulled out from dock with only the faintest hum of power, only audible to nearby dock workers, following a circuitous path through the port's berthing area, then out past hedgerows of defense emplacements into open space. Another change in its phased linkage to the universe and *Alfred* was gone, leaving little more than the briefest glow trail of charged graviton secondary emissions to mark the ship's departure.

Twenty-three minutes later they dumped velocity to rest at a rendezvous location just off from Kraken's small moon, a point in space only three light-seconds out from dock and well within the star system's ecliptic disk. Course settings, critical status-point updates, and velocity relative to Kraken's primary, displayed over a clear-vision of the outside starscape with the bridge wall displays setup for a direct view of the exterior panorama. A fuzzy swath of light composed of billions of unblinking multicolored pinpoints spread across the heavens highlighting the ecliptic plane of the milky way. Their destination lay ahead and, as they approached, five bright points of reflected light grew in intensity. Five merchant ships waiting at rendezvous in the compact pentode parking formation used by merchants for deep-space waypoints.

There should have been eight.

Decatur scanned the bridge from a command chair positioned for clear observation of every officer and their station on deck.

He liked this bridge. It was an improvement over simply viewing each station's readouts or, worse yet, having to wait to be notified of a problem. A captain who could physically see each officer on station quickly became familiar with their body language. Their unconscious physical response to questionable situations. The subtle hints that allowed him to react instantly when milliseconds might mean life or death in combat. Everything seemed fine except for his XO whom he sensed was about to look his way.

Decatur rose before she could comment, calling out as he crossed the bridge, "Commander Hopewell, I'll be in my office. You have the bridge."

He cycled through the plastisteel blast doors of the bridge and into the command deck passageway. His office and quarters were adjacent to the bridge, the door opened as he approached revealing five merchant captains already in attendance and awaiting his entry. They had been expecting him and had appropriately linked into his conference room from each of their commands.

Decatur examined their faces as he crossed to his seat. Two of them he knew, a third captain was young and obviously excited about being here. Decatur's HiveTab AI began an overview that only Decatur could hear, *"You know Captains Thomas and Hooke. The smiling younger captain is Ares Coswell who is running a Morris Industries mixed shipment of trade goods. His ship's field is a bit dense for their manifest, most likely he's smuggling extra tonnage for personal black-market interests, a bit more than his charter would permit."*

Captains Beverly Daniels and Hans Blinkman have enforced access blocks so I couldn't bring up their exact manifests but both are seasoned officers with strong political ties on Kraken.

"Good morning ladies and gentlemen." Decatur greeted the merchant captains as he approached his seat, "Three of your brethren are missing."

"Why?"

Decatur's eyes were drawn to a muscular bald-headed man dressed in Jasper workman's clothes and a crumpled captain's cap who sat upright as he began. *"Captain Hans Blinkman of Jasper Transit, senior ranking merchant officer,"* came into Decatur's cognisance from his HiveTab even before the fellow started speaking.

"They've launched on their own. Preferred not to wait, they have. Claimed they had little to fear and would take the chance. The rest of us obviously disagree and welcome your protection although we now find ourselves a bit skeptical. Your ship appears to be little more than one of the newer Antares-class freighters. You must realize we're taking a chance should we be stopped and boarded, worse if you attack and fail us. What could you hope to accomplish against a real military vessel?"

Another captain's voice cut in, "More likely, he'll turn tail and run."

Decatur's attention ratcheted over to the woman, focusing like the targeting turret of an ion cannon emplacement. Her record flashed into his consciousness, *"Captain Beverly Daniels, Jasper Transit and former Lieutenant NAU space force."*

Jaws clenched, as he stared at the rude captain, *Well, no sweet words of courtesy from this one. At least I can expect an honest reaction from her.*

Then spoke, "We don't know each other Captain Daniels so I'll allow the insult to pass."

"This time."

"Please restrict yourself to positive commentary if you have something to contribute."

The freighter captain's reply was immediate, "That was positive commentary, Captain Decatur."

"If you can't perform or should you grow weak when things get bad, we're the ones who will suffer. I expected an older class destroyer escort at the very least, something a bit more formidable."

"I looked up your record. You have no military service background. What's more, you have no background earlier than a few years ago when you mysteriously appeared midway up the captain's lists."

"Favoritism, most likely."

"I'm here against my better judgment but such are my orders. First foul-up and we're gone, orders or no orders."

Decatur sat and poured himself a cup of black coffee from the flagon, pointedly ignoring the captain's rudeness as he briefly wondered how his galley managed to have a flask of fresh coffee waiting for him at this unscheduled meeting. The thought reminded him there are times when one needs to be grateful for the small things in life.

The captains seemed puzzled. Ah, that was the reaction he had hoped for, a suggestion they would later notice his calm demeanor when under attack. One more sip.

"Thank you, Captain Daniels, but I am not here interviewing for a job so there is no need to evaluate my perceived qualifications. That is the purview of your ship's owner and my own chain of command. Now, let's get down to business."

"The names of the missing captains have been transmitted back to commerce central. They have forfeited their insurance bond for ignoring orders as will any of you who choose to leave the convoy. Should you depart and encounter trouble, we are not duty-bound to go to your aid."

"Captain Coswell, you are running over mass allotment. That's between you and your company. My only concern is that you be able to maintain pace with the rest of us. If you find you cannot keep pace or maneuver properly because of it, then it becomes my problem and you will jettison enough items, those not on your original manifest, to remedy the problem or you will be left behind. I will make the appropriate entries in my log. You will not be permitted to delay or jeopardize the safe arrival of the convoy."

"Captain Thomas, you are senior and know the course. Please take point. Captain Hooke, it's nice to see you again. I welcome your experience. Please position your ship at the rear of the convoy. Watch for strays and take advantage of the excellent sensor package I know you have on board."

"*Alfred* also has a few surprises including an advanced, long-range sensor suite augmented by a drone swarm distant early warning sphere."

"Expect *Alfred's* position relative to the convoy to change constantly. Call out if you encounter any unusual activity."

"Thank you. We launch in forty-seven minutes."

Decatur sat in silence while sipping his coffee, watching each captain's vid-entity disappear. Brett Thomas was the last to leave. Decatur could see his friend wanted to say something and wondered briefly why he didn't. Then, he too was gone. Decatur double checked connections by linking directly into ship's status to make sure no live channels to the room remained open and no telltale whisper cookies were left behind by his recent visitors.

Forty-six minutes, now. More than enough time for operations to launch the microdrone net. Ah, there it goes, our advanced warning extending a full two light-seconds ahead of the convoy. Even this close to home is not a safe location, most boarding and crew impressments occur within three light-minutes of disembarkation or port approach. I'll feel more at ease once we are en route and at supralight. Space is too large to find, much less intercept, even a million-ton vessel traveling at many times the speed of light.

"XO, take position upwave and slightly abaft their course. I want to keep the weather gage so we can quickly rush to their assistance should problems arise. If something does happen, every second …"

A warning ping from the microdrone net ripped through his command string.

"… belay that order, XO. Our drones are returning a hot detection."

An image solidified as data streamed in from thousands of remote autonomous sensors, clarifying with each microscopic drone's added data packet until he could resolve every detail on its surface. His eyes took in the coal-black, dimpled oblate spheroid typical of a CTAC warbird. Unlike the flatter, saucer-like shapes of the NAU, this ship was nearly spherical. Surface dimples characteristic of a Chinese design they claimed provided superior gravitonic field tuning. Then, the captain spotted something different about the dimpled patterning. The surface wasn't uniformly pocked like a golf ball, there were regular interruptions in the pattern.

"Yes sir," His XO, replied. "Identification lists it as a CTAC pocket destroyer commanded by Captain Xi Hsu, a twenty-year military academy veteran. They're at near proximity on the opposite side of Kraken's moon. That explains why they haven't spotted us and ripped into our convoy. Good thing you released the drone net so early."

Potential options washed over Decatur like the release of a floodgate's waters.

This is all happening so soon, we're not even out of Kraken system and my people are new to each other.

My first duty is to the safety of the convoy but if that CTAC warbird takes after us, I'll lose all advantage.

One moment. Good, the drone signal clears as more of the swarm rises above the satellite's horizon. Hsu's ship is locked to a merchant. Why, it appears to be one of my wayward captains. One who decided to try the voyage on their own.

I am charged to defend all in this convoy but if I go to this merchant's aid, I leave the others unprotected and risk losing more of them. It's true, that captain chose not to rendezvous with the convoy so … no, there is more to this than a single merchant…

My general orders charge me with stopping the taking of our shipping and impressment of our spacers. If I allow Hsu to depart, they will be free to move on to create even greater atrocities.

Decatur knew they had little time left, "XO, they are boarding one of our merchants. Notify the convoy to alter the alpha leg of their course to segment one-one-point-seven, that vector will take advantage of the lunar shadow and mask their departure. Return to their original course, at beta waypoint T-32. We'll rejoin them shortly thereafter but for now, we have business here."

"Alter the drone swarm path to continue shielding the convoy."

"Set **Alfred's** course for the CTAC vessel. Keep the moon between us as long as possible and then come upon them indirectly as if we have yet to discover them."

Decatur could feel his XO's agitation in her reply, "We're going to confront a CTAC war vessel and leave the convoy on their own? Respectfully, Sir, our responsibility is the safety of the convoy."

It is the duty of an XO to make sure the captain understands the alternatives to any situation, but Decatur sensed her concern went beyond a simple sense of duty. They had an unproven crew and he had proposed taking on an experienced CTAC pocket destroyer.

"If we leave that ship, it will continue to prey on other merchants. This is a good chance to blood our people."

"Aye aye, Sir. Course set to near pass abaft CTAC vessel."

"Very good. When we have them in direct sight don't try to be sneaky. Wait a while then do an abrupt course change as though you just spotted them. Notify me when you do, I'd like to speak with that captain."

"Find Major Walters, give him my regards and ask him to contact me. I have immediate need of his team's services."

"Aye aye, Sir."

Steve Walters' contact came in less than a minute, "You don't waste any time, Decatur. We're not even beyond satellite orbit and you're calling us to action. You know we're all itchin' to go. Your orders?"

Jankin Decatur wasn't as excited on the prospects as the major, "We're going to be a bit sneaky on this one. Let me fill you in ….."

Boarding Party

Local Space
Near side of Kraken's moon, ecliptical

The familiar waft of lemons with a touch of gun oil was there again as Major Steve Walters completed his high-vac suit's final checks and he switched over to the mix of high oxygen and activated Xeon trace elements optimized for combat. As if on cue, the team's ready room 'strike range' warning flashed across his HiveTab. Time for one last, critical scan of the area and his people before launch.

The tactical mobile launch bay was big. Big enough that the local weather patterns within it had to be controlled. His special ops team and their equipment were clustered off to one corner of the bay, occupying only a small fraction of its area, the air wing took up most of the real estate.

Unlike most engagements in the abyss, this promised to be very personal and in a relatively confined theatre.

"Fourteen sleds loaded and ready, Sir." Corporal Mike Yatsko reported as he approached Lieutenant Travis Strake and Major Walters. The major silently nodded. He'd run his own personal checklist and his mind was reviewing everything that could go wrong on an operation like this one. A part of him wondered if that old, now familiar smell that came on just before an operation was only in his imagination. How could sixty-seven rangers manage to stink of fear when suited in hard-vacuum combat suits? Then again, maybe the odor was his and his alone.

Being early in their first mission, they would launch as a heavy platoon, more than sixty-seven rangers. Ship-to-ship operations were always a challenge and there were a thousand and three things that could go wrong using these delivery systems the grunts called 'Slug Shots' even though they were of simple design. Each was a small, cylindrical rack-like delivery cage shaped a bit like an elongated rifle slug, little more than a central tube with cradles welded to it. The cylinder will support a combination of up to four warriors, robot drones, or man-portable heavy equipment packages lying parallel to its long axis.

He waited, watching a corporal and lieutenant slide into their racks, snuggling into compartments barely wide enough to enclose their shoulders. The slug's translucent surface became opaque as they entered, each ranger nearly disappearing before his eyes as the active camouflage came to life, with the entire slug eventually fading piecemeal from view. All but one of the delivery systems were loaded and ready, it was time for him to squirm into the last open compartment, his would be the last slug of the load. It would be a FIFO launch. First-In-First-Out, with his command slug bringing up the end of the firing sequence.

Walters squirmed headfirst down along the slug's central tube that contained the miniature slipdrive, wrapping around it with the other three rangers like one of four pole-dancers. Shifting his weapons rack and supplies to the side, he placed a 'ready' command directly into their slug's receptor using his HiveTab interface. The rack emitted a high energy mist that enveloped the entire craft, instantly solidifying into a smooth monomolecular skin, shrink-wrapping the four rangers and cargo within.

All was dark for a few seconds then a hollow hum rose from the central tube as the tiny slipdrive came to life, ripping open the electron shells of everything in its field – equipment, gas, and human alike. It was a dangerous field, able to exist only by the placement of that thin, single-molecule thick skin that permitted the drive to fire up even though it already existed within the stronger drive-field of the *Alfred*.

Without that protective monolayer, the slug and the entire vessel would have instantly converted to a cloud of expanding subelectron particles and gravitic energy.

With a range of millions of miles, the slug-ship's slipdrive provided both transport and an impervious barrier that absorbed all emissions radiating from the passengers including body and systems heat. Except for a slight background distortion during movement, each Slug Shot was invisible to any biologic or manufactured external sensors since the field created a deflection barrier of all particles and wavelengths external to the carrier, including photon and neutron particle beams.

Control clusters and tactical scenario displays came to life surrounding the major in a universe of stars overlaid with status reports. He released a 'Rangers Loaded and Ready' flag across the bridge net. Then, Major Walters steeled himself for the worst part of the mission, waiting for bridge release and start of the launch sequence.

The call came sooner than expected, "Major Walters, your team is green to go. Good Hunting." Captain Decatur's voice command sent wide open across the ranger net startled him, he'd expected little more than a green-flag release.

A synaptic subroutine in his HiveTab initiated the release sequence as he considered the start of operations, *Captain must really think this is something special. Well, I guess it is. We're finally striking back in a slap fest they started.*

The first of many deep rumbles followed by a jolt racked his frame as the first slug shot broke its linkage to the rail and sailed out into the universe. Walters prayed there would be no hang-ups, no failures that might result in **Alfred's** complete disintegration or, personally worse, an internal fire cooking those waiting to launch and trapped in their frames.

Even though it would be a bit longer before he launched, an external view, courtesy of that first-launched slug, surrounded him. His universe expanded, details clarified as more of the slugs emerged and spread into formation. Eventually, he was able to change the angle of observation by combining data packets from several slugs.

A tingle flipped across his subconscious followed by the stronger jolt of his own slug's release. His was last but he was free, a nearly textbook platoon release with Kraken's small moon dead ahead and his rangers, formed into a teardrop-shaped formation of invisible cigar-shaped slug ships, as they sailed directly for the satellite's center. The slug swarm didn't need call signs since all were linked into a secure phased-frequency hopping, burst-transmit HiveNet that input directly into each pilot's brain with a tag identifier.

Major Walters initiated a platoon link that overrode their displays and conversations, "Okay, here's where practice pays off. We're on stealth from here on out and you will hold transmission and formation discipline. No fancy wave-skipping today, you hear that Ramrod?"

"That was a good release, now follow the course laid out in mission briefing."

The CTAC warbird lay directly ahead of their formation but on the opposing side of the heavy-metal satellite as they swarmed downward directly towards the moon's surface. Without creating a ripple in the ethereal waves of lunar gravity, they covertly slid in nice and easy by tacking over to a lunar-primary gravity wave and sliding down its gravity well.

The flight dove for the surface, leveling off so close they raised a small dust-cloud on the airless surface and had to fly around all but the smallest lunar peaks. Like swarming hornets, they banked to follow a curving longitudinal course directly over the dead sphere's northern pole and down the opposite face, expertly wave skipping from wave-crest to crest as they coursed over the strong pull of lunar gravity to stay aloft without striking any rock beds or crater rims. Crater images blurred past as they skimmed the surface across half the planetoid until a bright point of distant, reflected light rose over the lunar horizon. Their target lay ahead, physically visible now. Still, caution ruled and they didn't immediately vector directly towards it.

The attack swarm minimized all chance of detection by going the extra distance and not altering their approach to the CTAC destroyer until they could hop to a vector that placed the lunar surface to their backs and their target directly ahead.

"Prepare to link to a galactic core wave and warp in for the bogey. Keep a tight formation. Three, two, one, now."

The CTAC destroyer's image grew as each second ticked by until they could make out details. It appeared a mottled-gray form, surprisingly irregular in shape when viewed by any merchant captain accustomed to working with smooth, nearly saucer-shaped ships devoid of sharp edges or bumps, that would complicate the slip-drive field calculations of the external particle repellant shield.

His eyes scanned the surface bumps housing weapons pods that mottled the warbird's surface along with standard CTAC markings that flickered red and yellow across its surface as they searched for the best points for entry boarding.

A call from *Alfred's* bridge came across, "Major, I've linked you into the external communications channel. I am going to contact the CTAC ship and confirm they are conducting an attack rather than a friendly visit. Your rangers are to approach to minimum safe distance to the objective and wait for either an attack or withdrawal command. If I cannot contact the merchant captain or if they demand to board us, consider that a situation flag for you to initiate action."

Margo Stoudt's voice broke in over a private link into Decatur's HiveTab startling him, "Captain Decatur, I appreciate the privilege of you allowing us to sit in on the bridge, but I feel I must speak up. You can't just issue an order to open hostilities and begin a war without a formal declaration. You have no idea what's happening over on the two ships."

The journalist immediately regretted her interruption when Captain Decatur's eyes ratcheted over to her seat in the high gallery at the rear of the bridge, "Sergeant Orlop, if Ms. Stoudt or Mr. Mason speak a word or directs a HiveTab transmission to anyone on the bridge but each other, you are to forcibly remove them and deposit them in the brig until further notice."

"Ms. Stoudt, I will forgive this one interruption. We are not initiating hostilities. We are addressing that CTAC vessel's actions. In any case, our ship looks exactly like a commercial freighter so they will have no fear of us, and I expect they will quickly confirm their hostile intentions."

"Please refrain from interruptions and I will gladly address them when not on duty."

"Easy people. Hold this course a bit longer." Decatur's voice carried across the room. His people were unproven and on edge, it was obvious in all but perhaps his pilot, Lieutenant Nauman, who appeared as cool as ever. A few words were in order.

"Remember, we look like a merchant. We want them to think that's all we are. Mr. Nauman, when I signal, I want you to vector indirectly for them. Luff her a bit and change course sloppily, let them think we just spotted our merchant brother who was stopped by a CTAC destroyer."

"Communications, if they don't initiate contact, I'll ask you to hail them. Keep it audio-only, let them think we're having trouble with the MultiVid, send an error-tag with the audio. Ready now, here we go."

An exceptionally bright star rose above the distant lunar horizon and was immediately highlighted on their walldisplay as 'CTAC Destroyer *Xuchange* and merchant *CSS Grimes*' along with their present course listed as 'stable lunar orbital'.

Nothing happened for one minute ... two ...

The captain's Tactical Display lit up, a sparkling haze surrounded the CTAC vessel marking the location of his ranger platoon as 'ready and waiting'. Decatur broke the growing tension on the bridge, "Let's see if we can draw their attention. Helm, make your course bogie intercept."

"Aye aye, Sir. Bogie intercept." Repeated across the bridge in an age-old tradition that managed to survive from the days when commands had to be heard above the wind, wave, and shots-fired on an open deck. A part of Decatur's brain listened, aware that their actions over the next few minutes would mean survival or failure but his concentration focused on learning as much as he could about the capabilities of the CTAC ship they were engaging.

Well, that answers one question about reaction time. Didn't take them ten seconds to pick us up when we changed to intercept. Haven't said a word so far. Good, the closer we approach, the easier they are making this ...

"Unregistered Kraken merchant vessel, this is CTAC warbird *Xuchange*. Continue your course then bring your ship to dead stop relative at ten kilometers. Comply or be fired upon."

Margo, looking for telltales in the captain's reaction, was amazed to see a smile cross his face. A grin, so feral it enlightened his visage and sent shivers up her back. His reply was totally out of character as he meekly submitted, "Aye aye. We will comply and be glad to provide any needed support for our sister ship."

"Is the Captain available? I'd like a few words with him."

"Captain is not available. Obey the command." Was their curt and final reply, Alfred's AI confirmed, "***Xuchange***, transmission ends."

On station just off from the CTAC ship, Major Walters acknowledged Decatur's command and the swarm of Slug Shots uniformly angled in upon both merchant and warbird. They had access to the layout of the merchant and therefore knew the locations of each cargo hatchway. The CTAC ship wasn't much different in layout, containing multiple visible hatchways, representing weakened entry points through a ship's hull.

Major Walters synchronized his slug swarm, "Move in, nice and easy now just like in maneuvers. The gravitonic field of the two cable-linked ships will pull you in easily if you just ease into it, let it settle your slug into contact before you dismount."

Like a settling swarm of nesting bees, the slugs melded to the exterior of their targets until the CTAC destroyer bristled with the long torpedo-shaped, sinister black forms sticking out from its skin like deadly parasitic eggs on the back of a caterpillar. Then, on cue, the field drive of each slug ship shifted, gradually phasing into that of the destroyer as they passed through their spindizzy region and began releasing their deadly load of rangers and munitions.

Timing from this point on was critical, they had a few minutes before the CTAC's bridge would notice the imbalance of their reduced slipdrive field caused by the additional load of dozens of the tiny slug frames that attached to the ship's outer hull.

The slug's skins dissolved and its occupants exited into hard vacuum while staying close to the hull and within the spindizzy as each team immediately set to unraveling close-packed bundles of wire, laying them out to form a network of enriched tungsten filaments surrounding the perimeter of the nearest ship's hatch. They moved swiftly, taking great care to hold the filament bundles close to the metal surface because even under low power, a slipdrive's debris repellant field could rip both ranger and wire-netting off-ship if it were lifted more than thigh-high above the ship's skin, ripping both out into the abyss like a bird flying into a jet-prop. Gliding silently across the hull so those inside would not hear their passage, they completed assembly within a few seconds then waited until Major Walters received the 'ready' call from all the slug-teams. On his signal, sixteen tungsten nettings activated a shunt field that drew in the ship's own gravitonic field forming a shaped barrier around the hatch-plate. Pre-programmed tungsten atoms transformed their molecular lattice initiating a molecular reaction with the ship's hull. The reaction dissolved the plating of the hatch by sinking active, high energy tungsten ions into the metal's atomic matrix. It required only a few seconds for the circular hatchway frame to separate from the ship and be sucked out into vacuum but restrained by the tungsten netting. The CTAC vessel's computers saw this as nothing more than a minor hull disturbance and sounded no alarms.

The ship's internal atmosphere gushed out into the air-tight netting forming a human-sized blister projecting out into vacuum, even with the expansion, it quickly equalized to ship's pressure. Inside the target vessel, there was little more than a sudden flutter in local pressure with only a minor drop in the compartment's temperature from gas expansion but the simultaneous release of sixteen entries was enough for the CTAC ship's systems to shut all airtight doors and the CTAC bridge now knew something was wrong but they didn't know what for all their sensors were once again reading normal.

Sergeant Jaeger cursed with admirable fluency to himself in frustration as he waited, watching a section of the netting on his squad's blister surface shift color. A few seconds of eternity and the transformation stopped but no portal opened for the rangers. What lay before the sergeant wasn't a door but a transition swatch.

Moisture adsorption pads inside his vac-suit worked overtime removing the sweat from his palms as he cursed under his breath, flipped his weapon's safety off and took his first step forward. This was the part he hated. Eyes wide open, he pressed his body against the activated tungsten netting. It withdrew from the suit's contact and, like walking into a soft wall of descending water, the netting reformed and flowed around him without releasing a molecule of internal atmosphere from the blister as he transitioned inside and the netting eventually sealed itself once again after his passage.

Sergeant Johann Jaeger was the first Kraken Ranger to enter the CTAC vessel on that ominous day. Every nerve on edge, but he was prepared as he stepped inside.

The two astonished CTAC crewmates however were not prepared for the black apparition that appeared behind them.

Jaeger didn't ask questions, there wasn't time. His finger pulsed once on the trigger of his shoulder weapon. Officially termed a 'Remington Needle Gun', it was an antipersonnel weapon designed for shipboard encounters that directed a stream of delicate, almost glass-like crystalline projectiles that would fragment against the dense shell of a ship's bulkhead and, except for cosmetic disfigurement of the ship's interior, they inflicted minimal damage. Striking something soft, like human skin or the soft flexure seam of a hard-vacuum suit, and the results were very different.

His trigger-pull released a burst of energy inside the needle gun, a short-lived eruption of pulsing energy from a tiny internal gravitic generator, created a rotating electromagnetic field strong enough for each pulse to shave a few molecules from the surface of a caseless ammo slug of silicon. Energized molecules ripped free by each pulse followed pulse-field lines that spun them into an elongated tube of hot plasma, solidifying in microseconds as the plasma packet exited the barrel as a stitched flight of elongated, hypervelocity needles.

Jaeger brought the crewmates down with one single burst of flechettes, ripping blood and tissue from the throat of the nearest crewmember and shredding the midsection of the second. The force of the midsection blast was enough to splatter bile and gore across the far bulkhead before slamming what remained of her into the bulkhead.

Five rangers entered behind him bringing with them a crew-served weapon.

"Jones and Madison take your system and establish a barrier at the cross corridor. McFiely, station your weapon there and watch our six. Keep Jones and Madison for support."

"Flagler take point. Our objective just changed. We now have the privilege of targeting their bridge. Move out."

A smile formed on Jaeger's face as alarms began wailing down the passageway. *We caught them with their pants down. With any luck, most of their armed spacers are over on the* **Grimes***.*

Crossing into the next section, he dropped a crippler into the door's closure track, they wanted the ship open from one end to the other for the next phase. Flechettes wailed past from a side corridor just ahead, sparkling against the bulkhead. His squad flattened themselves against the bulkhead and waited. They didn't have long to wait.

Moving in deadly silence, blue-suited figures entered from the side passageway, they were also following the howling sound of flechette fire. Flagler's arm went out in a balled fist. With measured time, he released one finger followed by a second and then a swift chop and the squad fired in a single blast. The slight delay was long enough for every CTAC blue-suit to be out and exposed down-passage.

The fusillade caught them by surprise sending blood, shredded skin, and cloth in a spray across the forward bulkhead. A mournful cry lifted, followed by a mangled groan, quickly silenced with the impact of a combat knife to the throat. Outnumbered ten-to-one, they brooked no chance. They could afford no niceties and a wounded spacer could still kill.

The ship's lighting flickered then died and the ranger's low-light vision kicked in. Ignoring all glideways and lifts, the team scrambled up ladders through two decks with not a soul to be seen.

Jaeger was getting nervous, *Where are they? Officer's country should be full of spacers by now.*

Ahead lay a corridor lined with vids, now completely blank and on their static default screens. At its end set an ornate door, obviously an armored bulkhead.

Jaeger motioned for them to spread out, wide-station. Kiely sidled up to the door and started placing shearing charges when the bulkheads surrounding them flickered and shook. Three loads of old-fashioned buckshot went down-passage, catching Kiely in the back and shoulder, throwing him to the deck as wild, undulating screams filled the corridor.

The corridor right before the bridge's armored door was wide open to the surrounding passage's which converged upon it leaving no cover for the rangers. Jaeger flipped the safety on a gas grenade and lobbed it. Red smoke, saturated with flashing yellow-bright particles, filled the passageway, blinding the charging blue-suit spacers.

"Suppressive fire," Jaeger shouted, his voice harsh and rasping. The heads-up displays of the rangers highlighted each squad-mate's position to minimize friendly fire casualties as they released bursts of flechettes, sending them down-passage at waist level. They fired once, twice then charged forward, slamming the enemy with an oncoming wall of fire.

A ragged scream cut the air on Jaeger's side, he twisted and saw a ranger struggling with a CTAC spacer. Swerving, he knifed the spacer then pushed forward barely skipping a step. Screams and calls filled the smoke-laced passageway. Something hit him, slamming him to the side, spinning him and his world about. It hurt; he had a hard time breathing but the load hadn't pierced his vacuum suit. Though his head was spinning, and pain filled every movement, he was looking for a target when the double-thump of the shaped charge bracelet placed on the armored bridge entrance by Kiely spun him in a two-step into the bulkhead. Ignoring any blue-suits who might be ahead, he turned to the now mangled doorway of the bridge and ran head-on into a concussive blast coming from its interior.

"Rush 'em, now." Corporal Covasa called over the general push and they charged through the shattered bulkhead into the bridge.

Her screamed commands came out in Mandarin, echoing across the bridge, "Drop your weapons. Facedown on the deck. Anyone so much as moves a hand will be fired ... "A shot rang out. Chaos erupted amid the sparkling red smoke still spreading from the last grenade. Screams and curses in Mandarin rang out but their resistance was short-lived for only bridge security personnel carried arms and they had all been eliminated.

A moan-filled hush filled the room. The smoke dissipated slowly, revealing white-suited officers spread-eagled on the deck at their stations across all three levels of the bridge. Four black-suited security guards lay in expanding pools of blood and smoking gore. Jaeger spotted Kiely face down in the center of the bridge. He must have been the first one inside despite the wound he'd already taken while setting the charge. Kiely wasn't the first squad member Jaeger lost in action, but the feeling never stopped the hurt. It was then he realized, he'd grown too close to his people.

Mourn later, right now they needed firepower at their backs, "McFiely, bring your stitcher to the bridge, and cover the entry."

The static-slap of flexwrap shackles flipping around the wrists of CTAC officers filled the air for a few moments. Jaeger double checked every one of them as they underwent a final shakedown for hidden weapons. Then he spotted his target and walked over to the uniform with the greatest cluster of gold cauliflower on it.

"Johnson, wait. Don't shackle this one." Prodding the supine figure on the deck with the hot-tip of his pulsar, Jaeger barked a command that his suit translated for him, "Stand up, Sir. No sudden moves. Nothing in your hands. Fingers spread wide, I'm a bit nervous right now."

Hate-filled orbs, black as the inside of a flechette barrel, lifted and turned, staring into the eyes of this peasant who dared to speak to him in this manner.

"Are you the captain?"

There was no answer, but Jaeger's suit had already identified the officer, "Come now, Captain Hsu. There's little use in silence. I already know all about you."

"I'm sure you monitored our boarding before we took your bridge, so you should know there's no chance of continued resistance. Command your people to drop their weapons. Surrender now and minimize bloodshed. You will be well treated and repatriated as soon as we can establish a prisoner swap."

"Prisoner swap? You impudent little pup. This is piracy. I'll move mountains to attend your hanging. You obviously aren't NAU even though you speak their language. Who in hells dark realm are you people?"

"I'm Staff Sergeant Johann Jaeger of the Kraken Rangers. Now surrender your ship or must I give your XO a field promotion to captain and see if he is more reasonable?"

The CTAC captain's face turned a bright red, his hands began shaking. Jaeger's finger lightly caressed the trigger of his weapon.

Suddenly the captain seemed to gather his wits. Hsu's attention turned to the monitors still operational on the bridge. There were patches of conflict on both the CTAC ship and the *Grimes* but it was obvious, both vessels had fallen.

The fire fled Hsu's eyes, replaced by a cold hatred of the sergeant and the situation he found himself in, "Ching Tau, open an all-circuits command." The words translated instantly into Jaeger's ears.

The sergeant gave his ranger a nod and released the communications officer's wrists, "At your command, Honorable Captain."

Hsu's head shot round to communications like he'd been gut-punched, while fury again blazed in his eyes as they ratcheted over to the small officer like a targeting laser. It lasted only a moment, his shoulders fell as he mumbled a single near-silent oath that the pickups in Jaeger's suit interpreted as one simple, devastating word, 'honorable'.

Taking a deep, jagged breath, he returned his attention to the Kraken sergeant, "How dare you. You are nothing. Not a country much less a unified, independent people. You have no economy to build and support a star-going military."

"You will live a short life but, I assure you, it will be an interesting one, pirate."

His eyes defocused for a second as he confirmed the CTAC ship's communications status then, "This is Captain Hsu. I have surrendered the ship. Lay down your weapons. Resistance is no longer required."

One-by-one, hot spots of resistance faded. Two held on a bit longer then abruptly, simultaneously went dark.

They converted a drone repository on the CTAC vessel into a brig, it takes a lot of room to hold, control and catalog nearly four hundred CTAC spacers. Less than forty CTAC raiders taken on the *Grimes* survived to be shuttled back to their ship. The Rangers followed the plan with the precision expected of an elite force, delivering them in small, controllable groups to the CTAC holding bay, even as other teams began repairs to both ships.

A thousand needed chores screamed for attention in Captain Decatur's mind but he restrained himself, this was a time to delegate authority and his people needed to be organized. After what seemed like an eternity, he called his XO over, "Commander Hopewell, you and Lieutenant Osaka are to shuttle over to the *Grimes*. If, in your estimation, their captain is no longer capable of taking command or he is deceased then you will take command until I decide how to proceed."

"If you find the captain well and hardy, then extend my greetings and inform him that I wish to speak with him, immediately. He is to return directly on your shuttle. Should he balk at this order, you are to request assistance from Major Walters. Have the rangers bring him over under guard, in flexwrap and trussed like a pig if you must."

"At first opportunity, have Mr. Osaka perform the same duties on the CTAC warbird.

"I would like you to begin an independent appraisal of the merchant's vessel. Find out how they came to be here. Correlate their cargo with their manifests. Determine if she is still flight capable. I want your personal assessment on this, not that of some merchant captain without enough sense to stay with the convoy."

"Then do the same for the CTAC vessel." Jim suddenly remember his crew, many of whom signed on even with their reduced wages, "Document the condition, survivors, and assets of our capture for our ship's records. Remember, Kraken has adopted the Earth's ancient admiralty law that dates to sixteenth-century international codes in configuring our service. This entitles us to return any equipment, vehicles, cargo, and vessels captured during armed conflict and open a prize case for court determination of their status and disposal. Per our service papers, we are entitled to up to sixty percent of the worth of all assets and you, as the executive officer, will personally see a nice percentage."

"Eventually, you will select and take a prize crew of no more than thirty spacers and return both CTAC and merchant's vessels to Kraken for award. I imagine this should improve spirits among the crew and our rangers. Do not transmit news of the victory on your own authority to anyone but our line staff, let the politicians determine how they wish to release the information."

"Returning of the *Grimes* to port may be a bit sensitive, politically. Return her only to our own command. Let the politicians handle any objections from her owners and remind them that this happened because she refused convoy escort."

"I'll embed formal orders in your file. Congratulations Captain Hopewell."

Hopewell's head turned and her puzzled frown transformed into a broad grin as she realized that this was to be her first independent command. The title was appropriate. After all, field promotions often became permanent.

~~*~*~*~*

Ship's log, Monday 2180.0803 1400 hours.

The recovered merchant vessel **Grimes** *and CTAC destroyer* **Xuchange** *currently stand in our lee with prize crews upon both. Our convoy proceeds onward with a three-fighter escort sent out after the* **Grimes** *action to support their drone shield. We intend to rejoin them shortly, as soon as our merchant and prize vessels are properly and safely discharged.*

Commander Hollen will return both vessels to Kraken for the court's disposal auction or induction into the Kraken fleet. I do believe ....

A priority ping from Major Walters on the TabNet command channel with a link to the XO interrupted his log entry. "Captain, could you come over to the Xuchang. I've found something you may want to personally handle, and I'd rather not discuss it over channels."

"I'll be right over, Major."

A quick call to the chief bosun's mate, "Boats, make ready my launch and invite our embeds, they may be interested in seeing a CTAC warbird. I'm on my way down."

The takeover of a fully functional CTAC Destroyer requires careful planning on how to handle a hostile contingent of several hundred spacers, as well as CTAC marines using a small prize crew. It was a complex and delicate undertaking that, if not done properly, could degrade into mutiny and loss of the prize. Transport back to port was complicated by the rule that Standard Operations Procedure (SOP) allotted no more than forty to fifty spacers assigned as prize crew for this size vessel.

Decatur took the lift from the heart of officer's country to the lower levels of *Alfred.* Throughout the entire transit, Major Walter's cryptic request for Decatur's physical attendance occupied his thoughts. The request was unnatural since Rangers pride themselves on being able to handle any situation. The captain expected a substantial problem. Yet, on the way to the hanger, he exited two decks above level. His boson would need a few more minutes to ready the captain's gig and Decatur believed any chance he had to walk through the working decks should be taken. Decatur was in familiar country since he'd spent years doing these same chores as he worked his way up the ranks.

Three spacers working on a magnetic rotator strap stopped to greet him as he passed. A formal interruption of work to come to attention with salute was not customary when onboard *Alfred* but it was usual for crewmembers to acknowledge the rank in passing with a slight nod and brief redirection of their attention to see if the officer required anything. Their reaction and body language conveyed more to Decatur than any ensign's morning report.

To their surprise, he stopped to speak to them, "Working the straps can be a pain in the arse if they aren't fitted properly but it looks like you have the chore well in hand. People are waiting for me so I don't have much time, but I wanted to convey my congratulations on a job well done, please tell your crewmates. This is *Alfred's* first engagement and, although we aren't through it yet, I'm proud of the job and the crew's level of performance."

"I know the scuttlebutt is flying about regarding prize money and, while I haven't the final say on it, I expect we'll all eventually see a nice bonus. It isn't every day an intact enemy destroyer is taken as a prize."

There's nothing like the mention of a few extra thalers in a spacer's pay to bring up spirits and their faces recorded that exact reaction.

"How much do you think it will be, Sir?" Decatur's HiveTab identified her as common spacer Jenkins. He knew what they wanted to hear, particularly the shy youngster visibly holding back his questions in awe of his captain.

"Lord, I don't know. That's up to the courts but I suspect a spacer even as lowly as you, Jenkins, can afford a politician's vacation next leave and still come back with a jingle in your pocket. Just a thought, but if you invite Chief Geer along and talk him into contributing, you'll vacation like kings."

"Sorry, but I must leave."

Their excited voices echoed far down the passageway until he passed through the safety airlock into the flight bay and a 'gig ready' ping sounded in his HiveTab as the door opened. It was a smaller bay than that used by the rangers but still more than a brisk five-minute walk across deck. The ship's external bulkhead was active and oriented so that he could see the surface of Kraken's larger moon partially occluding the blue and green sphere of their home planet. The brilliance of a milky-way unimpeded by a planet's atmosphere filled the sky with a billion multi-colored pinpricks of light. His eyes automatically went to a few barely resolvable points that managed to display as something more than a single bright pinpoint. The brighter spheroid was the merchant's ship and nearby, appearing to the naked eye as a faint, double star companion, was the dimmer CTAC warbird, barely visible against the firmament.

In time-honored tradition, a bosun piped him aboard with the announcement of '*Alfred* arriving'. He entered without greeting the six spacers seated inside. Hitching a transit over to the CTAC vessel on a captain's gig was frowned upon in the service. It was a rule Captain Decatur preferred to overlook when critical matters were involved. However, bending rules did not go so far as to permit access to his private cabin and, as he moved forward, he could hear voices from within.

Margo Stoudt and her fellow journalist, Mark Mason, rose to greet him as he entered, "Captain Decatur, thank you for letting us come along. This is an opportunity we've been hoping for."

Surprised, Decatur responded with a noncommittal answer, "Ah-yes." Still, public opinion for their mini-war and his ship's mission was important and journalists have a way with swaying public reaction. He wasn't sure just what they were heading into but decided it would be wise to humor them.

Within bounds of course.

His reply was intentionally cryptic, "You may find that you wish otherwise. I remind you of your contract. I have the right of first-review before you transmit anything. Should you ignore this rule you may find yourself excluded from future embeds. If the infraction carries enough weight, the penalties can be severe."

"Do I make myself clear?"

A thirty-second warning interrupted any answer. The gig shifted to internal gravity and lifted a millimeter above the deck plates. Decatur directed their attention forward in anticipation, "Now please watch the forward bulkhead, you don't want to miss this."

The wall ahead of them disappeared as the gig's walldisplay imaged the external space ahead through the active skin of his ship. Decatur watched a thirty-foot square area on the outer bulkhead began shimmering as though it imaged the starry universe surrounding them that was reflecting from a watery surface. Without a sound or feeling of acceleration, the gig passed through the distortion and emerged into the crystal-clear cosmos of stars.

Margo strained to draw nearer the view, a part of her listening to the quiet strains of an ancient musical piece called 'Pictures at an Exhibition' playing in the gig's background until she broke the silence, "I've seen the universe from many transport lounges but I've never felt so close to the awesome raw beauty of it."

Not wishing to waste a millisecond of his time, Decatur was reviewing the status reports for both ships under his charge, his interest focusing on the list of injured and dead. A partial list of items on the manifest of the CTAC vessel caught his attention, but he couldn't go into detail because of her interruption and besides, they were now on final approach.

He rose and crossed to stand behind the journalists, his HiveTab reacting to a point in the display where his attention focused, "If you look very closely in the region I've circled, you can see our destination. There are two ships there looking rather like a dumbbell, two slightly ballooned weights at the end of a short crossbar handle. They are the merchant ship *Grimes* and a CTAC warbird. They are connected by the CTAC's vacuum transit gangway. As we draw in, the resolution improves to the point that we can image the slug shots used by our rangers sticking out from the two vessels like spikes on a medieval knight's mace."

Minutes passed before their destination filled a larger portion of the walldisplay, "Look closely now. Adjacent to each spike is a cylindrical tube extending into the abyss, its end is formed by the circular slice of ship's skin removed by the rangers to force entry into the target vessel. The glittering, silvery net you see acting as the walls of the cylinder is composed of our Active Tungsten technology. It was used to remove the cylindrical cap and now acts as an entry point into the ships."

"Active Tungsten is an invention of Kraken National Labs and is confidential. You will not mention it in your releases nor will you discuss how easy it is for us to repair the entry point by simply performing a molecular weld of the cap back into the ship. You'll be able to observe that part of the operation after we have both vessels under control and just prior to departure, perhaps you'll be able to use that information in the future."

Mason was familiar with military operations, the concept of Active Tungsten was unheard of but the advantages were obvious, "A warbird's skin is like that of a tank yet your rangers have a way for a boarding party to penetrate it without blasting a ragged hole in the ship?"

"Yes, and without losing internal pressure. The method carries a bit more risk for the rangers boarding the ship since enemy combatants within might be a bit shaken, but they are not harmed by the entry. Our advantage is their forces cannot cover every square inch of a vessel's exterior surface so they have no idea where we may choose to enter."

"Now, I must depart at our first stop which is the CTAC vessel where Major Walters awaits. That ship is not yet a safe area for civilians. You will disembark to the **Grimes** where Commander Hopewell has assigned you an escort. I'm sure you will find plenty to write about over there since they were in the process of being boarded when we interrupted."

A wave of relief flooded over Decatur as he left the journalists behind. Politics was the purview of admirals and he had more than enough "tactical" problems to manage.

This was the first time he'd entered a CTAC docking bay, it was gray and plain, like most of their architecture, but otherwise resembled the hundreds of other Kraken and NAU bays he'd landed on. Major Walters was waiting with a squad of fully armed rangers standing at ready. Surely, this was overkill.

"I thought the ship was secure, Major."

"Yes sir, it is but the situation here is serious enough to warrant tighter security. Allow me to show you."

The major walked them past a group of CTAC spacers bound with flexwrap shackles, sitting cross-legged in a corner under guard, his curiosity grew as he passed by without the expected flurry of questions. Following a gray, humorless passageway, they down traversed two ladders to an area that he surmised would be akin to the lower flight bay on an NAU military vessel.

A team of combat medics exited a vacuum hatch that remained dogged open for easy passage, he was surprised to note they were not vac-suited and the passthrough didn't lead outside as any normal vacuum hatch would. The major carried a scowl on his face that Decatur had rarely seen in the serious but good-natured officer, "Watch your head, Captain. This isn't a standard ship's hatch."

Interior lighting was insufficient, and the rangers had supplemented it with portable sources that threw sinister dark shadows across a large bay filled with cages. Open drains lined the floor, an obvious runoff for the cages cleansed with recycled water under pressure, although cleaning was evidently not a regular affair for the area smelled strongly of urine, feces, and rotting meat.

The far bulkhead held four large cargo doors vacuum fitted for use in space as well as the atmosphere-dockside. Major Walters noted Decatur's scrutiny of the doors and commented, "The doors are electronically linked to the cages. They seal the hatch we just entered then, and after pumping most of the air out of the bay, they flush the contents.

"Each cage is designed with specialized piping for cleanout providing easy and very effective flushing of all debris into hard vacuum. A very efficient way to police a large area, quickly."

"We believe they were nearing the next cleanout cycle when we interrupted the process."

"Please, follow me."

Then something caught his eye. Someone in the far corner of the bay, was setting up to digitize the scene. Decatur wondered why the major hadn't asked for authorization then, as they drew nearer, was shocked to recognize just how advanced the equipment was. This was not a simple three-dimensional virtual recorder. His surprise grew even more when he recognized Mark Mason carrying the latest in full emersion technology. Worst of all, the journalist hadn't requested permission and had been told to debark on the merchant.

The captain was taken aback, *Such impertinence and a blazing disregard for orders.*

A red fury churned inside him only to be subsumed by an epiphany initiated by a thread of cold calculations. Forgetting the journalist for the moment, he turned with a growing dread of the question he must pose, "What is in the cages, Major? What has been going on here?"

"There's quite a mix inside but so far we've identified more than eight hundred individuals from the NAU, Kraken, Jasper, and even CTAC regionals. More than seventy percent are dead, hence the smell and their desire to 'police' the area."

"Initial autopsy suggests they died of cold and starvation. Outright neglect rather than torture."

"CTAC officers yielded no information but our interrogation of surviving prisoners and CTAC spacers helped fill out the picture."

"If a CTAC spacer has not performed to standards or behaves in a subversive manner, they end up here. Captured NAU spacers are given a chance to sign on as CTAC crewmembers. If you have a needed skill, you become a CTAC spacer whether you want to or not, they are given no choice. The same offering is presented to the Kraken and Jasper merchant spacers whose ships they board."

"Spacers who do not sign allegiance to CTAC and all captured officers end up in here for interrogation until their knowledge is no longer needed."

"Space is a vast abyss. Debris ejected from these cells continues to follow the ejection vector indefinitely or until radiation dissolves the material or it falls into a star or encounters an obstruction. The ejection of debris is a shotgun blast of unwanted humanity. Clean, efficient and ready for the next load."

"This is more than an intelligence-gathering effort. CTAC must be running low on experienced spacers so it's to their advantage to intercept our commercial shipping, the benefits are threefold. They press new spacers into their service, they confiscate cargo and supplies for their own use by simply declaring it contraband shipping and then they have the option of taking the entire vessel to fill out fleet losses due to the conflict."

"As to our pressed spacers, repercussions are minimal since the NAU is too busy with the in-system conflict and cannot afford to dedicate assets to defend the distant colony worlds. Of course, they always manage to have the resources to collect tariffs and taxes."

Decatur noticed the major was waiting for a comment but his carefully controlled silence said volumes.

There was considerable activity in the bay and he noticed armed spacers clustered in a few areas, "Are you using CTAC spacers to police the area?"

"Aye, Sir. Spacers as well as selected officers. They're doing a good job of it too because they know they are preparing their new homes."

"I see. Where is their captain?"

"We have him secured in the main mess hall. That's the place we figured would be the least likely to have hidden long-distance communications devices."

"The medics removed a HiveTab class device from his mastoid, very similar in design to our own. Engineering is analyzing it now. Didn't want to take any chance of them communicating with the ship or with their chain of command. They made it a bit easier since none of the spacers or noncommissioned officers had the devices. CTAC apparently doesn't trust their people."

"Status of the captain's quarters and bridge?"

"The captain was very anxious to be returned to his quarters but, as per operational guidelines, his quarters and the bridge are sealed with guards posted. Ship's AI access to sensors and controls is restricted to life support. We're waiting for specialists to arrive before attempting a sweep of the software, circuits, and sensors."

"Very good. Let's go speak with their captain."

"Yes, Sir. Before we go, I recommend you speak with two merchant captains who were incarcerated here. They've been very helpful and have said some things you should hear for yourself."

"Lead on, Major."

Major Walters led him up four ladders where the passageway opened on what appeared to be the officer's mess. He could hear raised voices inside, then spotted two men and a woman in merchant uniforms engaged in very active conversation.

"Ahem!" Captain Decatur's simple clearing of his throat was enough to stop the conversation. "I didn't expect to meet you here Captain Esperanza. I was under the impression you had a damaged ship with crew and cargo to care for."

"However, since you are here, perhaps you will introduce your fellow captains?"

A short, gaunt older man in a tattered uniform that hung loosely from his shoulders pushed back his chair and stood, not wishing to wait upon another's introduction. He'd been well into a carefully portioned platter of reconstituted Chinese cuisine when the argument had interrupted his meal, "My apologies, Captain Decatur. I'm Captain Benjamin Straits of the *Milldover*, eight months out of Jasper. Excuse my companion, Captain Jason Leeds, for not rising. He's been here even longer than I and is a bit weak."

"But, apparently strong enough to engage in a shouting match," Decatur frowned towards the still seated captain.

"As you are apparently quite brazen enough to think your actions legal and justified," Esperanza blurted out, "and ..."

Esperanza's rant stopped when the fire in Jankin Decatur's eyes redirected to the impertinent merchant captain, "Illegal? Unjustified? This from a captain we just rescued from a CTAC boarding party."

"We would have been alright. It was an inspection. Nothing more and the *Grimes* has a clean manifest without contraband."

Decatur's eyes defocused for a fraction of a second as the information he requested flooded through his HiveTab, "Clean manifest without contraband ... yes, so I see. Have you asked your fellow captains just how it is they find themselves in such a sorry condition? Incarcerated?"

"Just where are their ships?"

Esperanza began to backpedal, "I have no idea how they came to be here. I and my officers were escorted to the mess hall awaiting the return of Captain Hsu when you attacked, and all hell broke loose."

Decatur let the silence hang for a moment as he turned to look around the mess hall, "I don't see your officers here. Where are they?"

"They were escorted back to my ship."

Decatur frowned, he already knew the answer but turned to the Major standing next to him in his blood-stained tactical vacuum suit and raised his eyebrows in question.

The reply was short and simple, "Three were tortured and did not survive the interrogation. Two others reported already spaced."

"Such is the hospitality you received upon this ship, Captain Esperanza, yet you attempt to deny the circumstance. One of your ports of call included the Mexico City Starport, an NAU facility. This qualifies your cargo as contraband in the eyes of any CTAC warbird."

"You were about to find yourself in a cage next to your fellow captains and your condition would soon have been as sorry as theirs."

Esperanza's face paled as Decatur spoke. She turned a questioning stare to Captain Straits. His reply was a simple nod of assent.

"Records show you broke protocol when you didn't notify Kraken Shipping of the boarding. Please explain."

"It wasn't necessary. We were assured it was a contraband inspection. Routine, nothing more."

Captain Straits let out a short laugh, "Contraband? Routine? I know Captain Esperanza. She's been running cargo to both sides, most likely ran into more than expected this time."

Decatur turned to Major Walters; an eyebrow raised in question.

"Yes, Sir. That was to be the next item on my list of items to show you. The captain has numerous items in cargo that are not on ship's manifest. Munitions, heavy weapons, and military ordinance. They also carried this …."

Walters netted a file over to Decatur with a 'Confidential' tag seal prominent on its digital envelope. Inside was a report of Kraken manufactured equipment and munitions classified "Top Secret" that included one of Kraken's new AI semi-autonomous torpedoes labeled 'Item AI-7'.

A rare look of surprise came over the captain, quickly adding to his growing fury when Walters commented, "Yes sir, an 'AI-7'. Our Techs ran a scan and discovered something I thought you might find exceptionally interesting on this day of great finds. We identified DNA fragments on the packing belonging to John Bucker, a corporate officer of one of our military distributors."

"I well remember Mr. Bucker, thank-you Major for a very timely revelation," Decatur responded blandly not wanting to leave a hint of their earlier clandestine mission into his voice.

"Captain Esperanza, you have lost your officers and a good portion of your crew ..."

"You murdered them!"

"Don't be ridiculous. They were dead before we arrived, you can thank your CTAC friends for that. I'm sure you were slated for the same fate. Now, no more interruptions."

"Captain Esperanza, I'm placing you under arrest. We will return your ship to port. We'll let the lawyers determine what to do with the cargo and how to deal with the ship's owners."

"CTAC's colonial prisoners will be repatriated on Kraken unless they wish to sign on as crew aboard the Grimes."

A sudden question interrupted the captain, "What are you going to do with the CTAC spacers and officers?"

"I don't understand your concern for them, Captain Straits nor do I see it as any of your business."

"It certainly is my business. I'd like to see them all flushed into space as they were about to do to us."

Decatur was a bit surprised, "Ah, I see."

"I understand your feelings, but Kraken needs these people."

Captain Jason Leeds finally spoke up for the first time, his voice emerged weak but determination filled his eyes, "I have ..." A fit of coughing interrupted his great excitement.

"... know where they are keeping them." He sputtered.

"Where they are keeping ... whom?"

".. don't kill all merchants. My son he's ... alive ... I can show you where."

"Save him ... them. Don't know how long they can ... can survive."

STRATEGY

Waiting in the captain's conference room for his staff, Decatur was acutely aware of each precious minute lost by his indecision. He decided to make the best of it and use this rare gift of a few free minutes to step back and meditate.

His thoughts, entered in his personal log, wandered across all possibilities, in support of and against the restrictions of his defined mission.

*As captain of the **Alfred**, I am charged to safely escort eight merchants to Jasper. Five of the eight now proceed on their own with little more protection than that provided by our drones acting as an advanced warning escort.*

Three merchants did not make rendezvous, the whereabouts of two are unknown since they have shut down their transponders and do not reply to our hails.

*Side note, I wish to commend the actions of my crew, particularly those of our valiant rangers who boarded and took a CTAC destroyer, the **Xuchang**. A ship that waylaid several of our merchants and was in the process of taking as* *prize the third missing member of our convoy, the* **CSS Grimes** *under Captain Catherine Esperanza.*

Captain Esperanza is currently in the brig for smuggling weapons, details to be found in ship's log, the file link is attached.

While securing the CTAC ship, we uncovered records of their taking several other of our ships. We rescued Captains Straits and Leeds, who survived the encounter and now reside safely in our care. Captain Leeds disclosed the existence of a CTAC internment camp holding an estimated eight hundred prisoners, among them the captain's son.

Mission directives would have me return the CTAC warbird and Esperanza's merchant ship to homeport using a prize crew and thereby releasing **Alfred** *to continue convoy support. However, our discovery of the colonial prisoners and the harsh conditions of their internment presents a problem. Does my duty lie in the continued escort of the five merchants to Jasper or am I bound to attempt a rescue of Kraken and Jasper citizens incarcerated, their lives in dire jeopardy, in a fortified internment camp reportedly located, of all places, within the astral bounds of Sol System?*

The arrival of Commander Hopewell, Major Steve Walters, and CPO Rendall Gleason interrupted Decatur's entry. He began speaking even as they were taking tea and coffee from the sideboard. As they each took a seat, the walls and ceiling of his office slowly transformed into a clear view of the surrounding universe until it appeared as though they sat on a patio located above **Alfred**. The transformation marked the activation of a broad-spectrum frequency shield that would provide an area for the free exchange of information safe from external sensors and probes.

Decatur began speaking directly, "Barely out of port and we find ourselves in an unexpected position. Our orders do not provide guidance for a chance encounter with a CTAC warbird this close to port much less one in the brazen act of taking one of our merchants. The audacity of such actions can only be attributed to the liberties they have enjoyed in attacking our merchant fleet these past few years. Hopefully, we can put an end to such behavior."

"Major Walters, operational status of the CTAC vessel."

"All but one of the Slug Shot boarding portals cut through the ship's shell have been repaired. The molecular welding system used to repair and mate the entry plugs we removed has worked like a charm. The problem portal arose when its creation penetrated a central synapses junction of ship's AI and is taking a bit longer to repair but should be completed shortly."

"The vessel itself received relatively minor damage to the interior."

"There are four hundred seventy-five CTAC survivors. Counted among them are a hundred eighty-seven former NAU or merchant spacers pressed into CTAC service. All but twenty-three of those pressed signed enlistment papers for CTAC service. Under duress, so they claim. Twenty-four CTAC spacers request asylum and are now being held separate from their shipmates."

Decatur nodded, the tally was about what he expected, "Very good. We have use for experienced spacers. Let's see what we can salvage."

Walter's wasn't finished, "They've been on this mission for nearly a year now and could have continued. Their life support and operational supplies are more than adequate, they obviously have been scavenging from waylaid merchants as they have gone along."

"CTAC munitions are at near full levels. Their operational model must be a simple intercept followed by rapid boarding and takeover, with the option to either send the captured vessel back home or simply derelict it and dump its spacers into the abyss."

"Thank you, Major."

"Commander Hopewell, status of the *Grimes*."

Hopewell sat straight-backed and tense in her seat, stern-faced she broached a subject obviously not to her liking, "Captain Esperanza demands to speak with you. She's restricted and separated from the others as per your orders. Her first mate also knew about the arms smuggling and apparently was benefiting from it. I've taken the initiative and confined him as well."

"Their illicit arms cache shipment is more extensive than we had envisioned, all are Kraken manufactured. There's a load of Niobium in the hold that is not on their manifest and appears to be destined for CTAC refractories. There is a shortage of the mineral in China and it's critical for the manufacture of the heat resistant ceramasteel alloys used in slipdrive designs."

"Sir, the CTAC destroyer's attack on the **Grimes** just doesn't make sense. Esperanza planned a stop at a CTAC port anyways to offload the contraband. I can only surmise, since the CTAC ship was understaffed, it was critically short of experienced spacers."

Decatur was shaking his head, "No, that may be part of the reason, but they may have also seen the merchant as an easy mark or simply didn't suspect smuggling, seeing it only as a possibility to bring in some extra prize money. Esperanza may eventually have been released to continue onward."

"Esperanza, of course, would not call for help for fear of discovery."

"Yes sir," the XO replied but Decatur could see something was bothering her. She continued, "The ship is in great shape. The boarding, as violent as it may have been for the spacers, left a whole and intact ship and cargo."

"I've submitted a list of the munitions found on board. We questioned the crew and ran serial numbers found on the weaponry. The contraband is confirmed from Bucker's warehouse."

Decatur let out a soft whistle as he glanced over the long list, "The tonnage of contraband they were shipping is staggering but that pales before the description of the contents. These are some of Kraken's most advanced designs, many of them held in secret even from the NAU."

"I want you to unseal and inventory the contents of their entire ship. Do it safely but don't assume 'hazard' signs or other warnings to be truthful to their contents."

"I'm also changing your orders, Commander."

"Lieutenant Osaka will return the Grimes to port along with a skeletal crew and evidentiary documentation of our discovery. He's to take the merchants rescued as well as the NAU and CTAC crews. It's going to be a bit crowded, but they don't have far to travel. All must go …. except for any NAU willing to sign on as spacers."

"I do not want any of this on open broadcast, Osaka will return directly to homeport and remain silent to all but our direct chain of command. We may have prize rights to the vessel and cargo since it was shipping contraband. Ask Mr. Osaka to inquire into it. You can let the crew know about the new prize; it may make them feel a bit better when they hear the rest."

"I have decided to allow the convoy to travel to Jasper on their own. They're already at supralight speed and will have an early warning shield and the defensive screen provided by the drones as they approach Jasper. Their risk is now minimal."

"You are to take advantage of Esperanza's supplies. Take whatever you need from the merchant ship to support ongoing actions. That includes whatever exists on the list of contraband items but let me review your selections first. Anything we don't require will be returned with the **Grimes**."

"We are paying a visit to the Solar System and will be taking the CTAC warbird with us. She will be renamed the **Revenge** and commissioned to our service. Before our departure, you are to isolate, but do not wipe her AI systems. Install one of our spares as a replacement. I realize this will present difficulties but do your best, we cannot risk allowing a hostile AI access to ship's facilities. Reprogram any human interface, so our people aren't required to read and speak Mandarin in order to run it."

"Congratulations, Commander, *Revenge* is yours, but you will operate under my flag as acting captain."

"Major Walters, plan on ship-to-ship as well as extended dirtside action. We'll discuss the specifics as we learn more."

"We are going to attempt a rescue of those held prisoner. Should we succeed, our actions here will be forgiven. If we are not successful, some of us will most likely face a court-martial."

"*Revenge* will travel with us. We need her power. She's a solid, fast ship and I wish to have no connection with any ship that does not sail fast, for I intend to go in harm's way."

RAIDING PARTY

Three point eight days later
Outbound and below the galactic ecliptic
The Deep Expanse

Soft lighting inside the officer's lounge did little to mask the innumerable jittering pinpoints of light piercing the now transparent chamber's broad ceiling and walls, each point crystal clear and set against colorful silk-like curtain-folds blending into an aurora borealis of flowing colors from radiation-ionized particles visible only here, in the pure black abyss, far from any stars. The expanse immersed Captain Jankin Decatur in a universe of billions of stellar points. Swirling fractal patterns clustered off starboard-aft into a broad sombrero-shaped band of stellar mist, from here a man could gaze into the distant heart of the Milky Way. A hotbed of pinpoint lights jittering ever so slightly as ship's sensors sampled the slower moving photon streams surrounding their swift, supraluminal passage.

Jankin Decatur's eyes shunned the spectacular display to stare at a lesser but more significant, tiny replication of the galaxy slowly materializing on the opposite quarter of the lounge in the form of a distant star system. For this was their destination.

It lay more than one point six lightyears distant, lit only by the reflected glory of the brilliant yellow dwarf star at its center, Sol. Its planets displayed as less obvious points of light spread across a tight planar orbit lying at the heart of broad bands of dimly lit debris and radiation-haze formed by the cometary junkyard of the Kuiper Belt and Oort Cloud extending out into the surrounding abyss nearly half the distance to its nearest stellar neighbor, Alpha Centauri.

A comforting aroma of fresh-brewed Jasper coffee rode the airwaves of the chamber already vibrating beneath the musical strains of Mussorgsky's "Night on Bald Mountain". The wicked mood of the music suited Jankin Decatur. He had just returned from a visit with his new crewmembers and had spent more time than he had allotted with those recently signed on from the ranks of former CTAC prisoners.

Their sad stories had hardened his resolve.

The sound of an opening door distracted him, crewmembers rarely intruded when he was in the lounge, particularly when he was in such a foul-weather mood. Decatur looked round to meet the smiling visage of Margo Stoudt, one of the two journalists who managed to talk their way into staying aboard over his objections. He groaned at her entry with a bit more vigor than intended but if the dark-haired reporter heard, she showed no reaction, "I'm sorry for the intrusion Captain but your guards tell me I'm forbidden to interview the new recruits. I wish you would have taken me along to speak with them. I'm concerned about what they endured as prisoners of the CTACs. God knows, they certainly appear to be physical wrecks, why in the world did you let them sign on?"

As she droned, Decatur casually closed three of the reports he'd been reviewing. He didn't particularly care if she read those remaining. Looking up; her smile was pleasant, and her manners were first class as usual, so he decided not to frog-walk her out of the chamber. He hated politics but the sensitivity of this mission was high and he must do his best to ensure she remained on his side.

"I can't argue against your observation, Miss Stoudt. Their health is atrocious, so much so they would not have been enlisted from a dockside application. Those we accepted have bodies that will recover even though the scars and hatred forged by their captivity will last a lifetime."

"Unless, of course, they agree to undergo a memory wash when they return to homeport."

He saw a chill pass through the journalist at the thought of a drastic erasure of a human's memory.

If they return home, Decatur reminded himself before continuing, "In truth, I took them because I need experienced spacers to pull this off. Spacers are tough, they'll manage this because they want to, and their participation may even lessen the mental damage inflicted by their captivity."

Margo sat across from him, her palm up and shading her eyes as she consciously attempted turning her back to the stellar display, "God, how can you work in here with that? I didn't notice them at first but their constant jitter, it creeps into your brain like a million tiny strobe lights exploding inside a person's consciousness. I can feel the headache coming on already. What is going on?"

"We're traveling many times faster than any photon wave. If you were outside now, your eyes would attempt to gather photons from the streams of light coming towards you. If your unshielded eye somehow remained undamaged, you'd still see nothing since your brain couldn't interpret the view, it's called photon overload. It's rather like sticking your head outside the open window of a moving vehicle and attempting to shout. There are too many photons coming into your eyeball."

Turning your view aft, you'd see absolutely nothing at all since we travel faster than any lightwave."

"The image you see now is reconstructed from ultrashort photon samples taken by ship's sensors. The sample is only a small fraction of the total number of photons impacting them. Since we travel at a much greater velocity, sampling results in an apparent flashing and shifting of the image of each star and is called photon jitter."

"These images actually flash less intensely since we are in deep space and far from any stars because here the waves of gravity are long, uniform swells and the photon packets change little between samples. The stars seen now increased their jitter but moments ago and with good reason. The little critters are shaking because we've entered the extreme outer envelope of the Solar System's Oort Cloud. An area filled mostly with cometary debris and conflicting sources of gravity created by the sun, planets, and other heavy objects, so the photon sampling sensors gather a mix of distorted and phase-shifted photon packets with each sample taken. It's like trying to obtain water samples from a motorboat speeding through a small bay filled with wave-chop from other boats moving in all directions."

"The view upsets even experienced spacers. I've grown accustomed to it over the years. Jitter intensity will increase as we speed sunward across the ecliptic of the solar system and the density of planets and debris increases. Then, I will have to turn off the display and slow the ship in the turbulent waves found close to the heart of that star."

"Our destination is Mars and ..."

"Oh, you look surprised?"

"Anyway, there's a good chance we may not reach Mars if we can't elude the automated early warning sensor arrays located in the orbits of Neptune, Pluto, and Charon."

Margo moved closer to him, "My family comes from the Mars colony. You won't be attacking civilians, will you?"

Five years passed since Decatur was last inside the borders of the Solar System, four of those were witness to an escalating conflict restricted to off-Earth locations. Colonists on the Moon, Venus, Mars, the asteroids and Europa, a large moon of Jupiter, all suffered from the conflict.

Citizens of Earth complained about the costs and shortages. Some relative few missed those who had gone off to war, but the direct pain of the conflict never struck as strongly as it did those who lived off-world and therefore beneath the daily fear of conflict. Ms. Stoudt had struck a nerve in Jankin Decatur for he had also lived beneath the fear of death and the suppression of an unjust government. He understood her concerns.

"Mars colony exists in a war zone. It's not a safe place to live with or without our coming. I do not war on civilians and have no intention of doing any more harm than is necessary, even if they are military."

An image of others waiting outside appeared next to the chamber's door.

"My staff has arrived. Ms. Stoudt, I want to apologize if I've been overly curt and harsh at times. Unfortunately, I cannot afford to be affable when lives I am responsible for are at stake. You and mister Mason present a pointed hardship because of your notoriety to the general public and, should something happen to you, the damage to our cause could be serious. That is why I must ask you to refrain from taking risks."

Decatur didn't give the shocked journalist time to respond but released the security latch, his people were waiting.

"My staff members are here for a tactical briefing. You may stay but do not distract us with questions. We have much to do and little time to do it."

Decatur motioned towards the waiting coffee and tea as the room's illumination rose, diminishing the distractions of the universe. A miniature of the solar system materialized in the space at the center of the ring-shaped conference table with an oversized miniature of **Alfred** tracking in towards its center from the extreme edge.

"You've all met Ms. Stoudt. She will be staying for our planning session."

"Jasper steak and double-yolked eggs for breakfast, gentlemen. They serve the same fare in all the mess halls this morning. Eat heartily, your next meal may be far off and yes, Chief Gleason, you may have yours with a side plate of SOS, special order."

Margo's head flipped up and turned to the captain in an unasked question. A smile came to Decatur's face, she was learning to follow orders, but he knew her question and his mood was improving, "Thank you for not interrupting, Ms. Stoudt, I assume you're wondering about 'SOS', It's a very old wet-navy breakfast favorite. Creamed chipped beef on toast, something lovingly called by servicemen for ages 'Shit on a Shingle', hence the abbreviation."

"I suggest you try some, you'll be surprised how good it tastes. Most of all, it will stick to your ribs and will hold you over."

The captain's meal came out, Margo noticed the meat was already cut into the bite-sized pieces allowing him to eat without wasting time and distraction.

Taking a chunk of brisket small enough to allow him to speak and eat at the same time, Decatur continued, "In case you haven't met everyone. Major Steve Walters heads our Rangers with his second, Captain Mike Favorsham. My XO, Commander Harriet Hopewell will be acting captain of **Revenge** and our CPOs Bogan Geer and, the great hulk at the end of the table snarfing down his SOS and steak, Rendall Gleason. Everyone, of course, knows our pilot, Lieutenant Scott Nauman."

The lieutenant heard his name and looked up, a quick warm smile coming to the young man's face. He was otherwise engrossed in going through the conference background material.

It was then Margo noticed there wasn't much discussion at the table, most everyone was gulping down food and flipping through files with some of them using the habitual eye-blink as they set a document to permanent memory or highlighted a section on their HiveTab.

Gleason called for a second serving and Margo turned in haste to her meal, she was barely into her yogurt and chopped fruit.

There was no official end to the meal as Decatur began speaking, "We're going in using the CTAC AI's flag signals decrypted by our own AI from *Revenge's* records. If we're detected, our profile should appear as a CTAC destroyer bringing in a merchant ship as a prize. That should get us through most of the CTAC hurdles but if an NAU warbird comes upon us then we must consider them to be hostile."

"Remember, any merchants we encounter are to be left free to go their own way. We are here for more than prize money. Keep your people focused, our prime objective is to free colonial spacers taken prisoner."

The display before them seemed to brighten a bit as a faint course vector extended from the *'Alfred'* token. Decatur continued, taking but the slightest pause, "Some of you may have noticed our course took us considerably out of our way. This was so we could approach from the galactic north by northwest."

Unfamiliar with directions, Margo queried her HiveTab and the reply was instantaneous, *Interstellar course descriptions are derived from old-Earth wet-navy terminology for simplicity. 'North' refers to a vector with its base at the gravitic center of the black-hole located in the heart of our galaxy and base pointing in the direction of Sol as of January 1, 2100. South, East and West vectors lie in their conventional positions within the galactic ecliptic plane containing its hub and stellar arms. 'Azimuth' designates the vector height above or below the ecliptic with positive vector values using RHRT for the sign designation.*

'RHRT' puzzled Margo, so she followed its link, *'RHRT' refers to 'Right Hand Rule of Thumb'. Using it for galactic coordinates, the user orients their fist with fingers pointing in the direction of galactic rotation. Extending the thumb outward designates the direction of positive values and negative values lie on the opposite side of the ecliptic.*

Decatur's explanation continued, "…. they've placed wandering AI-enhanced monitoring stations at six locations in the Oort Cloud with most of their sensors directed above the ecliptic plane. The NAU has fourteen stations across both the Kuiper Belt and the Cloud, they follow the same strategy that provides an effective early warning for enemy task forces that may be trying a surprise attack from the less closely monitored but longer attack routes rising high above the plane of the galaxy."

A new graphic and course vector plot appeared, "Using data from our NAU commercial database and the CTAC supplements, our tactical AI determined this point of entry. It's a vector that will provide us entry through an area having only moderate NAU attention."

"We'll deploy a drone shield as we approach Charon's orbit and use it to guide us through a gap in the orbitals leaving Neptune and Jupiter stations on the far side of the sun. We only need worry about a small NAU research station on Saturn's Titan satellite.

"Remember, we'll be rendering CTAC flag colors so if we are challenged just let the ship's artificial intelligence units do their job. The facilities on Mars will know we're coming by the time we pass Jupiter and enter the asteroid belt, but we'll be moving nice and easy so as not to raise alarm."

A long, offset elliptical orbit appeared on the plot, "Mars currently is very close to the asteroid belt and this highlighted orbit belongs to one rock we've been tracking. We are timing our approach so that it coincides with that of the asteroid. We're going to disappear behind it on our final approach to our objective."

"Our objective is the cave complex located under an old vent in the floor of the Martian volcano Pavonis Mons. CTAC has established a major dirtside port there complete with atmosphere enhancement so that life there is no worse than living under an Earth-standard moderate altitude climate, rather like living in Nepal."

"We need a way to emerge from behind the asteroid and slip into that complex without their knowing it. This is where I need your suggestions. Our timing's right, we can land under cover of darkness, but the complex is situated in a flat plane and the nearby volcanic cone's sides are glazed and smooth. We don't know just how extensive the complex might be and this opening is only wide enough for a shuttlecraft so forget about trying a direct landing with one of our ships."

"Our rangers will drop in while maintaining the element of surprise. There is a major base within an hour's distance, so the minimum window of opportunity is about forty-five minutes to take the cave complex, land our shuttles, and transfer as many captives as possible up-ship."

"Suggestions?"

Major Walters slouched back in his chair, unconsciously running a hand through his hair, "There's not enough room to maneuver inside the crater walls for slug shot deployment. Jumpsuits should do the job if you can get us to a low orbital release. Landing will be complicated by the low atmospheric pressure but we can do it. I estimate a seventeen percent casualty rate because of the tight confines but that's better than having rangers slide down the soft surrounding crater walls. There's also a question of how we exit with all the ..."

"I know how you can get in there." A soft voice lifted from a seat offset from the discussion table.

Decatur turned a cross stare at the impertinent journalist that lasted but a moment as he chided himself for letting her attend a meeting with the expectation she wouldn't interrupt, "Well, I did ask for suggestions from anyone. Go ahead, Ms. Stoudt."

"I lived in this area several years before the war. There's a CTAC landing field on the other side of that glacial moraine to the west of the volcano. They are really uptight about that area, wouldn't let anyone approach the field, particularly a young and inquisitive reporter." A hint of a smile on her face.

"The level of traffic in and out of that isolated landing strip sparked my curiosity at the time since the base appeared too small for the supply tonnage passing through it. So, I did some research and found an early geologic survey map of the area. The region is honeycombed with lava tubes and caverns some of which extend under that landing field, others lead out in the direction of the base that is your objective."

"I'd bet they have an entrance for their complex under that landing field."

The major was shaking his head, "Doesn't add up. There aren't any roads going to the airstrip. You can't hide an underground military base with all traffic heading in and out of a single little airfield. There's just too much activity and we'd see signs of it."

"I never said it was a military base. It's just an airfield that has landing strips too big for local transport and there's no good reason for it to exist in the middle of nowhere. No camps, resorts, or farms are nearer than a hundred miles. Yet for months they had flights going in there and ships landing from orbit."

"Then, one day all the activity stopped but they cared enough to keep automated guard posts surrounding the area."

"Can you bring up aerial images of the area?"

Lieutenant Nauman answered the call, "I can do better than that. Our drone network just arrived on target."

Decatur linked his HiveTab to ship's resources and projected a full-depth image with a topographic map overlay of the area.

Margo sat up straight in her seat, obviously concerned, "Aren't you concerned about detection?"

"Individual drones are small, very small. Each one brings in only a fraction of the data that our computers sample and combine to form this image so there's no single source for the probe or data being transmitted back to us. No, they'll never know we are visiting until after we make ourselves known."

Rising from her seat, Margo walked over to the edge and around the display, "Well, there's the volcano. See these sets of long, straight, parallel ridges? Those are glacial moraines. Ancient glaciers pushed piles of stone ahead of them and left those steep ridges when they stopped growing and began melting. The meltwater is responsible for carving out some of the newer caverns."

"We know the caverns are there along with the lava tubes from the first Mariner landings, but no one has explored the caves since CTAC claimed colonization rights to the grounds."

"Zoom in on this dark patch, right there. That's the field, it has but one or two old buildings on it. Note the landing strips are clean despite the blowing sand so they're obviously still in use."

Decatur magnified the view, "The building looks old and has big, oversized doors. They certainly placed them out in the middle of nowhere. Let's take a look inside ..."

"Well, look at that. They've installed blocking measures. Can't scan the interior at all but I bet they didn't think of this..."

The captain directed an echolocation neutrino activated pulse and a layer of semitransparent tunnels appeared as an overlay of the image.

"How about that, a short length of tunnel leading off into an irregularly shaped labyrinth of caverns. Those rectangular structures you see are additions not matching the bedrock. They laid it out nicely."

"Ms. Stoudt, I do believe you just paid your way. You saved us a great deal of time and most likely lives."

Major Walters commented, "She may have helped us even more than you know, Decatur. Look, there's activity further down the string of caverns leading to a complex of reinforced blockhouses. That, most likely, is their military base."

"Everything down on this far end appears to be storage facilities but with a lot of additional areas that appear to be providing environmental engineering services. Maintaining a big space like that even at earth sea level normal atmosphere is expensive, there's no need to apply it for most storage."

"I suspect there's more going on in there. In fact ...."

Walters switched over to a different angle of analysis then mumbled, more to himself than the others, "Yeah, that's our target."

He turned to the others, "Our cyberwarfare team operating on the link just found the records for ... hold on. Let me recheck this number."

"Yea, more than we thought. By their own records, there are more than twenty-three hundred captives, most of them are NAU but only by a slim margin. Maybe that's why they've begun spacing those they catch. Their cells are full, so they're only keeping prisoners that display further usefulness. Our cyber team did a good job. I have names, service numbers, ranks, and interrogation logs and the list is building as I speak."

Decatur was deep in thought, "Great but go easy with the probe, I don't want you setting off alarms."

"We are here for colonial prisoners. Can you identify the sections where they are being held? Speed is essential and capacity limited even with **Revenge** accompanying us. We need to strictly limit the scope of our theatre of operations or this will grow out of hand really quick."

"The good news is this point appears to be a back-door. The section it opens into has a small armory right here as well as a series of rooms with more activity than I'd expect."

"Yep, this is our entry point and target. Once we're in, we'll play it by ear. This must be a touch and go operation. In and out. Quick, efficient, deadly."

"How do you plan to take the site, Major?"

"Major Walters, are you with us?"

Steve Walters was deep into visualizing threats and options. There were more unknown than known and what you didn't know could get you killed. He spoke, but it was more like a continuation of his thought process rather than an actual answer, "We have three objectives. Priority is gaining silent entry so we can identify the areas where they are holding our people. Then, guard suppression and blocking the subsequent CTAC response coming down the central tunnels of the base. We must be efficient and ruthless, no time to play. It'll be tricky because we don't know if they have our people in one location or scattered all throughout the base. It's gonna take time and it's gonna be messy."

"Don't see how we can do it in forty-five minutes."

Jankin Decatur's mind raced across the problems laid out by Walters, folding his observations into a much broader scope of threats, "There are too many prisoners to shuttle into orbit, even if we only take a quarter of the estimated number. This quadrant of the planet's going to be swarming with CTAC air and warcrafts. Unfortunately, this won't work unless we get out of there quickly."

"Major, as your people begin operations, have your engineers secure and establish a landing strip where we can safely ground **Revenge**. That means soil stabilization and compaction as well as the removal of any silicon spikes so the soil-matrix can support a two hundred thirty-three kiloton starship. The activity's going to raise alerts across the entire planet."

"Ah, Sir?" The diminutive lieutenant, Marion Purdy, broke in with great trepidation, "Orbitals, Sir. Their first warnings are going to be the automated stations on Deimos and Phobos."

Major Walters turned with questioned surprise to the young flight leader, an obvious reaction to the interruption but Purdy maintained course, "CTAC has stations on each moon. Depending upon their relative locations in orbit, they cover all approaches to Mars. Supporting them are seven satellites in high orbit. They're going to know we're here before anyone sets foot on red soil unless …."

"They'll be taken care of, Lieutenant." Walters dismissed the young officer."

"Yes, Sir. I see your plan to eliminate them all at once. They'll respond by sending up a hundred sky-bird orbitals. Small and not nearly as powerful as ours but they'll see our presence and be on us with suborbitals munitions."

"Even with a fighter umbrella, you'll have less than forty-seven minutes and they'll hit while our starship is open and loading on the ground."

Jankin Decatur waited a few moments for her to continue. When there was no response, "And your solution to this is what, Lieutenant?"

Purdy's flushed face revealed her nervousness but with the tenacity of a bulldog she took a deep breath and, "HiveBot simulations, Sir. We'll micro-torpedo a swarm of HiveBots into the satellite net. They'll never detect the torpedo casings at the distance we release the NanoBot swarms. The swarms will move in and record an orbit's worth of planetary scans at each satellite station. Chen, in crypto-programming, tells me they can modify the signals, creating minor changes in the data stream so they don't appear repetitive. The HiveBots will be tapping into their circuitry on the molecular level as they reprogram the data readings. When you're ready, we'll sync the new data stream, injecting it in place of the sensor's inputs, rapidly updating only those pixels covering our landing area."

Walters grumbled a bit to himself and was about to comment when Jankin Decatur spoke, "Pretty slick planning, right Steve? We don't have to reprogram all the satellites, just those that will be over this hemisphere of the planet. Even if they suspect something, it'll look like a system problem rather than an all-out attack, giving us time to establish our fighter umbrella. With any luck, we'll be done and gone before they catch on."

"Timing and intelligence gathering are going to be critical for this operation."

"We'll move in behind asteroid 162173 Ryugu, it's one of several that pass close by the planet each year, that will protect us from their deep space scans. Remember, they are already in a war zone and will be on the alert. First sign of detection or a mess-up and I'm pulling the plug and you tell your people that if I give that signal, everyone drops what they are doing and returns to the ship. Any ship. Or you will be left behind."

"Questions? Good."

"Operational outlines including force coordination by 0500 hours. Wait for last-minute updates until 0600. We'll finalize the time clock for launch at that point. Dismissed."

MARS

Decatur pushed back into his chair, unconsciously releasing a groan in response to the ache that had spread across his lower back. A complex series of three-dimensional plots, success probability projections, and tactical options folded in upon itself then faded from the plotting void of his workspace. Illumination remained low with a cool slip of ship-freshened air wafting by, carrying the sweet boxwood scent of his Kraken home.

Whether by mutual agreement with the NAU or a CTAC belief that the secrecy surrounding the existence and purpose of their base guaranteed its safety, it didn't matter. His people had found a weak spot. Still, the chance they were about to take was great.

A simple plan just wasn't in order since the complexity of tactics grew as his battle scenarios anticipated potential CTAC responses. Operations would involve coordination of teams covering tactical near space, low orbit, ground, and a subterranean first strike by rangers on the CTAC base.

Decatur checked the time … nearly twenty-one-hundred hours Mars objective local. Enough for a brief induced sleep period before the oh-one-thirty final launch review. Mentally tired, his body ached from the abuse of hours of inactivity and intense concentration. One last glance at ship's stats and a tight grimace formed upon his face when he noticed the IT-linked review of **Revenge's** status.

Their operational and defense systems were nearly eighty percent converted from CTAC functionality and projected to be nearly eighty-five percent at start of operations. It would have to do. Armament and capacity would be critical in the coming hours. Decatur's mind turned, reviewing tasks yet to be performed as he flung his body into the null-gravity sleeping tube and his HiveTab slowed cognitive response, enforcing a reduction in thalamus activity as it injected the cortex with images, sounds, and subtle sensations to relax his musculature and invoke a dream-state.

Two hours later he awoke refreshed. A quick check to confirm the readiness of his four task force commanders then, without bothering to disrobe, he walked into the EM enhanced low-frequency shower that cleaned his body and refreshed his uniform, its creases were once again sharp as a ranger's battle-blade and looking like his day-suit was just removed from the manufacturer's vacuum packing, no one would have guessed that he had just spent an evening in them, gulping down coffee and sweating over tactical alternatives.

A brief walk to the bridge marked the beginning of Captain Jankin Decatur's day.

"Captain on the bridge." Lieutenant Josh Osaka, the acting XO called out as she vacated the command chair.

Decatur didn't bother with the customary greetings, his HiveTab actuated the necessary readouts as he turned to the sensor station, "Are we still in the EM shadow of asteroid 162173 Ryugu?"

Lieutenant Scott Nauman replied immediately from the pilot's station, "Aye, Sir. Sailing in straight, true, and silent. Looking like we belong. Drone swarm gamma confirms no awareness of our approach by satellites located on either of the moons or orbitals.

"*Revenge* countdown to breakaway has initiated. We are at T-minus thirty-eight point three two minutes and counting."

Alfred and *Revenge* were two Astronomical Units (AU) inbound to Mars, electromagnetically shielded by the rock that conveniently led them in an extreme elliptical trajectory, eventually swinging them into a pass-by of the red planet. Four swarms of microscopic droids ranged far ahead of them: already in Mars orbit with two of the swarms focusing on the planet's tiny moons, Deimos and Phobos. They'd been there for nearly twelve hours, recording background and environmental radiation across the visible and lower end of the

EM frequency spectrum, information that would soon be put to good use.

Components of the swarms monitored the random skip-frequency communication jumps of the CTAC military stations as their encrypted transmissions bounced from frequency packet to packet. One thing about cryptographic techniques is that it's impossible for a programmed computer to create a truly random number stream, so at some point the strings repeat. CTAC programmers were clever enough to get around this by selecting two irregular pulsed quasars. They convoluted the quasar frequencies with their pulse packets to generate a more chaotic marker for frequency skipping. It was clever but still capable of being cracked if one had the time and computational power. *Alfred's* drone swarms provided such an analysis capability when deployed and now CTAC military and civilian transmissions were all open to their swarm monitors.

Decatur paced the bridge from its lowest to its uppermost levels, checking status and providing encouragement all while still being deep in thought. A part of his concentration eventually became aware of the presence of the two journalists in the top tier, silently watching with Mr. Mason busy recording bridge actions for posterity.

Should the recordings survive, a complete record of their actions would be at the fingertips of all who might be interested, whether friend or foe, news or courts-martial.

They were drawing in, less than one AU from the red planet, as close as the distance from the Sun to the Earth, a third of the distance between Mars at its closest approach to Jupiter and had remained undetected.

Still pacing, Decatur didn't bother to look up at communications as he initiated the next phase, "Ensign Feign, inform Captain Hopewell, *Revenge* is to begin their run."

"Aye aye, Captain." Ensign Litel Feign confirmed, "*Revenge* to initiate action."

~~*~*~*~*

Over on the **Revenge**, acting Captain Harriet Hopewell was seated in a rather crude command chair located at the rear of a gray-walled bridge. This was her first independent command, her hands were sweating as she chided herself that a good commander delegated authority and did not micromanage, or so the academy professors preached but she found it difficult not to hover over each critical station's shoulder.

Some of the most crucial bridge stations were partially converted, translated to the language understood by her crew but many sections still contained flurries of temporary tags hurriedly placed over the formal-Mandarin stampings of the starship's previous owners. Eighty-seven percent of the systems were recalibrated and interfaced to Kraken drivers, but Murphy's Law promised they'd discover all the critical functions missed in the next few hours.

As **Revenge** initiated her descent, two platoons of rangers in the special operations bay of **Alfred** entered final checklist preparation on their sliders. The rangers would engage from low orbit using HALO, 'High Altitude Low Opening' technique. SCOS, 'Single Combatant Orbital Sliders', are designed for stealth atmospheric entry facilitated by a small, limited function wavedrive module providing enough power to reach ahead of the warrior as they pierce the atmosphere by pushing aside gas molecules forward of their path. Since the molecules are accelerated to the side only a short distance, rather than pushed ahead and creating a bow-wave that would compress the atmosphere to form a shock wave, entry is silent and without frictional buildup. Their descent is unpowered and without the resistance of atmospheric drag, allowing the combatant to accelerate groundward unhindered and in stealth at speeds far exceeding terminal velocity.

"Listen up jarheads. Check your fittings two times, then check your neighbor's as well." Ranger Sergeant Johann Jaeger was scared and responded to it by being pissed, "This isn't some training stunt or game. You're supposed to be professionals, act like it."

"Trooper Hsu, remove and redo your SCOS fittings. I swear if you frag up and kill yourself, I'm gonna do my best to have Doc bring you back long enough for me to chew your arse out and if someone else dies because of your sloppiness, I'm gonna shoot you when I'm done. What the hell are you waiting for? I said redo that sloppy battledress … now!"

"Everyone check your buddy, make sure all air tanks are full. It's gonna be night down there and black as hell. If your tanks run dry, you're gonna be breathing Martian air and yer insides are gonna flash-freeze solid. That means you're gonna die, Hsu, it ain't funny and it ain't gonna be pleasant so wipe that damn grin off yer face."

"Look sharp, here comes the louie."

"G'day sir," Sergeant Jaeger didn't salute, they were on board ship. "Rangers ready, Sir."

"Rangers Ready, Sir!" the warriors echoed in unison.

"Bad arse, ah wouldn't expect less. The majors on his way down and it's a go as soon as the captain sez so. Remember when you get down there, look before you shoot but if they move first then you be the one who finishes it. I don't want to hear of anyone getting fragged because of friendly fire."

"Okay rangers get ready for the man. Suit up."

Lieutenant Travis Strake was as nervous as anyone. They were initiating a surprise attack that could easily escalate into a full-blown conflict and, if Captain Decatur continues to follow his stated intentions, they could find themselves in an all-out cat fight. The captain certainly knew how to pick his battles, all-out war with the CTAC, a country able to challenge the might and resources of the

NAU. And even the NAU, their mother country, hadn't been able to bring CTAC to its knees after years of struggle.

At the same time, the captain wants to hit the NAU to force them to stop the pressing of spacers into their service and halt the confiscation of Kraken shipping. That spells rebellion in its gentlest terms, every single one of them could be branded as a traitor and hanged.

Strake forced himself to focus on the mission. His platoon was slated to converge in low orbit before grounding directly upon the landing strip. Since Mars has no significant magnetic field in the northern hemisphere, they'd set their path using pulse packet communications synchronized to HiveBot swarms concentrated at three points in synchronous orbit.

Lieutenant Strake stepped into his hard-vacuum suit letting the armor close around him, cocooning him in a layer of flexible bio-foam. His thoughts were on the battle plan as the bio-foam molded to him like a thin layer of body fat beneath a skin able to withstand the extremes of moderate stellar energy, vacuum cold, as well as the deadly radiation of open space, and the lethal atmosphere and climate of Mars. He'd been suited so many times, his mind hardly noticed the tube insertion slipping into his colon and, since he was a male of the species, the soft skin attachment folding around his penis that would handle any defecation. A clear, warm active liquid beaded over his eyes, flooded his auditory canals, and enfiladed the HiveTab patch saturating his left mastoid bone. As a final step, the cavities of the headpiece filled with a variable density, programmable gas capable of transition to a highly oxygenated liquid mix for high-pressure environments. Similar to the molecular programming of the larger HiveBot swarms, the gas molecules were semi-autonomous NanoBot swarms capable of combining to vary both composition and density to provide both survival and battle enhancements in any hostile environment ranging from hard vacuum, with its low cosmic background temperatures of minus two hundred seventy degrees

Celsius, to the high pressures of a gas giant or even a deep-sea excursion.

Strake's face shield cleared as he exited the chamber. He slapped on his personal sidearm, a Lepton Pulsar, and slipped into the shoulder cage supports of his weapons rack. He'd suited up in less than a minute, then walked out and into the bay where his eyes spotted a strangely suited ranger, then he looked a bit closer, "You're out of uniform. Where's your patch, ranger?"

"I'm not a ranger, Lieutenant. I want to drop with your group and my rack package's all I need to take. I won't be any problem."

"Mason? You're insane. You ever drop before?"

"Aye, Lieutenant. I've gone the whole course. Ten years in the home guard with four hot drops."

Strake stared at the journalist. His suit looked okay. He knew how to don the outfit. Still, hot drops or not he was sure the journalist had never dropped into something like this. What the hell, none of them had …..

Mason figured the lieutenant was waiting too long to respond, "Captain approves but says the final's up to you."

"Yeah? Well, it's your funeral. Slide into SCOS seven. It's a bit temperamental but beggars can't be choosy."

Strake pushed the journalist from his mind as he walked across to the loading platform. He stepped up, snapped into his flitter cage, the human containment for the 'Single Combatant Orbital Slider' or SCOS.

Deployment was but minutes away when his SCOS projectile loaded into the ship's ejection rack, then rotated up into a chambered revolver operating on the same multi-cylinder principal as a Gatling railgun. He began sweating and tried to concentrate on the task at hand but couldn't. This was the worst part, the loss of control and the waiting. They were in a FIFO load and ejection process, 'First In,

First Out', and his capsule would be the last loaded. He'd be the last of his platoon ejected into space.

Until ejection, he was locked in a tube and barely able to lift his hands. A tightly bound captive, capable only of waiting and praying nothing went wrong. His entire platoon would launch ahead of him as he lay trapped in his cocoon, plenty of opportunity for an enemy response. Should the ship be disabled, he'd find himself entombed in a drifting derelict until death freed him in a thousand slow ways.

Making a desperate attempt to divert his mind from these thoughts, Lieutenant Strake opened a ship's 'status and environmental' window. Mars still wasn't in sight although they'd just passed a solitary cluster of rocks, inhabitants of the famed asteroid belt. He scanned each rock in the cluster. Some Yoyo spacers on a mining station noticing their approach could ruin the operation with a simple call to Mars central. Fortunately, these rocks were supposedly dead, common rare-earth composites not worth mining.

Major Steve Walters' voice injected directly into his brain, linked through his HiveTab, the officer had opened the channel to all the rangers, "All sections, rangers reporting ready."

Strake was surprised to hear the Captain himself respond, "Well done, rangers. We'll see you below. Give 'em hell. Let's get our people. Let's bring 'em home."

"This will be snatch and run. You are authorized to bring back anything you deem critical for Kraken's future operations. Let's see what we can learn as we rescue our brethren; *Alfred* out."

Strake's immediate, self-contained world consisted of his battle suit and the SCOS frame. For now, it was dark, and he was warm but helpless inside his capsule waiting for launch. The subtle whisper of ventilation filled the silence; he could sense currents of air swarming through the room outside as well as the faint rattle of some piece of debris in the tubes or perhaps the angry buzzing of a droid pest control unit. His suit transmitted odors; the sharp, tangy but oily scent of silicon lubricant wisped by for a moment. Creaks, groans of a live ship echoed in the dark surrounding abyss, enhanced by battle-suit pickups. A warning echoed through his brain, "Launch window, one minute."

Another personal warning followed. His suit began detailing the telltale signs of anxiety. He was breathing hard, hands sweating. A sudden whine ramped up the audio spectrum, followed by sharp clangs. The first ranger, Sergeant Jaeger, had launched. His SCOS lurched into sudden weightlessness follow by a jaw wrenching stop as the Gatling cylinder rotated into the next position. Again, and again the procedure repeated for more than twenty cycles as the rangers in his cylinder ejected into hard vacuum, joining the simultaneous ejections of other launchers.

One last rotation, a gut-wrenching jolt, and local gravity dissipated into the smooth weightlessness of space as his SCOS rumbled into the firing chamber of the electromagnetic cannon. Mixed feelings raced through him. Elation at the realization that control would soon return with the start of action was tempered by the near mind-numbing fear of a launch chamber jam. He'd seen it before and could envision the crushing as his capsule twisted around him and was ripped apart by the ejection field of the EM accelerator. He envisioned his suit transforming, hardening, altering to keep the body within it alive only to prolong the agony of slow shredding and a final blast into space when the automatics cleared the cylinder. Hands shaking, he waited. When it came, the ejection was more the smooth acceleration of a dropping rollercoaster than the violent blast of a shotgun. It lasted barely a second and his SCOS was free, the cartridge ejection capsule opened, releasing their frame into the void before pushing off to return to the ship for reuse.

"… formation. Alpha squad reports formed and on course." The universe was alive with chatter. The lieutenant visually spotted his team, they appeared only as suit-enhanced specs of light highlighted as each of the squad leaders updated the status of their thirteen-warrior squads. A glimpse of *Revenge* off in the distance flashed by, still close enough to be craft-visible.

Strake called over to CPO Rendall Gleason, "Chief, gather your people and assume independent course C232.1 for your objective."

A side conversation started as the CPO called over some last instructions to acting squad leader Corporal Wendy Covasa. The CPO and corporal would be sailing into separate landing zones nearly two klicks off from the field entrance where the ships were to land. Their mission; pinpoint the location and depth of the tunnels connecting to the main base. Then assemble the ground penetration charges and seal the main base from the operational areas.

One last check on the health of the SCOS armament module following them down. The module contained a self-propelled aerial defense platform for securing their eventual extraction.

Lieutenant Strake began reviewing the battle plan then stopped. The academy cautioned them about overthinking a plan. It wasn't good practice and could lock him into actions that they could not survive. Travis turned his eyes to the stars, searching for the constellation patterns seen by his ancestors. This was his second trip back to the Solar System and he wondered what it must have been like living on old Earth. At this point, nothing separated him from the universe but this thin living shell protecting him from instant death as his body plunged through space. He was tens of thousands of klicks from the next human lifeform, solitude at its finest.

Strake's HiveTab highlighted a distant red point of light shining just a bit brighter than the other stars. Standard issue mark-one eyeball saw only the pinpoint of light, but he could have pushed up his battlesuit's magnification to see details on the distant Martian surface. But chose not to. He felt alone in the universe and forced his body to relax as the SCOS functions carried him onward. There would be plenty of time for action soon enough. Now was time to let the suit carry him while he settled into sleep. Sleep when, where, and while you can.

The SCOS passed nothing of significance and the distance he traveled was more than three times the distance covered by Earth's first explorers to the lunar surface. Radiation and microdust were his only companions, the suit took care of the radiation and the SCOS frame shielded the deadly microdust particles. He was alone and at peace, a tiny spec of human creation bringing war to the still far-off world below.

Invasion

Ranger Lieutenant Strake awakened within a bee swarm of sparkling pinpoints covering his external display and marking the flight paths of his SCOS platoon. Each point referenced the location of a ranger sergeant and his two squads sailing groundward, already formed into an ellipse currently in low Mars orbit, it's foci converging along a conic section in a thirty-two-degree cone to a single distant point on the surface.

There was little chatter as their flightpath coalesced in a low angle entry of the atmosphere even though they still lay half a planet away from the landing zone or LZ. Rapidly they entered the ethereal layers of the carbon dioxide laden upper atmosphere, visions of cloud tops and hard ground ahead grew in distorted contrast as the planet's upper atmosphere thickened and was pushed aside by the gravitonic shield of his tiny wave drive with a force strong enough to warp even the trajectories of approaching photons causing his uncorrected forward vision to blur while leaving his peripheral clear and undistorted.

Swift, silent, and deadly, they passed into the lower atmosphere at tens of thousands of kph in a formation maintained by each ranger's HiveNet interface with individual warrior course adjustment override capability, leaving only the slightest disturbance of the surrounding atmosphere in their passing.

Day became night as the rangers crossed the terminator. Their Landing Zone (LZ) would be dark when they set down and already the atmosphere was thickening rapidly. Soon each SCOS took on a faint multicolored glow, increasing in intensity until it enveloped the entire flitter and eventually extended behind each SCOS. The glow was illumination created by carbon monoxide molecules ripped apart as the drive unit forced the atmosphere's gas from the path ahead, ionizing the molecules and releasing bursts of electron energy that emitted pastel-colored, short lifespan photons. A radiance faint enough for Chief Rendell Gleason to see the stars beyond ... and something else.

He called out as they approached six-kilometers altitude, "Bogey approaching on intersection course. It has a military signature. Permission to engage."

The lieutenant was quick to respond, "Engagement sanctioned but no weapons release. We are stealth."

"Aye aye, Sir. No weapons release."

CPO Gleason made the slightest adjustment to his course. The bogey was military shipping and the correction brought him onto an intersection dead center to the transport, he figured the impact would be interesting.

His SCOS's graviton field, extending less than an arm's length ahead of the slider, contacted the transport's graviton field. It easily pushed the transports vulnerable side shield away until it impacted the physical vessel's surface three pico-seconds later. The field then began chewing apart the metal fuselage molecules like a chain saw ripping rotten wood at more than five hundred times the spin-velocity of an EF5 tornado, spitting hot atoms to the side as it chewed into the craft.

Molecular bonds were ripped into raw atoms, electrons, and waves of raw energy from the slider-sized hole rocketed out from ahead of the SCOS in a lateral trajectory, instantly accelerated to thousands of kph. All in the transport, including its AI, died instantly, ripped by angry clouds of millions of molecular-sized pieces of hot shrapnel until the transport disintegrated into a fine, high-energy coarse-particle cloud that quickly dispersed. The SCOS slider itself continued onward in its self-created vacuum tunnel made wide and long enough to permit the unhampered passage of the one-man craft, leaving in its wake a remix of ionized Martian atmospheric particles and the transport's atoms.

"Bogie scratched." CPO Gleason reported. "Continuing final approach to LZ."

Major Walters' reply was hard and cold., "Confirmed, bogie down. Maintain formation."

Randomly placed and widely scattered across the heavens, the warrior flight paths began drawing together, eventually forming into three platoons sailing onward in near-circular formation and closing in on a single, still-distant objective on Mars' surface. Moving relative to each other like skydivers attempting to join hands in a circle, the diameter of the circle-shaped formation diminished as they plunged groundward until there were but three lateral meters separating each ranger. Each SCOS individual module now reoriented to hold its occupant in a prone position relative to the ground while slowing descent to 400 kph. Each individual flitter's long axis now lay parallel to the surface of the landing field below with the ranger's head pointing outward from the center of the circle, they raced downward silently until final deceleration kicked in at the last meter. A feat only a wave drive transport could do without killing the occupant.

At two-handbreadths above ground, their drives shut down and slider cages opened releasing their occupants. Rangers rolled off and onto the ground, a hundred rangers facing outward on the ready, forming a placement of defensive rings each nearly a hundred meters in diameter. Anything within the landing circle was neutralized by the sudden blast of compressed air created by their arrival.

A distant observer on the ground would not have seen or heard their descent except for a single blur of motion and a final ear-splitting crack as the tight defensive formation materialized on their objective, willing and able to join the fight.

"Alpha squad, clear." The first of the squad status calls were followed by each squad reporting no opposition. This night's ground temperature was a hundred degrees below zero Celsius as Walters' directed his suit's sensors upward like the targeting beam of a laser emplacement scanning the sky for threats. Mars' two moons were in near conjunction and nearing the horizon. Phobos, the larger satellite appearing half the size of the Earth's moon, glowed faintly in the Sun's reflected light looking more like a battered, pocked, and irregular shaped golf ball than a proper moon. Even though the satellites would soon be below the horizon and no longer a threat, he prayed the drones were successful in masking the sensor stations located on the two moons.

The surrounding barely moonlit plane was made of smooth soil artificially graded and star-port stabilized all the way out to the low foothills of a nearby set of worn, grey mountains in the direction of their objective; the mouth of the cooled lava tunnel, was located at the edge of a planar field just ahead of them at the far end of the main base. The major already knew tunnels stretched outward from it, forming a much larger area extending out to the roots of the nearby hills. Six small mounds of soil interrupted the planar surface, they didn't look natural and could be sensor stations, spotting posts, or defensive emplacements.

The rangers watched and waited.

Without rising, Tech Specialist Izzy Cooper reached out to her flitter cage and opened a small cargo hatch. Sliding her gloved hand inside, she then extracted it taking great care not to touch her suit while swiveling her arm forward and up until it was just above her head. A multicolored sphere materialized and engulfed her hand, its surface spinning, pulsing like a dim ball of blue lightning in the faint light of the stars. It emitted a weak hum in the thin atmosphere, changing in pitch and volume as it calibrated until the spin-stabilized and its surface smoothed.

A flick of her wrist and the sphere launched outward across the Martian surface to join similar releases from other techs. Like a dandelion puff flinging seed heads into the wind, the flight of energy-balls wafted out from the defensive perimeter in all directions across the Martian sands, bobbing erratically and sending back information on ground cover, changes in soil density, and gravitic pull. A detailed volumetric map began forming from indications of material changes corresponding to roads or artificial hillocks and voids beneath the surface; as well as artifacts that could be tunnels.

The display, injected into Major Walter's occipital lobe by his HiveTab implant, was taking form. He shifted it to the side with a simple thought while still maintaining a visual of the plane ahead as the mapping of the area's surface and underground took shape, highlighting hidden entrances, guard posts, and defensive emplacements.

No big surprises. The bunker doors are airtight, and blast reinforced with a second set of environmental pass-throughs behind them just like in an undersea colony. Hmm, it has two suborbital ships resting right inside the main doors.

Reinforced guard station just inside, no heavy armament above fixed machinegun emplacements and shoulder weapons in the locker located just off a set of rooms that look like living quarters for the guards and some possible interrogation rooms.

Cheez, they have a four-lane highway going through the tunnel to the main base-cavern. Makes you wonder just what they are doing over there. Again, a guard post with blast doors at the internal entrance to the tunnel. But why?

Perhaps, they're more interested in keeping people bottled up inside, rather than someone breaking in. Good, that makes our job easier.

Linking over the operations feed to the second and third platoons, Major Walters began setting the people of the Second Platoon into action by calling its lieutenant, "Quest 6, 1 to Beta 6, 1".

"Beta 6, 1 reporting rangers ready," returned instantly.

"Beta 6, 1 you have a go, seal the tunnels."

Then, contacting the lieutenant of the third platoon, "Gamma 6, 1 neutralize the topside guard shacks. Engage on the 'qt' then form up with Alpha."

Last, the officer of the platoon that the major would follow, "Alpha 6, 1 hold silent formation until we hear the report from Beta. Initiate a sensor sweep then immediately move in and install the airlock portal when clear."

"Rangers, move out," Major Walters called. They rose cautiously and began moving towards their objective, while keeping a low profile.

Lights suddenly erupted from the south guard emplacement, followed closely by a second set, and then the big blast doors of the facility began to slide open forcing the rangers into a dive for cover.

"Quest 6, 1" the call came directly from **Alfred** on the encrypted ship's channel to Major Walters as commander of taskforce Quest, "Be advised, bogie incoming."

"Copy that. This is Quest 6, 1, all hold in place. Repeat. Hold in place." Walters gave out the command that would halt all operations. The rangers dissolved into the landscape.

A yellow glowing orb formed on the horizon, correcting course as it approached before settling into a smooth glide path. Rangers hugged dirt, unseen in their camos. The settling starship was a graceful thing of beauty descending through the thin atmosphere until it floated above the landing strip and illuminated the stabilized field below, it then settled to a stop. Streaks of Elmo's fire ran across its surface as they bled off the static charge, then four portals opened and extruded low ramps.

Interior cargo doors of the ship smoothly opened, releasing seven self-contained environmental transports, followed by four open cargo haulers. The transports immediately set a course for the underground facility as the ship continued offloading supplies onto the stabilized surface.

Major Walters realized that things had just grown in complexity, but *Alfred* wasn't about to break communications silence. He could wait until the CTAC ship departed then continue but the base was going to be a beehive of activity in a few minutes. He began to consider alternatives.

Perhaps I should call it off until later. Unfortunately, that increases the chance of both Alfred and Revenge being detected when we attempt recovery of the rangers. Not a good option.

He was admiring the graceful lines of the ship, waiting for the right time to start their next move when a third possibility hit him.

"Beta 6, 1 hold in place then recommence when Gamma 6 starts a ruckus. Gamma 6, 1 hit 'em as the last bus enters the tunnel airlock. Take care when targeting, transports may contain prisoners.

"Alpha 6, 1 objective has changed to the starship. Board and take objective but minimize damage. Activate on my signal."

The rangers who had dug in before the tunnel entrance waited as the caravan unknowingly passed Gamma platoon's perimeter. Walters watched the bus caravan approach the cavern's airlock and enter. Nothing happened.

Strake should have hit them, what's he waiting for? Well, he knows his duty. Here's hoping we don't engage only to find CTAC reinforcements flooding out from the tunnel.

Walters called First Platoon to action. The CTAC ship had touched down at a point nearly surrounded by the rangers of First Platoon, providing a clear opportunity to take the ship.

The major rose to his feet and started their move forward, behind him waves of rangers lifted from the shadows like wraiths of the dead rising from the depths of hell out onto the hard-packed, artificially lit field and heading for the conveniently open, unguarded loading ramps.

Running with a crouched ground-covering trot, Walters passed a group of six CTAC spacers unpacking a supply skid. They turned in surprise when they heard him coming. "Down, hands on your heads and get down," he screamed at them while motioning with his pulsar. His suit directed the amplified Mandarin translated cry of his voice into the thin Martian air. The spacers looked at each other then slowly slid down to one knee. Walters motioned to the nearest private who ran over to one still standing and knocked the spacer to the ground with the butt of his pulsar then turned threateningly to the others, forcing them down.

Lieutenant Jose Catalan called out to third squad, "Alpha 6, 3 you're on KP. Round up these spacers, shackle 'em in place then follow up for more."

Walters ran up-ramp to the partially empty storage bay of the ship that lay open to the Martian atmosphere. There were tracks on the floor where the transports had rested but entry to the ship proper was blocked by sealed doors, "Forget the airlocks, use NanoBot cutters." He couldn't afford to wait for the pumping sequence; they wanted to take advantage of the chaos and confusion. A tech specialist ran to the bulkhead and removed her backpack. She pulled out a flexible line of grey putty and, with a flip of her wrist, flung it out into extension. The material was memory programmed and extruded into a long, thin, coiled snake about the thickness of her little finger. The tech grabbed an end and placed it onto the bulkhead about a finger's width above the deck. The material activated, and she could feel the growing heat through her battle suit's gloved hands as she shaped and molded the long string of NanoBots onto the bulkhead, forming a line that traced the periphery of a rough-entry rectangle.

As she worked, the putty-line began melding with the high energy atoms of the doors surface. The preprogrammed nanotechnology robots, each barely the size of a helium atom, sent out bursts of energy that broke the atomic forces holding the surface molecules and atoms of the bulkhead directly in contact with them. Splitting the bulkhead molecules into particles, they absorbed the released energy and material from the crushed atomics and converted them into even more NanoBots. The tech completed the circuit, then removed a small pen-like device from the pocket on her arm and touched its tip to the end of the NanoBot string and stood back.

The NanoBot string disappeared, melting into the bulkhead, extruding a grey foam covered with a shiny, oil-sheen surface behind it, that soon ballooned out from the channel it had just created. In less than two heartbeats, the bulkhead segment blew out under the higher-pressure present inside the ship and flew across the cargo bay to slam against a pallet. A flow of high pressure, oxygen laden atmosphere from the passageway on the other side of the bulkhead gushed out through the hole, screaming like an elephant passing gas and sparkling with ice crystals which formed as the warm air's moisture mixed in with the cold Martian atmosphere.

As the flow began to ebb, the tech lobbed a flash-bang into the passageway and rangers followed into the breach leaving Martian dust floating in swirls of mixed oxygen and carbon dioxide in the cargo bay behind them.

The well-lit interior had more than a dozen spacers inside, with two lying on the deck close to the entry. Three spacers down the passage were wearing Mars surface-suits so they survived the sudden freeze and were in the process of opening a cabinet door, the major's HiveTab interpreted the script on the door as "Emergency" but his attention was focused on the big spacer charging directly for him. The attacker's left hand wielded a tablet server and he was in the process of launching it when the ranger fired. The three-round burst of hypervelocity slugs walked up the spacer's chest, mushrooming on contact, passing through his flesh and bone while still expanding, creating a softball-sized exit wound in the spacers upper back. Meat, blood and gore spattering across the far bulkhead and ceiling.

Rangers sped down the passageway, flooding in from the portal cut in the bulkhead like black water rushing into a sinking ship. Two rangers were into the emergency supply cabinet opened by the spacers. They began hastily passing out the respirators and filmy pressure suits to the spacers who had survived because of the residual warmth in the ship but were already gagging on the oxygen-poor mix of carbon dioxide filling the passageway. They kept a wary eye on the enemy spacers as they waited for a ranger medic to come up and slap on flexwrap restraints, followed by an air-supply hood over their head, before throwing self-heating blankets over themselves.

Sergeant Jaeger approached the sealed hatch at the end of the passage. He put his vacuum-suit protected ear to the metal already chilled by decompression and the influx of the freezing Martian atmosphere but could hear nothing. Grumbling to himself that they'd trash the entire vessel with a second NanoBot string, he lifted the mechanical lever that unsealed the airtight door and jumped to the side as he flipped a gas and smoke grenade through the opening. Two seconds passed and shots sailed through the doorframe just to ricochet off the bulkhead. A surprised, muffled yelp sounded off from behind the sergeant. The spent shot had impacted on one of the bound spacers. Two fleeting thoughts raced through the sergeant's mind. The prisoner was lucky the rounds were ship grade slugs and not hull penetrators, so the spacer's wound was probably not very serious. Second, that spacer in the other compartment was experienced. Instead of immediately firing after the grenade toss, they'd waited a moment. Just the right amount of hesitation for an attacker to come charging in, Jaeger was thinking, he wouldn't make the same mistake as he tossed in a ship's munitions grenade. Its tinny blast shattered the thin atmosphere in the passageway as its detonation slammed the door shut.

The sergeant's reaction was immediate; he kicked the hatch back open, dove through the opening, and rolled across the deck only to bump into a body. Twisting his head, he spotted a grenade laying a half-pace away from the body's extended, shrapnel-shredded hand, with its safety still in place. He had been just a wisp faster.

Sergeant Jaeger secured the airtight behind him then charged deeper into the passageway. He chanced upon another airtight and cautiously opened it. The passage behind it was empty and the far door undogged but still latched to the bulkhead. Voices were shouting from the compartment on the far side. He and four other rangers entered. Hugging the bulkhead, as they chanced a peek into the compartment. It was full of tables set out in mess hall fashion. With people crowded against the far wall, struggling to escape through a small door leading into the next chamber; obviously panic-stricken.

"Everyone down on deck, face down or I'll fire into the lot of ya!." His suit-enhanced shout, translated into Mandarin, rang across the chamber. Startled, some in the crowd pulled back without turning and lay on the deck. Others simply stopped and stared, as those nearest the door pushed, even harder to get out of the room.

Since they were originally going to attack an underground facility, Jaeger's pulsar was dialed in to deliver titanium jacketed penetrators. Not healthy for shipboard use if you wanted to save the vessel and those in the next few chambers. He looked to his squad and, with a nod showing their readiness, they pushed forward across the chamber screaming commands as loud as possible. Descending upon the backs of the struggling crowd, they plied titanium pulsar rifle barrels, still hot from use, against the backs of their knees and with a flick of the wrist they slapped a flexwrap around their arms as they fell backwards. Disabled, their prisoners were dragged back into the center of the chamber. Those who turned saw the camouflaged battle suits of the rangers, their flat-black featureless helmets, menacing as a black banshee bringer of death. They surrendered quickly or received a rifle butt to the head, throat, or solar plexus. Most complied with the amplified commands and submitted silently.

"Hey, Sarge," a red-banded ranger leading three others carrying bundles of flexwraps called out. "LT assigned us to police duty. We'll clean up the mess. You guys move out."

"Hold on," Jaeger pointed to a bound spacer with officer's pips on her shoulders. "Bring her over".

Stumbling under the shove of the ranger, the officer refused to look at the sergeant, "I need your help, direct me to the bridge."

She didn't respond. Jaeger knew the suit's translation into Mandarin was correct.

"Corporal, use your flechette gun. Shoot her in the leg, right about here." She jerked involuntarily as he poked her upper thigh with the tip of his rifle. "Now hold still. This is a first for the corporal. Never shot a real person at this close a range before and he seems a bit nervous. You don't want him to hit anything particularly tender, do you?"

"I'm pretty sure we can find the bridge on our own. I just don't want to waste time, and more people are going to get hurt the longer it takes us to get there. You can help with that."

The CTAC officer turned to present an ugly, sneer-covered face as she answered, "What do I care about such peasants? Tell your dog to relax. Come, I'll show you the way."

~~*~*~*~*

CTAC spacers had been in the final stages of unloading cargo when the rangers commenced their attack. When the rangers hit them, they were unprepared and had their cargo holds wide open.

A CTAC military ship of this class typically staffed several hundred spacers. However, this one was modified to handle the transport of prisoners, so their staffing and weaponry were less than what was normal. CTAC wanted to keep their hoarding of both colonial merchant spacers and NAU prisoners quiet, thus the secrecy of the CTAC camp, a modern-day gulag.

Rangers moved quickly to subdue the cargo decks in the lower sections of the ship and those also on the perimeter, but resistance increased as they pushed inward to the central bridge at the ships heart.

Pushing his way onto the bridge, Major Walters and his people entered a passageway where grey bulkheads and decking stretched out farther than any they'd encountered previously. Adjoining passages formed intersections at several points down its expanse, each a good ambush candidate.

Private Izzy Cooper took a deep breath as she knelt to unfasten a corded belt from her waist. The snake-like belt twisted and flipped before squirreling down the passageway in drone-serpentine fashion. She directed it to halt and carefully peer around the corner of the first cross passage. Nothing of interest, sealed doors lay at the far end.

The second intersection also had a sealed door only this one was guarded by two spacers, standing weapons ready behind a makeshift barrier of cabinets. The droid silently slid around the corner but was immediately spotted. They fired, splitting off a segmented section of the drone that flipped around then back against the bulkhead where it took on a life of its own and squirmed quickly forward to rejoin the larger segment already snaking down the passage. The spacers now had two targets to contend with and hesitated when the first droid suddenly flipped, rolled to the edge of the wall and then squirmed around and under the barrier of cabinets.

The guards jumped and were screaming by the time Izzy came around the corner. The first droid was entwined around one guard's arm and he was frantically attempting to rip it off with his other. Both had dropped their weapons by the time Izzy was able to reach them. She calmly began pulling the cabinets back. One guard had given up, his arms tightly trussed together by the drone that had transformed into a longer and much thinner droid segment to tightly bind him. The second guard was hopping around, his face white as a sheet, eyes wide and screaming at the top of his lungs. Izzy went over to him, with one hand rummaging through her pockets, "Don't like snakes? Margie sure does look and feel like one, doesn't she? Now hold still, you could break a bone if you keep going like that. Hey, I had no idea you Orientals could turn pure white. Here, let me help you."

She withdrew a thin tube and lightly touched it to his neck. His eyes rolled up and he sank to the floor. The droid immediately released its victim then moved, coiling on the floor out of the tech's way but with a raised head that seemed to stare at the second, still struggling guard.

Izzy was examining the door as Sergeant Jaeger and three other rangers arrived pushing a CTAC officer ahead of them.

"You beat us to the bridge," he said, smiling at Izzy as he passed. "You got anything in your menagerie to unlock this door?"

Izzy smiled as she called the coiled snake back into position around her waist, "Just checked it, Sarge. Don't think it's locked. Give it a try."

"Really? Okay, Cummings you just volunteered. The rest of you, to the side, out of harm's way."

Private Cummins twisted the handle and pulled the door open to the breadth of one hand holding it secure with his stretched-out foot as he stood to the side.

"Come in sergeant. Stun or gas charges are not necessary. Yes, I've been watching. Your people seem to have the advantage. We surrender, for now anyway."

They entered the bridge. A few still active displays of the ship's exterior and interior corridors filled the walls.

"I'm Captain Jinzing Hect. Your uniforms and weapons aren't standard NAU issue. Who are you people? What is the meaning of this unprovoked assault?"

The sergeant was cautious not to approach the apparently unarmed ship's captain, "We'll answer questions later. First, order your people to stand down so we can put a halt to the bloodshed."

"I already have, sergeant."

"Good. Hands behind your back and order your people to follow suit."

"Is this really necessary, sergeant? It's so undignified."

"I assure you; it is needed. Now, we can do this the hard way ..."

"Yes, yes, I know. Alright."

Major Walters entered the bridge as they finished securing their prisoners, "Good job, sergeant."

He turned and motioned Lieutenant Catalan outside to an area where they could talk securely, "Lieutenant, secure the prisoners inside the bay of our first entry. Set up a minimum holding force then report with all available personnel to the cavern entrance and support second platoon. I think they may be heading into a situation worse than anticipated and I'm frankly surprised that we haven't seen a major CTAC response from offsite."

"She's all yours, lieutenant. I'm going to take a squad and check on what's happened at the tunnel entrance to the cavern. Strake may have run into some problems. Be ready for a fast response if I call in for reinforcements."

"Sergeant Jimenez, Follow me."

Walters was exiting the ramp when he turned his gaze towards the tunnel. All was peaceful, no scattered debris or bodies. No blast scorches on the rock face. Puzzled, he opened a channel to the drone umbrella and played back the sequence of events that followed their boarding of the CTAC ship.

The major watched as the caravan peacefully entered through the open blast doors of the cavern. They entered casually and unhampered, the last transport was on the ramp when a distant column of barely perceived figures materialized, marching in formation behind the caravan. They followed up the ramp and into the facility. The world again lay deathly still, then all hell broke loose within, Gamma 6 had just walked into the compound through the wide-open front door. The peaceful world outside continued as the maelstrom of bedlam inside the tunnel faded behind the closing armored doors of the cavern entrance.

He pushed ahead to a point in the recording tagged by his HiveTab. The scene continued unchanged then shifted to the north to follow plumes of debris flashing across the distant sky, climbing much higher than they would have risen on Kraken. Second Platoon had just launched deep penetrators into the far tunnel entrance hopefully shutting off tunnel access from the distant main CTAC base.

"Sergeant, follow me on the double. It looks like they're in a real catfight down in the cavern."

THE CAVERN

Thick blast doors squealed like a banshee's cry into the thin Martian atmosphere as guards opened the underground detention facility for the approaching CTAC caravan. Unknown to them, their caravan was passing through the perimeter of third platoon's camouflaged rangers who had gone to ground as their ship landed.

As they passed, Lieutenant Travis Strake risked a glance back at the CTAC ship. Sure enough, Major Walters had already launched his assault on the CTAC warbird and rangers were streaming into one of the ship's cargo holds. The convoy apparently hadn't noticed a thing and that provided an opportunity.

Strake hand-signaled 'formation' and forty-three rangers brazenly stood-to, their camouflage suits shading over to a flat-black texture as they formed rank behind the last of the passing cargo haulers. The caravan's transit lifted a cloud of dust that carried high and settled slowly in the low gravity, obscuring the dark shadows of Gamma platoon's march past the outer guardhouse. Three black-suited forms broke off from the marching legion as they entered, slipping to the side of the bunker's firing port to wait for the last of their band to pass inside.

Atmospheric pressure rose, and with it, oxygen content increased steadily as the caravan penetrated deeper into the tunnel until readings were nearly Earth normal. The cavernous interior of the detention center was huge. Martian gravity is only a third of Earth normal. Eons ago, the planet's thin, cold atmosphere let the ancient pyroclastic lava flows of Pavonis Mons quickly stream downslope while maintaining a flow thickness greater than any on Earth. The lava flow's exterior cooled quickly and the high feldspar, pyroxenes and the olivine content of the peripherally solidified mix acted as an insulating heat barrier that eventually emptied the last of the molten rock, leaving behind broad chambers with smooth floors covered by a glacially smooth, high-roofed impervious ceilings easily maintained at Earth's atmospheric standards.

A startled officer noticed the unexpected visitors and began shouting loudly in mandarin as he approached from across the room, "Identify yourselves. Who's in charge here?"

CPO Rendall Gleason stepped out of formation, the featureless black surface of the approaching figure's battle suit facemask infuriated the officer and, as he drew up to scream down the insubordination, the CPO's arm flashed out like a striking cobra. The blow easily flicked past the officer's defending reaction and lightly touched the bare skin of his neck where it exploded with a wicked snap. The officer's mouth opened wide, his tongue flicked out releasing a high pitched but short-lived scream just before he collapsed to the ground, even as Gamma platoon broke ranks. Some rangers spread out to guard stations lining the walls. Others ran down the sides of the caravan, ripping doors from the hands of drivers. Those stunned into inaction were rudely yanked out of their cabs.

Three brain-rattling thumps crashed in from the entrance of the facility and the CPO knew that the guard station had been neutralized. Surprise as well as the ferocity of the ranger's charge spread confusion. Pulse rifle discharges, amplified and repeated, carried by the cavern's acoustics, and crackled within the facility. The rangers quickly overran the guards and anyone lifting a weapon or turning to run was promptly shot down or stunned.

A second, even greater blast shook the facility followed by a great cloud of red dust and rock that bellowed out from deep within the cavern. The discharge scattered vehicles and people across the floor. Sgt. Winn Washington looked to Lieutenant Strake who replied, "Second platoon just sealed the tunnel to the main CTAC base. The cats out of the bag, they'll be screaming for help. Send a squad back to prepare for Alpha's arrival. Keep all the prisoners in the vans; we'll sort out ours and theirs later. When Alpha team arrives, have them unlock these cells. There should be a control at the end of each cell block that can open all the doors at once but if you can't find it then cut your way in. Pack as many of the cellmates as you can into the vans."

"The rest of us will continue to push inward and secure the cavern."

Washington sent a squad back to the tunnel entrance then called out, "Corporal Cassava, find the control center for this block, I'll take the next. Let's get them out of here, carry anyone who can't walk."

She then stopped and considered her last order to the corporal then added, "Unless they're dead or too far gone, of course, corporal. It's your call."

Prisoners, packed into cages like animals, filled the cavern. Filth on the floor suggested a stench in the air that none of the rangers chose to experience, so they continued using the filters of their battle suits, yet its putrid presence was obvious in the reaction of the new caravan arrivals. Calls and questions came at them in a dozen different languages while other prisoners, a bit quicker on the uptake, began cheering. All were pale and weak. Even those newly arrived were little more than skin and bones with some so feeble they had to be lifted from the vans.

Many, far too many, were too far gone.

Lieutenant Strake sensed something was wrong as he rounded the cellblock corner and walked into an explosion churning towards him from further down the cavern. Its cause was quickly evident.

The tunnel to the main base hadn't been completely blocked and fresh CTAC troops were flowing into the cavern. He saw them ripping into the backs of his rangers, heard their screams rising with the sharp whine of shouldered laser weapons emitting picosecond bursts of deadly coherent photons. He'd have to act fast.

~~*~*~*~*

The situation was increasing in complexity. Captain Jankin Decatur didn't like it one bit but could not see a way out of this morass into which the fates were drawing him deeper and deeper with every passing second. First, the unexpected arrival of the CTAC prison ship. Then their surprise at the sheer numbers of inmates in the prison and now their failure to completely seal off the tunnel from the main base. Too many fronts were opening. His resources were limited and theirs seemed not to be.

His office door opened upon his approach and, without preamble, he began speaking with the projected avatars of Major Steve Walters, who had returned to the bridge of the newly captured CTAC ship, and Acting Captain Harriet Hopewell in her new command, the **Revenge**.

"**Alfred** and **Revenge** are about to lose the cover provided by our meteorite. The CTAC prison ship's arrival complicates things but also presents an opportunity for increased capacity for what prisoners we can save."

"And prize money," the major mumbled.

Decatur looked up at the major, annoyed at the interruption for such trivia, "Ah, yes. Of course."

"On that note, I've sent Lieutenant Scott Nauman over with a prize crew to take possession of the CTAC vessel. It is renamed the *'Aries'.*"

Have some of your people stay and assist in securing the prisoners and with repairs. I want that ship flightworthy, loaded, and ready for liftoff, Stat."

"Captain Hopewell, **Alfred** resembles a merchant more than a ship-of war so we will use that to our advantage. **Alfred** will be shutting down one slipdrive and detuning its mate. You are to approach and secure **Alfred** with gravitic links as we enter Mars high-orbit. I want to present the obvious to CTAC Operations. The appearance of a damaged merchant prize, towed in by your ship."

"Let's keep them guessing as to what is going on down below, who our rangers are and where they come from. Major Walters, do you think your …"

An alert-one message from the drone swarm interrupted his words, "Launch detected: three transports and a full fighter wing. Destination: Pavonis Mons."

Captain Decatur's mind raced ahead, "Well, we half expected this but perhaps not so soon, nor in such force. We're vulnerable right now. Our rangers are spread too thin between **Aries** and the prisoner compound. Those in the compound have more prisoners to handle than expected, particularly since the fighting in the tunnels remains in question."

"Major, have them lay charges and pull back. We're through trying to minimize CTAC casualties."

"As far as prisoner selection, there's no time to pick and choose whether they be colonials, NAU, or CTAC. Press those willing and healthy enough to help into service, ranger discretion on the selection. As to anyone else except CTAC, if they were in a cage and can survive a move then transport them to the **Aries** using any means possible. Lock the CTAC guards into the cages, all of them, even if they claim to be NAU or pressed colonials. Exceptions of course for enemy staff officers or any guards our rangers feel know too much about us, they need be returned in shackles."

"Major, regarding enemy personnel on the **Aries**, you are to bind then transport all CTAC personnel to the compound and cage 'em. There's no time for interrogation and intelligence agenda. Keep their captain, XO, and anyone else our people think we need as well as any pressed NAU spacers who want to return home or enlist, no prison guards though. For those prisoners you retain, shackle 'em and pack 'em in tight with a minimal guard. We'll worry about pleasantries later."

"CTAC command must be unsure of the situation or they would have simply launched against the landing field. I want them to remain in the dark when they arrive, let them see only **Aries** and the tunnel entrance; anything to gain us time."

"**Revenge** will set down near **Aries** but can't get there before the CTAC force arrives. I am ordering an immediate fighter launch to counter the threat, stealth of course. We need to do this before we lose the cover this asteroid is providing us. The fighters should be able to slide out from behind our shield without detection and, with any luck, will catch CTAC in the middle of unloading with their pants down and hatches wide open."

"Any questions?" When none were forthcoming, "good luck, let's give 'em a bloody nose they won't soon forget and bring our spacers home."

GARYOWEN

Journalist Margo Stoudt stopped when she heard the captain's command to bring the fighters online. She'd been inside the bay to see them but was never allowed in if any of the Wraiths were awake. The good reporter that she was, she knew an opportunity when one appeared and sprinted to the launch bay. Breathing hard by the time she arrived, she could see a closing but still activated transit hatch ahead. With any luck, she'd be able to slip inside where she hoped to find a dark, quiet corner off from the flight crews who she hoped would be busy enough to ignore her presence. Her hands shook with excitement as she brushed the passkey threshold, praying it was still programmed to admit her passage.

As hoped, the passage plate transformed into a pressure chamber portal that opened by molecular reconfiguration of the bulkhead like an ice cube melting in a pot of boiling water. A universe of alien noise abruptly saturated her world as she entered, not even noticing the portal's closing behind her.

Alfred's fighter bay shook beneath a low, ragged hum. Excitement filled the atmosphere wafting along on ozone-filled streams and the pungent smell of human sweat. Margo had observed this in the vids of crew maneuvers a dozen other times during mission prep. But today was different; never had the sound been so threatening or the tension of the prep crews so obvious.

Menacing charcoal-grey forms pulsed in rigid formation, floating just a hand's breadth above the flight deck. Wraiths, each roughly three times the length of a human. Elongated, menacing pellets; slightly flattened to a sharp ridge that threaded their circumference, channeling a ribbon of energy sparkling in flowing malevolence, like a ruby-red stream of lava down a volcanic slope.

The background specs for these wondrous machines were beyond anything she had encountered before this assignment. The components of a Wraith fighter are grown in incubators as three-dimensional boules of crystalline metallic lattices, programmed to function using electrically conductive shear-planes of the atomic metal-lattice framework to define information pathways and logic gates. Emulating the construction of animal bodies in nature, they contained structural bone-like segments that moved using flexible plastisteel 'muscles' capable of both expansion and contraction.

Wraith bones and muscles communicated using a network of single-crystal plastic conductive threads joined into logic nerve bundles and linked using neural transmitters, operating much the same as synapses in the human body. Unlike an animal body, there was little or no initial learning curve for these components, for they are preprogrammed to base functionality during their growth phase. Their performance improved with use and experience to the point that a mature Wraith could extrapolate future results based upon their current evaluation of stimuli, even in completely new situations.

Much like Homo sapiens, they were cognizant, although synthetic animals.

A faint, blue-green field emanated from the surface of each Wraith, active telltales of powerful supralight slipdrives, adding their deep whine to the controlled chaos of the flight deck as they spun up to greet the gravitic waves of the universe. Powerful, single-pilot fighters that, for now, rested safely enclosed within forcefield packets shielding them from deadly interaction with their mother ship's gravionics.

Air particles ionized at the juncture of these unnatural realms of carefully controlled energy, cutting a sharp almond-scented tang deep into the nostrils of pilots and their support teams. Churning like a disturbed hive of Kirelian blood wasps, nearly two dozen Wraith Fighters growled at their restraints as their pilots nuzzled into their cockpits.

Excitement flared deep within each pilot's blood, as they approached their mounts, heavily spiced with the fearful knowledge that while drive physics shielded a pilot from high G-forces of combat and the deadly physical projectiles of interstellar conflict, they could do little to block the raw, deadly energy of the fermionic weapon's emissions release that would soon lace the skies above the red Martian sands.

Today, death would course the skies above this blood-red planet.

Across the deck from Ms. Stoudt, Flight Leader Alvin Krozel approached his Wraith. He was a small man with a quick, deadly mind and even quicker reflexes. His team looked up to him as a leader but, in his own mind, he was simply trying to live up to their expectations. Known to his fellows as 'Kronski', he was first to dive, belly down, into the grey-white swirling liquid that filled his Wraith's cockpit. Mounting his warbird in such a manner had become second nature for any pilot of a Wraith squadron. Krozel had performed this feat so many times he no longer noticed the fluid saturating the pores of his skin, flooding ears, eyes, nostrils, and lungs as he entered. His world blossomed into a cosmos of information, sensory clarity, and an awareness of surroundings near and far exceeding any gathering of a human's simple biological senses.

Kronski entered the addictive reality provided by this pseudo-liquid that was classified as an intelligence all on its own, one which was composed of swarms of molecular-sized NanoBots. A liquid robotic intelligence dedicated to protecting his delicate body and keeping him informed of the surrounding universe while enacting and, overtime as they grew to know one another, anticipating his commands.

His body flowed into a supine, face downward orientation relative to *Alfred's* deck. Completely ensconced in a Wraith-womb, protecting and providing the needs for all bodily functions encountered during intense combat including an awareness of every datum of information provided by the sensors of his bird and the mothership.

Humans interface to their universe with their eyes, ears, hands, and body, psychologically desiring tangible feedback, a solid response for every action. Kronski's Wraith provided a tactile yet virtual interface to all his motions even if his movement was nothing more than a momentary glance at a target or subconscious desire for an action to occur. Kronski's Wraith responded intimately to his desires. Some thought it to be devotion. Kronski himself knew it was true devotion and even claimed his warbird could feel the excitement as the ancient refrain of "Garyowen" began echoing throughout the bay;

We know no fear when duty raves

Take us away far from our home

Where Kraken's sons fly o'er the waves

That carry us off where ere we roam.

Our land, our lives, our people and faith

Know our souls belong to Kronski's Wraiths

So it matters not where we be goin'

As we sing the stars of Garyowen.

A song of duty and home, that was also a warning to the Wraith support teams. It was time to clear the bay. The opacity of the mothership's walls dissolved as they prepared departure, revealing the cosmic grandeur of a red planet on a bed of multicolored diamonds. There was no pump-down, no loss or change of atmosphere when **Alfred's** wall transitioned to a state called 'ship-permeable'. Although pilots were safe from the radiation and vacuum of space, the bay would soon be dangerous for unprotected spacers.

As the Wraith's excitement grew, their drives began emitting activated molecules that grew to envelope the whole vessel. The action could rip a lost wrench, dropped screw, rogue fly, or cockroach into a string of hot molecules flung out in all directions as the fighter's field encountered them. Occasionally a lost rod or wrench of the right length would be left behind, one end of it to be taken up and ejected from the ship's surface while the other was drawn to it causing the object to spin in place. This parasitic spinning continued until shutdown occurred and the object was physically removed.

Almost imperceptibly, the Wraiths, already floating a hand's-breadth above the deck, began to bob and flutter lightly in excited anticipation as they lifted even higher. They were now flying on their own in a personal vacuum created by the active drive field envelope of each Wraith, extending out from each fighter that had ejected even atmospheric molecules.

VSF-1, the first Space Fighter Squadron trembled in readiness.

The human eye sees nothing that occurs in less than a thirtieth of a second, so when squad leader Kronski's craft shot across the bay and out from the *Alfred*, it moved so quickly that any onlookers simply perceived it as a disappearance, sensed only by the sharp ripping of disassociated air molecules ejected to the side in its transit forward and the popping of vapors refilling the vacuum tunnel-wake created by the fighter's departure.

The molecular metal-matrix computers that composed the ship's bay hull had sensed the Wraith's approach and fled laterally, deforming their metallic matrix at blinding speed to avoid collision with the craft like an octopus morphing to squeeze into a soda bottle nearly half its size.

With the exactness of a nanomaterials engineer, the hull's atomic matrix retracted far enough to avoid contact with the fighter's drive field surface, parting less than the breadth of an air molecule away from the Wraith's deadly drive field then retreating as quickly to their original, solid metallic atomic matrix as the ship passed without the loss of a single molecule of the interior gas-mix.

With its transition into hard vacuum complete, the Wraith drives adjusted their link to the universal waves of gravity. The powerful gravitic drive field bent any passing photon streams and fermion energy packets as they sailed outbound rendering the fighters invisible to visual and most radiation sensors. The Wraith's only emanation was a briefly visible trail created by secondary electrons ejected during the interaction, shedding their energy in the form of low energy photons.

This faint, blue line marked each Wraith's passage on an orbit spiraling inward to a dead landscape turned red from oxidized ferrous ores on the Martian volcanic plane where the small, outnumbered force of colonial warriors would soon challenge the might of a rich nation nearly as old as the pyramids of Egypt.

~~*~*~*~*

"Captain on the bridge," bellowed out as Decatur entered, habit guided him across the bridge to his command chair while his eyes took in the body language of his crew, watching for the earliest sign of potential problems. His concentration, however, remained laser-focused on their greatest problem, logistics and there it gnawed at the complex knot of options available using methods gained from hard experience.

First, clarify the problem by laying it out logically for recording in his personal log. Fortunately, the services of his HiveTab allowed his brain to silently multitask and assign his log entry to a background process of his enhanced mind.

My rangers are groundside fighting to control a panicked herd of humans three times their number. Who, although mostly colonials and NAU, include a mixed force of enemy combatants as well as CTAC spacers. Of course, the inmates we release, even those from Kraken, may not be friendly to our cause and this increases the procedure's complexity since their allegiance must be determined on an individual basis or, with even greater risk, assumed.

Our primary objective remains deceptively simple. Release the colonials from their illegal incarceration and take them home to freedom.

Our forces, initially insufficient for proper management of the unexpectedly large number of prison inmates, were split early on by the arrival of a CTAC transport delivering even more prisoners. The ship dropped into the middle of the ranger's position without warning and its capture diverted nearly a third of our available ground force while adding more hostiles and prisoners to the mix.

In the cavern, Major Steven's people stirred up a hornet's nest of battle-hardened CTAC troops that are now streaming in from their main base using a tunnel the rangers failed to fully seal off.

The situation is complicated by our own moral convictions. Our first duty is to Kraken colonials and second to the other incarcerated colonial citizens. Yet, we all have a natural affinity to the NAU prisoners in the compound and even the few CTAC citizens held there because of their political convictions.

*Unfortunately, even with the inclusion of the capacity provided by the second captured CTAC ship to augment that of **Alfred** and **Revenge**, we do not have sufficient means to transport all prisoners.*

We have little time for a proper selection of who will go and who stays. Physical health is, of course, a factor. Many prisoners may be adversaries rather than supporters so a form of physical as well as political triage must be part of the selection process.

Intelligence just warned of CTAC transports and warcrafts heading our way, increasing the pressure and need for our early departure.

As for evacuation of the prisoners, it is suicide to attempt shuttle lifts into low orbit. Despite the objections of my staff, I have decided to take the unprecedented move of grounding both starships and loading them directly.

We place our hopes and lives into the hands of the rangers and our fighter screen. God help us all.¶

THE TUNNEL

A man-made shaft, broad enough to contain a four-lane highway, stretched for many kilometers beneath the Martian landscape. It originated within a huge natural chain of caverns formed by ancient rivers that once flowed beneath the mountains, extending down to the plains of the great Martian volcano Pavonis Mons. There it intersects a natural labyrinth of underground tubes formed by ancient lava flows, now terraformed for human habitation or, to be more specific, climate-controlled storage and the incarceration of prisoners of war and dissidents.

"Incursion from tube portal twelve, unknown strength. Sector three." Platoon leader Lt. Travis Strake received the call that carried data, a status flimsy, across the push on his HiveTab. As he brought up the flimsy, it quickly became apparent they were about to receive a visit-in-force from an origin they didn't plan upon, the tunnel leading to the main base.

There were troops within the tunnel, for it hadn't been closed off. The ranger sapper team assigned to seal the tunnel failed to achieve complete closure and CTAC forces were now racing past the blockage to settle what they apparently still believe to be a prisoner uprising.

"Sergeant Washington, to me."

Washington came running and Strake began immediately by flipping the flimsy over to her and opened it, the sector map of the incursion, "We're getting visitors and they are coming in behind us, from the tunnel from the main base."

"Let's see if we can contain, then push them back into the tunnel. Grab a heavy squad and circle around to the other side of the tunnel's exit. Lay some Leaping Lena's in the corridors you can't cover. You also have my authorization to release Ambots. Set them to allow the CTAC to pass by. When these guys reach your squad, hit them and activate the Ambots in ambush mode, but leave them an escape route. Push them back rather than entrap. Keep pushing them all the way inside. When you have them back in the tunnel, stop. Bottle 'em up and seal the entrance, I don't care how. This is a holding action and we need you back here."

"In the meantime, I'll hit them head-on. They'll be expecting us and will attempt an end-run. That should deliver them right into your ambush. Go."

Strake charged off at a trot, gathering rangers as he moved along. The cavern walls were glass-smooth, stabilized magma that led on for long, long stretches following the downhill slope of least resistance down the mountain. The path ahead curved little, if at all, with very few sharp turns. An occasional tight bend always preceded a narrowing on their side that opened into a much wider, round-domed chamber on the other side of the turn's blockage where the magma had formed into a pool before siphoning its way downslope.

Strake's charge carried them through a set of doors and into a massive, tear-dropped shaped chamber with high ceilings and a flat floor half-filled with prisoners silently staring at them from cages stacked two levels high. The silence was unnatural, with a saturating smell of human waste and fear that prompted Strake to tune them out with his suits filters. The chamber's upper end was still under construction with tools, parts, and crates scattered about.

"Sergeant, have Corporal Cassava send a break-out squad. Tell him there's ….. oh, forty more up here. Then …"

Like a scream at a funeral, the call interrupted his orders, "Corporal Strake, over here."

The lieutenant's head snapped to the left. The bellowed demand came from down among the cages. He turned back to the sergeant, completing his order sequence, "Then continue up to the tunnel entrance but take care, the door's wide open and they may be waiting on the other side."

Strake broke off on a short jog, wondering who the hell was addressing him as 'corporal'.

"Strake, hey buddy. I see you made louie, good for you. Okay, pleasantries over. Now get me the shite out of here."

The lieutenant looked at the human skeleton clad in tattered prison greys shouting at him. Then recognition came, "Captain Jenson? I never expected to run into you here."

"Say, how did you recognize me in this battle suit."

"We spent enough time together. Shite, I'd know you in your birthday suit. Now, cut the chatter and get me out of this damn cage."

Suspicion rose inside the officer, "Why are you alive? I thought they spaced officers."

The skeleton managed to look exasperated, "They do unless they think you know something they need. Now, please cut the chatter and get me out. NOW!"

"I'll let you out but listen up. We're in a tight spot. I'm in command and if you defy me, I will put you down without hesitation.

We are colonial forces, not NAU, and you have no authority over these men."

"You're in a tight spot, what do you think I'm …"

The talking skeleton was growing frantic, "Look, never mind. I'm sorry. Release me, we'll cover the niceties afterward. I'll obey. I can even help. You need me, buddy."

"Damn right you'll obey. Now, stand back," Strake shouted as he pulled a sachet off his equipment strap. Taking out a packet, he massaged it between thumb and finger then molded it to the locking mechanism of the cage like a wad of gum.

"Back up, don't touch the sides. Things are going to get hot."

Tapping it lightly with his index finger, he pulled back. The packet's surface became glossy, then rippled and, with a sizzle, melted into the case steel metal like a sponge soaking up a puddle of water. A puff of smoke shot out from every seam of the lock mechanism, then drifted off as the cell's door lazily swung open with the glow of still white-hot, deformed steel framing, the now missing lockbox.

"Remember, don't touch. Follow me."

Strake had no choice but to take the prisoner along and hope he could keep up. They ran up-tunnel, following the path through chambers already taken by his people, passing half-assembled cages, crates, and tools strewn across the chamber floor. A Chinese firecracker string of sharp cracks ripped out as they approached, echoing off the walls of the huge chamber. Hypervelocity pulsar rounds sang their angry buzz, splitting the air as they whizzed by, adding their deadly song to the mixed echoes of Mandarin shouts and screams filtered from the background chatter of rifle fire by their battle suits.

Strake ducked as a ranger stepped out performed a roundhouse arm-chuck that was followed by the dull, head wrenching thud of a concussion grenade thrown into the narrow passageway. A hammer-blow of smoke and debris erupted from the narrow tunnel along with a spinning boot, stringing a shower of blood from a foot dangling from it and spinning across the room. Three rangers immediately charged the narrow portal, the angry staccato of firing erupted then all became quiet except for some inarticulate groans that somehow managed to penetrate the blast filters of their suits.

"Okay, this is a good spot to seal the tunnel. Sergeant, run a team up-tunnel for cover while your people lay the ..."

"Strake, wait a sec." Jensen interrupted. "Let me pay my way. There's another chamber ahead and you don't want to blow it just yet. If you push, you might get there before they destroy everything. I told you they wanted me for information; ahead is part of the reason why."

"It's a holostorage unit with hardcoded datacrystal matrices and their library of cryptographic keys. That chamber is secure, a CTAC safe backup storage for their entire fleet."

Strake wondered just what this guy really wanted, "That's BS, how could you know about this?"

"It's amazing what they talk about in front of you when they figure you ain't gonna be around much longer. Look, you're wasting time. One chamber up and you can blow it. Then we all get out of here, ah ..."

"You can get me out of here, can't you?"

Strake's face shield had cleared within the cavern letting Jensen see his death head grin. A shiver went through the captain, "Cheez, you have gotten cold-hearted these past years. What the cust you been up to anyway?"

Strake ignored the question but called out over the command push of his HiveTab, "All units, belay that last command. Wait one."

Then stopped, his eyes went glassy as he reported to the major. It took but a few seconds, "All right, you keep up with me. If the lighting goes, grab onto my belt and pray the next chamber is lit."

Opening his push to the rest of his team, "Change of plans. We're going to take the next chamber up-tunnel."

"On your toes, ladies. The tables just turned, this time we'll be the ones in the narrow tunnel, and you can bet your sweet turtle's ass they'll be looking for payback."

"Move 'em out, Sarge."

They passed over the floor slick with blood, bodily fluids, and the occasional weapon dropped next to a still moaning or inert body. The level of moisture in the cavern must have been higher here for there were blue-green sections of mold lining the walls along the floor. Less than five minutes later, Sergeant Washington halted her unit and motioned Private Cooper onward.

Izzy Cooper advanced silently, reluctantly. She couldn't keep her eyes off the open portal ahead. The vision of an arm flicking in, followed by the arc of a hand-launched antipersonnel grenade sailing through the smoke-laced air sent shafts of icy fear through her veins.

Slinging her weapon, she reached back into her knapsack and brought out a flat coil of rope-like material. Flinging it out, it caught the air and sailed onward for several paces then flipped open like a striking cobra. It shot forward in a gliding arc to the ground sprouting dozens of mandibles from its sides. The weapon hit the ground running, weaving back and forth like a thick, black millipede and, like the arthropod, it carried a sting.

The millipede scuttled for the portal only to run into an emerging swarm of black, hairy spiders sweeping around the corner, moving more like drops of water skittering across a red-hot grill, than the controlled stepping of a live arachnid.

The millipede didn't hesitate and sent out a snowstorm of translucent white string that sailed out airborne. Spiders met the millipede attack with diode-pumped YAG laser beams, snapping wildly as they pulse-fired at the white streamers, the millipede, and the rangers.

A hand whipped out from behind the far portal's frame then disappeared releasing a black canister that rattled against the walls and onto the floor. Another snowstorm of string flew out, enveloping the grenade, pulled it in and in the blink of an eye, wrapped it tight as a fly spun into a spider's cocoon. The smothered explosive was strong enough to destroy the millipede but did no further damage. The corporal launched her own room-clearing grenade then charged forward, firing her pulsar. The rangers followed in a push through the portal, not a single ranger glancing at the biologic in thanks as they charged by.

This chamber was smaller than the previous, its walls coated with a weird insulating foam-like dimpled material that looked like it was crudely sprayed on. At first glance, the space appeared empty until their eyes noticed a milky, egg-shaped distortion at its center. It's very center for the distortion floated in mid-air. They could see through the object, though not clearly for it distorted the image of the wall beyond as they cautiously circled it to halt before the up-tunnel portal leading to the CTAC main base. But only the sound of retreating footsteps in the distance was there to greet them.

Strake called them off, "Let 'em go. Now, seal that tunnel and do it good and proper."

Strake walked back to the NAU captain and was about to speak when a dull thud made him skip a step. Dust and chaos flooded out from the uphill tunnel, but the lieutenant never gave it a glance. His attention was focused on the thing in the center of the room. A thing his eyes could not seem to focus on.

As their eyes adjusted to the apparition, they noticed translucent tendrils extending to the upper-walls and ceiling of the chamber. The tendrils squirmed and flexed between the points of contact, connecting the egg to the ceiling and far walls squirming like a fat-bellied, translucent earthworms trapped at both ends.

Strake copped back a few choice words, swallowed, and then turned to the prisoner, "Don't tell me that thing's your storage matrix."

"Yep, first time I've been this close but there sure was a lot of chatter about the contraption. It apparently gave them the green-willies too but at the same time they all spoke of it as something 'new and exciting'. They were obviously in awe of it."

Strake turned to the ex-prisoner, "Well a lot of good that does us, how do you expect us to remove the ... whatever it is?"

"Oh, that's not the holomatrix, it's a gravitic cusp used to interface to the storage unit. You can see it's gravitic because of the image distortion of things behind it. We have yet to see the matrix, actually we're looking right past the thing."

"Where's your tech with all the toys?"

Strake called out, "Cooper, front and center."

His hand motioned her attention to the NAU captain as she came running up.

"Ah, Tech Cooper. You were pretty slick back in the tunnel. Let's see what you have in your bag of tricks for that." He said while gesturing towards the holomatrix containment, "I need a gravitic field punch."

Cooper stared at him for a moment, "Shoot captain, what do you think I am? A destroyer?"

Her smile released a coppered giggle from the captain in reply that sent a shiver up the tech's back when he answered with, "Come on sweetie, you know what I want. I want a Dirac Delta Point penetrator. Nothing big, just something to punch a pinhole through that shaped gravity shell."

Cooper had involuntarily taken half a step back, immediately regretting her smart-arse answer. This wasn't a guy she wanted to piss off, "Yes sir, I get it. You want something with feedback too? How about this?" Izzy was solid and confident as she opened a cargo flap on her battle suit and pulled out a rolled piece of ragged, stiff fabric. "This usually requires a launcher but not when we're this close."

Taking his silence as consent, she rolled it into a tube then, holding it like a dart, her arm shot forward. The dart sailed across the narrow, open space, its fabric unfolding mid-flight then glided in to settle immobile above the lenticular aberration. It began swirling, releasing a black mist that eddied outward.

"A NanoBot swarm embedded in a delivery fold, special programming." She commented with a smile at the captain which she immediately regretted when he smiled back.

The mist thickened, and began churning, as thick tendrils of a knobby-oily-black fog grew outward, shimmering like drops of oil spreading across the surface of a still pond. Then the oil slick abruptly coalesced to a point above the holomatrix, growing smaller until it was but a black pinpoint floating in the air until there was a 'pop', accompanied by a burst of heat lasting less than a heartbeat.

Cooper smiled, she liked her job, "They compress until they can punch through on an atomic level, ripping through the gravitic field and then the surface energy of the atomic shell to leave a NanoBot link behind them. Couldn't crack open the whole structure but, for an area the size of a molecule or two in width, we can get through." Cooper said as she safe-sealed her weapons pouch, "Link to AZ-313, Lieutenant."

Strake's HiveTab enhancement linked into the channel. A portion of his mind could see a matrix that he recognized from its body-centered-cubic textured molecular surface. Beyond that, it made no sense.

"Okay Captain, what now?"

Tech Cooper knew this was coming and handed the captain a headband. He put it on, his eyes glazed over as he felt it linking to his own NAU HiveTab. Strake just had begun to feel the captain's entry into the data channel when the matrix began vibrating then disappeared and the channel disconnected.

"Now I know why they kept you alive, Cap …", Cooper stopped, the captain was ignoring her.

Her gaze returned to the apparition, finding that the force fields were gone. A small, black cube, the size of a human head, floated at the room's center for a moment before settling gently to the floor. Its surface glistened, releasing occasional pinpoint sparkles of light from an otherwise coal-black surface.

Captain Jensen put his hand out towards the tech, "Don't touch. Give me a permalloy mylar wrap, please."

Cooper dug into her pack and pulled out an envelope, extracting a poncho-like cloth. Jensen carefully laid it over the cube and then flipped the device into a fold.

"I shut the archive's field down. We should leave now Strake. If our CTAC hosts weren't upset before, they are going to be downright nasty from here on out."

"The captain's correct, Lieutenant." Captain Decatur suddenly broke into Strake's command push. Captain Jensen was privy to the conversation since he still wore the headband.

"The level of CTAC communications chatter just quadrupled. Clear the tunnels, get out all you can, but I want you out of there stat."

"Oh, and make sure your NAU buddy and his "gift" are in the first load, boarding of *Alfred*. Otherwise, keep him under guard like any other prisoner."

NAU intelligence officer Captain Jeremiah Jensen, a broad grin on his face, was on his way to freedom and home.

Or so he thought.

SURFACE ACTION

"This 'thing' I'm setting up is an olfactory sensory neuron channel. It's really nothing for you to be concerned about." Mark Mason replied to the CTAC officer behind the environmental field-'bars' of the prison transport cage, "I'm a combat-journalist and, once this thing's properly calibrated, I'm going to record the sights, sounds, emotions, and even the scents of Mars as you are transported into the cavern, solidifying a record of the whole experience for posterity."

"Ever wonder what it smells like on Mars' surface? So far, no one knows because we can't breathe the atmosphere. Even if it were warm enough to get into your lungs without freezing them solid, we couldn't do it. The atmosphere's mostly carbon dioxide and therefore thin enough to collapse your lungs. However, we will soon be able to experience this planet's environment using every human sense. They'll smell the rot and stink that fills your caverns. The smell of all the filth that resides there from all the caged spacers so poorly treated by you and your people."

He turned a frank stare to see the reaction of the prisoner, obviously taking him by surprise with the appearance of a sudden friendly smile undiminished by the near-invisible face-shield of his vacuum-suit's helmet, "Where you from, Sublieutenant?"

"I'm from Zhangjiakou, just outside Beijing. Look, I'm not responsible for prisoners. I've done nothing wrong, I'm just a communications officer."

"What's going to happen to us?"

A tinge of pity filled the journalist, "I know you are flight-crew and not part of the prison system. You don't deserve this."

"But then, neither did they. Shite happens and ..."

The journalist stopped, obviously reconsidering his next words, "Okay, you suckers are lucky. We won't be taking you along with us. The rangers are going to move you into the cavern's cells as they release our people and empty space becomes available. A human can go a month without food, you know. Not near as long if you don't have water ... need 'bout forty-eight hours I recall. You'll be okay as long as your own people don't flip a missile into the cavern, shoot you, or simply abandon you."

"I'm sure you'll enjoy the experience, and the smells if nothing else."

A ranger came over escorting two manacled CTAC officers jogging at double time, then stopped without saluting to address Major Walters, "Major, Sir. The lieutenant sent these fellows over, figured you'd want to take them back for war-crime trials."

"This one is the CTAC prison commandant and his buddy's the XO of the facility."

Mason overheard the exchange and altered the focus of his recording in time to catch the obvious storm of emotions flashing across Major Walters's face. The journalist stiffened as the officer's hand went to his sidearm, then hesitated. Walters seemed to chew on his answer for a moment then turned, giving Mason a hard look that said, 'I don't give a frag if you're recording or not'. His gaze seemed to zone-out the CTAC officers who were attempting to ignore him, stiffly glaring in defiance of their situation, as he turned to the ranger, "We're full up. If I take these two Zermonkies then its two colonials I need to leave behind. I have neither the time nor the capacity to deal with them."

"Neither do you, Specialist."

"Escort them back to the cavern, I'm sure they'd prefer not to leave with us."

Walters turned his back, returning to his original task. The exchange was obviously over, and the ranger was about to start when the major's final words came out hard, cold, and sharp as a ranger's titanium-steel blade, "Specialist, take the safe route through the west ravine."

"Report back directly to me in five minutes or I'll have your hide tacked up on my chamber's wall."

The ranger stiffened as though he'd just walked into a force field, hesitated, and then turned, "Sir, there's no way I can get back …"

"Specialist!" Sergeant Jaeger's boot camp bellow cut him short, "You heard the Major. Get to it and report back. Not a minute later, understand?"

Puzzled and confused at first, then an understanding crossed the face of the ranger along with a savage smile that would have chilled Old Nick himself. The specialist had been inside the caves, seen the prisoners. Seen and smelled all the corpses and mutilations.

Mason's eye turned to the timeline runback on his recorder. He'd captured the exchange and was reviewing it when the bust of a Pulsar rifle echoed through the thin atmosphere from beyond the nearby hills edging the ravine. He'd expected it but still jumped when it came.

Without looking up, Mason keyed the command through his HiveTab, removing the entire sequence and its archive from the recorder. He followed with a bit-level bit scrub of the dynamic memory section. This was one can of worms that wasn't about to see the light of day. An episode he could live with but one he'd just as soon forget.

Major Steve Walters pushed the incident from his mind and stared into the distance, across the field. The newest vessel of Decatur's growing flotilla lay on the stabilized field of iron-rich sand, nearly ready and close enough for him to feel like he could leave its final repairs and AI adaptation to colonial control standards to his subordinates.

~~*~*~*~*

A red haze softened the rugged terrain of the mountains ahead, their sharp bluffs backlit by the yellow orb of the planet's distant star that lay low to the horizon, framed between the two peaks ahead of their tracked vehicle. Mars has an atmosphere composed mostly of carbon dioxide, nothing much to speak of since it's a thousand times thinner than that of Earth's. Too thin for an Earth-standard hover car but strong enough to raise the fine red sands of the surface into a dust-laden fog capable of masking the approach of troop transports.

Mason continued recording as he followed on the major's heels. They passed rangers carving out slit-trenches that would protect and hide their presence, for he knew only a historian would have called them 'foxholes'. Hardly a stray ranger or cargo pallet was visible on the landing strip. Eventually, they had erased all traces of the destruction left by the savage assault of several hundred rangers.

Walters turned to the journalist, "Just received a drone alert. CTAC finally pulled their act together and sent out a surface response force."

"Captain believes they still haven't spotted our ships in orbit. We've shut down and buttoned up the captured CTAC transport and isolated its AI, it won't be sending out unexpected warnings. If we're lucky, they're still in the dark as to what's actually going on."

"Link up with Sergeant Jaeger. Keep your head down and stay out of his hair. Remember, you are an observer, not a participant."

Mason smiled as he jogged over to the sergeant's platoon. He wore a ranger battlesuit complete with all the trimmings including armor and active camouflage; all standard ranger issue, everything but the shoulder patch. A part of him shivered with anticipation, he'd never had the opportunity to experience this level of continued combat intensity during his time in service and that old feeling of excitement was returning.

His suit was officer grade, so his HiveTab had the full communications and battlefield tactical interface issued with a sternly repeated reminder that he was strictly a recorder of events.

Rangers spread out in the crest of low hills surrounding the landing strip, an area filled with islands of wind-worn rock separated by rust-colored dirt and powder that sailed airborne with the slightest disturbance. They quickly learned to avoid the smooth, level patches masking pits filled with fine dirt particles that could trip the unlucky runner or, it was rumored, swallow a man or even an entire vehicle.

Jaeger hyper-sensed his approach, "I was wondering when you'd get here, Mason. Hitch up with Jenkins and Loxley."

A pip appeared on the journalist's field map marking the location of the two rangers. They were tucked into what amounted to little more than a body-length shallow trench, not so much for protection against incoming munitions, as it helped them blend into the rocks and smooth surrounding terrain. Mason recognized Joan Loxley from onboard the ship but neither she nor Pfc. Rob Jenkins said a word as he approached. Even with secure communications, chatter was rare. They were taking no chance of disclosing their positions.

Working quickly, he worked up a slit long enough for him to slide into and waited.

Before long, a darkening of a red-tinged horizon quickly transformed to black under the approach of the foul weather front. The wind rose and gusts joined by stronger blasts of air hit them, constantly changing direction and, in gravity barely a third that of Earth's, lifting fine dust particles into huge rust-colored clouds that ascended impossibly high into the heavens.

"Watch your six," A whisper snuck across from the sergeant's push. A quick glance to his rear then Mason checked his battle status telemetry. Nothing had been reported, no sign of approach. The storm before them carried swirling clouds of red dirt and a high-pitched squeal like fingernails scraping down an ancient blackboard.

They had waited a small eternity when a black ghost materialized in the dimly lit sands ahead, moving cautiously amid the blowing debris. The journalist's eyes fixed on the apparition. It moved slowly, coming directly for him until it vanished beneath another gust of dry red ground. Two more figures materialized in the near distance only to swirl out of existence beneath the next banshee howl of wind and sand.

Bogies began popping up across his battle display without the automated identification tags, that would indicate an AI logged entry. They were manual entries from squad leaders as the enemy approached unseen, but for the proximity detection of a Mark I Human Eyeball.

The fury of the storm worsened over their slit trenches, turning the world black as night and inside its black folds it roared and sparked with strange firefly like lights. More sightings flared into life only to disappear beneath the black, red-tinged swirling curtain of the sandstorm. Mason's pulse rate grew with each new blip defining the enemy's measured approach. Onward they advanced, widely spread, yet converging to a point midway between the ship and the compound entrance. Then their approach changed as caution slowed their movements. The journalist saw a shadowed apparition drop to a knee to look and listen, still oblivious of the dispersal of rangers, now surrounding and interspersed within the CTAC contingent.

"Wait, pick your targets. Keep yer damn heads down," The major's voice stomped through his brain. Each ranger knew only of enemy sightings near their position, but it was obvious that a much larger force of CTAC troops surrounded the rangers. True enemy strength was unknown, and their exact disposition unknown as well.

The fight would be close, dirty, and personal.

Mason had just managed to get all the systems silently recording when he sensed an approach through the subtle shifting of the surrounding Martian sand rather than by sound or sight. Eyes straining, he saw nothing. Then a shape formed. A bulge, little more than a mound the size of his fist lifted surface outside his trench. His hand searched his battle-harness of its own volition, habitually searching for the weapon he no longer carried. Slowly, the sandy bulge expanded and was now pushing towards them like a mole's passage beneath the surface.

Something grabbed his shoulder, twisting him around. A cyclone of red sand screamed as it swirled around him and the dimmed figure of a ranger silently, but firmly, pushed him to the side. The ranger slowly crawled from the slit trench, arm extended, combat knife ready in his gloved hand. Mason heard a small grunt as the arm arched forward then down, ramming the vibro-blade deep into the mound cutting sand, stone, and ultimately into soft tissue.

The biologic convulsed, ripping itself from the ground. It carried the ranger up, his knife firmly still held in a one-handed grip. With it came a banshee's scream, rising above the wailing storm. Its convulsions revealed a snake-like android, thick as his arm and easily as long as Mason, with the ranger's blade still firmly transfixed right up to its hilt. It convulsed again, lifting the ranger higher into the air. Somehow, his other arm flashed out, swung forward and the muffled flash of a sidearm lit the swirling sand like a lightning strike but was absorbed just as rapidly as it came.

Six storm-muffled, ultra-high velocity reports split the air, screaming as they pushed their way through the sand-saturated air and ripped the ranger apart. The body dropped, disappearing beneath the blowing sands.

The presence of the rangers was now known, they'd been uncovered by the CTAC launched biologic drones, thick worm-like robotics scouting ahead by pushing their way beneath the sand.

In a fractional heartbeat, storm-dimmed Pulsar blasts erupted all around Mason from an enemy whose penetration had carried them unknowingly deep inside the colonial perimeter. Blowing ferrous-oxide laced sand brought darkness neither sight, nor sensors could penetrate. CTAC soldiers responded to ranger fire with a fusillade of their own at targets they could neither see nor sense. Chaos filled the battlefield. Dug into their slit trenches, rangers fired at any shadow briefly emerging from the blowing sands. Some blindly sending defilade fire at a target's coordinates as designated by the last update of their suit's battle map.

A hurricane blast of controlled energy filled the space above the ranger's shallow trenches bringing destruction to anything extending more than an arm's stretch above the surface. Then a new wailing-scream rose impossibly above the chaos of battle and was joined by a third, much more personal screech coming from beneath their feet. Pure reaction wrenched Mason around and his suit's sensors targeted debris-obscured shadows, struggling barely out of arm's reach; demon-shades, risen directly from the depths of hell, flipped and squirmed across the ground, churning within the maelstrom of debris.

The journalist launched himself blindly forward, relying more on feel than sight. He slammed into the thrusting shoulder of a ranger's suit, reached out, hand skidding across its wet surface to jam-up against a slick, thrusting tube, a worm-like thing had dug into the ranger's chest. He squeezed but it gave nothing beneath his death grip. Mason used two hands to firmly latch onto the slithering horror. He dug his fingers into its soft flesh and twisted with all the strength his legs could put into it. A blinding flash erupted, his training recognized it as secondary emission of flesh vaporizing beneath the beam of a pulsed YAG laser beam, another surprise weapon of the biologic bent on ripping its victim apart.

The victim screamed beneath the blast as a hole the width of Mason's thumb cut through her battle suit. Exploding with blobs of liquid flesh mixed with liquified sand slagged into glass before losing their energy in the far wall of her trench.

As Mason reached for his knife, his eyes caught sight of the pulsar at her belt. Too far. His only defensive weapon would have to do but would it be enough?

The biologic snake began retracting from the wound; he knew it would turn on him. The blade activated automatically as he unsheathed it, a familiar deadly vibration in his grip that increased angrily as he thrust forward. It hit the hardened skin of the snake, he could feel it penetrate, and vibrate wildly as it deflected off something surprisingly dense inside, then was nearly wrenched from his hand when the blade chattered and lodged tight upon encountering something truly solid inside. He twisted, straining with his whole body, a deadly-twist he'd been taught many years ago would maximize internal damage and hopefully free the blade.

The worm shuddered, whipping around in a spasm that threw him back. He was deep in the shite now as both ranger and CTAC pulsar loads screamed just over his head, ripping the ground at the top of the trench, a hand's breadth away as Mason scrambled backward to escape the death throes of the biologic. A fleeting moment of amazement crossed his mind at the life-like reaction to death appearing in the man-made drone.

Something managed to grab his shoulder. Twisting, pulling, lifting him from the trench then slammed helmet-to-helmet with a shout, "Stay with me, Mason! Up and out!"

They ran, stumbling over the body of the dying ranger, feet pumping, straining for purchase within the soft, shot-churned Martian red sand. He felt naked running out in the open and only trained reaction drove him onward as he blindly slid a hand over his harness and confirmed the recorder sensors were with him and operational. They jigged then jagged, constantly shifting direction as the sergeant led a crossing of the open landing field.

The storm seemed to ebb, clearing as they ran. Mason set a mental note.

Passing across the open plane, I see many more CTAC casualties than colonials. Some rangers still were hunkered down in trenches since the initiation of firing. The sandstorm blinding friend and foe alike but only the CTAC troops were fully exposed to the murderous fire erupting from both friend and foe. Results are horrendous.

They circled the **Aries** and crossed into a maze of stacked, recently unloaded storage containers. Bounding like fleas from box to box, they worked their way across the field towards the nearest ship's ramp but were stopped by an earsplitting, head rocking blast. The sound of the weapon's report followed the head-splitting jolt of a hypervelocity wavefront whose passage screamed across the higher octaves brought on by the thin Martian air. The journalist's head throbbed in pain despite the automatic sound and shock dampening of the battlesuit's helmet. Mason knew instant death had screamed past less than a hand's breadth from his own helmet.

The ranger running in front was not so lucky. A second and third blast from the sniper and he saw two more rangers drop in his peripheral vision as he dove for cover.

One of those on the ground, out in the open was Sergeant Jaeger.

Somehow a human groan seeped eerily through the ringing in his ears. Mason risked pushing his throbbing head out enough to see beyond the container. The sergeant and one of the rangers lay there exposed and wounded but the sniper hadn't fired, didn't finish the job. Mason thought it didn't make sense, why didn't the sniper finish them off?

He assessed his situation.

That sniper managed to drop everyone in the group ... except for me. Why? Did the CTAC see me dive for cover and doesn't want to give away his posi ...?

A crack from a hypervelocity slug ripping through the thin atmosphere was followed by a scream that carried across the squad's communication's push. Startled, Mason jumped back, then poked his head around the corner. Instantly realizing his mistake, he pulled back. The hypervelocity pulsar round struck the edge of the container as Mason pulled back, passing so close he was thrown back and could feel the burn of a track of instantly fried flesh created by the deadly slug as it scorched its way past his neck.

Mason's suit reacted instantly, releasing a liquid-like powder that sealed the leak. He ignored the process for he now knew what was going on.

No damage beyond a bruised face and neck brush burn. Lucky me, I lost nothing more than my pride.

That sniper intentionally wounded one of the downed rangers. It wasn't a kill shot. He intended to wound him, picked him so he'd yell out and get me to expose myself.

He's waiting for me.

Mason could hear shouts in Mandarin from approaching soldiers.

Time to leave while I can.

Can't. Can't leave them lying there like that. He's going to waste them just as soon as I bug out.

His mind replayed the recording just taken. There it was, the flash of the sniper fire coming from behind the ship's landing strut. *SOB's tucked away, up in the knee of the strut.*

Mason noticed the boot of the ranger. He reached out, pulled the body back until he felt the shot's impact. His hand felt the body spasm; a kill shot this time.

Frantically he searched for the ranger's weapon, found it on the ground around the corner. Just a pace away but it might as well have been a hundred. He'd never make it.

The ranger's vitals are flat. Small comfort, she was dead before I pulled her in. Check her gear.

One sidearm, slug clips full. Two grenades.

Close combat weapons but more than I had a minute ago. Now, right now. I gotta do something, anything. Right now! But what?

Mark turned and ran back three lanes of cargo crates then turned again going out of his way so to hide his retreat. Running full speed, grenade in one hand and a pistol in the other, he circled around. He felt like a rat in a tub as he raced across the open space between the crates and the ship, but no fire was directed his way. Without hesitation, he crossed down and circled behind **Aries** until he could see the landing strut ahead. Then, he slowed and started jigging back and forth, moving silently until his eyes caught movement.

Screaming at the top of his lungs to draw the sniper's attention, he fired as he ran with only the barest effort to properly aim. Then, close enough to lob a grenade, he skipped once to set his footing and flung the grenade, completing the roundhouse swing with a crash dive for the red Martian sand.

His head hit something hard. The grenade went off and he rolled before the blast. Mason looked at his hand, numb fingers still held the ranger's pistol. His scream came out a ragged, deep-throated squeal, that painfully rocked between the waves of pain in his head.

Something dropped from the strut to the ground, closely followed by the sniper. Mason launched himself onto the sniper, digging his shoulder into the trooper as he landed on the CTAC marine's back, then grabbing the neck from behind, he felt for the soft spot at the base of the skull where it joined the spine.

Two thumbs jammed the sniper's soft vacuum suit into the spinal nerve bundle. The sniper convulsed, flapped an arm then relaxed. Mason pushed harder until the breathing stopped, then just a bit longer to be sure.

His thumbs ached, but no time to rest. The journalist flopped to the ground, looked around, and quickly picked up the sniper's rifle.

Checked its load … half a clip.

He had one grenade left in his pocket but also found and pulled a concussion grenade from the sniper. A quick scan of the area, someone was coming. CTAC troops emerged from around the edge of the ship; they had yet to spot him when he fired into them. Some dropped, while others ran for cover.

Mason moved in a running crouch over to the nearest downed ranger. But it was too late, he was gone.

The second ranger was alive. Mason picked him up in a fireman's carry and sprinted for the nearest box, and dove around its corner as a hail of fire raked its side. A sentient part of his mind thanked the stars for whatever was inside this container and that it was capable of stopping a hypervelocity round.

He didn't bother to roll the moaning ranger against the box but instead spent those precious seconds ripping a patch from the victim's belt pack. Bending over, he squeezed together the hissing tear that the man's suit had been trying to seal and slapped the patch over it without stopping to check. The suit should be able to take care of the rest. The ranger would be okay where he lay unless … Mason failed, otherwise, better cover wouldn't help.

Mason got up, his gut hurt as he pulled out a frag grenade, let the pin flip and round-housed it around the container. The blast rocked him back but he charged through the swirling sand headfirst, screaming at the top of his lungs. Two CTAC troopers lay on the ground; he could hear the other's screams as he pulled his remaining grenade. He considered it a lucky choice as he round-housed it. It wasn't a frag but the concussion would still be dangerous, even in the thinner atmosphere. Anyways, it gave him a better chance of survival.

He didn't stop to look where it landed but grabbed the nearest ranger's harness. It was Sergeant Jaeger. The man's eyes were wide, angry and he was shouting something Mason couldn't hear.

Mason manhandled the sergeant to his shoulder, they staggered for a bit with the sergeant screaming as he swung his arm over Mason's shoulder. Mason snap-fired one last burst behind him, then ran for the shelter of the stacked cargo containers. Nearing exhaustion, he let the ranger bounce painfully to the ground near the other survivor then twisted around as he dove for cover and brought his weapon up.

The sharp crack of hypervelocity slugs cut the air in front of him. He ignored them and aimed a burst that walked across the front of the CTAC charge. Three fell as he brought the pulsar around.

The world around him exploded. Shrapnel and shots filling the universe, something slammed into him. Then all became quiet. He was bleeding, he could feel a flow of blood across his right eye, the tear-alarm of his suit squealing at him but there was no movement to his front. A muffled shout behind him, reaction swung him around, his finger tightened on the trigger … and stopped. There was no visible target.

Screams and firing rose to his side. He twisted feeling suddenly weak, dropped a weapon that was suddenly too heavy to hold and then darkness came. ¶

Martian Airs

A solitude, few have ever experienced surrounded Wraith Flight Leader Alvin Krozel as he passed beneath a distant black-velvet canopy, pierced by billions of colored pinpoints of light. This was true isolation, with no sense of movement. The lights didn't twinkle or sparkle, that would have required an atmosphere. They were constant, pure, never visibly changing but he knew they moved, so slowly as to appear to not change at all.

A luminous band of haze lay ahead, forming a broad stream of brightness that surrounded him, with points individually so tiny and numerous they appeared as a thickening layer of glowing mist that widened to a great central bulge. It was as though he floated at the center of the band of a cosmic diamond-studded ring.

With enhanced vision, the misty bulge resolved into trillions more brightly shining pinpoints, each its own unique color, burning fiercely upon a fainter background of yet more distant flares. Focusing within this bulge, his eyes gazed upon the grandeur of the center of the galaxy, a clear, airless abyss yet filled with more stars than particles of sand on all the beaches of Earth.

In the near distance, to the left of his flight-line, floated an irregular, highly pocked rock that was shaped much like a Neolithic chipped axe head. From this angle it appeared sharply shaded into a bright crescent. The rock's name was Phobos and it orbited a much larger, red object named Mars, a little further off and a bit to starboard but still distant enough for his fist, at arm's length, to cover the sphere.

Though enmeshed within a skeleton of molecular-programmed materials massing several tons, the Wraith pilot's gaze could move in any direction and still experience an unobstructed view of the universe: for the visual reality of the Wraith was, as he now willed it, invisible to his visual and tactile senses.

A soft chime sounded bringing faint regret as he dulled the starry vista using a thought-command that replaced the display with an array of screens and controls. Their images materialized directly into his occipital lobe, appearing tucked off to the side of his direct vision and displayed in a manner set by his preferences and unspoken desires. The continued existence of his dimmed vision of the starry expanse was also by his choice, their presence made him feel a little closer to the stars; made his own existence seem a bit more real.

Kronski could see, feel, and touch every control in his fighter if he wished. They were as real as the mug of coffee that he'd had last night, but as substantial as a dream since the Wraith injected their reality directly into his brain.

A desire to open communications linked him directly to his flight team.

"Starburst, deploy an orbital net-in-depth drone swarm, then hold them on station-alert." His communication went out over a sideband encrypted, sliding frequency wave-packet to the squadron, "I want to know about anything and everything that moves. When Hometeam moves out of the meteor's shadow there's bound to be a CTAC reaction. Let me know if it's anything more than a verbal greeting."

"Alpha-ray, you and I are ground assault. All wraps are off when CTAC spots Hometeam, we are weapons free at that point. Remember, allow nothing to exit the CTAC base."

"Mind the ranger IFF designators. Strike authorization danger-near is granted but I'll have your slowly-skinned hide as a rug on my cabin floor if I find you responsible for friendly fire casualties."

Kronski took his flight out of formation, breaking off in a long, easy slide down a gravitic wavefront that minimized even the subtle photon emissions of its passage, which by far was the easiest way for an enemy to detect the presence of a Wraith. They passed through the gravitic wave-chop region forward of Mars' orbital path, where the planet's gravitonic emissions collide with the ether-current of the Sun and galactic core. The ride smoothed as they descended until the flight was little more than a swift transit across the swells and steep wavefronts of the planet's gravity well.

Riding well below the crest of a fast-moving gravitic wave crest, Kronski circled for a fly-by of a nearby NAU base. Recorders on, he documented the strength and disposition of their assets for future reference. Aside from some ground troops exercising outside the broad geodesic dome, there was nothing to indicate they were aware of the growing problems of their CTAC neighbors.

Drawing near the objective they were still a quarter of the planet away and moving at 'ground-crawl' speed of only several times that of sound when Hometeam, **Alfred's** war room moniker, patched Kronski into a conversation from **Revenge** already in progress with CTAC flight control, "... welcome home, **Xuchang**.

"You are cleared for landing on corridor Jensua Two."

Hometeam's AI automatically recognized the CTAC hail using the original name of their captured CTAC vessel, now renamed '**Revenge**', and translated the conversation. It decided the approach wasn't acceptable, "Request alternative flight path, we bring 'guests'."

NanoBot interrogation of the prisoners discovered the CTAC site was not to be directly mentioned. The incarceration of large numbers of NAU prisoners was forbidden by the treaty's defined rules of conflict. They had to wait a few moments before the reply came, "Maintain orbit, *Xuchang.* Display a yellow token flag and await local controller instructions."

Kronski smiled to himself, *So far, so good. They just told **Revenge** to hold formation. That means they know there's trouble at the prison but are hoping the local guard can handle it.*

Wraith pilot Alpha-Ray's call came through five minutes out from their target, "Bandit, bandit, bandit. Unidentified flight trace suborbital, intersection vector two-seven-two-point-niner-two."

Kronski's call immediately went out to his VSF-1 squadron Wraiths, "Blueblood and Nighthawk, intercept, warn them off. Crash bandits if they do not comply."

"Rodger, confirm contact 'crash directive'."

The flight leader's tactical display marked the departure of the two Wraiths as they shot out of formation, accelerating in-atmosphere to near a thousandth of lightspeed. Phosphorescent fireflies briefly lit the trail created by the sudden acceleration of the departing fighters, marking their passage through the planet's thin upper atmosphere at nearly nine thousand times the speed of sound. Kronski immediately regretted sending them off , for with their unavoidable maneuver, the enemy now knew someone unexpected was crossing into CTAC airspace.

~~*~*~*~*

He could hear voices, distant voices. Important voices he felt he should be listening to, but he was so tired, so … Not voices, screams.

Mason snapped into pain-laced awareness. His mind numb, ears ringing so hard they throbbed. Someone was screaming at him. He jumped, agony flooding every joint and pore of his body as something grabbed his shoulder, pushed him back and held him there until he relaxed. A pressure against his arm and a moment of relief flooded over him before the world went into blessed blackness again.

~~*~*~*~*

Heavy words softly spoken pierced *Alfred's* Combat Information Center (CIC), "Captain on deck." There was no outward reaction from those in the room, but every spacer and ranger could feel the change as he entered.

This was as it should be and Jankin Decatur brooked no notice. They now engaged in war and, when in the CIC, one focused on business not protocol.

Encapsulated in this darkened chamber was a universe of conflict orchestrated by the gods of war. It was here, Decatur directed four theatres of operation, including a space flotilla, an air tactical umbrella, their subterranean penetration, and its supporting above-ground defenses.

Ensign Molly Trumble didn't bother to look up much less wait for the captain's command as he approached her control sphere. All four theatres, gathered from across half the Martian globe, existed as faint virtual spheres of operations surrounding her. A sphere solidified, clarified into reality as her attention focused on it or the onboard AI highlighted actions requiring her notice. The sphere she highlighted upon the captain's approach was one of sharp chasms of red rock with two CTAC fighters weaving low, fast, and deadly between the peaks, "The bogies CTAC launched will be on target before our colonial Wraiths arrive. The good news is they sent only two."

That sphere diminished as her attention shifted to another view that moved to envelop her station. It solidified into a bird's eye display of a red-colored plane with a lone starship resting on the stabilized landing field.

"Control of the starport remains in question. There's no front, forces are mixed, and the conflict fluid. Major Walters is ready for the flyover. His people are under broadband visual and deep infrared wavelength sensor camouflage. The CTAC troops also carry individual IFF transceivers, we can expect the incoming CTAC flight to work close support."

Decatur stepped into the ethereal construct and his world transformed. He gazed across the field from a point suspended high above, "There isn't much any CTAC air asset can do unless they swing into a live-fire pass, which is sure to take out their own troops as well."

"Unfortunately, we're in the same boat. We can't bring airpower into the equation for fear of hitting our own and we can't start prisoner evacuation until CTAC ground forces are neutralized."

"CTAC command now knows something serious is happening. But most likely they still suspect a prisoner uprising. They'll fly over and call for additional ground support."

"Withdraw Kronski's crash authorization but have him maintain a stealth monitor of the CTAC fighters. Authorize Walter's rangers to engage the flyover using surface-to-air. We need that captured CTAC ship. Protect it. We need to keep them thinking it's nothing more than a prisoner uprising."

"Watch for any reaction. Most likely their next move will be either another land approach with armor support or an airdrop. We can't afford to be blindsided."

A 'Captain Only' (CO) missive interrupted continued discussion. It was a message from the **Revenge**, sent with crypto-encoding using signals reflected from random bursts of gamma rays, "CTAC starship approaching. Boarding attempt anticipated.

"Your orders?"

Captain Jankin Decatur closed his eyes. The entire situation had just managed to spiral down even further.

They were about to be uncovered.

~~*~*~*~*

Acting Captain Harriett Hopewell suppressed a groan as she rose, wiring harness in hand, from beneath her operations console. Pain shot across her back as she stretched, using the effort to run her eyes across the others in the room. Nothing in **Revenge's** CIC worked properly and there were times when even as the captain she had to dirty her hands.

Mired in a swamp of frustration, apparently few things in this ship worked properly. Nothing here could meet the clean, efficient functionality of a typical colonial freighter, much less a ship-of-war. Information flow and the logic encoding of these systems seemed absolutely alien, overly complex. She couldn't believe how much effort the former owners expended to compartmentalize each crewmember so each one knew only as much as absolutely needed.

The CIC of her captured CTAC vessel lacked even the open visualization of combat space she'd grown to expect in **Alfred**. They had no concept displays beyond a few primitive three-dimensional plots using abstract tokens for enemy assets.

CTAC spacers at their stations were incapable of adding their interpretation of data gathered for analysis; the entire ship might as well have been automated with slow electron-valve computers or with the primitive integrated circuits of centuries past.

Ensign Connelly, still down on his knees, had no compunctions to letting out a groan. It was a freedom the captain envied the technician, along with his liberty to openly grouse, "How in Finagle's pox-laced universe do these ships stand against a modern NAU combat vessel. This backup system's as inoperable as the primary, God forbid they follow any concept of redundant self-repairing systems. Half the spares don't work. Intelligence personnel can't share information, can't even communicate with each other unless we render the isolation barriers of their workstation inoperable."

"Via, the curst system is design-locked so all information flows in only one direction, up to the captain's station."

Hopewell smiled at Connelly while covertly rubbing her back, "Make do, ensign. Keep at it and try not to get frustrated."

Long, frantic hours of modifications had resulted in something passable for a room designed to wage war. Their CIC still lacked the sophistication and power of *Alfred,* but it would do. It would have to even if it made her feel like some storied captain of an ancient steel man-of-war on the seas of Earth, using cryptic sensor display symbols for combatant identification and lacking the powerful visualization scenarios and simulations of a modern battlespace.

"We're being hailed, ma'am. Apparently, it's 'audio only'. Shall I patch it through our AI translator."

The captain shivered in disgust, "Finagle save us, it's like going back to the industrial revolution.

"All right ensign, patch it through, audio-only."

They'd managed to jury-rig a colonial AI translation module to the communications shunt and it, thankfully, interfaced beautifully. Still, Captain Hopewell felt a tinge of dread as the call began.

"Captain Hect, welcome home. Unfortunately, there is a minor problem at the starport that will delay your landing. I'm sure you understand the sensitivity of cargo shipments to this destination. Please do not be offended but I have been directed to perform a check of your manifest."

"Hold orbit to receive a customs shuttle."

Not knowing Captain Hopewell now commandeered the vessel, the customs agent expected to speak with the registered captain of the CTAC ship,

Hoping the AI would properly phrase her request as well as mimic the CTAC captain's male voice and oriental phrasing, "I understand and will comply. Space on our guest-ship is at a premium, may I ask how long you anticipate before we receive clearance to land?"

Their reply was slow in coming and Harriett's anxiety grew with each passing second until a call arrived directly from their main base, "We have no information to share regarding wait time. Inspectors are en route; you are commanded to hold station until further notice. CTAC Central out."

"Captain Hopewell," Decatur's words, erupted from the speaker startling her. The whole antiquated communications method felt so unnatural and Jankin's words came through harshly, "We aren't about to wait for them."

"Prepare to break orbit in eight minutes. Control of the field below is fluid. Anticipate landing under fire. Prepare for immediate loading of prisoners and casualties as soon as we dump static charge."

Captain Hopewell's reply was immediate, "Aye aye, Sir."

Calling over to her XO on the bridge, "You heard the command."

"Break orbit in seven minutes, thirty-two seconds. When we touch dirtside it will be a contested LZ so keep us in on a vector adjacent to *Alfred*. Keep a low profile and ignore any further hails."

"We are 'weapons-free' status at the point of departure."

Acting Captain Hopewell's attention returned to the orchestrated chaos of her CIC, *Barring any of Finagle's tricks, we should be able to present a suitable response. Some first command this is. This flying bucket is held together with spit and luck. Next thing I'll open a circuits locker and find it lined with strips of ancient duct tape.*

"One-minute mark," announced the newly installed ship's AI.

Harriette Hopewell was too deep in concentration to hear the actual departure call, but her subconscious sensed the change in HiveTab activity as the ship's field altered its tack-link to a new gravitic wave pattern. Her communicator highlighted their flight and current position relative to Decatur's vessel, then flagged an incoming hail from the customs vessel. She ignored it, as well as their second demand for obeyance of their order. A quiet smile formed on her face that came from knowing her XO was on his toes, anything to gain a few precious moments and increase the CTAC confusion.

Thin Martian atmosphere engulfed the ship as they approached the planet's night terminator. Receptors embedded in the captain's HiveTab displayed the glow from the distant Sun now perched below a far horizon. Twenty more minutes until touchdown alongside their sister ship.

An alarm sounded inside the CIC. The weapon system's bosun shunted a visual to the chamber wall, "We have incoming. Two CTAC launches using reaction rockets.

"Targeting just came on, they locked onto our path. Punch-rocket signature, Captain. Estimated time to impact, one minute twenty-seven seconds."

Hopewell stared at the rocket's projected course plot as her HiveTab brought up a slipsheet of the weapon's capabilities, "All right, they must be desperate if they are sending conventional rockets up against a starship."

"No, ma'am." The ensign's voice replied both auditory and across her Hive-Channel, "The rockets have a modified delivery signature. It's a Hive-Mine nose cone adaptation."

Revenge's speed, though great, was limited by their proximity to touchdown. There was no hope of outrunning the missiles which had a much shorter distance to travel. The rockets would intercept the ship's course with enough time to deploy the aerial mines into a broad cloud of tiny but deadly particles, each smaller than can be seen with the unaided eye but capable of triggering the entire swarm into a fatal attack.

Captain Hopewell had a choice, deviate course or push through the mines on a wing and a prayer.

She stared at the image of the oncoming missiles. The rockets resembled two huge poles. Ancient telephone poles, like the ones she'd seen at the First Settlement shrine on Kraken, coming up to meet her ship.

"Ensign, arm the Ionic Phalanx."

The reply came instantly, "Aye aye, ma'am."

Ion-Phalanx stations were distributed over the ship's bulbous shape like quills on a porcupine, each site was flush with the skin's surface during normal operation. But when activated, they extended outward just enough to remain within the ship's gravitic spindizzy field. The newly installed Phalanx was a last-minute and untested addition. Hopewell prayed its limited scope would be enough. Even though Phalanx operation from this point onward was automatic, Hopewell wanted to hold her breath for some silly reason in defiance of logic that said the system would simply work or it would not. In either case, it did no good to worry. She and her ship would either exist or not in just a few short minutes.

Captain Hopewell sensed the disturbance in their drive field as the Phalanx deployed. She ignored it, attempting to focus her thoughts on the complex problem of a Martian surface touchdown adjacent to, and in synchronism with *Alfred.*

"Wombat fighter launch." The warning seemed to hang in the air of the CIC like a rotten smell.

CTAC Wombats, dreaded suborbital fighters capable of delivering a wide spectrum of munitions over great distances, could challenge even a frigate in low orbit.

"Plot solution completed. Wombats are on course for the prison starport, ETA twenty minutes, and ..."

A ripple passed across the surrounding bulkheads before transforming into an audible ripping sound as the Phalanx exploded into action sending packets of charged, heavy-particle ions at individual targets smaller than the human eye can resolve, ripping the gravitic ether surrounding them until it transformed into erratic physical pulses penetrating the soles of their deck shoes. All eyes turned to their captain.

Hopewell was as surprised as they, "It's the Phalanx. We're under attack but this is new to me too. I never expected anything like it, although scientists predicted a massive release might be felt. They warned it can't go on indefinitely since the Phalanx rods are quickly depleting. At this rate their sub-microscopic, charged ion-particles are leaving each rod in such numbers that the cores are losing noticeable mass and the reaction to their mass ejection is shaking the ship, like the recoil of an ancient warbird's rifled guns."

The ions of the Phalanx were relatively dumb particles barely capable of tracking a charged Hive Molecule. Directed bursts, streams of charged ions fled out before the *Revenge*, traveling more than three thousand miles through the thin upper atmosphere to intercept small but deadly individual Hive Molecules.

As the particles shot through the upper atmosphere, they gradually bled charge from near contact with carbon-monoxide molecules and cosmic alpha particles leaving illuminated trails of rapidly fading photons. Many of the charged ions missed their target but even a near miss could be enough to discharge the Hive Mine molecule or implant a small string of code, or a virus that could disrupt the mine's simple operational program.

A clear tunnel opened through the mine-saturated sky ahead. Sensors showed the surrounding air glowing an angry red and green as the tiny mines shattered releasing angry-red bursts of energy as photons.

A section of the CIC's bulkhead, roughly the diameter of a human head, flashed brightly. Screams pierced the air and its bright flare flashed momentarily blinding Hopewell while knocking her flat to the deck. She used a console to pull herself up off the deck.

Revenge lurched again, "Gravitic field breach, Captain. Defensive spindizzy particle clusters inside the field were able to reassemble and reinforce the weakened defense shield. In addition to the hull breach, we have weakened structures in sections H3 to H4."

She took the luxury of a deep breath in the fume-filled chamber before calling out, "Chief, medics to CIC. Remove those bodies. Ensign report, damage … watch out where you're stepping, ranger, I don't want gore tracked all over my deck. Break out a silica-gel pack. Soak that mess up so no one slips."

"Ensign, damage report."

"Nothing ship-critical. Spacer Haward and Technician Hsu are dead, casualty reports from elsewhere still generating."

"Breach repair is active."

CIC external sensors came back to life displaying a flash off in the distance ahead generated by a silent shockwave, strong enough to be visible on their screens as a front of highly compressed air centered on the blast site. They passed through it; all ill effects blocked by their drive's field isolation.

"Wraith fighters took out the missile launch site."

Captain Hopewell relaxed just a bit, "Very good, let's focus on our mission, Ensign."

Ensign Collier updated their position, "Touchdown in three point two-five minutes, fifteen seconds behind original ETA."

Hopewell sighed then said aloud, "Error is acceptable."

"Lieutenant Yamoto, you will take point and establish a perimeter so our spacers can begin loading."

"Ranger's Ready, and itchen to be bitchen, Captain."

A bosun's voice echoed across the com, "All jump portals, prepare for latch release in three, … two, … "

Revenge passed from atmospheric cruise speed to a dead stop in the blink of an eye. Its shockwave exploded out across the starport as the ship materialized, instantly displacing three million square meters of Martian atmosphere as it came to rest on the stabilized red soil of the starport. A slow heartbeat of inactivity passed as waves of lightning danced over the ship's surface, discharging all the static energy created from an entry at nearly four times the speed of sound.

Cargo doors snapped open so fast they seemed to launch the rangers out across the Martian plane. They were greeted by weapon's fire from two enemy armored personnel carriers. Their solid, antipersonnel rounds impacting the ship's hull, screaming as they deflected off into the thin atmosphere. Two shells managed to penetrate an open portal directly into the ship, crashing through four bulkheads setting off a blast that rocked the ship and deflected through two upper decks, killing forty-two spacers.

Walker's rangers responded from their dirtside hides where they had taken shelter during the ship's landing. The major didn't waste more than a glance at the black smoke coming from the **Revenge,** for his attention lay focused on the ship his people had captured, where two pockets of CTAC spacers still held out in a cargo hold.

He turned to the distant prison tunnel entrance, anxious to see the caravan of prisoners emerge.

His prayers were answered when the tunnel's blast doors opened and a convoy of tracked vehicles emerged. Battlesuit clad rangers rode on the vehicle tops or clung onto their sides, the inside of each vehicle packed with the released prisoners. Time was short.

Returning his attention to the holdouts, "Chief Geer, give those CTAC holdouts our last offer. They don't have time to think it over, our passengers are on the way and I won't breach any distractions when we take off."

"Ranger Ready, Sir." Came the reply.

Enemy spacers had sealed every entrance and com input to the defiant compartment on the CTAC ship in a desperate last stand. Chief Geer placed a gloved palm on the bulkhead and, with a thought, activated his AI translator, the sound waves from his palm speaker were conducted through the bulkhead by sheer vibration, "Last chance. Thirty seconds and then you are out of time. Open your doors, you will not be hurt. Save us the trouble of having to scrape out the mush that will remain if you don't."

He stepped to the side and motioned a tech forward who removed from his utility pack a glob of putty-like material the size of a handball which he slapped onto the bulkhead.

As the tech spread a clear cream over the flattened glob, Greer again placed his palm on the bulkhead, "Last communication, fifteen …"

The doors slammed open but no one emerged. A ranger edged around the corner, spotted one of the spacers with a weapon and hit him dead center, the ship's round he used shredded the spacer and two others behind him.

Survivors dropped to the floor as though they'd been cold-cocked. Their inaction gave two rangers a chance to step into the doorframe, "Empty hands on yer heads and keep 'em there. Now, stand up. Nice and slow."

Greer shouted to two other rangers, "Bring flexwraps, bind 'em as they come forward. There are carriers waiting in bay two, pack 'em in. It'll be crowded but they will stay airtight long enough for their buddies to pick 'em up. Move it, pack 'em in."

A distracting communication interrupted, "Wait one .... Yes, Sir."

"Captain sez hold anyone claiming to be an NAU or colonial spacer but keep them bound and outta our hair."

"Don't fool around, CTAC just launched another ground assault. Shoot anyone who resists."

LIFT OFF

Major Walters was frustrated, the captured CTAC ship didn't have forcefield environmental encapsulation and that was a problem when loading refugees quickly and efficiently. It took too damn long to go through the pumping cycles.

In typical ranger fashion, he took the simplest approach and popped open the hatches. Earth-normal air bust out into the cold Martian, carbon dioxide laden atmosphere. The blast of relatively high-pressure air was brutal, violent but thankfully short, throwing crystalline shards of ice across the landing field from the moisture-saturated, high pressured expulsion.

"Corporal, we will be enacting an emergency liftoff. When I give the word, button up the doors but open the blowout valves during liftoff, you'll have to bleed in oxygen from the emergency reaction tanks to displace the carbon dioxide in there as we lift. Think you can balance the intake and bleed-off?"

The corporal looked a bit unsure but her words were steady, "Never tried it before but it'll get done. How hard could it be, Sir?"

A call came over his unit push, "Inbound, hostile floaters with aerial support."

Walters brought up a tactical plot, sharing it with the sergeant, "There they are. Looks like light cavalry floaters, Sergeant. Strengthen the perimeter facing their approach but keep an eyeball on our six; they may have slipped off a roundabout penetration squad."

"Rangers Ready, Sir." Was the immediate reply.

One more thing to check, the tunnels, "Lieutenant Strake, how are your people doing?"

Strake's reply was concise and crystal-clear as it cut through the surrounding chaos deep in the tunnels, "The first of the caravan should be unloading any minute. I've ordered them to discard the mobiles and board on foot. No need returning the mobiles to us."

A sharp crack split the air, so loud Walters could hear it inside the CTAC vessel. **Revenge** had just landed.

"Good timing, Lieutenant. We now have both ships down but they'll be hot as your people load. Warn them but keep pushing."

"Rangers Ready, Sir."

Walters crossed over to the open hatch. **Alfred** was already open with its loading ramps extended and ready. Tornado-like clouds of dust swirled out from the ship, backlit like patches of bright fog on the ocean. The Martian soil lifted into the thin atmosphere by the sudden, violent arrival of **Alfred**, which was laced in a constrained lightshow of bright red-white flashes; discharges of static energy with the warbird's unmistakable shape at its center.

"Sergeant, a second wave is incoming and this time it's their cavalry. Time to evict these CTAC spacers. Anyone with an environmental suit on, out and onto the airstrip. Tell them to head for the tunnels. If they hurry, they might make it before their buddies begin firing on them. Have two men watch them leave, shoot any that stray from the path"

"Chief Greer, forget the cleanup. We're due a full load of new passengers from the tunnels. Don't bother unlocking their vans as they enter, it can wait. Pack 'em in as they come, we'll sort everything out after liftoff."

"Aye aye, Sir. What about the NAU or colonial officers? There aren't many but they all have ideas of their own."

"They are talking cargo. Ignore any commands. That's a direct order from the captain if anyone asks. If they continue, you have my permission to constrain them by any means you deem necessary."

"I'm heading out to greet our new arrivals."

Major Walters flashed a nod and a knowing smile at the chief before sealing his helmet and entering the airlock. The small airlock leading into the cargo bay was much too slow and too small to satisfy his urge to pace back and forth while its sublimation pumps transferred its air into a solid stored in a pressurized container. Frustration grew as he waited.

The CTAC warbird's bay was near empty and open to Martian air. His footfalls pounded hard and tinny on the super-cold metal flooring of a chamber filled with the thin atmosphere. They'd thrown out any noncritical cargo, which meant almost everything.

Outside in the distance, transports moved rapidly across the blast-pocked starfield with rangers clinging to their sides or roofs. The first of them was just arriving as the major disembarked, watching with admiration and pride as the rangers leaped from their slowing vehicles rather than waiting for them to come to a stop and climbing down the ramps. It was a difficult feat under low gravity, but gracefully accomplished.

Frantic screams sounded off, first over his command push then immediately followed by more shrill, shouted commands from outside when an arriving transport's cargo door exploded open, releasing a puff of white vapor that instantly crystallized into the mushroom cloud of cold air and rapidly transformed to slivers of sparkling ice before sublimating into gas. Walters ran over to the vehicle, there must have been near forty people inside. Packed together standing, now frozen in position; their faces white, marred by streaks of red running across them from their skin capillaries rupturing as they froze. They'd died soundlessly with terror frozen on their faces. Throats and lungs instantly solidified by an air-mix more than a hundred degrees below zero in an atmosphere that would have suffocated them anyways.

"Who the hell is responsible for this vehicle?"

A black-clad private slipped out of the driver's seat, "I am, Sir."

"Why didn't you warn them of the consequences of opening that door? You lost control, Private."

"Sir! They made it all the way but refused to wait. Perhaps one of them panicked. I could hear them inside shouting then screaming. There must have been a tussle, they rocked the entire transport and ignored my orders. One of them must have gotten to the door and … well, you see what happened."

The transport was a sealed containment, but one not built for carrying humans. Walters shook his head, they would have made it if they could have kept their heads for a few minutes, "One joker and they all paid the price."

"Leave 'em where they sit. Come and help direct the others. Quickly, we have floaters incoming and they are going to catch us before we finish."

As if on cue, cannon fire erupted followed by a low, resonating rumble. The major didn't have to look up to know the ordinance wasn't from a floater.

Walter's suit pinpointed the aircraft, that was but a speck to the human eye as it traveled silently.

The ground around one of the transports aside the foot of the ship's ramp suddenly blossomed into a thousand lethal fountains of debris ripping out across the field, mixed with deadly shards of shattered landing strip. Military ordinance impacted the area so rapidly it sounded like ripping cloth in the thin atmosphere. A transport transformed into a tattered, ripped hunks of metal, along with flash-frozen flesh.

Then came the long 'brrrrp' of the rifled cannon fired from a distant Wombat fighter. They had no place to go, no place to shelter from the distant fighter except for inside the starships.

Walters activated the local push, signaling to the nearest driver, "Don't stop. Ram that hulk out of the way. Clear that loading ramp and get your people inside."

A second angry burst erupted across the field mixed with a high-pitched squealing. Men were shouting, feeling trapped in the open as they desperately ran to the ramp. The major didn't have to look, he knew the pilot targeted one of the starships; the sound was the hardened metal of the rounds ricocheting off into the sky. The ripping sound of the fighter's gun firing was punctuated by an enormous explosion. He looked up and smiled, an expanding ball of black smoke with flares moving out in all directions filled the point where the fighter had been like a blossoming display in a Founder's Day sky. Then the delayed but expected roar arrived, one of their Wraiths had arrived on target.

"Stop yer gawking. There's more behind 'em, move out now." Screamed a sergeant as a line of troop-laden CTAC floaters came up on his suit's tactical display. A whirring sound cut the air around the field followed by the call, "Picket droids!"

Small, autonomous flight war-drones peppered the overhead in stealth, unseen by even the ranger suit's tactical sensors. They came in swiftly, targeting the transports.

Ranger's responded, launching small hunter-killers. Small semi-intelligent airfoils fired from their rifles, propelled by packets of solidified gas that, when launched, rocketed them forward. The drive could last up to thirty seconds, enough for an H-K to lock onto its target using only the object's bow wave, make course corrections and drive into it.

Transport loading went on amid bursts of gas and smoke. The chaos of conflict rapidly spread across the landing strip, punctuated by a near-constant rain of ice particles, deadly shrapnel, and flakes of depleted propellant that had solidified in the cold air.

Captain Decatur's call came as his ship's ramps retracted, "Last one loaded, button up."

"Rangers, hold and provide cover until all ships are filled."

Captain Jankin Decatur shook his head as he closed the general push and signaled lift-off.

Alfred released swarms of Seigfried Platforms as she lifted. Disposable independent weapons pods, they dispersed in a cloud, floating above the landing field to establish a defense-in-depth volume shielding the ship from above. Their sensors reported nearly a thousand CTAC cavalry approaching on another wave of floaters. Floaters, large airfoils capable of carrying five or six troopers over the roughest terrain as they elevated on cushions of air and were aided by the planet's low gravity. Floaters could easily switch to small jets when passing over deep ravines or if additional height was needed. Six of *Alfred's* Seigfried emplacements managed to lock-on targets. They fired, striking and downing nearly ninety percent of the incoming floaters in just one ion cannon strike.

Decatur commented, "Apparently, CTAC command still was not aware of the presence of an interstellar warcraft in the conflict."

"Unfortunately, they now know it's more than a simple escape with a starship now present."

"Q-code targeting is active." Echoed across *Alfred's* CIC. Decatur's response was immediate, "Monitor but do not respond. We're playing for time, remain in stealth mode."

Decatur knew they expected his ship to position itself above the cloud of Seigfried Platforms. He hoped that, by not responding to their targeting beam, they would hold their fire.

Alfred jolted as fingers of fire scraped the surrounding sky as the ship lurched hard to the side. *Alfred's* AI voice filled the CIC, "Drive field performance down seventeen point three-two percent, circumference batteries sections 'F' and 'G' are fused. Self-repair initiation ongoing."

Sensors shorted to zero, screens flashed white. A tech's voice rose above the din, "Coherent Ion Cannon. We are targeting incoming ion packets."

Another blast sent a short-lived but violent vibration through the ship. *Alfred's* AI replied to some unheard query, "Phalanx Defense response activated."

Ion Cannon fire, heavy metal ions, charged and linked together as coherent waves like a photon laser pulse, came at them at near the speed of light. Photons bled off along its path as the beam shredded the molecules of the thin Martian atmosphere, sending out cyan-colored pulses of visible radiation as a byproduct. The danger was in the relativistically enhanced mass of the near light-speed ion packet, a super-dense slug of heavy-metal ions compressed to unnatural density by the reinforced coherence of the beam. These were starship penetrators, modern versions of the ancient anti-tank sabot rounds.

The pulse bled off energy as it dug into the ship's Slipdrive field, penetrating the spindizzy region with enough force to punch through the stabilized titanium alloy skin.

"Finally, they know they're fighting a starship." Captain Decatur shouted, "Things are going to escalate fast. Launch status of our ground assets."

"*Revenge* has lifted and is hovering in place, providing cover for *Aries.*"

"*Aries* suffered portal damage to two bays. They report direct hits on several transports which were completely slagged as they were loading. They're attempting to cut away the …"

Decatur's command went straight to Lieutenant Scott Nauman, *Alfred's* pilot who had volunteered to fly the newly captured *Aries*, "Scottie, belay the portal cutoff. You don't have the time. Blow the door linkage and load your rangers. They can survive lift without closure, they're rangers."

"Aye aye, Sir." Replied the pilot.

Decatur engaged his CIC crew, "Recall our Wraiths, we need an umbrella. Layout a course to Phobos shadow-side but veer to remain in the ecliptic; the moon will provide initial cover for a rapid transit to the asteroid belt where we'll shift course again and warp to the heart of the Trojan cluster. Wraith recovery will commence near Jupiter's orbit. I'll update orders at that point."

A second flash preceded another defensive burst from their Phalanx system.

"Lieutenant redirect our Wraith's to target that ion cannon emplacement. Let's give our hosts something to worry about for a change."

Captain Hopewell called in across her private command push, "Decatur, the CTAC firebase is out of our designated theater of operation."

"I realize that, Harriett. Consider, we've already captured two CTAC vessels and are attempting to rescue a thousand or so prisoners that were not in our direct mission description. Kraken command can only hang me once but if that cannon scores another strike on Scotty's ship, they won't survive with only a weakened drive field protecting two open bays."

"Sabotage, Captain Decatur." Lt. Scott Nauman, interrupted, "A flight-check of our slipdrive set off a small charge in our drive capsule that ignited as it phased into high flux. We did examine that system preflight and found nothing, but it was an unknown drive so I insisted on a high-stress test before lifting. Good thing too or we wouldn't be talking right now."

"We aren't lift-capable and to sweeten things, more CTAC floaters are on their way. We're a lost cause."

"We'll draw as much attention from you as we can. I suggest you take advantage of it and get out with what you have."

Captain Decatur took a deep breath and stepped back, his mind racing.

*If I leave now, I can at least get **Alfred**, **Revenge**, and all the prisoners we've rescued back to Kraken. Scotty, Walters, and their people dirtside, in addition to their prisoner contingent, will be lost. They'll all become prisoners ....*

No, no they won't. That charge was set to blow when the ship began pushing upwave. They are all condemned. They'll die if I leave them behind.

Well, in for a penny, in for a pound.

"Scotty, have Major Walters establish a reinforced perimeter and hold."

"Make sure your entire drive capsule is offline and cut the slipdrive module from its stanchions. I don't care if you take it out in pieces and dump it in the sand but do it quickly. Keep all the interface conduits intact, we're doing a drive-swap. **Alfred** out."

"Captain Hopewell, lift and maintain **Revenge** in orbit on full alert."

"If things go badly down there, you are ordered to break orbit and return to Kraken."

Calling down to his CIC, "Ensign Trumbull, contact engineering. Have them perform a hot shutdown and dismount of drive two. I know I'm asking a lot but we can't afford to shut down both slipdrives so this must be a disassembly while still active."

"Dismantle the drive, modify it to fit the *Aries* configuration then transfer it to a floater and deliver it to their 'D' bay. Have Sergeant Orlop vacuum suit his teams for combat. We'll be setting down in a hot LZ, they are to set up a shield as we touch dirtside. Don't wait to offload, permission granted to charge weapons while still in the ship's bay."

As was his habit, Decatur took a moment to visually scan the stations on his bridge, knowing the task would fall harder on one young man's shoulders. The strain was evident to his trained eye, so he directly linked to the copilot's HiveTab.

"Toshie," The only sign that Ensign Toshie Foster received the link was a slight twitch of his shoulders. "Scotty's commanding *Aries*, so you just inherited the pilot's slot. I realize you've never grounded a starship much less put down in a hot LZ but then, few have."

"When we drop, I want you to hold the drive field until the last moment then drop her hard no matter who or what may be in the LZ. Come in fast; just make sure you collapse the field the instant before you ground. I'm not looking for elegance, drop us hard and fast."

Decatur switched to ship's push so all could hear the call, "We are going in weapons-free. Don't request authorization but choose your targets carefully. We have people on the ground and our air assets will be mixed with theirs."

"Mister Foster, begin our descent."

"Aye aye, Captain. Initiating landing sequence 'Hot Descent'."

Decatur sat back in his chair, letting his people do their jobs while keeping a prioritization app open for alerts on any of the theatres of action as he reviewed the CIC reports. There was a lot of activity at the CTAC base; they were assembling another wave of rapid response cavalry on floaters. The distant NAU base was also beginning to stir. Drone reconnaissance detected them readying a rapid deployment force, an obvious defensive response to all the CTAC activity.

The thought slammed into his mind with the impact of an ion cannon blast, *An opportunity?*

He sent a priority-one call-up to his Wraith Flight Leader, "Kronski, two CTAC floater contingents are inbound, vector your position two-seven-three degrees. En route, detach two assets on attack vector stealth zero degrees but do not directly engage. Have them circle 'round the NAU base and complete a low fly-over with full exposure. I want you to get their attention then immediately assume return vector two-six-niner relative and eliminate floater threat."

"Aye, Sir. Please confirm we are to conduct an obvious hot strike on NAU facilities."

With a mental jolt, Decatur's eyes widened slightly in surprise. Oddly enough he hadn't considered an attack on the NAU base. After all, Kraken was an NAU colony.

So, do I now order an aerial strike on our own motherland's fleet? It would guarantee a response. They already are guilty of hijacking Kraken shipping and they press our spacers into their service and have continued to ignore our appeals as though we were the enemy. This mission keeps escalating; perhaps it's time to ...

No, a half-hearted effort is one better not taken at all.

He entered his command into the formal record, Decatur wasn't about to let his pilots suffer for following his orders, "Confirm VSF1-1, hot-strike authorized. Repeat, hot-strike authorization on NAU base. One pass, minimal damage but let them see you leave. I want them buzzing mad."

"Aye aye, Sir. One pass. Kronski out."

Decatur muttered, perhaps a bit too loudly, "Cry havoc, and let slip the dogs of war."

"I'm sorry, Sir." His pilot returned, "Please repeat the command."

"As you were. Ignore the comment, Mr. Foster."

Meanwhile, Starburst Squadron Leader confirmed his new mission directive, "Aye aye, Sir, breaking off two assets. Initiate target loop around base NAU II for an open strike then rejoin assault on objective one floaters approaching *Aries* and **Revenge**."

"Nighthawk, Blueblood this is yours, hotshots. Initiate command sequence Foxhound."

Two Wraiths broke off from the squadron, circling north on a path that swung far around, beyond the coming wave of CTAC floater cavalry. Turning to a vector that would lead them directly over the NAU base they began their approach. Unlike the CTAC facilities, the NAU facility was older and had more above-ground facilities but there the similarities ended.

Nighthawk feathered his Wraith's gravitic force field, distorting it to trail behind him, and then called to his wingman, "See that Blueblood? The distorted field completely changes our visible outline if you detune the photon redirection phase. Looks kinda like a superfast CTAC cavalry floater."

"If you say so, I just see a big blur and ... whoa, did it. This makes the whole world look freaky and she flies like a fat boat. Switching to opaque viewport, instrument only navigation."

"Approaching first objective.

"There's pressurized storage containers set off from the rest of the field. Sweet, the Old Man said he wanted us to deposit a bit of chaos with minimal damage. Just enough to stir up the hornet's nest, so those containers are our target. Go in low; make sure everyone gets an eye-full as you give it a burst of old-fashioned armor-piercing depleted uranium penetrators. Veer off immediately to assume final CTAC attack vector but remain visible so they can track our approach and departure. We'll drop back into stealth as soon as we pass behind the mountain peaks."

Nighthawk fired a twelve-round cannon burst. Its abrupt violence vibrated the Wraith briefly until their fiery tracer stream touched something sensitive. At that point, the sky transformed into a piece of the solar heliosphere that swiftly passed aft their course.

Phasing his fighter back into stealth mode, Nighthawk softly commented over their private push, "Well, bet that got their attention. Objective phase one accomplished."

Back on *Alfred*, an app-priority message highlighted the surface-flash rising from a point below. A rare smile of surprise formed on Decatur's lips. It was more than he'd asked for, but he swore not to worry over possible consequences. The pilots had achieved their first objective. With little effort, he returned his gaze to the snooper screen he'd set to monitor *Alfred's* pilot station, assuring himself that the young ensign wasn't having problems. Good so far, anyway. The trickiest part would be in the last moments of their landing.

Meanwhile, Nighthawk and Blueblood vectored in on their primary objective, assuming a skirting approach that raised dust clouds in their wake. Their photon-enhanced sensor bank highlighted the fast response cavalry troops in the distance ahead riding broad, flat arrowhead-shaped vehicles with heavy iridium armor in the bow and below. A thin armor shield enclosed the top of the cargo bay and two powerguns extruded from the bow, each capable of forward aerial or ground targeting. Neutrino surround analysis confirmed they were light cavalry without any heavy support.

"Blueblood, I just received a target dispersion plot. They're spread out and slowed by the terrain despite their air-cushions. The count is thirty-three floaters, estimating a force maximum of a hundred fifty troopers."

"Let's make this short and sweet so we can return to the party. A bit of overkill won't hurt. Target them all."

"Roger Nighthawk, target all. Initiate."

Blueblood's targeting aid appeared. He took a moment to highlight all thirty floaters as targets and promptly forgot about them when a laser-like cyan shaft of light shot up at them from the target. Just missing his fighter, it passed close enough for its field to briefly short out several instrument sensors while slamming his entire craft to the side. The pilot's attention turned to focus on evasion and survival.

"Systems NAV32 and MOD43 reboot," announced in his ear but the pilot didn't need to be told what was happening. Pure reflex swerved his craft and immediately set it to jinking an erratic flight path. Another jolt, his Wraith jolted from a second beam passing so close he could see the energy release of the atmospheric molecules blasted apart by the hot passage of a coherent beam of deadly copper-cobalt ions fired from a floater-mounted powergun.

As the Wraiths jinked high above the enemy at Martian Mach 4, the speed of sound being only two-thirds that of Earth's warmer air, the warcraft's munition targeting system independently released a single spinning globe. The globe powered forward, then drifted losing little altitude at first when a single braking-jet fired to dump velocity and adjust its vector until its path carried it just forward of the CTAC cavalry floaters convoy. A fine cloud of tiny cylinders ejected from the spinning globe before it disintegrated into a fine ash that dispersed into the thin Martian atmosphere as silicon dust.

The cylinders, miniature osmium sabot charges, individually locked onto their designated target cluster, each taking great care to select a floater with the fewest number of designators from other sabots. The munitions then fired a burst of highly compressed liquid nitrogen that projected the sabot charge into a ballistic path straight to its target.

As the sabot impacted the floater, kinetic energy liquified a pinpoint channel into the floater's iridium armor and the tiny, dense osmium penetrator shot forward, cutting deeper into the interior, expanding as it went in while liquifying a pool of armor ahead of it that eventually exploded into the floater's interior and then solidified as hot shrapnel, losing enough energy to bounce around the interior like a tiny billiard ball, shredding all in its path.

A crackle of death ripped through the valley's thin air like a string of Chinese firecrackers erupting in an empty oil drum, as the entire convoy of floaters slammed into the Martian surface. No survivors walked from the wreckage that now lay scattered and embedded in the rocky surface. The wrecks exhibited no outward damage, but each floater's interior had been transformed into a charnel of mashed bile and human hamburger mixed along with plastics, iridium, and other metals.

"VH1-1, mission accomplished. Rendezvous Hometeam, twenty minutes."

"Rodger Nighthawk. Well done. Sensors confirm kill."

The hundred-thousand-ton starship *Alfred* descended into the Martian atmosphere, penetrating with the speed of a hypervelocity pulsar shot. Not a ripple, soundwave or trace of frictional heating marked its passage since the ship's slipdrive field gently pushed off individual air molecules in its path, swinging them around the vessel and swiftly redepositing them in its wake. Off in the distance, a huge sandstorm churned over a continent-sized area, sensors reported it traveling on a course that would intersect with the landing field. They'd have an operational window not quite wide enough to finish repairs on the *Aries* and complete the loading of the rescued prisoners.

Alfred dropped under programmed power to the surface faster than any pilot's reaction could respond, crashing down to a point less than the width of a finger from the highest projection of the rough packed surface directly beneath it. Smoothly, the ship's engine shut down and the starship abruptly dropped the last centimeter into contact with the red iron-oxide laden and stabilized surface of the landing field, sending off a thump that shook everything like a low-grade Mars-quake.

Captain Jankin Decatur's command voice shouted out on the general push, "Wait one, hold for my order before disembarking. **Revenge** has yet to touch down."

As he finished, a low, near-silent thump rocked **Alfred** and was immediately followed by Decatur's order of disembarkation. Doors flew open and ramps ejected to smooth their small step to the Martian surface. An anti-grav floater waited in the transfer hatch carrying the dismantled gravitic drive, with a weight greater than that of a two-person speeder, it slowly began crawling down the still extending ramp.

Chief Greer urged his people on, "Watch yer p's and q's. This here drive's delicate and I'm nervous as a newborn Kraken winged-snake with its butt exposed to the world."

"Simpson, did your mother drop you on yer head or don't you know how to listen? I saw you stumble, you good for nothing piece of karstyle shite. Pay attention to where ya plant yer big feet."

They managed to jockey the big drive midway across the open expanse between ships when a blast from **Alfred's** automated defense sent them reeling face-down in the red sand. The chief looked skyward in time to see four distant flashes that marked the vaporization of three incoming supersonic missiles. A wall of hot vapor, intensified by the following roar of the oncoming missile's wavefront, slammed into the crew knocking anyone still standing off their feet. They would have been flash-burned had it not been for the harsh surface of the planet which forced them to wear these vacuum-rated battlesuits.

Rangers, hardened by training, were the first to rise after Chief Greer, his head still throbbing from the blow, shouted, "To me, to me." Ignoring the threat of incoming munitions, they leaped over dazed spacers, and took up the dismantled slipdrive, guiding it across the field and up a ramp into the captured CTAC vessel surrounded by the low-passage roar of two Wraiths as they disappeared off into the distance in pursuit of the attacker.

A marine corporal was kicking and screaming at those still on the ground, "Get up you slovenly excuse for a human being or I swear you'll buy the farm right where you lay. Now's not the time curl up sucking your thumbs and feeling sorry for your lily-white arses." Dazed and shaky, spacers rose to follow, stopping only to help their mates while searching for those whose skills were needed to perform the engine swap.

Some paused to gawk at the incoming prisoner transport convoy. Half a dozen of the sturdy vehicles down the field had been blown over or scattered by the force of the thwarted attack. Transports with ruptured containment became sudden silent tombs, their occupants flash-frozen in the planet's poisonous atmosphere. Decatur had lost nearly two hundred souls in the moment of the blast.

Greer called out to his sections, "Begin rolling up the ramps soon as the last load enters. Follow inside and keep them quiet and contained. They have no idea what's going on and the *Aries'* bay is wide open to Mars's atmosphere."

Spacers in the bay ran to the transports as they came to rest. Placing their palms flat on the doors to project their voices inside the vans, "DO NOT open the doors. You are inside a ship but open to Mars atmosphere. Open the door and you will die."

Greer noticed two figures long-step jogging towards him in the low gravity. He recognized Lieutenant Strake's battlesuit but the spacer following him was in a CTAC vacuum suit with a white bandana fastened around the neck to signify surrender. Then he noticed an odd thing, the CTAC spacer carried a pressurized security briefcase.

Lieutenant Strake waved, calling over on their private push, "Chief, I'm bringing Captain Jensen, he's NAU military. He and his briefcase are important. No one is to obey orders from this man. NAU officer or not, he is a prisoner. Get him inside and keep him under guard until I return. *Aries* loading has a problem that I need to address."

"If I don't return in fifteen minutes, personally take this guy to Captain Decatur. Do not delegate this, do not let this man roam freely, and do not let him speak with anyone other than the captain."

Strake tapped the stranger on the shoulder and Greer could feel the sudden presence of the stranger as he joined their push, "Jeremiah, this is Chief Greer. I'll be back in a few minutes. If I'm delayed, he'll take you to Captain Decatur, our commanding officer. Start without me but show only Decatur what you have."

Greer gave his lieutenant a look questioning the level of informality extended to the new 'captain' but didn't venture a comment, simply returning, "Aye aye, Sir.

"Captain Jensen, this way please."

Strake paused to watch Greer lead the NAU officer up the ramp and disappear into the ship then set off at a jog to see what was causing the delay at their newest acquisition, the *Aries*.

He had jogged only a few paces when the blood-red soil ahead erupted. A long, dark, snake-like object as thick as his arm flew up out of the soil with a banshee-like scream that injected chills into his spine. The thing struck a nearby ranger in the small of her back, hitting with enough force to penetrate even through her hardened battlesuit. She must have been set to transmit for her scream saturated communications as she slammed to the ground. The stricken ranger convulsed as she tried to reach her back, squirming on the ground, screaming until the front of her suit blossomed outward, flowering into a spreading blast of blood, bone, and gore. The screams abruptly stopped when the monster's head emerged, its body launching out from her abdomen then twisted to target another nearby group of rangers. Strake's pulsar sidearm fired, its hypervelocity round solidifying as it left the barrel. The solid impact transferred the kinetic energy, blasting into the metallic brain-case of the tactical snake-drone.

Shrieks filled the landing field, giving name to the deadly drones suddenly appearing everywhere. Rangers dodged behind cover or dove flat to the ground. Shrieks were tactical droids. Millipede-like figures thick as an arm or leg and the length of a human, they burrowed at high speed through the ground using hundreds of flexible appendages to attack any warm figure or moving object using iridium alloy hardened grinding wheels.

The head of the drone fell to the ground but its body continued forward, driven by the independent circuitry of each body-segment until it also was blasted into slag. Lieutenant Strake called to the spacers, most of whom were unfamiliar with the weapon, "You have to sever it right at the neck or the head will continue the attack. The head's the deadly part. Don't worry about the bodies, most they'll do is trip ya or break yer leg if you're clumsy."

A chill ran down his back, out of pure reflex, he swung around in time to see a Shriek erupt from beneath the Martian soil just four paces away with its legs churning ground and air so fast they screamed as it sailed outward. Reflexively he brought his sidearm around, it discharged automatically sending a hypervelocity-slug down the gaping maw of the droid effectively rendering it inert...

Momentum threw the mangled body into him, lifting him off his feet and ripping the air from his lungs.

Stars flared for a moment, he shook his head and ran a quick suit check. Strake instinctively rolled only to be thrown sideways by a glancing blow came across his back. Continuing the roll, he brought his weapon around in time to see the last segment of the droid bury itself into the ground where he'd lain. Another was coming directly at him, he fired. His burst caught it square on, ripping it into pieces and sending the hair on the back of his neck on end, as a detached part of his mind envisioned the Shriek that had gone to ground erupting directly beneath him. But in actuality, another segmented body was coming straight for him, flexing across the ground like a snake before glancing off his shoulder to skitter across the field, already a headless, useless weapon.

The wail of the ship's recall sounding the harsh strains of 'Star Rangers' as it rang out through the thin air and with it, the lieutenant knew he'd never make it to *Aries*.

Strake rolled to his feet and took off at a run. He made it up the ramp passing through *Alfred's* already closing bay doors and managed a glance back towards *Aries.* It was already buttoned up, except for those bays now without doors.

Atmospheric readings appeared, flashing into a display registering at the side of his vision, the huge bay was nearly up to the proper pressure and gas mix, and temperatures would follow soon after the gases ceased expanding. His legs, back, and shoulder ached. It'd been a long, hard day since he climbed into that SCOS cartridge early last evening.

The lieutenant didn't wait for bay atmospherics to stabilize but used his authority to pass through a smaller pressure lock. A few of the younger spacers inside stepped back, staring as he quick-stepped to the glideway. Strake didn't approve of their stares, then a thought forced him to look down. His battlesuit was dented, scarred, covered with freeze-dried gore, mud-stains, and sand. The sight of it and the sudden inrush of relief that came with being relatively 'safe' inside the ship suddenly seemed funny as the reason for their stares dawned upon him.

Breathing in the recycled air of his suit, he didn't notice the terrible smell that followed his transit. His suit, now coated with a film of offal that had been fried, liquified, and then flash-frozen, now was open to the ship's air and warmer temperatures.

Strake needed to get to Captain Decatur. He needed to be there as his old friend Jensen told his story; needed to hear the full tale and confirm it for himself.

But he also knew Jensen was not a man to be trusted.

He turned a corner, found himself in ranger county and decided he had better spend a few moments and shed his battlesuit for a cleansing shower. Once inside the locker, he didn't bother with the dressing capsule but pressed the emergency release button. The seams split and the active armor became as limp as cloth and fell to the deck as he removed his helmet.

Yeah, smells bad but it's sure good to breathe ship's air again.

Flipping the suit inside out, he swiped it across the deck, trying to pick up some of the gore it had deposited. The deck was self-cleaning but boot camp habits die hard. A quick, two-armed fling into a cleaning port and he strode into the ionized sonic shower which was little more than a quick walk to the exit, where he could grab a clean utility cover before continuing.

There was a note in his HiveTab inbox from Chief Greer telling Strake he had left the NAU captain waiting in the bridge security ready-room guarded by two rangers. Decatur trotted up three levels taking the glideway lift to the center of the warbird, and to the bridge.

The rangers stood to greet him as he approached without saluting, "Thank you, rangers."

"I see someone was nice enough to get you coffee and a sandwich, Jeremiah. Go easy on that. Your stomachs not used to eating anymore and you'll suffer for it."

"I know. This is three days of rations for me. Been like that for five months now."

"Well hopefully, you're through it." He turned to the ranger guards, "Has the captain been notified? Can I get entrance to the CIC?"

The corporal replied formally, "Chief Greer said the captain's orders were to hold our guest here, but I'll call in for you, Sir."

A slight hesitation as the guard contacted the CIC controller then, "Prisoner stays here, Sir. You may enter but remain in the gallery until Captain Decatur calls for you."

The Bridge Section CIC's grey plastisteel door signaled his pending admission then confirmed Strake's DNA nodal sequence as he grabbed the entry lock-bar. He entered an upper gallery arching above a CIC teeming with near-silent action. Though the room was at the physical center of **Alfred**, the landing field visibly surrounded them as though they resided on a patch of decking beneath their feet floating at any height above the battlefield as desired by the captain. Off in the near distance, hovering at twice ship's height, was **Revenge**. Just a bit higher and off to the north, directing fire at unseen targets beyond the nearby mountains.

He could see **Aries** had yet to lift. They hadn't completed the installation of the new drive and Captain Decatur was in conversation with Lieutenant Scott Nauman, acting captain of **Aries**, "…. Scotty, you don't have time. Forget the abbreviated checklist, just confirm the activation basics."

The journalist, Margo Stoudt, stood forward in the gallery, standing in rapt attention of the activity across the CIC below. He walked over beside her as a beam of raw energy flashed from **Revenge** to a target on the other side of **Aries**. A grey cloud erupted from the spot, slowly lifting into the thin atmosphere. Display graphics appeared as the lieutenant's attention shifted to the action, marking it as a man-portable anti-ship missile launcher that a three-person team was setting up for a firing solution, but the team was now just a rising cloud of gas.

The raw energy of the Ion Cannons combined with fire from a ship-borne battery of Yttrium-enhanced X-ray Pulsed LASERs targeted line-of-sight threats across the field, flashing a deadly light-show across the entire landing strip as dusk slowly overtook them.

Margo turned her head, smiled briefly then quickly returned her attention to the action below without a word.

"Drone screen Betty-Three reports NAU strike force redirected to our position, ETA arrival in seven point two zero niner minutes." Sounded across the CIC push.

Decatur called out, "Lift the damn thing, Scotty. Our NAU cousins finally woke up and our time is up."

Aries rested below them unmoving, encased in streams of energy chaotically rippling across its surface as the new slipdrive attempted to recalibrate its gravitic field to its new misshapen host. The energy field suddenly blossomed, transforming into a translucent shell, though still filled with the red flashes of a poorly tuned drive, briefly sloshing back and forth like a carried bowl of water for a few heart-stopping seconds before it settled down and assumed a visible Coriolis swirl. The ship began its lift with a sharp pitch, rocking it fore and aft until the drive-field cleared the ground effect layer.

"NAU strike force entering energy weapons maximum range, ETA two point seven minutes."

Decatur called, "*Revenge* and *Alfred*, NAU passive targeting only, we don't want them seeing us as the threat. Hold your fire for my command."

"Threat warning, CTAC fighter squadron is inbound Zulu three-seven-oh. ETA weapon's maximum range at five point three two minutes."

Except for his white-knuckled grip on the arms of the command chair, Decatur showed little strain as he ordered, "Passive targeting only on threat addition from CTAC fighter wing. Wait upon my order."

A minute passed and *Aries* still had not settled into a stable drive field. Decatur's mind raced, "*Aries*, make ready defensive armament and for God sakes, stabilize your drive."

"You need to lift now."

"Scotty, you have about forty seconds. Take off now."

"NAU wing divergent to new course plot for interception of CTAC air wing."

A smile formed on the corners of Decatur's mouth. He suddenly realized how dry his mouth had become as he ordered, "All hands, do not repeat do not fire upon or use active targeting on CTAC or NAU incoming."

"*Revenge*, ride shotgun on *Aries*. *Alfred*, lift out, assume position between *Aries* and NAU wing but maintain course. *Alfred* will run Tail-End-Charlie acting as a shield for our sister-ships. Do not conduct active targeting on enemy airborne assets even if they redirect towards us, we are not to pose an active threat.

"*Aries*, sensors indicate you're loaded with soil deposits caught in your spindizzy field. It's tricky but you're going to have to chance a shutdown and purge it ..."

Ship's AI announcement cut him off, "Defense systems active."

Decatur stopped, interrupted by the NAU wing that just opened fire upon the CTAC fighters. The incoming CTAC force returned fire at nearly the same instant while maintaining some of their directed weapons towards the three colonial ships. Tremendous flashes of energy and ordinance filled the sky surrounding the colonial ships, still so close to the ground that Strake felt a momentary tang of pity for the exposed CTAC troops below.

Alfred's outer field glowed with a rainbow bullseye under the impact of a close-quarters TEA LASER pulse of invisible light whose coherent photon stream was scattered by the intense gravitic field of the rising ship.

"Hold fire, do not respond."

NAU fired first. Their salvo, impacting the CTAC air wing, flared over the horizon. The CTAC response was immediate, quickly spreading across three degrees of the distant skyline.

"Now *Aries*, dump ..."

Slipdrive glow surrounding the *Aries* disappeared. The ship slid upward carried by the momentum of their ascent while leaving a grey cloud of shed debris in their wake. With near-perfect timing, *Aries* reactivated her drive and a visible field returned, surrounding the ship with a healthy, and nearly uniform blue glow. *Aries* shot off like a racehorse leaving the starting gate.

Hell-fire on the horizon from the air battle continued far below the colonials as they lifted on a course that would carry them around the larger moon.

"Captain, a new threat just emerged from behind the satellite, appears to be a CTAC frigate."

A com transmission from the frigate opened on the bridge, "Unidentified vessels escorted by CTAC *Lingley*. Assume Phobos orbit at dead slow relative and prepare to be boarded or you will be fired upon."

Captain Jankin Decatur didn't hesitate, "***Revenge*** and ***Aries*** leave now. *Alfred* will engage and shield your departure."

The CTAC vessel, previously occluded by the satellite, managed to come upon them so close they could see it emerge without sensor enhancement. This was not to be a battle of starships conducted light-minutes from one another. The engagement would be toe-to-toe, the equivalent of a starship knife fight.

"All hands, prepare for …"

"VSF-1 inbound awaiting orders," Came in unbidden over the captain's command push. The Wraith fighters approached in stealth and were already in striking distance.

*That's a fully operational CTAC frigate and, this close to Mars, most likely has an unseen fighter screen of its own. They'll be on **Aries** and **Revenge** soon as they break off.*

"VSF-1,1 *Alfred* will engage the CTAC vessel. Veer off, provide cover for *Aries* and *Revenge* as they withdraw. No CTAC fighter assets spotted yet but you can bet your last thaler, they are out there somewhere so watch your six."

"Roger, *Alfred*."

Decatur examined the enemy frigate lying off his bow so near he could see details on its matte-black skin without sensor enhancement. He must destroy or disarm it quickly or it would have support from orbital or ground assets. Should he fail, his fighters would have problems even if they survived the coming engagement since neither of the captured vessels had carrier facilities. That meant the pilots would have to ditch their fighters and be individually rescued. A time consuming and dangerous task; even in peacetime. Near impossible when under attack.

A touch of pride glowed inside him for his 'Garyowen's. They knew what the order meant and still accepted his command without question.

Launch alarms screamed across the bridge. Decatur's eyes went to the frigate but could see no threat until his HiveTab highlighted the danger. The CTAC frigate wasn't waiting for them to comply as ordered. It launched a stealth attack so insidious and hidden that Decatur wondered what unknown magic of sensor-science Ship's Architect Josh Humphrey had managed to install in the *Alfred* and had neglected to tell him about.

A second alarm shrieked, giving him a single heartbeat to counter the automated threat response as the systems initiated and, before the captain could react, the system independently launched into action.

A dozen energy tubes shot out from the ship's outermost skin, each one extending across their external spindizzy field just far enough to stretch beyond the gravitic field's edge and immediately launch thousands of small, Hive-Capable Droids (HCD) into the surrounding abyss.

On this mission, the tiny droids searched for WAIEDs, CTAC Independent Wingmen, deadly tactical AI entities, much larger but fewer in number than the colonial droids.

Alfred's entire bridge crew watched in fearful fascination as the vacuum of the expanse separating the two warbirds exploded into glowing strings of energy as the defensive colonial network of molecule-sized HCDs aggressively located, tracked, and hunted down the finger-sized WAIED attack elements. Each HCD depended upon its HiveNetwork, a droid hive-consciousness now spread across an area covering half the volume of space from Phobos to the Martian surface.

Individual HCD were assigned a WAIED element target based on proximity. Already closing at lightspeed velocity, they set off a small gravitic field within its shell upon contact that disbursed the targeted WAIED as a hot burst of sub-electron particles releasing clouds of energetic photons, resulting in the glow. Soon the entire region between the two ships was filled with glowing, swirling strings of linked-particle gas that eventually blocked sight of the CTAC frigate like a dense, glowing fogbank but that lasted but a moment. Yet, at the height of the detonation the entire space was still empty expanse, a vacuum harder than any capable of creation upon any planet's surface.

Captain Decatur, a man who thought he had seen it all, was stunned when *Alfred* reported the successful HCD countermeasure launch and attack. A moment's silence passed, broken by Ensign Feign, "They're either desperate or suicidal. No one would have survived a WAIED detonation at this distance. Not their ship, nor any of ours."

A successful WAIED attack left no survivors for every atom within the expanding gravitonic field, whether it be metal, ceramic, plastic, or flesh, it was ripped asunder at the electron level. The encapsulation of energy needed to perform such a reaction dwarfed the fires of nuclear fission and the mass of a starship converting instantly to highly energized subelectron particles that would have consumed all three colonial ships as well as the nearby CTAC vessel.

Jankin Decatur commented in a calming, easily carried voice although he found his hand shaking perceptibly, "Yes. Well, easy now people. Concentrate on your stations, this isn't over."

His HiveTab interface highlighted nearly a dozen tiny puffs of light out at the fringes of the vapor cloud causing him to release a nearly silent grunt.

Well, they are expected. It's what I would have done.

"The WAID attack was a distraction. Major Walters, prepare to repel boarders. **Aries** and **Revenge**, leave now. We'll hold them here."

Repel Boarders

Alfred stood toe-to-toe with the CTAC frigate. Controlled havoc reigned on board until Corporal Mike Yatsko completed the positioning of the last of his squad in their 'repel-boarders' stations located near the outer shell of the ship. In short order, the rangers, spacers, and the ship settled back to wait for the coming storm.

Repel-boarders stations existed inside the ship. A ship's defender couldn't pass out an egress tube and stand on the outer skin of an energized vessel to wait for borders. Even now, though simply holding position in Phobos orbit, their slipdrive was active as they moved to keep the Alfred at a constant distance from their CTAC antagonist. Rather like two motorboats upon a river of gravity-waves maintaining their relative distances. Standing on the outer shell with one's legs extending down into the spindizzy region to the ship's skin was not healthy. The field would simply remove the legs molecule-by-molecule in an instant leaving the rest of the body to float off on its own trajectory, minus the dangling appendages.

Harsh treatment, even a Ranger would object to it.

Less than forty paces above the corporal, a five-combatant CTAC boarding module approached *Alfred* under cloak. Then, nearly touching the vessel, it fired a fine stream of chafe into their target's spindizzy field. The solid chafe particles were instantly ripped into a cloud of molecular particles that glowed faintly as the atoms were energetically ripped from their metallic bonds. The glow was Bremsstrahlung radiation caused by the sudden injection of energy used to break the molecular bond and, measuring the wavelength of the radiation released, the boarding module analyzed the phased frequency clusters of the elliptically polarized magnetic field of *Alfred*'s spindizzy.

Rainbows of color flitted about the boarding module for the moments it spent matching the protective field of its target. Five CTAC marines inside held their breath, hoping the analysis was correct as the module slid into the spindizzy zone then magnetically clamped onto their target's skin like a tick settling in upon a dog. *Alfred's* protective field changed its flow to cover the boarding module, gently enveloping the sudden appearance of the cylinder, accepting it as though it was simply a wart upon its skin.

The boarding module stamped a manhole-sized reactive film onto the ship's metal hull then covered it with a pyroplastic patch designed to focus the coming charge and protect the CTAC boarders who waited, praying the module's next action wouldn't be their last moment of life.

A loud blast shook the compartment followed by a moment of relief that flooded each marine. They'd survived. Their crash couches flipped open as did the boarding hatch located aft of the compartment as an explosive charge slammed a layered disk of ship's metal into the compartment below. It flew from the overhead, slamming into the deck with a force that injected a deadly wavefront of compressed air across the compartment while leaving a smooth-sided hole from the ship to the CTAC boarding module.

Screaming, the marines charged across the module, gave a quick glance to a suit display that told them the orientation of ship's gravity relative to their module and each boarder grabbed a steel bar on the bulkhead to swing forward feet first in a much practiced leap through the portal.

An angry swarm of flechettes screeched their deadly, sizzling zap as they met the first boarder, shredding her from thigh up through torso into a mist of blood, bone, and frayed material that coated the bulkheads and the deck.

A second boarder followed, skidding on the offal coated deck and stumbling over the still screaming remains of the first marine. He was followed by a flat, silver disk floating down through the boarding tube. It whined a banshee's wail as it abruptly changed direction, targeting the two colonial spacers who managed to survive the blast of the initial entry. The disk abruptly switched direction in an eyeblink, cutting through part of the bulkhead to reach the nearest spacer, a spinning hyperfoil blade capable of shredding plastisteel as well as flesh and bone. The nearby CTAC marine dropped, screaming beneath the blast of a Lepton Pulse Rifle or 'pulsar' firing ship-load munitions that shredded both invader and disk but bounced off the bulkhead leaving little more than gouges in the hard plastisteel as the colonial spacer who fired, immediately pulled back from the chamber into the relative safety of the ship's passageway.

"Riley hit the deck!" As the words met him, his muscular reaction sent him slamming to the hard surface saving his life. A heavy, crewed pulsar's blast ripped a hand's breadth above his head, scouring him beneath a scorching hot blast of air. The burst went on to splatter a CTAC marine, sending packets of body and blood down the passageway. A second marine fell wounded, her collapse to the deck had saved her life as a Colonial pulsar blast sent ship-load slugs through the portal to fragment against the bulkhead and ricochet into the breeched compartment like a swarm of deadly wasps.

Riley's head was spinning from the blast but he managed to grab his Pulsar and crawl back to the door frame, snake the tip of his rifle around it and blindly fire off three more rounds before risking a view into the compartment.

One body lay slumped at the opposite end blocking the door. He rose cautiously, ran to the edge of the frame and risked a quick glance into the back room.

Releasing a long breath of air along with his tension, he stood erect. Ears ringing, shouting back to the others, "Clear. All clear!"

~~*~*~*~*

Alfred's CIC AI entity released an action summary to Decatur's HiveTab, "Quadrant three sections charley-two-dash-niner to charley-two-dash-fourteen, boarders eliminated or taken in custody. CTAC marines established a foothold in Wraith Launch Bay Alpha. We have not been able to halt their incursion but have slowed entry. Quadrant two has six entry points, four now blocked with two still presenting a threat.

"Thirty-two boarding platforms were eliminated by battle drones released by your command and seven by Wraith deployed launch. No additional platforms detected."

The last statement caught Jankin Decatur's attention, had he heard right?

"The Wraiths were ordered to shield **Revenge** and **Aries**. Who disobeyed my command?"

"Flight Leader Krozel is responsible for the action. He did obey your command. Krozel logged a release of three Wingman Drones for on-station defense of the **Alfred** prior to departure in anticipation of such enemy action. Apparently, he failed to appreciate the full extent of the enemy's launch and should have released more."

"Ah, maybe so. Still, his action saved lives. Put an entry in my personal log to keep an eye on the flight leader, he shows promise."

CIC's AI wasn't finished, "The CTAC boarding launch was illogical unless we assume, that they did not recognize **Alfred** as a warbird. At that point their action's logical conformance probability rises to eighty-seven point six-five percent."

Jankin Decatur looked over his officers on station in the CIC and found no apparent signs of distress. Active resistance was ongoing at three separate ship locations and Rangers, with colonial spacer backup, were addressing the problem. It was only a matter of moments before the CTAC captain would respond to the departure of the **Revenge** and **Aries**. Decatur wondered just what that response would be. Would he let them run and deal with **Alfred?** **Alfred** was dangerously close for a graviton torpedo launch. Even precision firing directed at **Alfred** from a Mars-based cannon emplacement would endanger their ship.

Unless there happened to be an emplacement on Phobos itself, then a precision strike might be attempted.

Then again, if the CTAC captain still believed this may all be a prisoner insurrection supported by the NAU, the CTAC captain might let his forces continue their assault on the **Alfred** and decide to chase the escaping prisoners now running ahead.

"Helm lay in a course for …."

The CTAC vessel suddenly disappeared and, in that instant, the onboard wave scanners recorded its graviton wake vector's correlation to the course set by Decatur's two fleeing vessels.

Cursing the hesitation that allowed their enemy to depart before him, he decided he had one advantage. Since the CTAC captain didn't know the rendezvous point, they would track the residual graviton ionization wake left by the departing ships currently engaged on a pre-planned indirect traverse. Decatur, however, had already plotted their rendezvous point in the asteroid belt. He would take a direct path to it.

By taking a direct vector Decatur knew he'd lose all chance of escaping untracked but the CTAC captain had just removed that as an option, so he didn't waste a second moment, "… make rendezvous on the asteroid belt's Trojan Cluster. Fully engage both drives, let's push the redline."

Alfred's drive clamped down on the crest of an upcoming primary gravitic wave before his pilot confirmed the order. In place of the confirmation came a reply that, in a different situation, would have invoked a captain's rebuke, "Aye aye, Sir. Drive Alpha engaged but we no longer have a second drive."

Decatur cursed his own forgetfulness. How could he have forgotten they'd dismounted one drive and moved it to the **Aries**?

"Thank you, Ensign. Just give me all you have, redline the wave-linkage. We must be at the Trojans before our sister ships arrive."

"Torpedo room make ready two graviton torpedoes. Set them to maximum yield with a half-phase separation, safeties off for immediate tactical AI launch."

"Upon our arrival at waypoint one, expect **Aries** and **Revenge** to emerge on the instant and in deacceleration from their wave-link. You will target back down their wake to a point danger-close but aft of our ships and immediately release on bearing."

"Do not wait for or request pre-launch confirmation."

In the gallery, Margo Stoudt turned to Lieutenant Strake releasing a loud, angry whisper, "Is he crazy? He's going to fire on our people."

The journalist's stared at the captain then turned to Strake, fear and horror evident in her face, "He's going to kill off thousands of our people on those two ships just to get that CTAC ship yet look at him, giving out orders cold and calculating as a machine. Doesn't he care?"

The lieutenant's recent, still very raw experience replied although he couldn't bear to look directly at the journalist, "He cares, Ms. Stoudt. Duty first. The self-recrimination comes later, assuming we survive, along with all the self-doubt and self-criticism of actions taken."

"The nightmares can only be worse if his choice proves wrong."

They felt a quiver marking the engagement of **Alfred's** engine. Mars and Phobos vanished astern replaced by the universe's fiery points of light performing their jittery dance for but a few moments. Then the dance ended, replaced by a blinding, blue flash illuminating the velvety blackness of the stellar background with the immediate launch of two graviton torpedoes. Ship's sensors recorded only their residual wakes as they reappeared bending the photon-images of the distant starfield beneath the violent distortion of their gravitic-fed launch. A wailing scream enfiladed the CIC then rapidly faded with the unfiltered remnant of their high energy departure.

It was as though two bright stars went supernova, their instant image already a disk quickly fading before the human eye. **Alfred's** CIC's walldisplay zoomed in on the area of the still distant **Revenge** and **Aries**. They appeared in focus for an instant before succumbing beneath an impossibly black tsunami that swelled over them and the distant stars as the gravitic fury of the blast swept all lightwaves from the area.

As quickly as the blackness formed, it was gone. The images of distant stars once again settled into place, wobbling strangely relative to one another for a second or two because of the localized chaos in the gravitic ether bending all radiation passing through its deadly forcefield lens before settling into their proper, stellar positions.

Revenge and **Aries** reappeared but were no longer in formation. They drifted dead, lifeless in the passing ether of the universe. Aft of them lay a sparkling ball of glitter looking much like a tiny expanding nebula of fireflies, slowly succumbing to the all-encompassing blackness of the universe.

"Ship-to-ship tightbeam from **Revenge**," Communications Specialist Ensign Feign announced as Acting Captain Hopewell's bridge appeared before them.

"**Alfred**, our slipdrive has shutdown. **Aries** is also dead in the ether and we have not been able to contact them. We lost headway and ship's gravity when our wave linkage phased out. We are attempting a drive reset."

Feign responded, "We will be there momentarily, **Aries**. Complete your checks and reset but await our arrival."

Strake released his white-knuckled grip from the support rail then turned with a knowing smile that startled the journalist, "Captain's crazy like a Kraken tree-weasel, ma'am. You're right, the torps released a graviton implosion that disrupted local gravity waves like a boulder dumped into a stream. Fortunately, our people had already begun decoupling from the local wavefront as they approach rendezvous. When the torps detonated and the wavefront hit, it washed over them from astern, broaching their aft shell and carrying them forward like wet-sea surfers on a wave, causing only their drives to shut down."

"The CTAC vessel wasn't so fortunate. Their ship was coming in fast, heavily linked to the wave crest it rode for an intended interception. So, although the torp didn't strike it directly, the warbird smacked directly into the oncoming blast wave with full linkage to their drive wave."

"The chaos caused by the torpedo's blast shredded their frigate into pieces that reflected light, forming that tiny nebula we saw flaring briefly in the wake of our ships."

Decatur finally addressed the gallery, a look of relief upon his face as he said, "Now, let's hope they can quickly restart their drives. We are out of spares and have not enough room to accommodate all their people. I expect we'll be seeing CTAC assets arriving soon and I'd prefer to be far from here by the time they arrive."

A tickler from Jankin Decatur's own HiveTab blossomed into a prioritized reminder; *there is an urgent meeting waiting for you in Captain's Quarters.*

Prisoner of War

"This way, Major Jensen; Captain Decatur commanded we wait for him in the captain's conference room."

Captain Jeremiah Jensen of the NAU marines was not Kraken military commissioned but there is only one captain on a ship so he would be addressed as 'Major', an honorary promotion.

The ex-prisoner was mildly surprised to discover that, what appeared as a finely finished wood door was a hardened security portal with pressure seals. The 'conference' room could double as a reinforced bunker. Its interior was synthetic light-wood paneling, complete with sculptured knots and smooth grain texturing that went well with lighting from some unseen source, providing a relaxing illumination free of shadows on the tabletop.

Strake motioned his guest over to a cushioned office chair as he crossed to the opposite bulkhead, "I'm gonna have some java. How about you? Are you hungry or thirsty?"

"Coffee? You have honest-to-goodness coffee? With cream?"

"Well, it's synthetic but pretty good even by my standards. How about a small sandwich or cup of soup, too? You've gotta build your system back up to eating regular ration levels again."

"Yeah, anything."

The rear door opened and in stepped a huge, broad-shouldered figure in a uniform Jensen didn't recognize. The guy looked familiar but, "Gleason?" Jensen blurted out as he stood up, "Fireman Gleason? Shoot buddy, what in Finagle's Weird Universe are you doing here?"

A big smile covered the CPO's face as he extended his hand, "Yer an officer now? I had ta come and see it with ma own eyes. Jensen, by the tar in me, it is you and yer a captain? Who'd ya have ta kill to get 'em ta make you a gentleman?"

A shocked look came over Jensen's face, but he recovered quickly, "Hell, I never thought of it that way and no, I didn't have to kill anyone. CTAC took care of that. In a conflict like we're in, the promotions come quick and ..."

Jensen stopped as the door opened and a short, broad-shouldered man in a captain's uniform entered. Cold, steely hazel eyes seemed to identify and lock onto their target, reading into every niche of the NAU officer's soul as he pulled back the captain's chair, "Be seated gentlemen. I assume you're Captain Jeremiah Jensen."

"You have a good record but there seems to be a lot missing from it. Even our systems couldn't access some of the files so that tells me you're most likely NAU Intelligence."

"This ... is what makes me nervous."

"I said sit down, I'm a busy man. The lieutenant tells me this is important so let's not waste time."

"First, how is it you survived becoming a CTAC prisoner when they have a policy of eliminating captured officers. Then, we'll turn to that case you seem to be so attached to."

A broad smile came over Jensen's features, "Yes sir, but would you ask Mr. Gleason to also have a seat. We used to know each other, and I know what he's capable of. I'd be a lot more relaxed if he sat or stood where I could see him."

Decatur could see the attempted hidden smile on the CPO's face. He was obviously enjoying this so, "No, Captain. It's because Travis and Rendell also remember you that we choose to take this precaution. If you are honest with me, you have nothing to fear."

"Now, please continue."

Jensen continued with an obvious level of discomfort, "I'm alive only because CTAC also figured out my position and thought I had access to sensitive information. CTAC Ministry of State eventually discovered that I've been record blocked with a cryptokey." Oh, they tried to crack it at first, I've got the scars to prove it, but no one can force information out of me if I can't remember it myself."

Decatur saw the CPO become tense and silently shift his balance towards their guest. The captain shook his head ever so slightly before taking up the conversation, "So, this is the reason for using my time. You think you know something. Okay, who or what has a key that can unlock this information. One that even you can't get?"

"Oh, well. Except for certain preset conditions, that would be Commander Mark Fields, commandant of Lunar Area Seventy-Two. However, there is information NAU headquarters needs in that briefcase we brought back, it contains not only CTAC message codes and armament storage but also something even more important."

"I had no time to be choosey when Travis freed me, so I grabbed the entire data cubit. Finagle himself only knows how much information is on it. But I do know it contains lists of prisoners and their location of incarceration as well as documentation of actions; call them atrocities, performed during several raids on the colonies. Travis implied this was part of your mission. Naturally, I'm very glad it was, or I'd still be in the caves."

"There's one more thing I discovered during my stay that I can share with you, CTAC operates a network of black-market arms sellers that extend across the NAU and into our colonies."

Decatur tried not to show his surprise, *Bucker. This man has incriminating evidence that can put a tight noose around John Bucker's slimy neck.*

Jensen flipped open the lid to his briefcase and turned it so the captain could see inside. The briefcase-style box was lined with a soft, black fur-like fabric. Within it floated a black cube containing an eight by sixty-four, single-layer matrix of yellow translucent crystals each of which held a small universe of sparkling, multicolored stars.

Captain Decatur rose from his seat and bent over to look closer at the matrix, "You stole an entire quantum-spin platter? How did you manage to remove it without frying every molecule in the matrix?"

"Ahh," CPO Greer broke in with the exclamation he typically thought was the politest method to interrupt a conversation. "Beggin yer pardon, Captain, but what's a quantum-spin platter?"

Decatur wasn't surprised by the question, "It's a quantum array storage module. This is an exceptionally big one. It uses spin linkage to align electron spin tachyon entanglements for data recording. A module of this size could hold a tremendous amount of data."

Jensen relaxed back into his chair, the pleasure of cradling a warm ceramasteel coffee mug in his hands radiating from his features, "There is a lot of information in that data cubit, I suspect much of it will not be critical but there are some things I do know about. You see, CTAC is short on technical support. They have few engineers familiar with this level of technology and, since the technology was stolen to begin with, there's a lot about the science even their 'qualified' engineers won't understand."

"CTAC actually had a file on me, can you believe it? Their records said I had worked with the technology so, when they raided our base, they were kind enough to allow me to survive. It seems they had a need for my services. They shipped me off-planet, all the way out to that god-forsaken place beyond the edge of civilization. Even went so far as to put me in an underground bunker, for Finagle's sake!"

"Last thing I ever expected was to be rescued."

"Out of boredom and pure spite, I defeated the callogen-lock on the data module during the last system maintenance. That was nearly nine months ago, and I was wondering how I could use my minor victory."

"It was like a genie had come to my rescue when Travis magically appeared behind a cloud of smoke from the blast. I couldn't remember his name at first but recognized his face and knew I was rescued."

"Now, if you will bring in a tech with a maintenance interface, I'll see how much data we can map out of this thing and where it will take us."

"Ah, there is one thing. You realize I must work this interface alone. Colonials are not security graded for access to this level of information. Fear not though. I'm sure central command will make it worth your while when you return me to the NAU."

Captain Jankin Decatur's eyebrows formed a scowl which spoke volumes. Leaning forward to steeple his fingers before him, elbows on the conference table, his eyes stared into the NAU captain's, holding the man's gaze. He then said only, "Mister Jeremiah Jensen, allow me to ask where you hail from on Earth?"

"Why, I'm from Virginia sector."

"Southern or northern part of the sector?"

"Why, southern but I don't understand where this is leading, Sir."

Decatur relaxed and sat back then casually inquired, "So, your ancestors were rebels?"

Jeremiah was obviously becoming annoyed with the personal prying of this strange captain, "If you mean from before the Great Union during the Republic? Yes. My ancestors fought for the Confederation during the Civil War and their fathers before them struggled for the founding of the Republic itself. We have been true and loyal citizens of the Republic of the United States as well as the North American Union that followed."

"Even though there is very little of the Republic left in it?" Decatur quietly replied.

Jankin Decatur gave the captain a rarely bestowed smile, his blue eyes twinkling in delight at the officer, "I mean you or your family no disrespect; rather I would mean to honor them for being a rich source of patriots who value freedom and liberty."

Jensen visibly stiffened. This colonial captain's words bordered on sedition, perhaps even treason.

CPO Gleason's deep belly-laugh snapped the rising tension. Jensen turned to see a broad grin on the spacer who leaned forward a bit and stage-whispered across the table, "The man has no idea where you're going with this conversation, Captain. Be kind to the gent, he ain't so bad and he's been locked in a dark cage for much too long."

Jankin Decatur began lightly tapping the edge of the data briefcase with his index finger, "We certainly welcome any assistance you may choose to provide. I am most grateful for the knowledge that you've already defeated the collagen security shield. Our people should have no trouble accessing the information from this point forward."

"Our ship comes from Kraken and, try as hard as the NAU might, they have not succeeded in isolating us from technology and science."

"Your experience and your training make you a very valuable asset. At the end of this, I'm going to give a gift to you. One the NAU does not have the grace to provide for our people."

"I don't want a decision from you now since I'm giving you the highpoints only. First, let me fill in recent events since you've been out of circulation. I'll leave it to the chief and Lieutenant Strake to fill in the details about who, what, why, and when."

"Kraken and Jasper are no longer colonies of the NAU. We have declared our independence. In spite of its appearance, this ship is a warbird of our own design and construction, a frigate to be precise."

"We are here to rescue colonial prisoners shanghaied because of the NAU-CTAC conflict. You were lucky enough to have been one of those who made it aboard. The raid we just conducted could just as well have been against an NAU prison compound performing the same atrocities."

"You, sir, are a prisoner of war. You will be treated with respect and your condition will be considerably better than the colonials your Union currently incarcerates."

Jensen seemed stunned at first, "You turned against your homeland?"

"No, Mister Jensen. Our homeland has turned against us."

"Your family will be notified of your well-being. You will be confined to locked quarters. I will not put you in a cell. If you give your word of good behavior and parole, you will be allowed free access to parts of our ship until we return to Kraken. Eventually, you may be exchanged and returned home."

"Your family has a history that shows their love of freedom. Perhaps you may eventually decide to join our cause."

"Chief, take care of our guest. You know what to do. Lieutenant leave the briefcase with me and resume your responsibilities."

"Thank you, gentlemen, you are dismissed."

Captain Decatur stood as they left the conference room, he then returned to his seat while absentmindedly running his fingertips across the briefcase. He had this uncomfortable feeling. He knew the worst was yet to come.

THE WAY BACK

Communications Officer Ensign Litel Feign's melodious voice cut through the subdued chatter of the bridge, "Haach imaging reports final munitions preparation for the launch of three warbirds, location backside of Mars, foothills of Arsia Mons. ETA fifty-three minutes. Identification confirmed as a fleet destroyer, a frigate, and a striker star-sloop."

Decatur cringed at the use of the 'Haach' acronym; an ugly, unfortunate name that stood for **'High Altitude Atmospheric Crest Holography'**.

Shaking his head, Decatur called over to Lieutenant Nauman, "*Aries*, status report."

Scott Nauman appeared inside a bridge still exhibiting the damage of a violent takeover by rangers. Technicians had also contributed to the mess with several consoles obviously ripped out of their control clusters because of the danger of a loss of command control should the ship's CTAC AI regain access. New consoles littered the aisles, jury-rigged in all but one location. Decatur wondered just how the pilot had managed to lift off from the surface and up to their rendezvous under such conditions and while under hostile fire.

Scott's report was crisp and clear, "The massive stern wave created by your torp broached us astern, blowing out our drive field. The ship attempted to compensate resulting in it shorting three superconductor rings on the outer field rotator."

"Repairs proceeding, we're about ready to attempt a restart. We should be seventy-two percent flight-ready in fourteen minutes."

"If it doesn't work, plan on leaving without us."

Sometimes you just had to let things slide and the captain was in a hurry, "Well, we will address that should the time come. Keep us updated."

Decatur didn't like wasting time, *Fourteen minutes. That gives our CTAC friends fourteen minutes to gain on us using a strong ion trail.*

Habit returned his attention to the status of his own bridge, *all seems well but we are short the presence of one ranger sentry, I …*

Rangers. Yes. Let's try something.

"Major Walters, do your people still have that scuttled drive? Could you still fire it up? It doesn't have to be up to spec."

Walters signaled reception of the message and, less than thirty seconds later, was the answer, "Aye, Sir. The old CTAC drive here on **Aries** was forcibly dismounted but is still functional, barely. But its operation is as glitchy and dirty as Finagle himself, but it'll run. I wouldn't want to spend any time in its field though, the secondary radiation will be a killer."

*A stroke of luck having the old drive from **Aries** available and in the hands of already vac-suited Rangers.*

"Better than I'd hoped for major, a ship's drive no less. Here's what I want you to do …."

~~*~*~*~*

Lagrange Points are positions where the gravitational forces of a multi-body system tend to balance. Within the Sun's asteroid belt, planetoids tend to form major clusters at two of Jupiter's Lagrange points where they orbit the sun in synchronization with the gas giant. The points are well known and named *'the Trojans'*. **Alfred's** current course targeted one such cluster lying just sixty degrees ahead of the planet, sharing its orbit. This one cluster contains over a thousand unusually dense rocks greater than a kilometer in diameter, a composite mass equivalent to the rest of the asteroids in the entire solar asteroid belt combined.

The three colonial starships made rendezvous here, disappearing from CTAC sensors by laying in the shadow of a two-hundred-kilometer Trojan asteroid, named *'Hector'* by early astronomers. Roughly a tenth the size of Earth's moon, it is one of the few asteroids able to boast having its own orbiting satellite.

This small satellite was the objective of Sergeant Winn Washington and PFC Rob Jenkins as she maneuvered her two-seated scooter in for a soft rendezvous. It wasn't an easy approach since the rangers had to perform the delicate maneuver with a one ES-Ton, or 'Earth Standard Ton', gravitonic drive secured abeam their scooter. Although their cargo weighed nothing out in the expanse, its sheer mass and momentum could crush a careless ranger and scooter very easily should they lose control.

Deftly adjusting course then fine-tuning each correction with a trim command from her HiveTab interface, the sergeant drew inward for the rendezvous. It was a task that need be performed carefully for, should the mass of their scooter and drive impact the tiny rock improperly, it could throw the small satellite out of an already unstable orbit putting a quick end to their mission.

Approaching slowly, she pulled back again and again, each approach adjusting their closing and acceleration vectors. Each adjustment of the controls drew them nearer to the perfect approach solution until they 'kissed' the satellite's surface with just the far base of the engine.

"Ready," Washington called to her mate. "Fire pitons."

Five puffs of propellant silently burst in a ragged cloud from their side, each explosion sending a dense-metal rod deep into the satellite's surface where tiny fins at its tip opened, preventing them from pulling out. Automatically, straps on the drive reeled in the titanium cables attached to the pitons, securing it and the scooter to the satellite.

"Well done, begin drive activation prechecks."

Captain Decatur's voice interrupted her concentration, "Excellent job, Sergeant. Now fire up the drive but keep the field at minimum. We'll monitor from here until it stabilizes. Then I'll signal you when we're about to pull out of station. You follow. Stay within the group until I give you final instructions. When I tell you, unlatch your little scooter and return to your ship as quickly as possible. Waste no time, you will be in a high radiation area."

"Aye aye, Sir."

"Captain Decatur, you know this is my first independent command? May I name her?"

"What? A ranger sergeant commanding a Kraken vessel? Well, I ... perhaps it isn't any crazier than everything else that's been going on."

"Acting Commander Washington, congratulations on your new command. Please feel free to name your ship and you may so log it, listing you as ship's commander into our records."

"Now listen, I know you are still a ranger at heart, so I need warn you. You are to keep the name appropriate ... keep it clean, Winn. This will be in the official record."

"Call if you encounter problems."

Jankin Decatur set an alarm that would notify him when the asteroid's drive field stabilized. He then checked on the ETA of the three CTAC warbirds – forty-one minutes to clear their weapon's ranging.

The notification popped up, he called over to their asteroid, "I see you are ready Sergeant Washington. Good Job."

"Commander Washington reports Kraken Special Vessel **Robert Rodgers** running stable, although the drive field's radiation envelope runs a bit dirty. Ready for departure."

Decatur chuckled quietly at the formal response with its subtle correction of rank, "Well done and accept my apologies, 'Commander'."

"Excellent name selection for your first command. Robert Rodgers, the commander and founder of the original special forces Rangers Battalion in what would become the United States. He is a legend worthy of the ship and your mission."

"All ships maintain a tight formation. The course set into your systems will lead us to Jupiter, where you will get new directives."

Decatur finally felt like things were moving smoothly and under control as they entered the miniature 'planetary system' of more than a hundred moons surrounding Jupiter, their next waypoint. Rising from his console, he took advantage of the free moment to stretch and look over the stations of his bridge. All seemed well. His small fleet was in a tight formation that promised to carry them quickly to home port.

A program-status note from his HiveTab appeared, reminding him it was time for one final command to the sergeant – 'Commander'.

"Commander Washington, you should be feeling a smoothing of drive performance since we just exited the heavy gravitic wave chop of the open solar system that limited our in-system acceleration.

Stand ready, you'll soon receive a pre-coded course adjustment; install it into your drive's processor."

"Our new course will take us directly into low Jupiter orbit where, as you draw closer, your vessel is set to accelerate steeply as it whips around the planet, gaining as much speed as possible using the calm region of gravitic wavefronts created by the huge Jovian Gravity Well."

"At that time, **Robert Rodgers** will split off from the rest of the group. Its drive will detune as it accelerates leaving a clear trail of secondary ion residue in its wake for our CTAC friends to follow as we quietly shift to a divergent course."

"Before that first acceleration kicks in, you must detach and depart. Do not waste time. You will not survive the radiation if you stay with your rock. Free your scooter and rendezvous with the *Revenge*. Don't waste time with *Aries*, their docking is blown."

"Aye aye, Sir." Acting Commander Washington returned.

Decatur continued, "Major Walters, we still have Wraiths out there who wish to come home. What is the status of enemy boarders in my landing bay?"

Walters took a virtual eternity to reply. When he did, Decatur was surprised to see the major breathing hard, "Landing bay is not secure. We are attempting to nullify boarders but are hampered by the need to minimize facility damage. They've put up stiff resistance to any thrusts on our part and refuse to negotiate."

"Major, I don't care if you blow out half the facility's guts. Eliminate the threat so I can land my 'Owens. We need to leave, and I want those birds inside our drive field even if they can't dismount their Wraiths."

"Aye aye, Captain. It's your call."

Then, another call from Ensign Litel, "Captain, our drone screen reports two CTAC destroyers emerging from Jovian transit and bound on course intercept."

"Oh, Via! They must have a deep base on Io we didn't know about and must want to stop us badly if they're willing to expose its existence by launching two heavy destroyers against our little pack of frigates."

"All ships, manual adjust defensive formation. Use **Alfred** as a shield from approaching CTAC warbirds but maintain course."

"**Alfred** will engage. When we do, you are to initiate the previous directive for a return to Kraken. We will buy you time, don't waste it. Godspeed."

Commander Hopewell called for confirmation, "The three of us stand a chance against the destroyers. **Alfred**, by herself, does not. Request you rescind the order for us to break and run."

"Commander Harriett, you are no longer my XO and do not need to provide me with alternative actions. Our fighter shield is still deployed, **Alfred** will have our Garyowens to back us up. Please carry on as ordered."

Hopewell did not reply audibly but she obviously cared little about the visual she allowed to be transmitted. Then, she was gone.

Decatur forced the exchange from his mind, "Quickly, while they are still sublight. Fire Photon battery. Full coherence and monochromatic."

At this range, the Photon Laser Battery's pulse would be near-instantaneous in its transit delivery.

~~*~*~*~*

Acting Commander Winn Washington was unsure of her mission directive. Did her decoy mission even mean anything given the appearance of the two CTAC destroyers?

"Jenkins, our cargo feels like it's resisting, is this rock we're dragging misbehaving."

"Yeah, she doesn't like being dragged in this vector. Drive is straining but it should be able to take it."

"Hey Winn, don't you think it's time we break off and head home?"

"Any second now, as soon as the new course directive kicks in."

"Let's hope it's soon. I ..."

"Oh shite, you feel that. Yep, she's accelerating. Look back, her gravitonic field is splaying out like a stellar flare."

"That's okay, that's the whole idea. The drive is set to be run dirty leaving an ion trail a half-parsec wide in space. I'm gonna blow the linkage. Hang on."

The entire scooter shook as their captive planetoid sent out a following ring of debris into the abyss. Somehow, Winn felt the reaction should have been stronger, "What was that? You call that an active release?"

A quick inspection using two of their small drones provided the answer, "Only two of the links went. You try it, Jenkins."

"No response, Winny. Looks like we're gonna ride this one out."

"Oh, Finagle's got his evil eye on us for sure. Look forward."

Concentrating on their own problems, they missed the dull point of light distorting the far-off stars that had grown into an energized disk directly in their path. It reflected little light, but they eventually spotted it by the starlight points of the distant Milky Way distorting in the object's passage.

"Oh shite, we're locked onto this stupid rock and now this. That's gotta be another ship."

"Well, so much for riding this out. Probably better this way, anyhow."

"Hang on; I'm doing a course override. We're ..."

"You can't do a course override, we don't even have proper control with two of our pitons gone, Washington, what ..."

"Yes, I can. I'm commander and that's a logged fact that gives me command authorization."

"Redirecting to intercept course and you shaddap, I need to concentrate."

~~*~*~*~*

A pulsed photon laser-battery's discharge is little more than a packet of light particles screaming through space with their waves coherently aligned as a formation of soldiers on parade align their stride. But *Alfred's* primary battery, the Kraken Laser Pulse Battery was something more, much more.

Energy manipulation technology on Kraken secretly evolved to the point that particle behavior of a light beam could be controlled nearly down to the individual photon using pulse compression. The resulting transfer of high-frequency energy released when it impacted a target was deadlier than any conventional laser weaponry.

Alfred's main battery simultaneously released a dozen long, nine-nanosecond blasts of high-frequency energy pulses that went out screaming at the speed of light through the hard vacuum of space. They impacted directly on the nearest CTAC destroyer who's external gravitic drive field immediately began attempting to rip high energy photon particles from the condensed light packet.

A laser's punch comes not from a solid object built of atoms and molecules but the transfer of energy from the photon packet pulse. Two basic and irresistible forces met on the surface of the CTAC vessel where its gravitic drive ripped energy from the pulse, redirecting photon paths and changing frequencies but at a cost for the interaction depleted their gravitic field locally in a complex reaction whose timescale could only be measured in zeptoseconds, a unit-of-time so small it is equal to a single number one sitting twenty-one places behind the decimal point, a mere a trillionth of a billionth of a second.

The pulse was immediately followed by a second, then a third, and more. Flowing out so quickly human eyes saw them as a single, fire-hose deadly shaft of light.

Rainbows of light enveloped the CTAC destroyer marking their impact as the target's gravitonic field leeched energy from each of the canon's photon packets. Stray blasts of pure energy, running the full gamut of frequencies from invisible x-rays, through the visible spectrum, and into the deep infrared of a pure thermal energy were ejected into space. Rainbow arches of light flowed about the ship, enveloping the destroyer in undulating waves as though an aurora-borealis on steroids had attacked the warbird.

A barrage of graviton torpedoes erupted from the second destroyer, accelerating for the **Revenge** and **Aries,** who had ramped their drives for a grazing plunge into the security of the turbulent upper-cloud surface of the nearby gas giant that could have swallowed more than one thousand three hundred Earths and not shown a lump. Space twinkled visibly behind the colonial ships marking the release of two clusters of WAID anti-ship droids. Normally a poor choice for defense against a graviton torpedo, the droids anticipated the course of the fast-moving weapons, adjusting their velocity and shrouding their target's AI's sensors like thousands of swarming ants as the deadly munitions followed the colonial ships, disappearing beneath the swirling storms of the planet.

Visuals on the walldisplays of **Alfred's** CIC highlighted multiple blasts, silent but violently blossoming beneath the churning storm cover. Swirling tornadoes, growing in strength, converging until the area mushroomed into an angry red bulge rising from the deep.

Captain Jankin Decatur spared no time staring at the ominous display. He had a ship to fight if they were to survive these next precious minutes against the two freshly launched and deadly behemoths, each nearly half-again the size and four-times the firepower of his warbird.

"Wraith squadron VSF-1 forming for attack on CTAC bogie designated Sierra-two." Echoed through the captain's HiveTab. Decatur's reply was immediate, "Negative VSF-1, realign on Sierra-one. Keep it staggering and outta our threat zone. **Alfred** will take on Sierra-two."

"Aye aye, **Alfred.**" The reply was simple, short, and clear.

The Wraith must have been in the objective's proximity since the CTAC destroyer immediately lit-up in shield-reaction to high-speed sabot penetrators released by the 'Garyowens'.

Decatur didn't spend time watching. Calling his pilot, "Ensign Foster, change tack, take us across the bow of Sierra Two, move in close as you can. Let her see us coming, Toshie, keep their attention on us and away from our Wraiths."

"Laser batteries, lay in another barrage on Sierra One as we pass."

Alfred leaped upwards, jolted, lifting the deck beneath their feet to break legs and throw anything not secured across the platform. Decatur knew they'd been torpedoed but could feel the hit was indirect and, based on the direction of the jolt, was in the ship's southern hemisphere.

Groans and cries filled the bridge as they pressed onward to within a tenth the diameter of the gas giant, a distance equal to the diameter of the Earth. Once again it would be a close-quarters conflict, another starship knife-fight.

When unsure of what to do, do something, anything. Decatur's shouted command would have carried clear across a battlefield, "All railguns. Long and short banisters, continuous fire on target."

Streams of sabot-enhanced, depleted uranium shot from the **Alfred**, stretching across the gas-filled upper stratosphere like deadly icy-blue lasers, searching for a weak point in the target's field, leaving tornadoes of Jovian gas in their wake.

Before they even struck, the CTAC captain launched a flight of graviton torpedoes but the flight of the railgun salvo was already upon them causing one to detonate during ejection, still in its chamber.

A second blast shook **Alfred** side-to-side, "Hull breach. Landing dock Bay Three and two decks directly above are open to vacuum."

The bridge was littered with the dead and injured, Decatur noted they were streaming air and flotsam into the heavens above the gas giant as he ordered his third laser battery directive, "Main battery, redirect to …"

~~*~*~*~*

Flight Leader Alvin 'Kronski' Krozel's Wraith screamed its passage through the dimly lit, brown and red swirling clouds. A Wraith typically travels in silence whether it be in the atmosphere or under a liquid but, this deep into Jupiter's atmosphere, these gases were so dense their pressure caused his ship to pop and creak. He could hear the unnerving clatter above the atmosphere's shrieking objection to their fast passage.

The god-like vision of human-made sensors guided his course, and his prayers went out to the four fates with a plea he would find the target and it would not see him first.

Their flight now down to twenty-one fighters, they had sustained what the log had recorded as a 'moderate' loss. Somehow 'three lost' seemed less painful than three brothers, friends he'd never see again. In spite of the pain, Kronski knew the approach he'd selected was dangerous, a risk that could claim the entire squadron for they now sailed deeper into the gas-giant's cloud-cover than the penetration of any known craft.

He had decided a dive into the bottomless mists was their only hope of drawing near to the CTAC destroyer, remaining unseen and surviving long enough to perform an effective weapons release that might stand a chance of evading the ship's deadly counter fire.

After all these years, Jupiter remained a mystery. Telemetry had failed in its atmosphere and hardened, and deep-dive physical probes never returned. Some theorized that gravity, and maybe even the laws of physics itself, changed beneath the turbulent sea of gases. A few scientists were sufficiently brazen to suggest Jupiter wasn't a planet at all, but a micro-black hole and the visible cloud cover was composed of anti-particle interactions expelled by its theorized Hawking Radiation shell lying just above a much deadlier invisible event horizon.

Kronski sailed through a dim universe of dirty-red storm clouds like some ancient superhero. His craft, currently set to full transparency through direct visual input to his occipital lobe, delivered the experience intimately to his senses. For the hundredth time, he checked his wing-count, *All still in contact. Can't see my own wingman through my Wraith highlights his location. Weird place to navigate a Wraith… Must trust your instruments… more like flying by dead reckoning. Blind as a bat… maybe worse since we're restricted to passive sensors.*

Alarms sounded a fractional second before the dark, swirling gases surrounding him flared into brilliant multicolored brilliance jostling even his flight path for a few moments. Then it was over. Kronski checked his wing count, three fewer Wraiths registered, *They're gone. Just like that. No residuals, no calls, and no telemetry. Not even an automated distress-packet launch.*

"Bluetooth, your wingman is gone. Link up with Nighthawk and Blueblood."

"What happened, Sir. She was …."

"I don't know. Forget about her or you'll be joining them. Focus."

"Aye aye, Sir."

He sounded okay but Kronski knew Bluetooth was shaken to the core.

Pure frustration made the flight leader take the chance as he let out a single staccato EM microburst. Immediately he regretted his action. For it had raised their risk of detection but he hoped to find his lost Wraiths.

The worst possible result returned: nothing. Not even his wingman registered with the pulse. The only reason they could still communicate was that their telemetry used gravionics rather than electromagnetic radiation.

"Finagle take us but we aren't going any deeper, we're heading out even if it's by dead-reckoning alone," Kronski's decision came easily and with welcomed timing. "On my mark, alter your vector to fifty-two degrees southwest of Jovian north and set in a thirty-seven point five-seven degree up-bubble."

"Be ready for acquisition update just prior to clearing the cloud cover in estimated seven minutes from … mark. At instance, initiate to your new cruise setting and arm four Crest Runners for release as you confirm targeting lock."

"Do not, repeat, do not request release confirmation. Upon release, you are on your own to continue engagement."

"Remember, *Alfred's* on the other side of that bogie. Take care in targeting."

Weak shafts of sunlight now laced angry colors across the surrounding storms mixed with the unnatural scream of hot gases rushing past their Wraiths until the surrounding clouds faded to nothing. Flight Leader Kronski checked their formation. Time was short.

"Spread out a bit, targeting update in forty-three …"

The unmistakable brilliance of passing high-density railgun rounds cut through the thinning clouds above like a white-hot poker, its arc swinging towards them. He had time for a quaking intake of breath before a nova-like blast of yellow light erupted above them followed by an honest-to-goodness sound wave carried to them by the vaporous upper atmosphere of Jupiter. Kronski's ears were throbbing as the sky above abruptly revealed a patch of stars that faded as quickly as they appeared.

A thought flashed through his mind, *now I know what it's like when you're at the bottom of a deep lake and someone throws a grenade in above you.*

They continued their upward climb through the churning chaos, the black velvet of space suddenly appeared, surrounding them. Ahead lay a great expanding ball of light reflecting off residual gas and flotsam, that was once a ship. In the near distance, a tiny image reflected its brilliance. Kronski's AI highlighted the brilliant image and its coordinates flashed out to the entire fighter wing. Six Crest Runner missiles exited his spindizzy field, his Wraith jolted forward with their release and the heavens disappeared behind an angry-red photon blast as they each latched onto the crest of the first gravity wave to pass, then shot out to meet their target at speeds a full ship-of-the-line could never hope to attain.

An answering radiation wavefront slammed into them, while blurred images of storms and stars flashed through his brain. Flight Leader Kronski didn't even have time to form the question.

~~*~*~*~*

PFC. Jenson Holst couldn't believe his ears, "You are out of your mind Washington, this is a breach of orders that come directly from the captain and you are gonna get us killed!"

The sergeant's reply was immediate and sharp, "We're already dead, Holst, or didn't you notice we can't break free? Our scooter's locked in; fate-bound us to this rock and don't even consider jumping ship without some better form of propulsion. We'll never make it back without the scooter and they ain't about to send someone for us, they have their hands full."

"Better to go out this way, it's faster and painless. Besides, we'll be helping our mates. Now hang on."

Jensen stretched forward and out to look beyond the sergeant's vacuum suit, he could feel acceleration building as the scooter's reaction drive carried them to an obvious destination, "Hey, you're heading straight for the CTAC destroyer. They'll blow us out of the universe and then its 'goodbye Sally, life wasted'."

"Stop being dense, Private. What did you think I intended? Dive into Jupiter and be slowly boiled and squished to death as we are gradually drawn down into the planet?"

"They won't fire on us. They're too busy trying to take down **Alfred** and we don't pose a threat since I've set a course that will miss them. They'll ignore us as a stray chunk of rock and when I shift direction at the last second, they'll have no time to react. With any luck, we'll weaken or unbalance their field enough to give **Alfred** a clean shot. Now shut up, I need to concentrate."

Soon they were near enough to see details on the skin of the destroyer surrounded by the thin, blue aura that marked the edge of its spindizzy shield. Off in the distance, **Alfred's** field suddenly rippled green fire at a dozen points. Washington had seen this before. **Alfred** just released a 'Gravitic torpedo assault' and it was bound directly for them. Confirmation flashed through her mind as she watched pencils of red-sparkling fire stab out from contact points with the CTAC vessel's spindizzy barrier, momentarily disrupting the destroyer's shield.

Winn added her suit jets to those of the scooter, jolting the rock to vector inward. The destroyer abruptly veered towards them and Private Holst's nerves exploded as their direction shifted. His hand flew to the physical retainer belt and pulled the emergency ejection tab. A flash of compressed gas particles ripped his body out from the scooter, sudden acceleration slammed the wind from his lungs and his world went black.

The universe Holst returned to was a wildly spinning starscape. A thought-command set off the attitude gas jets of his suit, slowing then stopping the gyrations of the all-to-close cloudbanks until the massive cloud-wall hovered over him, filling half his universe with malevolent bands of storm clouds.

Screaming in pain, he'd defecated under the impact and the suit's air stank as it noisily worked to scrub the stink and fear pheromones from his recirculated air supply.

Using precious ejection gas reserves, he reoriented until vision centered on a small, distant but bright disk silhouette lying against the swirling storm clouds of the huge planet.

As if on cue, the disk blossomed into a small sunburst, ejecting swirling strings of energized gas that twisted off yellow and green snakes of raw energy, slithering out into the surrounding abyss, briefly licking the Jovian cloud-tops below before vanishing as quickly as they appeared.

Sergeant Winn Washington had rammed her command, the asteroid's moon, into the deadly energy barrier of the CTAC destroyer's field. The field didn't ripple and sputter releasing rainbow colors in the controlled fashion of a spindizzy redirection as was normal for an external matter strike. Weakened by *Alfred's* torp launch, it flared so brightly Holst's eyes registered afterimages despite his suit's blockage of the deadliest emissions.

She did it, I never believed we'd get through their defenses much less penetrate their spindizzy. You goddamn pure-luck bastard. You did it, Sarge.

But Private Holst's elation was short-lived.

Sergeant Winn Washington was gone, vaporized along with the CTAC warbird.

Jensen noticed his suit highlighting a distant, rippling disk of light. Identification of it as **Alfred** came a message packet that appeared in his HiveTab interface as well as a summary of the ejection matter required to push him home and a readout laying out a potential course.

Holst checked his reserves and ran a quick calculation. He didn't have enough propellant to return for he already floated within the deep gravitational pull of the Jovian Gravity Well. Eventually, his orbit decayed to a tumbling descent into the exosphere of the gas giant. Great clouds swirled around him and friction with the planet's gases heated the struggling environmental synapses of his suit. He would die from friction heating long before striking anything solid.

Or so he thought.

The super-compressed gasses of the huge planet were now noticeably constricting his vacuum suit; a device designed to maintain pressure in the absence of any atmosphere rather than protect him from ultrahigh compression. Pressure increased as he descended, the surrounding storm-clouds grew in strength and began violently whipping him in all directions, threatening to beat him to death within his own rapidly compressing suit even as the compression climbed, compacting suit and body. Reducing bones, protoplasm, and muscle to a tiny, super-dense particle of inanimate matter that fell until its mass, now ripped to pure elemental atoms, equaled the buoyancy of the surrounding atmosphere and floated off into oblivion, forever more a part of the Jovian cloud structure.

~~*~*~*~*

Decatur watched the huge CTAC warbird morph into a cloud of high gravitonic energy elementals, radioactive gas, and flotsam. *Alfred* jolted as the resulting gravitic wavefront struck. The blow rattled every joint in the ship's frame and, for a second time, punched a depression into the tops of the clouds far below. Jankin Decatur caught a glimpse of a small piece of the ship's hulk before it too disappeared beneath the swirling storms below, it was all that remained of the mighty warbird most of which had instantly transformed from energized physical elements into sub-electron particles.

However, Decatur's war was far from over, "Laser battery, belay that last order. Redirect fire to Sierra One."

His acting XO called out, "She's not directing fire, Captain."

"She hasn't surrendered. Continue as ...."

Sierra One erupted, splitting into pieces as the captain watched in disbelief. His eyes ran across the battlefield monitors then caught on the section assigned to monitor Washington's nearly forgotten moon they'd stolen and renamed *Robert Rodgers*. The sensor's tracking had merged with that containing the expanding gas cloud of Sierra One. He didn't have to review the recordings to know what had happened.

"Ship's Log, record names of Sergeant ... ah ... change Sergeant to Commander Winn Washington of the *KS Robert Rodgers*, and Corporal Horst Jenkens who gallantly gave their lives today for Kraken."

"Ensign Feign, we still have three CTAC vessels on interception course. Move us to our last known contact coordinates with *Aries* and *Revenge*."

A QuickCode message receipt from his HiveTab delivered a two-line summary of the Wraith squadron's actions and last known location. Jankin Decatur squeezed his eyes closed for a moment, *Ah*

Finagle, you play a fool to the hilt and now you focus on me. I'm deep in enemy territory and you've managed to trick me into spreading my people across a volume the size of half the solar system.

Decatur opened the general command push, "**Aries** and **Revenge**, make your course for home. **Alfred** will follow when we can, do not wait."

"VSF-1, job well done and I'm glad to see you still with us. Next problem before we bring you home, we have three CTAC warbirds inbound from Mars."

"Draw them off then break contact and rendezvous at point Oort Zero," Decatur reluctantly gave the order to meet at their original staging point at the edge of the Oort Cloud, the outermost boundary of Sol System.

"Aye aye, Sir. Operation Swamp Fox then Oort Zero."

Jankin Decatur let escape a rare, quiet chuckle, Kronski's a good officer who needs very little direction if you can accept his dry humor.

Unfortunately, our fighter bay is out of commission so there's no place for them to land and Kronski knows it. It's a suicide run. He also knows that. I've sent them off, like so many others, to their death. How many have died since this operation began? A thousand? Most likely I've started an all-out war with CTAC and on my shoulders alone rests the blame.

PURSUIT

A lesser sun, barely a tenth the brightness of that viewed from Earth, emerged from behind the eternal storm clouds of a planet ten times the diameter of humanity's home. The star's bright rays were visibly distorted by the huge gravitic waves released by this nearby planet humans call 'Jupiter', a ball of super-condensed gas with enough mass to place it on the delicate threshold of igniting its own internal nuclear fires and the potential of becoming a small star.

In the great space surrounding this giant planet, exists the Jovian Gravity Well. A region where waves released by Jupiter, ride strong and smooth with great peaks and deep troughs to carry a ship forward with a strong, smooth, and agile grace.

Further out, forming the greatest extremity of this protective shell, gravity waves thrash in eternal chaos as great rollers from the nearby mighty planet meet the rushing torrent of its sun. A flood already churning from the ethereal contribution of every mass in the solar system, their violent clashes forming sharp crests and abrupt shifts of wavefronts that thrash and swirl into concentrated regions of intense gravitic chop. Compact regions where the solar radiation tears light-bending wisps of gravity into short-lived, deadly streamlets capable of ripping a slipdrive ship apart.

Alvin 'Kronski' Krozel linked to his squadron, "VSF-1, rig for rough flight. Enact uploaded vectored flight pattern K-2. We will swing into that deep trough ahead then warp through what should be an interesting gravitic wisp and emerge within striking distance of the CTAC squadron."

Eleven Wraith fighters, riding within the calm gravitic shadow of the gas-giant, banked headfirst into chaos. Warbirds, normally able to change direction on a dime and return a nickel in change without notice, would now be sailing through a region where flight would be treacherous and mind-jarring.

Wraiths were not creatures of the universe but creations of human concept. Many considered their warbird as not only alive but intelligent and, by the ancient definitions of intelligent life, perhaps even sentient except for one critical element, they were not independent beings. The Wraith warbird was a conscious augmentation of human physiology, which intellectually as well as physically bonded intimately with its pilot.

Nothing binds a human more intimately to the raw power of the universe than a Wraith fighter. All concepts of a flight capsule consisting of exotic metals and plasma-nanoelectronics vanish when a pilot mounts their warbird by diving into the liquid colloidal suspension of NanoBots saturating the cockpit.

As a pilot enters, NanoBots stream into every orifice and pore of the humans' body, passing through cloth, skin, muscle, and veins as easily as an owl soaring amidst the trees of a forest. The pilot's mind rapidly hive-links to the corporeal and neural centers of the Wraith organism. The Wraith pilot's perception of the universe expands as information flows between the junctions of their host's neural control centers and the human mind. Senses, memory, and computational powers melding with those of the Wraith to create a super-entity with enhanced reaction time, vision, intellect, and cognizance.

While protecting Kronski from radiation and the extremes of the surrounding universe, the Wraiths shell surrounding him was no more noticeable than his own body. Traveling through the hard vacuum of space, light-seconds distant from his farthest squad member, he could feel and see every member of his squadron as well as the surrounding gravitic 'sea' of chaotic waves churning the universe ahead.

Lieutenant Jack 'Starman' Shane called in their first contact, "Bogie, bogie, bogie."

"Three warbirds in loose formation with swarm sensors deployed. Signatures confirmed as a fleet destroyer, frigate, and a starsloop."

Flight Leader Krozel linked into Starman's web channel and immediately could see, hear, and 'smell' the CTAC squadron's approach even though they lay physically beyond Jupiter's horizon.

They knew the exact position and composition of the Martian CTAC squadron but couldn't break their Chinese communications encryption. Success lay in the solitary hope their quarry had not sensed his people waiting in ambush.

Captain Decatur's call erupted over his private push, "Alvin, it's worse than I'd hoped. That's not a destroyer, they have a heavy fleet cruiser leading them. It'll swat us out of the way and hardly even notice. I've ordered our ships home, but they aren't far enough out. I must assume that cruiser has seen their passage and, since it is faster than *Aries* and *Revenge*, they will bypass us and launch against them at the Oort Cloud rendezvous.

"Our people have to make it back home and report on all that's going on. We need not be there. Stand by for new orders for a coordinated attack alongside *Alfred*."

Activating his key stations, Decatur called out on his ship's general push, "Rig for hard-vacuum combat. Security, full lockdown.

All noncombat personnel are to be secured in quarters and wearing vacuum-suits."

"Precharge gravitic torpedoes and Crest Runner missiles."

"Launch HiveBots and initiate a counter NanoBot mesh aligning to Jupiter's crescent at three-hundred mega-klicks."

"Wraith leader swing your flight around and prepare to follow course Iota-One as downloaded into your navigation. Wait for my order before initiating final course deviant."

Decatur examined the officers in the CIC as they implemented his directives, *now, let's hope our CTAC friends have sensors no better than ours.*

In the gallery of the CIC Bridge, a puzzled look flashed across Journalist Margo Stoudt's face as their new course appeared courtesy of her HiveTab interface. Lieutenant Strake was standing next to her and noticed, "Keep the faith, Margo. The captain knows what he's doing."

Yet, things were not moving smoothly and Strake himself allowed doubt to cloud his reasoning, *I fear the captain may be cracking under the stress. God knows it's been beating down on him for long enough and we just seem to be sinking deeper and deeper into the shite as we go along.*

This course-change will take us deep into the Jovian stratosphere in a crippled ship that has a breached landing deck and two other levels partially open to the universe. Even if we maintain control of our spindizzy shell, I don't know if it'll withstand Jupiter's tremendous pressures. These ships are designed for travel in a vacuum rather than the intense compressive atmosphere of a gas giant."

Two torpedoes slid from Alfred's tubes, softly stabilizing into a powered orbital drift that would carry them below the broad span of debris-filled space between Io and the Jovian cloud-tops. Moving in stealth with little more than an encapsulating energy sphere to minimize drag against the upper atmosphere and defend against the millions of dust-to-small-moon sized chunks of rock reminiscent of the rings that once were supported by the planet, they swung in a wide arch releasing but a single deviation-pulse that aligned them into a long ballistic orbit on an intercept course with the oncoming CTAC ships, an objective more than four times the distance from the Sun to the Earth.

At zero-point-two-seven AU from target, the torp's fired a directed mist of millions of HiveBots into a boomerang-shaped arc that blossomed into a uniform shield formation ahead of their track moving at nearly four-tenths lightspeed. Traveling in formation, the HiveBots began their attack.

Shimmering curtains of blue, red, and white fire surround the southern pole of Jupiter, a huge natural EM-dynamo, formed by the expulsion of long strands of excited particles into the heavens of the small universe surrounding Flight Leader Krozel. The auroral display was magical, mind-bending as it danced about the polar tip of the gas giant like a liquid crown of will-o'-the-wisp excited gas. A display the Wraith pilot found much too distracting as he pushed the sensor-enhanced sight of his warbird to its limits searching for tell-tales of first –contact, an event he didn't have to strain to notice when it finally blossomed.

It began as a silent but sudden, intense, ruby-colored patch blossoming across a distant region of the sky, sparkling as it expanded against the billions of multicolored, but fixed intensity, distant starry points. The sparkle transformed into a dark-ruby mist, dimming the stars behind it until the glow tinted even the cloud tops of the planetary storms below. There, it rolled and churned for minutes before fading and leaving behind a myriad of churning, rainbow-colored miniature nebulae.

This first sign of conflict surrounding Jupiter arose from the clash of modern-day pickets. CTAC NanoBots, running ahead of the squadron, had just met a force of much larger HiveBots silently waiting in ambush. The colonial HiveBots allowed the NanoBots to advance, penetrating deep into the dispersal perimeter of space they occupied. AI-enhanced HiveBots net-linked, they patiently assigned targets so that not a single enemy NanoBot would be missed. When the time was right, they struck as one, delivering streams of charged particles at targets up to a thousand klicks distant, each designated mark no larger in diameter than the width of a human hair.

The HiveBots struck using charged particles that penetrated the strong atomic forces of the surface barriers surrounding each NanoBot, piercing its electron orbits, disrupting programming, and breaking energy bonds with a characteristic ruby-red release of energy marking each successful strike.

The resulting lightshow saturated **Alfred's** distant CIC Bridge and was followed by an energy front that threw Margo Stoudt into Strake's arms. The ranger enfolded her shoulders, providing a moment of support before releasing her with an unspoken apology.

NanoBot survivors of this first strike were quick to respond, deviating their flight path by grabbing at a passing cosmic ray or changing linkage to an alternate wavefront but their numbers had been greatly reduced. Strake continued as though nothing extraordinary had just occurred, "That flash was our HiveBot picket shield taking out their NanoBots. They just lost their early warning service and now our turn at 'em is coming."

When Lieutenant Strake turned to Margo, he was surprised by the reporter's intense reaction, "Pretty spectacular considering we could probably walk through the middle of that battlefield and not be touched by a single combatant. The picket NanoBots are spread so thin through space it requires special sensors and thousands of cubic kilometers to see their presence but, as we just experienced, their decimation resulted in a total release of energy so great it was able to jolt our ship."

"Mission accomplished. Now our CTAC friends will be partially blind until they rebuild their network, giving our Wraiths a chance."

Distant from **Alfred** by nearly a third of the giant planet's diameter, 'Kronski' Krozel willed his Wraith into a long arc that would carry him nearly out to Io's orbit, taking his squadron in a loop around the still sparkling region of the HiveBot - NanoBot conflict.

Kronski brought up his tactical, it materialized as a semi-transparent mapping resting against the heavens ahead, he willed it to remain in that position relative to his warbird's vector so he could move his eyes without it following his gaze, then called to his wing-leaders, "Ignore the starsloop. Blueblood, you are nearest the frigate so that's your target."

"Starman and Blueblood, bring your flights in. Flank mine and follow my lead. Once we engage, you are free to deviate. Primary objective is the fleet cruiser. If we can disable it, we stand a chance of surviving this."

Meanwhile, **Alfred** had set her course and was now racing onward through Jupiter's swirling cloudbanks when suddenly their universe blossomed dark red. Again, the ship lurched and twisted within an over-strained spindizzy barrier attempting to protect those compartments open to the Jovian atmosphere as well as move the ship forward beneath the planet's deadly storms.

Strake again resorted to one hand on the supporting railing and the other around Margo's shoulders, "Unfortunately, we are now lifting directly from Jupiter's cloud cover and that's just what they expect at this point. Unfortunately, we're the diversion for our Wraiths and we won't disappoint them. There's going to be hell to pay for it but, if our luck holds, all they'll see is **Alfred** coming directly at them."

"By now, our Wraith warbirds should have swung far around and will be coming in from behind the CTAC squadron. If they spot the Wraiths early, then it's a suicide mission the captain has sent them on."

The glow slowly faded and Strake sensed tension growing in the bridge. Despite it, commands and status updates remained calm, clear and the thick, obscuring mist-cover of Jupiter's clouds brightened and began moving past at an increasing rate. The lieutenant was surprised to see Decatur rotate the travel axis of the ship so that the damaged areas now faced forward, placing them under the strongest region of spindizzy protection.

Eventually, the clouds parted to the black expanse of the cosmos ahead. Over it lay a newly created swirling nebula of color. A dark-red mist covering a patch of the distant stars where the NanoBot shield had once existed. Leaving the CTAC squadron barely visible, highlighted by their sensors as three irregular disks of flickering light at a location on the starboard edge of the mist.

A staccato burst of bright flares leaped out from behind Margo's viewpoint towards their target, human-made comets trailing long-bright tails that swerved, swirled, and jinked ahead of deadly blue-white hot points launched into the vacuum ahead to leave a short-lived trail of luminescence from their secondary electron emissions.

"Crest Runner Missiles," Strake said. "They latch onto this planet's huge wave crests and skip from wave-to-wave for a bit, jigging to change their direction of attack, then come around to another tack to complicate enemy defenses and all the while they're accelerating. They're going to be hard to stop but ..."

A blinding white-light flashed from the edge of the red cloud created by an atomic particle release so great that even the ship's AI could dampen it quickly enough to save their eyes from the pain.

Strake continued speaking as he took a handkerchief from his pocket to dab the tears from his eyes, "That's only the first blow. Crest Runners are one of our smartest weapons. They are crafty and work in unison with a goal of destabilizing the target's spindizzy shield, so that subsequent torpedo releases can survive to complete a penetration, that will result in a graviton energy release and hopefully destruction."

Points of light flared out from the image of the CTAC cruiser. An opaque bubble of blue light enveloped the ship, the stars surrounding it blurred and twisted from the bending of light photons by the intense gravitational forces concentrated in the sphere. Then the image solidified and stabilized leaving a faint twisting comet-tail of blue-white light swirling out from its side into space.

Strake lunged. Grabbing the journalist by the arm, he roughly launched her into a crash chair. Physical straps enfolded her as he spun around and into the acceleration couch next to hers, hitting so hard he would have bounced out of it had not its straps secured him.

Their ship jolted like a sauromount that had just stepped on a rabid hypersnake. Pain shot up the lieutenant's left shoulder as **Alfred** lurched beneath a screeching, wailing groan amid the churning, swirled image of the surrounding heavens.

Damage reports were already gathering in bridge display as Captain Decatur regained consciousness. Pain rocked his head as the captain shot a glance to the side where a visual plot detailed the damage. Ensign Feign enunciated the worst of it in slurred phrases passed through swollen lips, "They were guessing and launched in stealth before our missiles struck. Ship's integrity holding but section 'C', decks four to twelve have decompressed. Casualty reports still incoming. Spindizzy barrier weakened by a loss of ship's symmetry but hold...."

Lieutenant Barry Sol overrode the status report, "They have a targeting lock on us. Looks like a frigate missile ... release, release, release. Assault course zero-six-niner point three-two mark three-seven-point niner-niner."

Decatur's command voice cut through the communications chatter, "Ensign Foster, make our course directly at them. Full thrust, no evasion. Collision course with a steady axial spin orthogonal to the thrust vector."

"Forward bearing railguns, short and long banisters, alternate stations reload and fire. I want as much continuous flack down-target as you can throw."

"Captain," Lieutenant Svenson, Acting XO called out. "As forward railguns come about to align on target there will be railgun mounts located above the damaged flight deck. Structural integrity may not hold."

"I'm aware of that XO, but we have little choice. I've begun a forward spin, so they need but hold up for a short time-on-target firing before new emplacements are brought to bear. A bit unconventional but should be an easy maneuver since we are on a fixed course."

Ensign Trumbull broke in, "Section 'C' decks thirteen to sixteen just collapsed. Internal lifepods with a forty-three percent successful initiation. Railguns 'Banister D' have come to bear and are awaiting ...."

"Do not await orders to fire. Fire as you bear, I want them pounding that CTAC cruiser."

"One minute, twenty-three point, ah, two seconds to collision."

"Ion Cannons, fire as you bear."

Alfred began jolting with a regular pulse that reminded Margo Stoudt of the beating of an excited heartbeat with the stars ahead jittering in tempo. She turned to the ranger strapped securely in the seat next to her but didn't have to ask the question.

"We've just gone supralight on the attack plus the ship is spinning to bring batteries to bear on the enemy and that adds to the perceived 'jitter'. Ms. Stoudt, you may wish to prepare yourself. I suspect the captain intends to ram the cruiser at high velocity."

Decatur's voice ripped across the bridge like the funeral knell of cathedral bells, "Program all remaining Hive-Mines, behavioral command 'active search and destroy, with maximum release'. If we don't make it, I want to make sure they follow us to hell."

"All hands, rig for collision."

Decatur managed to hear someone or something screaming as he passed into oblivion.

Kronski brought his wing around, rapidly coming up aft of the small starsloop, "Lieutenant Purry, orders are not to engage the sloop, but they apparently haven't spotted us. Would be impolite to not leave a calling card, you're closest. Mind you, don't waste a second's time in gabbing as you pass."

Marion Purry's thoughts had been running along this same line. He'd prepared the munition but had hesitated to use it because of orders and now, waiting the one-point-seven minutes to calculated release of the package was as bad as waiting to open a present on Michaelmas morning. The time finally passed and, as a last-second afterthought, almost gleefully he initiated an event-following recorder and released it with the pod.

His focus immediately returned to business and the much deadlier frigate that lay in the distance ahead.

The pod dropped below supralight on a pre-programmed vector using the smallest, now nearly archaic, wavedrive technology available to maintain an excited sub-electron particle state while still maintaining speed and course. Completely stealth in flight, it floated silently on a wave-crest without even a hint of an ion bloom or electron fluorescence trail.

As it neared ten light-seconds of its target, its outer casing split releasing four iridescent munition bubbles that aligned into a linear-string attack formation.

At the last half-second of flight, nearly the distance from the Earth to its moon, the first munition-bubble burst and ejected a high-density slug that exploded as it lost the wavedrive's shield, its mass expanding beneath uneven relativistic forces that instantly dragged it further below lightspeed. High energy and now high mass relativistically enhanced pebbles fractured into existence in less than a nanosecond, impacting the forward outer bulkhead quarter of the sloop's slipstream spindizzy field with their released munition's mass still expanding in a manner predicted by Einstein himself.

The starsloop's shields flared through a rainbow of released-energy particle emissions that churned out-of-control and, in the next instant, the three remaining munitions rammed their excited-graviton fields into the weakened defense field of the craft.

In much less than the blink of an eye, tons of physical material, once composing a small warbird and its crew, transformed into deadly radiation that carried forward to slap aside Purdy's Wraith with a glancing blow that shut down all systems and dropped the warbird out of supralight, rendering it and its pilot unconscious.

The energy flare went on, bathing the aft sections of the CTAC frigate. Further on, greatly diminished in intensity, it struck the CTAC cruiser, and briefly overloaded the ship's external sensors.

The cruiser suddenly flared, its spindizzy field blazing uncontrollably in aurora-like waves that rolled across it like water being carried in a bucket. The apparition amazed Flight Leader Krozel, he wasn't sure what just happened but didn't waste a nanosecond, "Don't worry about what happened, they copped a load and are confused. Fire on the big lady now, engage, engage, engage."

Three wings of Wraith fighters swung into their preplanned attacks.

Krozel and his wingmen swung in abaft the CTAC ship, "Still no visible response from the objective. Releasing graviton torpedoes, foxfire, and foxfire bursts."

A flight of four torps dropped out of Krozel's spindizzy field, their own wavedrive field smoothly enveloping them as they emerged to spin off ahead, linking hard and close-hauled to the heavy gravitic rollers emerging from Jupiter. Confronting the enemy ship in a smooth line-of-battle, they fired active-sabot charges into the already wildly fluctuating spindizzy field of the cruiser, raking the weakened ship from stern to stem.

The entire warbird visibly shuddered, its spindizzy field flared wild, flashing, brightly   back down the ionization path of the torpedoes that had just struck it. Then four other flights of torpedoes fired in mass, coming up the ship's flank and firing chafe that drilled in, locally overloading the protective barrier of the field just as their drive-enabled sabot charges struck the bare surface of the wounded ship.

Of the thirty-two torpedoes fired, three managed a complete penetration. A fraction of a picosecond passed as a new circularly polarized magnetic field invaded the bowels of the massive warbird. The new field immediately spread within, energizing every sub-electron particle in the vessel. However, the ship was already under a slipstream drive and its graviton particles were already energized, so the newly injected energy ripped apart every electron in the ship including all cargo and crew, transforming molecules, atoms, and electrons into subelectron particles and pure raw energy.

The resulting photon release cast shadows of the distant moons of Neptune onto that planet's upper clouds. In a bit over eight seconds, the visible photon component of the wave struck the Earth, flaring as a man-made supernova briefly visible in the daytime sky and disrupting those few archaic EM entertainment broadcasts as were then in fashion.

There was no debris to mark the cruiser's former location except for one darkened Wraith fighter currently spinning out of control in Jupiter orbit.

The CTAC frigate was just recovering, its spindizzy field unstable but improving by the second. Flight Leader Krozel was analyzing the health of the enemy ship and was preparing a launch when he detected a transmission easily identified as a broadband request for assistance. He linked into the enemy ship's public wavelength and, with unexpected ease, drew up status and health reports. They had sustained damage and extensive casualties. The ship's life support was weak and their advanced systems and AI were both down.

Krozel remained under stealth discipline but the ship below had just issued an all-bands request for assistance. His decision was swift, and he was careful to strip all metadata and sourcing from his call, "Calling vessel in distress. Do you require life-support assistance?"

The answer returned immediately. Krozel could see a damaged CIC center with a spacer sporting a cap of pharmacy gel over a section of his head. The Wraith pilot knew the spacer could not see nor scan any identifying information as the image replied, Kronski's AI handled the translations, "We've been attacked. Requesting assistance."

Kronski smiled as he answered, "As we see it, you are casualties of a conflict you started. Now, do you have life support?"

"You, you are the ones who attacked us. You now play with us before committing murder."

"We have no intention of continuing hostilities, unless you choose otherwise. Surrender and we may be able to call in assistance."

"No, we do not yield. Do what you must."

"VSF-1," A vision of **Alfred**'s CIC Bridge materialized, they too had obviously taken damage. Captain Decatur appeared disheveled and favoring his right shoulder as he addressed the flight leader. "Do not respond. Objective achieved. We gain nothing by destroying them. They'll survive long enough for help to arrive. Return and …"

Decatur turned to look back across the bridge and said something that was not transmitted to Kronski then returned his attention, "Sensors report you are missing three warbirds. Two were lost when your objective exploded. The third is dead and drifting in the ether at the coordinates I've just transmitted."

"Rendezvous with the others at point Oort Zero and we'll attempt a pickup. Do not attempt to land, the flight deck is disabled. We are working on a solution."

"You must do this quickly, Jupiter's gonna be swarming with CTAC."

LONG WAY HOME

Captain Jankin Decatur was in a foul mood. "Ensign Feign, locate Captain Hopewell. The captain is not responding to my hails." Both bridges, Main and CIC, were a pox-laden mess with only half their systems operational.

Alfred and its Wraith fighter screen limped back at half-speed to the rendezvous at the outer edge of the Oort cloud only to discover the remainder of their squadron was not on station. Even worse, they were not responding to hails or even HiveTab communication pings.

The damage to his flight deck was too great for a powered landing and Decatur had briefly considered abandoning the Wraiths for a pilot-only pickup before proceeding onward. He neared the point decision to scuttle them but decided against it. Such an action would have been an immersion into hell itself as they attempted to extract the violently objecting pilots.

Alfred's rangers resorted to the arduous task of towing the surviving Wraiths back into an airless flight deck, one-by-one, using their Slug Shot ship-to-ship assault tubes. Even so, the screams of indignant objection raised by the Wraiths added to their humiliation and were only surpassed by the dirty temperament of their pilots.

Alfred lost nearly a third of its habitable space in the encounter and an even greater percentage of climate-controlled stowage. Its AI was reduced to the level of an idiot savant able to perform only the most fundamental command strings and totally incapable of insight or anticipatory actions. Food stores were being regenerated and the atmospherics techs had yet to stabilize microclimate fluctuations from chamber to chamber.

Ensign Litel's high voice lilted across the bridge, "Captain, no reply from Captain Hopewell but I have physical and sensor confirmation of both *Aries* and *Revenge*. They are airlock bound and dead in deep space within a single slipdrive field envelopment. Their position does not indicate a vectored attempt to return to Kraken or any other known destination. Physical damage evaluation suggests *Revenge* may have rammed *Aries*."

"I am not able to detect any external communication and long-range internal snoops are blocked by their field."

Decatur settled back in his command seat beneath a throbbing headache. *Obviously, something is wrong. Harriett had reported earlier on communications difficulties but this smacks of something more sinister.*

The situation can only deteriorate if I hesitate.

"Set a course at best speed for our sister ships. We most likely have a problem awaiting our arrival on site. I want all available weapons up to active-status and ready, this is our first priority.

"Major Walters, we need a Slug Shot insertion, how soon can you be ready."

Calculating as he replied, Walters returned, "Half of our remaining inventory is in stowage for return to port, that puts us at seven units locked and loaded for launch in forty minutes unless we require more than man-serviced weapons."

"Forty minutes," Decatur mumbled as he calculated options, which were few. "Situation involves a problem with both our sister ships. They are unresponsive and I suspect Captain Hopewell is either dead or dealing with internal difficulties."

"You are to initiate a boarding effort with most of your rangers focused on *Aries*. If anyone is watching, they know we are coming so stealth is not a consideration. Time is."

"A summary packet is coming your way. You are free to use your own initiative for final deployment after my review. I'll let you know of any changes in the situation."

Lieutenant Travis Strake received the recall to launch bay as he was on his way cross-ship to ranger country. Having come from the observation gallery, he knew something of the situation and could guess the rest.

"Sergeant Jaeger," he called ahead to his Top. "Hot Recall. Wake 'em up and make ready for vacuum insertion, stat. The major thinks we have mutiny on our hands."

He quick-walked down the moving central WebWay to the outer ladders of the launch bay. The bay remained under partial vacuum and cursed having to don a pre-launch vacuum suit from airlock supplies and the precious minutes stolen from him. Most of his platoon was already on deck and drawing weaponry. Vapors filled the bay, dissipating unnaturally fast in the partial vacuum, it was a waste of valuable supplies, but this was a 'Hot Recall', time was critical still a ranger took the time to do it right.

An update from the major flooded into his HiveTab and Strake ran an immediate review before passing it on to his top sergeant, "Confirmed, this is a mutiny fired mix-up. It's going to be dirty but don't let your people get trigger-happy. Situation is unconfirmed but we suspect factions of the prisoners taken onboard may be attempting to secure the *Aries* and are currently engaged with *Revenge* personnel. Fighting is most likely centered in *Aries* but may have spread back to *Revenge*.

"Be on your toes. Any uniformed combatant may be hostile. Pacify all encountered assuming they are hostile but minimize casualties. We'll sort 'em out afterward."

Lieutenant Travis Strake wasn't a bit happy about the situation.

Confusion reigns. Old Finagle's dancing with joy today and we're running right into his latest cluster-jack. This is dirty as hell, and just the type of situation that gets rangers killed.

The landing bay was a hive of activity despite it being under partial vacuum. Most of the damaged structures were repaired or stabilized but the portal to the universe, that used to be a nice uniform rectangle with blast doors, was now a gaping maw that even the ship's field could not seal tight enough to hold atmosphere.

Chief Gleason was on station at one of the slug launchers that had miraculously survived the onslaught. Despite the rigors of the last few days, his people managed to suit-up under the worst of conditions and were already queued, taking their proper positions on Slug-Shots cues.

"Morning Chief, I see you have loading well in hand as usual."

"'Morning' Sir?" The CPO didn't bother to look up at the lieutenant. "Didn't realize it was morning; hadn't even thought about the time of day for Finagle knows how long."

"The guys are tired, Sir, and tired makes one careless. Careless makes ya dead."

Strake knew this was the chief's indirect way of telling him to be cautious, "Thank you for your concern, Chief. Let's plan on sitting down for a nice quiet steak and beer when this is through, on me, of course."

"I'd like that, Lieutenant."

"Here ya go, this coffins got your name on it. Come on, I'll help ya strap in."

Strake was already reviewing his sit-rep as the Slug's door sealed. Everything around him seemed to bang or ring, each report just another assault on over-tired nerves. He felt the first rough spin as the Slug rotated to load in the next ranger, *that wasn't supposed to happen. I've never felt a slug launch rotation before.*

Calm down, ranger. Breath deep and slow. Your tired and been keyed up for way too long.

A call from Major Walters and the countdown began. Sudden inaction and the short but monotonous countdown nearly put him to sleep. His eyes closed for a moment. Then the first jolt as Alpha squad launched, followed by a lurch and sudden stop as the next squad chambered into the jettison catapult.

Hard jolts, regular as clockwork. One followed the other as ….

Strake's world lurched. Unexpected weightlessness twisted his stomach as his eyes opened in near panic. Sheer willpower forced him to assess his situation.

There, there. You fell off to sleep, all is normal. Control your breathing and get down to business.

He ran a quick-scan and was amazed. The captain had deployed them within hailing distance of their objective. All but one of his Slug Shots were performing. For now, that failure wasn't his concern. Gleason would pick 'em up.

Their Slug Shot maneuvered in under its own control, taking a moment to sample, match its field then settled in to slowly penetrate their objective's spindizzy shield.

The slug's skin dissolved and they exited into hard vacuum. Moving swiftly on their bellies, taking great care to hold the filament bundles close to the metal surface they slid across the hull, completing assembly within a few seconds. He waited until his platoon signaled the 'all-ready', then tungsten nettings activated a shunt field that drew in the ship's own gravitonic field, sinking activated-energy tungsten ions into the metal structure.

Fire met the first two rangers inboard. A corporal unloaded a flash-bang and followed its blast into the ship, "Flexwrap 'em all, even if they aren't moving. The rest of you, follow me."

If they fired first, you returned fire. Dead and wounded lay strewn down the corridor. Crossfire at an intersection erupted then abruptly stopped.

"Identify yourself," echoed from an unsuited figure at the end of the corridor.

"Rangers, **Alfred** delivery." The corporal replied then copped a look back towards Strake. Strake didn't like the informality but flicked a finger to motion the non-com on.

"**Aries** crew here. We'll hold fire, proceed."

"Glad to see you guys. Ah, sorry Lieutenant, didn't notice you there. This section's clear except for a pocket in ..."

"Yeah, we dropped right in on them. Pocket's neutralized. Go on."

"Good news. Most of the resistance is holed up in storage bay two, they knew that was transport stowage. There's a mixed bag of friendlies and hostiles goin' at it in there and ..."

A sudden 'whomp' rang through the ship's frame. The corporal saw the spacer obviously picking up a crew only HiveTab transmission that he couldn't receive. Relief flooded across the spacer's face as he reported, "You rangers don't fool around. There's goin' ta be a lot of guys with headaches down there, but that jolt was them taking out the bay. Now it's a matter of revivin' 'em and sortin' out da good, bad, and just plain ugly."

~~*~*~*~*

Less than an hour later, Captain Jankin Decatur stepped off the shuttle and walked a short way across the deck to an already open airtight door and entered without announcement. Like a targeting laser scanning a battlefield, Jankin Decatur's eyes ranged over the holding bay on the **Aries**.

There's a lot of people hurting in here. Better that than dead, I guess. These hostiles can count themselves lucky that there were friendlies in the mix. Where the cust is that journalist when you need him? Ah, yes ...

"Specialist, that man there; the one with the equipment racked to his uniform. Revive him first. As soon as he's coherent bring him to me and for Finagle's sake, give him a shot or something so he can speak clearly. I'm in no mood to waste time."

"Oh, and grab his equipment satchel, treat it like it was your own. It's your skin if anything happens to the contents."

Groans and whimpers filled the bay as he surveyed their handiwork. It was ghastly, smelling of discharged bowels and urine. He needed to find Lieutenant Nauman, the commander in charge of this pile of junk and human flotsam.

A tick mark appeared against the far bulkhead courtesy of his HiveTab. He smiled for small blessings; someone must have located the lieutenant and updated the system. He walked gingerly, passing over both silent and now moaning bodies when he noticed a feminine figure moving to intercept his path.

"Ms. Stoudt, this is no place for you. You should have remained on our bridge. How did you manage to ... oh, never mind. Belay the question."

"Captain, what happened? Why ..."

"Ms. Stoudt, we are short on time and lie here nearly defenseless even though we are now near Kraken. Please limit yourself to observations if you wish to remain. You will be updated in due time."

"Lieutenant Nauman, you seem a bit the worse for wear if that Flavian-goose egg on your head is any sign of your distress. Are you well enough to tell me just what the hell is going on here?"

"Captain, I ..."

"Scottie, there's no need for courtesies now. Sit down man, and report."

"It started here in the holding bay, Sir. Elements of the prisoners managed to conspire and overcome the guards. I suspect the gooks are a mixed bag of CTAC, NAU, and even some colonials. Sorting them out is not going to be easy."

"They made a bee-line for the bridge and, being a CTAC ship, somehow managed to open the blast doors. Took us completely by surprise and didn't take any pains to avoid bloodshed."

"Our rangers counter-attacked and Commander Hopewell ..."

Decatur's calm voice corrected the pilot, "Captain Hopewell for now, fleet courtesy Lieutenant."

"Aye aye, Sir. Captain Hopewell immediately rammed and boarded. I have no idea how she responded so quickly."

"Things were nip-and-tuck for a while and at that point, my world went black. I assume your rangers settled the outcome."

Mark Mason had just come over, obviously still a bit uneven on his feet. The corporal and two spacers followed behind with the journalist's equipment.

"Mr. Mason, I trust you were not too badly treated. I never thought I'd have to say this but, were you recording during the mutiny?"

"Yes, sir. Between my data streams and those of the ship, you should be able to identify those responsible and those simply caught up in the action."

"Thank you for your professionalism, Mr. Mason. Once again, I'm glad you came along."

"Corporal, if the medics have completed their work on him, escort Mr. Mason and his equipment into the captain's meeting room and gather Ms. Stoudt on your way. I'm sure she'll be interested. If she isn't, then ask her forcefully but gently."

Port Lagrange

Early 2180 C.E.
Civilian Outer Orbital Station- L2, Kraken

Kraken was a rich world boasting a major port whose size and shipping volume rivaled the greatest seaside and orbital harbors of Earth. The port resided at Kraken's Lagrange-2 point located in high synchronous orbit, called simply 'L2'.

L2 itself was much more than a starship wayport and holding area.

The station had grown famous for its amazing vistas, the breathtakingly beautiful colors of the seas and continents of the jewel-like 'garden planet' it orbited. When darkness fell, great natural displays covered the skies of the world 'below'; grandiose multicolored, exhibitions courtesy of the unique mix of metal-rich meteors which surrounded both port and planet, artifacts of their nearby heavy-metal moon. As a result, L2 quickly became a favored destination for travelers and tourists, flocking to its colorful domed resorts boasting of zero-grav swimming parks, swirling air-beaches and palatial multi-grav sports arenas that dotted the port's circumferential exterior extremities.

So, it happened that the many vacationers and business executives within these resorts were the first to observe the apparition. There was no broadcasted warning of her coming for she traveled in ethereal stealth. As she approached, all eyes focused on the strange, almost frightening visage of a ship emanating a nebulous light show of colors and long-tendrilled emissions rivaling the evening meteor display currently in progress on the mother planet far below.

Iridescent waves of raw energy snaked out ahead of the ship only to fall back upon themselves before recoiling for a launch into another forward lunge evoking greater spectator exclamations. These waves of pure energy washed across the star-pocked but airless sky, bearing the ship ahead like multicolored tentacles dragging some fluorescent animal across black desert sands.

Spacers in the crowd saw little beauty in the apparition, but recognized her as a slipdrive warbird, or perhaps the ghostly hulk of such a vessel with its drive fields poorly tuned and possibly distended. As the phantom drew in, fleet veterans were able to make out how badly she'd been scorched and battered with entire sections ripped open and left laid bare to the universe. Her spindizzy barrier was chaotic and fluctuating rather than the healthy, uniform blue-white aura that should have enveloped the vessel. She was a ship obviously incapable of controlled, much less interstellar, travel. Yet, there she passed, now risking a far spread of a barely contained spindizzy shield to tack to an erratic but controlled course down the harbor's inbound road.

Spacer disbelief turned to open mouth amazement as a second phantom materialized followed by a third, arriving up-tail as though in tight astral formation.

The bizarre convoy smartly laid into dockage, shutting down their fields in unison as if on command. Laymen sighed in disappointment of its end and returned to their holidays but experienced spacers raced cross-port to the harbormaster's office for news, while harboring the deepest feelings of foreboding.

A launch flaunting a captain's ensign emerged from the third, smallest vessel, moving with obvious intent to the commandant's pier where it deftly locked to the portal tube. Captain Jankin Decatur, his black dress uniform setting off the golden captain's piping along shoulders, sleeves, and pant-leg, disembarked with a long, confident stride. Saluted the flag, signed into office, then took the lift to an all too familiar waiting room.

Jankin Decatur knew it was over and he was glad for he carried the burden of every life lost, all because of his incompetence. This was indeed a rare occasion for he was uncharacteristically unsure of how to proceed for, unlike the clear-cut duties of command, this promised to be a meeting steeped in politics as well as personal criticism to match his own repertoire of self-accusations.

How do I tell the board I stretched ... no, be frank, I broke orders? I abandoned the charges of my convoy to take off on a wild chase resulting in significant damage to my ship with such high cost to both crew and materials. How do I reconcile the souls lost on my watch? Colonial, NAU, and CTAC lives terminated, all victims in an undeclared private war of my personal initiation?

His briefcase rested heavy on his lap. The tale lay here in its matrices, complete logs from his ship and the two vessels they'd taken intact. Decatur knew the best he could hope would be Kraken Courts Martial while somehow avoiding extradition to Earth for his sins.

Time passed slowly. After a period of self-flagellation, he linked his HiveTab to the **Aries** matrix and began another review. This occupied another forty-three minutes before the compartment's door opened. Decatur, noticing the commodore's uniform and staff braid, and snapped to attention. The commander greeted him icily, "You've caused quite a stir, Captain. The briefcase, if you please."

He turned to leave. Decatur ventured a question, thinking he couldn't make matters worse, "Commodore, am I to follow?"

The commodore let out a short chuckle, "No just sit tight until called upon. In all candor, Captain, we don't know what to do with you."

Time passed slowly. He grew anxious, keenly aware of the purgatory his people must be experiencing as they also waited.

Eventually, a missive arrived reading,

APPOINTMENT
TIME: SIXTEEN FORTY-THREE HOURS, LOCAL
PLACE: RDML SINC FLEET STUDY

Decatur figured he was in it deep if they were putting him up before a rear admiral of the fleet. He grabbed his cap and set off, he had ten minutes to travel to the opposite end of the port and lift a hundred twenty-one decks.

Knowing the distance required, the decision materialized characteristically quick for the young captain. It was going to strain his credit account, but he couldn't afford to be late for this appointment. Walking quickly out onto the banister plaza, he hailed a helo. The pilot confirmed his destination and docked the credits most painfully before proceeding. They climbed rapidly until he could see his ships still at tether, now joined by a medical barque. There would be no traffic in or out, no passing of the security cordon now forming about them. They were all under quarantine.

He also took note of three port tugs bringing in phased projectors, an unheard-of precaution. In a few minutes, no one would be able to see or sense his ships sitting there.

He briefly wondered how security would handle all the personal WaveCap recordings taken by tourists during their arrival.

The helo lifted across central port, between gleaming towers, direct to an interior balcony pad where he literally skipped off-board.

His HiveTab directed him down soft-floor corridors lined with the smooth, sleek images of slipdrive ships on the bulkhead walldisplays intermixed with visions of the stunning vistas common to the station and finally to a wooden door, elegant in its simplicity. Mounted on it was a bubble memory display reading, '**RDML John Bastian**'.

The name ripped through Decatur's thoughts as he entered,

Jack Bastian is now a rear admiral? It's barely been two months since I left port and good-old Stone Bastian COO is no longer a civilian but now a Rear Admiral sitting at the top of my own chain of command. How many hats does the old man wear? Will wonders never cease?

Just how could things get any worse?

All had changed yet little was different. The office was dark, files and folders lay strewn through the display volume of an ornate desk positioned off to the side of a short conference table. Bastian didn't look up to acknowledge Decatur's presence as he puffed away on a vapored cigar. The cigar bobbed as the old man grumbled a command, "Sit. Sit down captain."

Decatur placed himself in the wooden chair immediately before the desk. That got the rear admiral's attention, bringing forth a sigh and another low rumble that rattled the office walls, "How in hell do you plan to attend a conference sitting in that chair? Must I hold your hand, Captain? Sit at the table, the table. I'll be with you shortly."

Decatur flushed and rose, taking the next-nearest seat of the four possible. The admiral was not going to be able to yell at him for taking the first seat, the one he would obviously occupy.

Decatur nearly jumped when Admiral Bastian's graveled voice echoed off the bulkhead, "You are making a habit of this, son. We will speak to it later. For now, I wanted you to myself for a bit before I expose you to the wolves."

A few eternal moments of huffed silence followed.

Eyebrows rose in surprise, the admiral groused, "Roughly one point eighty-seven billion thalers, um … yes."

"Per ship mind you. Of course, the second CTAC warship might be a bit dated but still …"

A few more undecipherable comments, then finally, "I've spent the past hours reviewing the personal and ship's logs. You apparently don't know when to stop and …"

Bastian stopped, fire in his eyes drilling into the captain. Decatur twitched; you could hear his jaws clamp shut, biting back the noticed objection that lay unspoken but dangerously on the tip of his tongue.

"Good, you're learning … but I see it's a damned slow process."

"Ah-Hummph …where was I?... Yes. Captain, you don't know when to stop. You seem to charge forward where any sane commander would have withdrawn … and all the damn fools followed you with lust."

"We've barely begun the tally. You've brought in such a mixed bag of garbage and jewels, it'll take us weeks to decide who is friendly, who may be honest NAU but unsympathetic to our cause, and who's an outright enemy."

"You sir, are anathema to any sane service. What they at one time labeled as a 'loose cannon'."

Decatur could barely restrain himself, but self-control triumphed momentarily.

Another few eternal moments passed, interrupted occasionally by a sudden twitch of the cigar and a more felt-than-heard grumble, "But … you … are my loose cannon."

Bastian finally lifted his head, drilling focused attention onto the captain, "Now, I want you quiet and still. This isn't the same as when you and I were simple merchants and before you waste my time asking, I was recalled to active duty just like you. It's just somebody's perverse sense of humor that you landed in my basket and I'm making it my business to see they regret that decision."

"Do not react no matter what you hear, keep your thoughts and body-language to yourself if you value your neck. Do not say a word, unless I, and only I, specifically direct you to speak."

The stare lingered until he asked, "Am I understood?"

Captain Decatur simply nodded his head, the motion evoked a rare chuckle from the admiral as the ancient, scarred officer softly grumbled, "Good, good."

"They are coming. Sit up straight, dammit. Remember, all you see and hear stays in this room."

The far section of the office blurred, purely a warning sign for any faint of heart. As if it were a receding wave, the blur-interface slowly receded, revealing in its wake an extending virtual continuation of the conference table that eventually stopped with the eleventh new attendee, a full admiral, materializing at its far foot.

Decatur's heartbeat raced. He had to concentrate to conceal the realization that even the faintest hope of survival was gone. He'd heard rumors of them but never believed the fabled 'Twelve Apostles of State' existed.

Most were mixed-service officers with four additional in civilian dress. His eyes ratcheted across their faces, he nearly lost all composure as he recognized his 'friend', Commissioner Alexander Hollen.

Next to the commissioner, leaning close in slouched conversation sat another familiar face, the notorious John Bucker.

Bastian began in an uncharacteristically clear voice that carried the room, "Good evening, I realize this was short notice, but time is critical."

Two admirals stared. Their frowning eyes had been lock-focused on Decatur since materialization. Hollen sat stone-faced, withholding even a glance of greeting as he listened half-heartedly to Bucker.

Bastian grumbled, "Mr. Bucker, we are in session."

Bucker immediately stopped. Looking askance at the rear admiral, he slouched back into his armchair thus yielding to Bastian, "Good. Keep in mind, this incident is a bit more than we allowed for and …"

"Incident?" The admiral sitting next to Bastian rode over the rear admiral, "John, you are trivializing a military assault on a sol-system military base? How can …"

A man down-table, in civilian garb, slammed his fist on the table-top; Decatur was astounded to feel his own section vibrate under the impact, "Jennifer, you voted for this. Good grief woman, you're in the military, grow a few. Given our situation, did you really believe the expedition would not incur military action?"

"Besides, the worst of it took place on Mars. They never even approached Earth's neutral zones."

"They attacked an NAU starbase." Was the nearly shouted retort.

"No," replied a ranger three-star at the far end. "There was no direct contact. Their near-pass smartly drew NAU assets into the confrontation but Decatur had already withdrawn from the theatre."

"What of the actual cost?" Bucker obviously wanted to inject his two cents. "Our newly remodeled ship is ripped to a slagheap and he returns with two hulks in even sadder shape. I'll take all three but only because I previously offered. It will be a loss, mind you, so don't expect to get much at auction. Just leave them as …"

Alexander Hollen lifted his hand. The action was enough to stop Bucker and his follow-up insured that strain of argument was ended, "John, we well know the worth of the prizes. You aren't getting them. They are fleet assets and that includes the *Alfred*."

The admiral next to Decatur took advantage of the short but pregnant silence that followed, "This act places us into direct confrontation. You think things are bad now …"

"Enough," Bastian's commanding roar again silenced the conference, "I didn't anticipate having to remind you of our sworn commitment. We pledged our lives, our honor, and our fortunes to see this through be it resolution or revolution."

"It begins. Decatur followed what opportunities arose, unlike others who have simply been playing military escort for our commercial interests."

"At last count," His eyes hazed over for a second as he updated his memory. "The captain and his people, many of whom gave their lives in the endeavor, returned one thousand seven hundred thirty-two Kraken citizens and a yet undetermined number of Jasper colonials."

"The number rescued will increase as we exchange NAU ex-prisoners for Kraken citizens."

A voice replied, "Yes, but how many lost their lives …"

Bucker chimed in, "… and at what cost?"

"Hmm, I have a question," A lady in a formal business suit obviously wanted to make a statement. Surprisingly, the simple clearance-of-throat was enough to silence the discussion. She continued, taking no note of the other's deference, "John, I don't understand. We're going to return NAU citizens to their CTAC captors? How can we condone such an option even if we do recover a few of our people held captive?"

"Senator, I apologize for not clarifying. We intend to exchange NAU ex-prisoners back to their homeland, not CTAC authorities. In return, we will receive colonial spacers, we have learned thanks to the captain, that are being held in NAU confinement. We've held our silence for too long. These are our citizens, forcibly taken from our ships and incarcerated without trial, their only crime being a refusal to sign on as NAU spacers."

"The NAU has never admitted to the incarceration of our people, Admiral."

Bastian replied, "Many such political fictions are rapidly falling by the wayside, Adely. Initial processing of the matrices uncovered more than enough hard evidence. All thanks to Captain Decatur, I again remind you."

"I expect an announcement to your constituents detailing the rescue of so many fellow citizens should be a bright feather in your cap."

"Except when I give them the toll of those killed by his actions," she replied.

"Yes, and that can also work in our favor as you turn their anger against CTAC aggression, they bear the fault for abduction and the NAU is guilty of failing to protect and return them home."

The admiral residing next to Decatur ruffled through a few screens the captain couldn't see before speaking, "I have of course noticed Captain Decatur seated next to me. As you so forcefully reminded us, he is an intelligence asset? When will I be allowed direct access?"

"I also note he is present at a closed meeting. Rather a bit unusual, wouldn't you think? Just what are your intentions?"

Bastian shifted his stare to his captain. Decatur didn't flutter an eyelash. The rear admiral then shifted targeting to the full admiral awaiting his reply, "Now perhaps is the proper time to settle this."

Turning his glare to the entirety, "What say you? I want your positions clear, upfront, and on record. We have more than enough problems without backroom brawls emerging in days to come."

"Captain Decatur aggressively followed orders that came directly from this group. This is what we needed. This is what we wanted. We need more people like him."

The admiral across the table spoke, "NAU and Kraken citizens died because of him. We are now in direct conflict with CTAC. They are a superpower, for God's sake."

Another voice, "All of which we discussed at our last meeting."

"Ah-Hummph," Bastian rumbled as silence again descended. "This is as I feared. If we do not unify, do not firmly support his actions when we leave this meeting, then we lie to ourselves most dangerously. It screams that we may not really have the heart for this."

"Perhaps we lack the stomach; much less deserve the right of becoming a free and independent world."

The fires of conviction edged his voice, "Kraken will shrivel and die. Starved, choked out of existence by our own dotard motherland and mark my words, history will place blame for it on the name of every head present at this table."

"I warn you, if we back down now then we are ..." He hesitated, then, more softly, "... we are lost."

Another pregnant, silent pause filled the room followed by the bull's continued roar, "Need I make this clearer?" His black eyes drilled directly into the admiral next to Decatur, "We are committed, Jennifer, and if I don't have your full support then ... we will fail. Do not kid yourself. This goes far beyond financial well-being. You, I, everyone at this table will ... not ... survive."

"Read NAU history, it repeats itself. Ominous words, that were spoken by an old NAU founding father of centuries past named

Franklin, return in our time to drape heavily about our shoulders, 'We must, indeed, all hang together or, most assuredly, we shall all hang separately.'"

Bastian retreated into unchallenged silence. A moment passed, "No discussion? Then we go on record, vote your conscience."

A vote was taken, and assent was universal, although some votes came with obvious reservation.

"Good. If there's no more business, I propose we adjourn and return to our duties."

Jack Bastian watched silently, letting the office darken as the meeting dissolved. Conference attendees dissipated one-by-one, all except for one whose image shifted to sit across from Captain Decatur.

Alexander Hollen broke the spell, "I wish to extend my personal thanks to Captain Decatur."

"There is also a matter of intelligence we need to discuss, and it derives directly from his work. Would it be appropriate to touch on it with him still present?"

"Our captain is in this up to his waxy ears," Bastian was obviously returning to his daily persona. "We'll be seeing more of him in the future. Can't seem to avoid the man. Proceed."

Hollen wasn't about to let unsettled interests fade, "About the memory matrix recovered from the CTAC base and NAU Captain Jensen, an obvious operative of their intelligence. We don't need Jensen to decipher the matrix, but I believe he could be an asset. I'd like to attempt to turn him to our side. Ah, ... and for that I would require the services of Captain Decatur."

Bastian settled back into his seat, eyes drilling into the captain, then returned erect, "Our captain is going to be busy. I leave it up to him. If he can see the benefit of his services, then I will loan him to you."

"Occasionally, mind you. Please do not abuse the privilege."

Hollen seemed satisfied with the arrangement but Decatur for the first time showed deep emotion and was obviously uncomfortable voicing the request, "May I be allowed to speak now, Admiral?"

Bastian registered surprise then recalled his strict order, "Yes, of course."

Decatur began with obvious reluctance, "Both of you have admitted to knowledge of my personal history before coming to Kraken. If you recall, the incident that ended that segment of my life, and nearly cost me my life, involved a ship's mutiny. At that time, I discovered the mutiny was instigated by a man whose name has again come to my attention."

"From what I have experienced today, I must ask if you are also behind his mutiny and treason. Are you playing me the fool?"

Bastian practically sputtered his reply, "Treason? Why, we are all involved in treason at this point but not in such a manner."

"Under what evidence do you bring these accusations before us?"

Decatur looked to Hollen. The man showed no outward response beyond a sly smile. Turning to Bastian, the captain continued, "You will recall that during the recapture of the **CSS Grimes** we discovered Captain Esperanza was shipping Kraken weaponry and other contraband to CTAC. By her own admission, she confirmed her guilt and mentioned that the shipments to CTAC were sanctioned by someone high in Kraken government circles."

"Alex mentioned that the original CTAC capture of Jeremy's ship was orchestrated by an organization of the same name voiced by Esperanza. Finally, in the caves of Mars, Captain Jensen told Lieutenant Strake that he was tasked with tracking down a man selling black-market technology to CTAC."

"In all instances, the name that has come up was that of the same man sitting in conference with us, John Bucker."

Bastian sat back as though slapped, black eyes glared a threat into Decatur's soul. "You are out of your mind, captain. Bucker has been on our council since its inception. You accuse a patriot who may someday be a founding father of our nation of black marketeering and treason?"

Decatur was by now thoroughly disgusted with the politics and softly replied, "You forget bloody mutiny."

Hollen quietly replied, "These are serious accusations, Decatur.

"Bucker has friends not only on council but through other political ties. The name may well be a coincidence. After all, I've never encountered any instance, beyond your accusation, when a first name is given. How do we know the reference is not to some nebulous organization rather than this man?"

Decatur considered telling them about the midnight raid used to recover their stolen slipdrive. Bucker however, was known to them for many years. He was a known and trusted colleague. His only counter to the challenge would draw Gleason, Walters, and others into admitted felonious assault, and theft. He'd have to gather more proof.

"I am not at liberty to disclose the details, however I will suggest that we have had supplies and critical shipments disappear and Bucker's corporation is chartered for providing the most critical items."

"That and the named instances from here to Sol system …."

"That is not proof young man," Bastian broke in.

Alex replied, "No, it is not proof Jack, but it would explain a lot that has happened."

"Tie this in with my own suspicions and it all makes sense, except for the fact that I failed to recognize our own 'Bucker' to be the culprit."

"Bucker has several warehouses on Kraken and, I believe, a few on Jasper. They all maintain the highest levels of security, high enough to make his business dealings suspect."

Bastian appeared rather sad, "I knew his father. We served together. He was a crude man, but I just can't see his son doing this. Yet your concerns have merit and present a compelling argument even though both of you miss one thing."

"If his influence extends across the colonies and even to the NAU and CTAC, we are on the edge of an extensive operation and the corruption smacks of originating in the highest levels of state, perhaps in all the government circles. This would not be the first time that politicians engaged in illicit ventures supported by their lofty position."

Bastian let out a grumble, "Captain Decatur, I earlier called you a 'loose cannon'. It appears I underestimated your ability to complicate my life."

"Most likely, Bucker may only be a very small fish in a much bigger ocean of sharks. We must move carefully."

"Gather what you can on him, Alex, but hands off the little cretin for now."

Hollen was unfazed, "Yes sir. In that case, I'd like to clip the man's wings a bit, just enough to make him wary before encouraging mutiny for personal gain."

Baskin nodded, "Yes, I have no intention of letting him run roughshod across our realm but don't let him suspect who is behind it."

Alex seemed satisfied, "Good enough. Then, if there is nothing else, I'll take my leave. Good day to you both."

Bastian settled back into the chair, his characteristic scowl returning to his face as Alex's image dissolved. He continued staring at Decatur, who managed to not move a muscle.

Bastian rose, slowly walked over to his desk's sidebar, and opened a door, "Scotch or bourbon?"

Decatur projected a questioning look at the admiral without uttering a single word.

"Oh, for God's sake, it's over. Cut the crap and loosen up."

Flabbergasted, Decatur didn't say a word.

"You are military to the bone, aren't you? Must I give you a direct order to lighten up?"

"You survived but by the skin of your teeth. I suspect you came closer to death in this encounter of the last few minutes than at any point in these past months."

"But never mind that. No scotch today, we need something a bit more civilized. Here's a brandy. Limited batch direct from Jasper's best. It's time to loosen up and celebrate."

Decatur cleared his throat, "I must admit, I've never felt so helpless, Sir."

"We're off the record, Decatur. 'Jack' will do, and trust me, you appeared anything but 'helpless'. Put your mind at ease, your people are being taken care of. You deserve to give yourself a few moments. Enjoy them with a brandy."

"Am I to assume there will be no charges?"

"Were you sleeping during that meeting? No, no charges and there damned well won't be. You followed, no, by Finagle's guile you exceeded orders."

"Seems to be a fault you possess."

Decatur wasn't satisfied, "I'm glad to have saved so many but at what cost? As the admiral pointed out, I am responsible for many more lives lost. It's a burden I don't enjoy. I lost many nights' sleep because of a decision years ago to execute rather than release the survivors of a mutiny. My recent action was so much worse, so many more dead, injured. Many innocents killed and yet … this time it somehow bothers me less."

"This frightens me."

Bastian rumbled incoherently, staring into the captain's soul, allowing the silence to linger. Then came, "I suspected as much and have no easy answer except to say I know what you are experiencing. Many front-line commanders experience such emotions. Those who never do are the ones I need worry about."

"You will learn to live with it, or you must change your vocation. But if you decide to leave the service, then you will have to live with a growing knowledge that as this conflict continues many more will die and our great vision for our world may fail. And this may all come to pass all because you had not the will to stay the course."

"You and I will be working together in the days to come. Loosen up and consider things clearly. You've brought in an intelligence coup of epic stature and performed a great service for your colony, one that may eventually be an independent world, thanks to you."

"Consider this, the CTAC warbirds you brought in assay at roughly one point eight-seven billion thalers per ship; even more when considering cargo, munitions, and supplies. That will push the totals up significantly higher. Then, there's salvage recovery from the rescued commerce vessel. That, naturally, is added to all of this."

"Of course, Kraken takes a bit more than half the worth."

"Even so, your future is financially secure, and this will allow you to concentrate your full talents on the task at hand."

"What, no reaction? Are you dead man? Did you forget the statute passed awarding prize money? You and every swab under your command are going to come out of this with a very substantial bonus. It will make many others envious considering the level of wealth you and your people are going to assume."

"Unfortunately, this presents the possibility of some talent leaving service but then, there will also be no shortage of future volunteers."

"You've gained immeasurably in political clout since your direct chain of command participates in the prize reward and that includes the council members, whom I suspect have yet to consider the full impact of the prize decree."

"Except of course for Mister Bucker; whom personal fortune appears to be all he thinks about. I expect we'll see him courting your friendship in days to come because of it."

He stopped to warm his snifter briefly over an open flame, a twinkle in his eye, "Yes, they are going to be very supportive."

"I'll have the financial breakout for you and your people sent directly so you can convey to them the good news. The funds actual will take a while to trickle through the bureaucracy so don't go buying any yachts in the immediate future. You will, however, be able to get by until then with a small advance."

Bastian's eyes lost focus, though he tried to hide the fact by taking a lengthy sip of brandy.

"Damn, Alex wastes no time. I was wrong; another person on the committee besides Bucker was considering the financials. You keep a close eye on Alex, he's sharp.

"There, my office just issued new orders for you. I see you're properly dressed this time. You may stop by, but do not spend significant time with your command, you have business dirtside that demands priority. Then, Alex wants to speak with you, in person and in private."

"Decatur, we'll speak more of this in the days to come. I expect you will reserve an evening for a quiet dinner at my place. Informal of course, full civies. I need to know you better."

"You are dismissed, Captain Decatur."

Jankin Decatur passed from the conference room feeling like the world had just lifted from his shoulders and wondering if he should spend the money for a helo down to the main deck or simply take a lift until he remembered Bastian's speech concerning the prize money.

Then it dawned on him, *Why, the old coot ain't so bad after all. He even invited me over for dinner and a drink.*

Humphrey's Folly

Captain Jankin Decatur swung by the docks on his way dirtside. Rumors were high and several officers stopped him to present questions. He could tell them little and, being familiar with the service, they understood. Some of their scuttlebutt was amazingly wrong, others surprisingly so close to target he wondered what their source might be. However, be they right or wrong the captain could not speak to the subject.

Hopewell greeted him as he was formally piped aboard *Alfred*, "Captain, congratulations. I understand things went well but heard no details."

They exchanged little else as she ushered him to the captain's quarters where they could speak in confidence. The compartment's door closed behind them, sealing them from most of the noise and orchestrated chaos of repairs. A tray of coffee, tea, and a rare treat of dried seaweed cookies set in the table's center. "Harriet, one of the best bits of news I received was your confirmation to a captaincy and your coming investiture as captain of the *Alfred*."

Captain Harriett Hopewell nearly choked on her seaweed cookie upon hearing his words.

Decatur set down his cup, "Ah, your reaction … you have yet to be notified? Perhaps they left this to me … a gift for both of us. Well, I come prepared. Here, I'd be honored if you'd wear these."

He reached into his pocket and pulled out a small but ornate box crafted of rare Golden Jenkins Tree wood. Inside was a newly burnished pair of captain's pips, "These were my first military, given to me by Commissioner Hollen. I'm sure you will bring them honor."

The new captain's eyes sparkled, "I'll wear them with honor."

"We haven't heard a thing from outside, security is so tight. What news? I could see your concern as you left and now, you're losing **Alfred**. What …"

"Rest at ease, I originally feared for the nature of our reception. My concern was that charges would be levied upon me … and others."

"I received transfer orders. Thankfully, I retain my captaincy. More, I can't divulge except to say they are unclear as to my future."

"A bit of good news as to our fortunes in common, they haven't completed an assay of the value of the ships taken as prize and goods recovered, but last I heard it exceeded five billion thalers.

"You look shocked. What is the value of a star frigate? Five billion passes very quickly. Kraken will take half, mind you. Of the remaining, you get two percent as an acting captain, two percent is divided between the staff officers and another two goes to the spacers based upon their rating. Even a newly hired spacer will garnish more than two year's wages from the expedition."

"Proceeds are, of course, NAU tax-exempt," He ended with a rare smile.

"I must let you know, depending upon final orders, I shall request certain members of my people to follow my transfer. You would have been included but I expect you'd rather retain your command."

Rather than comment as expected, a worried look crossed Captain Hopewell's brow, "I've heard from my own sources, and no, I can't tell you who or how given the security shell we're under, but you've made strong enemies, political enemies. A few admirals, a commissioner and even a senator were in the naming."

Decatur played with one of the snacks without tasting it. He actually disliked the current seaweed fad, and answered, "Such is politics. I despise it, would avoid it if I could. Thank you for the warning."

"I expect we have unleashed a storm. It's coming was inevitable and our position on the forefront will bring new enemies, some of them quite personal in nature. With great risk comes great opportunity if we can but hold on and survive."

A reminder arrived through his HiveTab, "I have to leave. I have reservations on the Mare Elysium Elevator, and it waits for no one. Good luck, Captain."

Captain Hopewell accompanied him back to the loading dock through corridors strangely silent and devoid of all life. Construction had stopped. Not even a distant echo chanced to flee down the companionway.

The lift opened to the piping of whistles with the entire ship's crew and workers standing in silent formation. A tear formed in Decatur's eye as Chief Gleason's voice carried the bay, "A cheer for the captain, hip, hip ..."

"Hurray."

"Hip, hip…"

"Oi, Oi, Oi," The traditional cheer echoed as the band piped him off-ship."

~~*~*~*~*

"Cabby." He called forward to the pilot, "Thank you for waiting. The Mare Elysium Elevator, if you please."

"Yessir, Captain, that'll be another seven thalers."

Decatur replied with unaccustomed ease, "I expected so. Just do it."

A half-hour later he was resting in a private compartment on the space elevator, another exorbitant expenditure but his credit line somehow wasn't complaining. He had fourteen-and-a-quarter hours, by quick-line descent, to sit back, enjoy the view, and attempt to sleep as the elevator whisked him to the planet's far-off surface, still nearly two thirds the distance from the L2 Port to Kraken's equatorial station in mid-ocean. After that, a two-hour flight to the forty-second northern latitude and Pallentau City.

His eyes caught rare sight of one of the new, stealth orbital ion-cannon platforms currently under frenzied construction, an emplacement capable of erratic shifts in orbit along with gravitic-phased photon and E-M refraction to hide or blur its presence for a nearly invisible passage. It would be part of the planned network of defense-in-depth quietly under frantic construction around the planet.

Decatur had just settled in and was catching up on his mission report when his sealed and secured compartment's door slid open with a faint hiss; a dark form entered. Decatur's hand moved to the miniature needle-gun nestled in his waistband. He'd notified no one in advance of his reservations or method of travel.

"My apologies, Captain. I'm part of your security contingent. Normally, I wouldn't have bothered you, but I just received an alert that you are not to continue your dirtside flight segment arrangements, another will assume your current reservation. A decoy, if you will. Normal procedure, I assure you. No need for concern.

"When you arrive, take the down-lift to dock twenty-three. It's a private deck and someone will meet you there with a direct conveyance. I was told to say, 'Jack says it's okay.'" The words had barely left her mouth as the figure slipped from the compartment and was gone.

"So much for anonymity and a secure compartment," Decatur mused as he shoved an old-fashioned, wedge-lock into the track, "I didn't even know I had a 'security contingent'."

Hours later he was gracefully awakened by his HiveTab in time to see sun-drenched cumulous clouds spreading across a green-blue sky that extended until meeting the rim of a crystal-clear cobalt ocean at the far horizon. Though the elevator platform was far out to sea, the sky churned with feathered and leather-laden fliers attracted by the sea life below and a now visible landing platform obviously under expansion.

A thin tether glistened above the elevator, rising upward to some invisible destination in the heavens. It couldn't be seen but he knew it continued below, passing through the artificial port-island. His compartment's information screen sensed is interest and began describing the great depths that the cable continued into the sea below, all the way down to a link embedded deep in Kraken's planetary crust.

The final descent was nearly silent, without bumps or changes in momentum until a chimed announcement marked their arrival.

Decatur had only his briefcase, so he proceeded directly to a down-lift highlighted by his HiveTab. The doors swung open upon sensing his anticipated approach then down it went, transporting its single passenger to a private, secluded dock. There was a well-furnished waiting lounge there, fully automated, but his HiveTab urged him to a gate, then into an undersea chamber that opened blissfully with the sights, smells, and sounds of a tropical ocean grotto.

A sleek, private craft awaited his arrival and, standing beside it, a steward, "Welcome sir, this way, please. If there's anything you would like or if you have any questions, I'll be glad to address them as soon as we depart."

"We'll be leaving immediately unless you have reason for delay."

Decatur eyed him closely, "Are you sure you have the right traveler."

"Captain Jankin Decatur, identity confirmed," and with that, the steward flipped his wrist up, a small area on its underside contained Decatur's registration and security codes. Transport is courtesy of the commissioner, sir."

Things were finally going well, "This is a nice surprise. No reason for any delay."

The compartment was a bit tight and he had to stoop slightly as he sought out a comfortable chair. A work desk and fixed terminal were conveniently positioned nearby.

The steward brought in a warm face-towel and a tray of refreshments, "Now, what can I get you."

"This bottle of water is quite the welcome addition, thank you, I'm anxious to watch our departure," Decatur turned, his HiveTab automatically switching the bulkhead to an external display. They were already streaming submerged at a tremendous rate, a thin reflection marking the passing wall of water a few hands-breadths outside.

Decatur queried his HiveTab, *how does this vessel travel?*

The reply was instantaneous, *Super-Cavitation, according to the vessel's server. The craft's leading-edge moves with sufficient rapidity to separate the sea ahead into its component gases, highly efficient with only a negligible amount of energy that must be introduced into the reaction. This allows the craft to fly beneath the water's surface. A safe and most secure exit method, or so its security system assures me.*

He sensed the forward door opening. Decatur looked up, the synthetic was returning with water in an amber-crystalline beaker, "We have three hours remaining in travel. Commissioner Hollen requested you review the documents contained in the thumb-server on your tray, it is access-restricted to this cabin so leave the device behind when you depart. The files are secured so you won't be able to record or download their contents. This is eyes-only for your review and your memory segments of them will be interrogation blocked."

"Thank you," was the captain's simple reply. He was impressed by the level of security and, as he began a review of the documents, soon discovered just why the commissioner was being so guarded.

Time passed quickly as Decatur turned to a review of the background information of current events here on Kraken as well as in Jasper and Sol systems that led to their decision to resist NAU control. There apparently was no known similar movement of independence in Jasper. Kraken, it seems, would likely proceed alone.

A second packet contained segments of a declaration of independence, obviously a work in progress and drawing on the ancient foundations of the NAU itself for their inspiration.

A chime and the bulkhead illuminated with the entry of a yellow-green band of light filling the cabin courtesy of their home star as the craft erupted into full-flight, now following an aerial course.

Eventually cobalt seas led to beaches bordered by lush green countryside passing below rapidly, Kraken's majestic native wilderness resembled an exotic park packed with far-spreading herds of huge creatures traveling upon two or four feet, depending upon the momentary preference of each. Kraken was a planet that paralleled an evolutionary path taken by Earth's except for one very significant difference.

The calamity that struck Earth nearly sixty-six million years in the past eliminated nearly ninety-percent of the planet's species. In doing so it thrust the world into a climatic cycle of harsh, recurring ice ages and rapid tectonics. The saurian species were practically eliminated from a biosphere thrown into rapidly cycling periods of extreme stress. An environment that challenged survival and greatly sped up species evolution to the point that in less than a hundred-million years of the Earth's six-billion-year existence, more than ninety-nine percent of the planet's species had become extinct, and through it, Homo sapiens had evolved.

As species evolution on Earth was forced forward at a frantic pace, Kraken blissfully continued through the ages with a warm, stable, Eden-like environment retaining its evolutionary great biodiversity, a mix of saurian as well as earth-similar mammal species equivalents, each species free to evolve its life-form at a much slower pace in a benevolent, softly changing climate. The species mix and biomass abundance of this garden-like world made Earth seem, to Kraken colonists, a barren bio-desert.

Quite naturally, lacking the continued challenges of a rapidly changing Earth-like environment, sapient life on Kraken never blossomed and the slowly evolving descendants of their dinosaurs of ancient times retained dominance of the planet's ecosystem.

Decatur knew, by silent HiveTab broadcast, that his destination was drawing near. The craft followed the terrain closely, streaking down a steep-walled valley between jagged cliffs never touched by the smoothing-effects of passing glaciers or ice-sheets. The valley narrowed ahead; eventually drawing in so close the craft was forced to adjust its altitude until the wide section of its oblate-spheroid-shaped hull was near vertical and, in this tilted orientation, it slipped into a natural cavern.

The vehicle landed silently, and Decatur felt, rather than heard, the main-drive shutdown, as the hatch opened and the steward reappeared urging his exit.

Alexander Hollen, Grand Councilman of Kraken waited upon him. Decatur thanked the steward as he disembarked, his eyes habitually scanning his environment until he noticed several AutoSentinel defense pods cleverly concealed near the cavern's entrance. The remainder of the grounds suggested nothing military. Lavish decorations covered the walls and ceiling with an open-air lounge and bar at the far side.

"You may return to your hanger, Alfred, unless of course you require maintenance or would like recreation time."

Decatur, a look of mild shock on his face, turned to the commissioner.

"What? Is there a problem?" Alex returned the captain's unspoken query, then understood. "No, purely coincidence I assure you. I named the craft after a fictional butler who intrigued me in a piece of classic literature studied in my school days, about a caped crime-fighter who also operated from a cavern. Written by some fellow named H.G.Wells, I think."

The explanation clarified Decatur's query. Both craft and steward were one and the same, a single entity synthetic intelligence.

"Come, Decatur, we have little time to waste and I have a surprise for you."

"I would have had Alfred pick you up on L2, but I needed time to prepare for your arrival."

Alex led him through a jacketed door in the cavern wall, and into a second chamber. Decatur had never seen the man so excited, acting more like a kid on Michaelmas Day than a sober leader of state. Then, he saw the silent form waiting ahead.

Resting on the granite base, its sleek lines left no doubt, this craft was made to fly. It was small, a bit smaller than a Wraith but embodied definite sculptured elegance. Fanfolds of ripples coursed down its smooth, nearly cusp-like body, its skin a silver, nearly mirror-like finish.

Unlike a Wraith, a hatch lay open in the side. The interior held a four-seat compartment with an obvious head and mess unit set off in the aft section.

"Take the copilot's seat and ..." Alex noticed the captain's eyes fairly caressing the console and compartment. "Perhaps you'd like to take her up, Captain? She handles well and ..." The captain appeared surprised, "It's just an offer, Decatur. I'll pilot if you wish."

Decatur visibly grabbed control of himself, "This is ... a civilian craft? This is not what you wanted to show me?"

Laughter filled the politician's eyes, "No, no, no. I apologize for not explaining myself properly. This is one of my yachts, a bit of a personal extravagance for someone who loves to fly. I noted your reaction and thought you'd like to take her up."

"She isn't much in the way of automation, a toy for sporting about rather than serious travel but she is fun and has more than sufficient range to take us to what I want to introduce you to."

A sly smile crept across his face, "I'm going to keep that a secret for now, simply because I love surprises."

"Sit, either front seat. I'll link your HiveTab into the interface and ..."

Decatur's world expanded.

He could feel air fluctuations in the cavern; he knew the function of each system of the craft and its status. The control board before him blossomed with gauges, terrain maps and accelerometers like those of ancient machines of flight and he knew there was a library of virtual controls and gauges available for the asking.

"As I said, I like flying but not the total immersion of today's serious craft, I like to feel the machine around me and directly control it like the pioneers of old."

"Go ahead, take her up and feel the rush. Of course, if you want immersion flight, we can do that too."

With but a thought command, a virtual yoke swung out from under the console, it looked and felt solid to the point that he could rest the weight of his arms on it. Pulling back on a lever set to his left, the engine wakened and a set of cavern doors slid open as the craft lifted two hair-widths above the highest peak of the granite floor beneath. They were already flying even though they had hardly moved.

A slight nudge forward, he lifted then swung the agile craft into a tilt and experienced the change in momentum as they shot through the narrow cavern exit. Gaining attitude, he climbed into an open sky free of any prying eyes. Effortlessly, they sailed upwards, piercing the low haze and into a wall of stratocumulus storm clouds, ignoring the churning winds and shedding the static charge that threatened fliers of old.

A course vector appeared, directing them up. Pulling back on the yoke, the speeder shot upward on the planet's gravitic front with no more effort than if it were in a dive.

Kraken's distant horizon appeared, draped in the reds and blues of its distant haze shield then the universe ahead morphed into soft, velvet black. In less than two minutes, the L2 lay off their port bow and navigation asked him to accelerate.

"See what I mean?" Alex broke his awed silence. "Going will be a bit boring for a while but I think you got the idea. When we return, we'll have time so you can joy-ride around homeport for a while. Right now, a bit of pleasure that is also business."

They pushed outbound, skittering across the heavy gravitic chop of the inner star system. The craft was amazingly lithe and could sail close-hauled easily as it climbed far up the star's long gravitic rollers, seemingly disregarding the in-system chop and gaining speed as they sped off to some mysterious destination still masked by the commissioner.

A little over an hour later, Jankin was still enjoying the craft and learning how it handled in the rough regions so near a star when he noticed a singular bright point of light dead ahead was growing in magnitude and, as it resolved into a disk, Decatur recognized the familiar cupped ring-set of the largest gas-giant of the Kraken stellar system.

Flight smoothed as they entered the gravity well of the giant planet and their craft screamed as it tacked inbound to its ring-set like an ancient fighter locked in a crash dive. Suddenly, they were upon it. A hard bank and they broached to a relatively narrow open path nearly parallel to the plane of the planet's ring-set.

The universe transformed, their craft now skimming along the granular surface of the blue-gas giant's rings they gradually drew down just inside the nebulous surface of debris. Even with AI assist, maintaining a course through the many moonlets presented a deadly challenge. As they pierced deeper into the ring, the stars gradually faded, replaced by flickering shadows of their parent star's light peeping through the blend of rock and ice, mixed with glittering reflects from thousands of shining surfaces, a swirling storm of flickering lights, rocks, and debris increasing in density and chaos as they descended into the blend.

Alex seemed not to mind the surrounding visual chaos, "I'm sure you recognize this as Jennings' planet, our system's version of Saturn. The electromagnetic and gravitational fields of this gas giant form a natural EM dynamo that interacts with the heavy metal composition of its ring-band. The field created shields us from external snooping by even the most modern technology of the NAU. One moment, bring our approach around a bit …. you're gonna like this."

The universe swung about, shifting the overview display of the huge planet's ring belt and debris now saturated their universe, visibly thickening as they went on until ahead of them lay what appeared to be a solid mass, a near-solid wall of detritus.

Even this obstacle contained a hidden rift that magically appeared as they drew near. Then suddenly, it was gone.

They emerged inside a void; a spheroidal-shaped clear expanse of space bounded by ever-sparkling, churning walls that permitted but a ghostly external illumination to pass. At the center of the dark void lay an obvious pattern of lights and radiation marking ports, approach channels, office facilities, and manufacturing on a scale greater than any Decatur had ever witnessed.

"Our possession of all you have witnessed today requires advanced science and manufacturing on a level highly illegal under even the Kraken Colonial Charter. Off in the distance, you see our pride and joy, the font of all our hopes for independence and future existence, our most advanced shipyard."

"You're familiar with the Lagrangian stable-site starship ports used by Earth and Kraken for mil-spec ship construction. Well, Kraken's a young world and, because of past restrictions imposed upon our research and industry, we have no history of regulations and out-of-date assets to burden our infrastructure. What we now build must exceed the latest to be had by others if we are to survive the coming years. The technology within this shipyard surpasses any Earth-sanctioned facility we know of. Bureaucracy has not existed here long enough to restrict our ship designs or constrain construction techniques and our political base fears for their lives. Therefore funding, although always a battle, is less of a problem."

"An old friend awaits in the facility, Joshua Humphrey. He's a bit of a military historian and insists on calling the miracle of science sitting at dock ahead a frigate even though she is more than those you are familiar with. She is the first of her generation, radically different to the point that some engineers have taken to calling her Humphrey's Folly."

Decatur's experienced eye examined every line of the warbird below and, as he marveled at the sight, the specifics of the ship flooded in through his HiveTab. Alex's flier was obviously an early implementation of this new design concept; a like-generation of craft otherwise unknown in this universe.

Like a great frigate bird, it was of long sharp edges and swirls designed to reduce wave distortion and gravitic cavitation. The lines promised great stealth capability. Its surface wasn't smooth but held long, funneled furrows of a design radiating out about its center of mass and mimicking Alex's speeder.

Alex could barely restrain his pride, "The furrow-field is ground-breaking. Its period-length is calculated to optimize linkage to the waves of deep space and, hopefully, will allow it to travel at an even greater velocity within the environs of the abyss. The extendable spikes you see placed at regular intervals across the body and wings provide extra traction on the gravitic waves functioning like the studding-sails, or 'stunsels', of an old wind-sail square-rigger. However, these gravitic stunsels are tunable and can be used to steer the ship even when the waves of gravity grow weak."

"They will enable more agile response during course shifts, slipping to side or reversing direction by phasing onto a different gravitic wave."

Alex turned silent and sat back for a few moments, his attention focused upon the captain. Then a sparkle emerged as a glistening pride from his eyes as he continued, "She is all yours .... should you want her."

He hesitated, almost reluctantly adding as Decatur's head snapped 'round to meet his gaze, "But I must warn you. This is a new concept as well as design. So, she's less a gift and more a problem child. In addition to the demands of your mission, you will have responsibility for working out all the bugs and improving her final design. Trim her as you wish but remember you and your people will live or die by your decisions."

"Under no conditions is she to fall into enemy hands."

"You will be responsible for the selection and training of her crew, all six hundred and thirty-five of them. They are yours to choose and you will succeed or fail based on their quality."

"So, what say you? Are you willing to accept command?"

Decatur couldn't believe his ears. A frigate designed from first-concept, as a warbird no less. A ship-of-war able to strike out on its own far from the constraints of fleet action or supply shipping. A warbird capable of taking the fight directly to the enemy.

"What field of battle am I to prepare for?"

"Right now, merchant services are redirecting their shipments away from Earth and Sol system. We will restrict them to the colonies. Earth will gradually see fewer and fewer colonial shipments. This will incite the NAU to increase interdiction of our trade. Quite naturally we expect them to focus near the colonial ports because of the near impossibility of intercepting flights in deep space."

"Maintaining Kraken trade and independence will be your charter. Under broad directional guidance of the board, you will have an independent command to carry the war to the enemy as you see fit, subject only to baseline board approval."

"What say you, Captain Jankin Decatur?"

The End of the Beginning

ö~ö | ö~ö | ö~ö | ö~ö | ö~ö

Story Background

"**Quantum Surge**", its storyline and main character, are based upon the true-life accomplishments of John Paul Jones, Father of the United States Navy, who was born in 1747C.E. as 'John Paul' in Scotland. As in this story, the first military ship he commanded was named *Alfred* and in it, he was first to take the American revolution to the shores of the colony's mother-country.

As to John Paul's name change to 'John Paul Jones', read his biography.

I guarantee, you won't be disappointed.

APPENDIX :
TECHNOLOGY & ARMAMENT

Crest Runner Missile

Perhaps the most intelligent AI weaponry of the colonials, Crest Runners link to a gravitic wave's crest, skipping from wave-to-wave for a bit, jigging to change their direction of attack before coming around to another tack to complicate enemy tracking even as they accelerate to the strike. Crest Runners are designed for use as a first strike capability and work in unison, as they must in order to defeat a spindizzy field.

A spindizzy shield is strongest at the leading-edge of a ship, which could be at any point on a slipdrive ship that happens to be normal to their instant directional velocity vector. This is often called the 'bow', similar to the physical bow of a wet-navy ship. Similarly they also sport a 'stern' of aft segment but keep in mind there is no fixed physical part for either on a slipdrive since this class of ship can move in any direction and change it at any instant without the ill-effects of momentum.

Crest Runners are fired in muli-missile pods. As they approach their objective, each determines their probability of completing a successful attack based on multiple parameters including their position relative to the objective. The missile with the greatest potential for a successful attack, fires sabot-enhanced railgun slugs, optimally from astern the target.

Spindizzy fields are designed to deflect oncoming flotsam ranging in size from micrometeoroids to even large objects by molecular disassembly of the object. The field works less efficiently for impacts to the ship's 'side' and is weakest at its stern.

A Crest Runner under sail has excited-electron gravitic mass so it is not subject to Einstein relativity effects but the sabot slugs it fires quickly revert to simple objects subject to a relativistic-mass increase when moving at a significant fraction of lightspeed. The slug is released while traveling near or even above lightspeed so, as soon as they exit the missile's gravitic field, their relativistic mass balloons to near infinity. Thus, we weaponize the classic speed-of-light barrier for a rail-gun slug's striking force is proportional to the slug's mass multiplied by its acceleration relative to the target.

The railgun sabots are fired at grazing incidence to the target's spindizzy barrier which immediately attempts to reverse the intruder's direction and push them aside and astern. However, during an attack the target's spindizzy field now is faced with an extremely difficult task since the sabot's mass is tremendous and they come from astern rather than bow-on, the field must therefore attempt to reverse the full mass of the sabot's velocity vector.

A Crest Runner attack has a high probability of destabilizing the target's spindizzy shield so that subsequent torpedo releases can survive to complete a penetration that results in a graviton energy release and destruction of the objective. At worst, they weaken the target's defenses providing an opportunity for a well-timed attack by other munitions.

Graviton (Gravitic) Torpedoes

The greatest problem in starship warbird conflict is to penetrate the ship's spindizzy field, the energy barrier designed to move all molecules of matter out of the path of a warbird traveling at supralight speeds.

The preferred method is to sacrifice one torpedo if it can be maneuvered to impact aft of the target, striking in the objective's direction of travel where the field is weakest.

During a normal attack, a gravity-driven Graviton torpedo approaches the edge of the target's spindizzy field. At the first detection of a nearby target's field, it fires a blast of heavy-metal chafe enveloping a central sabot. The chafe locally weakens the target's field and the sabot-charge follows. The charge ignites using an internal atomic reaction to generate a small circularly polarized magnetic field. If the sabot has penetrated far enough, then its explosion creates a second gravitic field that reacts with the target and forms a gravitic sub-electron reaction within the objective resulting in a massive, explosive conversion of all matter in the target to energy.

HAACH VIEWER

Acronym for **'High Altitude Atmospheric Crest Holography'**. Adaptive Active Optics technology providing detailed remote imaging for viewing any point on any planet supporting an atmosphere using reconstructive imaging of airwave aberrations to recreate photon ray traces. The ray traces are used to reconstruct high-resolution multidimensional holographic images of the planet below.

This technology will also function at a water-atmosphere interface for imaging of sea-bed details.

HiveTab Interface

A small patch, thinner than a piece of paper with the diameter of a piece of chalk, is designed to rest on the skin just above the human mastoid, the bone located behind the ear. Upon installation, thin monomer tendrils are released. Like living things, the tendrils grow into the pores of the subject's skin, passing inward to pierce the subcutaneous and penetrate to the base of the brain. There they sample from every nerve synapse firing, pulling in the energy needed to run the miraculous organic circuitry of the HiveTab.

Twenty-four hours a day, the patch monitors body functions, and brain-nerve synchronizations. It contains an internal clock synchronized to the stable shifts of cosmic dark-matter frequency slides. It also accepts external data from gravitonic emissions, physical contact with external stimuli, and the emanations of other nearby interfaces including human hosts. In operation, the patch provides both interface and leading-edge technology for enhanced processing, data storage, rendering and transmission of information as well as other, more mundane functions.

The patch is not a computer, it's a human augmentation that learns from its host over time, essentially becoming a part of the host.

Hive-Capable Droids (HCD)

Each sub-microscopic, molecule-sized HCD is an autonomous construct that uses active molecular programmed components smaller than the wavelength of a blue photon to create a weapon of war able to think and react to counterthreats.

HCD interiors churn with constrained gravitic energy controlled by cognitive programmed molecules residing across neural bubble-nerve bundles to link and form a single, newly awakened hive-mind with one goal in its short lifetime, the unleashing of the tremendous gravitonic energies stored in the cumulation of its electron sub-particle bonds.

The drone entity projects a pattern-sensitive field ahead of it that can extend nearly a tenth of the distance from the Earth to the Sun as it searches for its quarry or for the familiar encounter with the sensor field of a sister drone. Each contact linking to another drone allows it to expand its hive consciousness and computational powers both in strength and in breadth to a swarm maximum that can extend across nearly a light-minute of space.

HIVE MINES

Programmed NanoBot molecules (HiveBots) designed to communicate and function autonomously or within a swarm. Each HiveBot component is roughly the diameter of a rare-earth molecule. They link together forming nebulous particle clouds but can remain constrained as tightly packed swarms, essentially an intelligent cloud deployed into a volume of space as anti-shipping munitions. They react to any matter within a designated proximity or to the presence of an external gravitic field causing them to track the target and, upon contact, explode into life. As the swarm density grows, the intelligence and capability of the hive increases.

Hive Mines penetrate a gravitic field by overloading it locally. If they can reach beneath the external spindizzy barrier and into the excited subelectron particle region of a slipdrive starship, they begin disassembly of the matter, instantly reprogramming the released molecules of the matter to create additional HiveBots. A successful attack will eventually cause the release of all the gravitic energy of the molecule's activated electrons resulting in a huge energy release.

LEPTON PULSAR

Light armament for sidearms and shoulder-weapons including both slug and needle gun adaptations using caseless ammunition. Larger munitions are also constructed for action against planetary emplacements and targets unprotected by slipdrives.

A small gravitic reaction is created inside a shielded chamber. Munition base material of any format -- metal, silicon, even heavy elements -- is stored as a solid bar or compressed powder in a clip-holder. As the gravitic field rotates, it shaves atoms off the top of the bar. The bare atoms form a super-heated plasma that is spun and formed into a hollow or solid projectile, depending upon device settings, by the accelerant field and exits the weapon at supersonic speeds while still a spinning plasma. The plasma instantly solidifies into a 'dumb' slug traveling at multiple times the speed of sound with spin stability given to it by the impetus of the rotating magnetic field. It delivers a heavy punch equivalent to having a hand-held Railgun.

The Pulsar's accelerator is a closed system. The pulses are shielded and won't interact with a ship's drive field as long as its magnetic bottle remains intact.

SLIPDRIVE

Graviton particles were first theorized in a paper from Stephen Poliakov in 2002C.E. Doctor Phillip Nolen initially used controlled magnetostriction of materials to both induce and detect very high-frequency sideband modulation in the extremely long waves of gravity as a communications device for submarines.

The field concepts evolved to other applications including a superluminal drive capable of linking to the gravitational waves of the universe, called the Wave Drive.

The Slipdrive, a second-generation improvement, was invented roughly fifty years later.

RAIL GUNS

An old but reliable favorite because of their compact design and minimal maintenance requirement. Kraken designs appear in both long and short banister installations with the shorter rails used for more rapid, close-quarters work. They fire an enhanced depleted 'uranium' sabot that is easily manufactured on ship as needed by molecular modification of any of the Actinide elemental waste products found in Fermi Class vessels. Being program enhanced, the sabots can perform minor course deviations using limited but effective molecular programming.

WINGMAN AI ENHANCED DRONE (WAIED)

Individuals drones used by CTAC forces composed of an exterior ablating ceramasteel crystal rod about the thickness of a straw and a finger in length, encapsulating a depleted uranium needle sabot.

A WAIED attacks a starship by driving into it like a missile. Their outer shell resists molecular disassembly by a ship's gravitic shield and, although it cannot prevent the field from ripping it apart molecule-by-molecule, the destruction is slowed by the drone's super-dense crystalline lattice. As its skin ablates molecule-by-molecule, the drone's core continues its penetration deep into the victim ship's slipdrive spindizzy region.

Upon contact with the vessel's outer skin, the ultra-dense uranium needle, or sabot, fires. Piercing inward through the ship's multiple outer shells until it explodes into life inside. The resulting hole is tiny, barely the width of a human hair, but through it the energy from the target's own protective slipdrive exterior field now had a channel into the interior.

This force, turned inward against itself, spreads through the target's innards by ripping apart the already energized electron shells that make up ship, crew, and cargo until the entire vessel disintegrates into a highly energized subparticle mist. Full conversion takes less than a femtosecond, that is, one quadrillionth of a second. The amount of time it takes light to travel thirty centimeters in the open vacuum of space.

THANK YOU

I hope you enjoyed this story as much as I have. If you liked it please take a moment and provide a review for others. If you haven't read all my other books in the 'Crucible' and 'Jankin Decatur' series then follow this link:

http://PhilipNolen.com/Books.html

Visit my website to read an unpublished tale from the novel, as well as discussions and background.

Also, sign up for my email list.

For more information including excerpts, excluded scenes, paleontology references, and technology discussions visit:

http://PhlipNolen.com

Where you will also find unpublished short stories from the universe of this novel.

Terrence Zavecz

PS: Perfection is impossible for most of us.

Send me a short email highlighting any mistakes in this text or to provide suggestions. Those who help me will get recognition in the next release and novel. Also, if you wish, you will have a part in my next novel as well as a preview of my next book.

As always, book reviews are encouraged for without an author cannot exist.

EXCERPT

QUANTUM
UNCERTAINTY

One enters life two ways -- from within your mother's womb or a creche tube. It's when it's time to leave that the Fates ply their twisted sense of humor in a thousand different ways.

Master Chief Petty Officer Rendall Gleason knew they were close on his trail. He was a big man, even by Kraken standards, and justifiably frightened. He couldn't help but marvel at how such big animals managed to travel so quietly. Kraken trees are tall with broad open spaces beneath their high canopy. They'd been lucky to get out from under those giant monarchs of the jungle before the predators latched onto their scent.

Back there lay a clear, open forest floor with no place to hide. The brush they'd just entered would protect them just a bit more but not enough. Unfortunately, with their passage through the low scrub-brush, came noise-prone movement and he knew it did no good to stop and hide.

It was obvious what was chasing them. He'd gotten the glimpse of a silhouette against the stars when one of them stood upright, its great head pushing through the high boughs to get a look-see ahead and taste the night air. Then also, even though he couldn't hear them, their stink and the occasional flutter of a tall tree was telltale for how close they were.

It was then he noticed a new scent. A different but familiar rank odor of rotting vegetation that confirmed what lay ahead. No options remained, they'd have to skirt it in the dark, *Da swamp. Our last obstacle and it will be slowin' us down. Too bad it's not gonna slow dem down. Still, if we can get across before dey catches us, den we just might survive.*

He shouldered his Lepton Pulsar rifle to free both hands and stepped to the side, ushering the others past with the faintest breath of a whisper tainted by a near-forgotten accent that emerged under stress, "Follow da ridge, do not shortcut inta da swamp or dey'll get us for sure. Step lively, now."

In doing this, the chief shifted to the back of the line. He was now 'Tail-End Charlie', the guy protecting their backsides and the one who'd be first to get it.

Unless he remained alert.

Ah ain't no dumb-ass ranger, dey loves dis kind of stuff. Unfortunately, ah've got a bunch of greenhorns, never been in da wild-lands before, exceptin' da major of course. Dey needs me here, ah'm the one most likely to survive the position.

The small dark form before him stumbled, Gleason's massive hand reached out catching her by the backpack and using but one arm lifted her to her feet without missing a pace. Just a whisper as she solidified her footing, "Watch yer step, Miss Stoudt."

Part of the chief thanked God for tonight's full moon, another portion cursed it since evenings such as this found the packs most aggressive. The light of Kraken's midnight moon's a bit tricky when it's full, particularly when the planet's asteroid rings are in phase. Such nights never get truly dark, there's just too much reflected light coming off the silvery surfaces of both satellite and rings. When the precession of its rings, formed by the asteroids of the Serpent Swam surrounding Kraken, also lined up, the illumination was … well, you could almost play cards under it were it not for the constantly shifting shadows created by lighting that played with your mind made worse by the blowing leaves of the jungle's canopy.

Branches rustled behind him. A hunting call followed; it was a cross between a freight train's leaky steam engine trying to stop on rusty rails. No point in being quiet anymore, "Go, go, go. Charge yer pulsars and watch yer feet. Anyone slips up and dey'll be on us all. If we can reach the clearings above the cliff, we just might live."

Weaver bushes snatched at pants and sleeves in passing, trying their best to rip a chunk of exposed flesh for dinner. They grew in thick, tangled clusters along these ridgelines, filling the surrounding air with the sticky-sweet order of their lime-color blossoms. Pretty but they made travel harder.

Sweat streamed down the CPO's back, pulling at his attention until a second bellowed scream throbbed through his brain as it split the air from off his port side. His eyes shifted from the rough footing as they caught sight of a second black shape to port as it lifted above the treetops then disappeared.

Just popped up for a look-see, Rendall thought as he picked up the pace, pushing the figure in front of him with a nudge from the stock of his rifle, it was the captain's back he'd just prodded. He'd either be forgiven afterward or it really wouldn't matter.

A shout rose that set his heart pounding. He pushed and twisted through the meshed jungle growth before emerging into a clearing.

"Stop yer gawkin'. Fan out along da cliff top den face aft. Watch ya don't flip over the edge."

He couldn't blame them for the obvious distraction. The black infinity of an open star vault enveloped them as they emerged from beneath the jungle canopy. Kraken's night sky held no pollution from city lights and here the sea breeze scrubbed most jungle pollen from the air. Stars twinkled above, even under the glare of the full moon sending its reflected shafts of moonglow directly at them. The vault above held far more sparkling laser points than they'd ever see beneath Earth's darkest night.

They couldn't afford to enjoy the view. The land before them was grass-covered, thigh-high, and it could hide a thousand hungry beasts cranky for being bothered. They crossed the narrow clearing, chests heaving under the exertion then edged up to what would be a nasty drop down a nearly vertical cliff to the rocks below.

Command transferred naturally as they set up their stand. Major Steve Walters' voice carried over the wind and crash of waves on the rocks far below, "We set anchor here. Hunker down. Pick yer targets but hold fire until ya hear my call then take time and aim for throat or skull, anywhere else won't stop them."

Steve Walters, a Major of Kraken Rangers, was frustrated and therefore quite annoyed. They'd been sound asleep when the perimeter alarms went off. An intrusion was unexpected for this time of year. Surprised, they had barely escaped their campsite and were forced to leave some of the gear behind. Nothing was going right.

This was supposed to be a fun excursion. A trip to the beach. A bit of fishing and crabbing. A quiet time to talk. But then, beautiful as it was, this was Kraken.

Walters consciously slowed his heart, reduced his rate of breathing. Now was the time for silence. Nowhere to go, at least they knew their backs were secure. They had an open field before them providing a good kill zone. Fortunately, any colonial realized you didn't travel unarmed through the wildlands. Unfortunately, whatever was on their trail was big and, knowing Kraken, it would be quick and lethal.

The jungle went silent, too silent. All night noises, the calls, even the rustling of small feet through the grass abruptly stopped. Walters found himself holding his breath, anything to improve hearing. Eyes strained against darkness filled with flickering shadows caused by the reflection of light from the moon's rings. Then he saw it.

Or rather; he saw its eyes.

Two yellow-green, glowing orbs with their iris split horizontally and diameters as large as dinner platters floating in among the palms and high limbs of the jidder-clumps. Silently searching, drilling their focus first at one point then flicking to another. Experience alone allowed the major to estimate the creature's size and even he was surprised for its eyes floated at roughly the height of four tall men and the predator wasn't stretched upright.

The creature moved, or rather a shadow-shrouded piece of the landscape in the distance seemed to shift. Walters marveled at the sophistication of their natural camouflage. Knowing what to expect and the fact that it was silently coming directly for them. Eventually, he was able to discern a form. At this point, one of Kraken's frequent meteors ripped the heavens, low enough to flare out in a burst of yellow light that flash-illuminated the landscape.

His eyes captured the image.

It was tall, walking on two legs but if it were to twist upright its head would pierce even the high canopy of the jungle. Its skin rippled and glistened beautifully, bronze colors flashing under the sudden blast of light so finely he could see through their downy feather covering to reptile-like surface scales bordered in feathered prongs. These were feathers much like some poor imitation of a sculpted bird feather but able to twist and slide among the scales.

Its head was elongated, thick with mighty neck muscles that worked jaws lined with ivory teeth the size of ripe bananas but strong enough to crush an opponent's thigh bone or skull.

Kraken's first settlers called them Trex and, at their first encounter, those early visitors thought they had come across the Tyrannosaurus Rex or T. Rex of Earth's ancient past. T.Rex, the infamous villain of so many old stories and prehistory. Later studies showed they were nothing of the kind.

This animal was not a primitive predator dinosaur.

In an amazing example of parallel evolution with Earth, for eons of time ancient Kraken's equivalent of dinosaurs dominated this world. However, Kraken's saurian species never suffered the extinction of their counterparts on Earth.

Kraken also had an Earth-like mammal equivalent but, since the saurian species here remained dominant, the mammal-like animals of this planet never had a chance to evolve and shape the ecosystem.

Kraken's Trex had tens of millions of years of additional evolution beyond the stage of their Earth-like equivalents. This new, improved predator was a bit slimmer than any T. Rex but faster and without any trace of vestigial arms. Here they continued to dominate the food chain and, along with the planet's mild climate, suppress the development of the Kraken's mammal equivalent species. Unlike Earth, this planet's weather never transformed from the early mild, garden-like world into one ripped by repeated cycles of hot climes and ice-age freezes that stressed the human species into developing intelligence on Earth.

Trex, Kraken's greatest killing machine, has the eyesight of an eagle and can track a mouse by smell and sound from the other side of a lake -- should they be interested in such a tiny tidbit. Even the new arrival of alien humans provided little more than an additional chance for a light snack.

The Trex stepped out into the open field as the sky began its slow transformation to daylight, moving in the changing illumination with grace and confidence as though it owned the place. As so it did. It was then the major noticed other dark forms waiting beneath the leafy cover and was able to spot four, no, at least six of them. He highlighted them with his HiveTab, assigning targets to each of his team members using their local HiveNet link followed by a silent message.

"The Trex pack's too large. If they launch a serious charge, we'll have to take our chances scrambling down the cliff-face and hope for the best. Hold fire unless I call it. I'm going to try something."

Walters knew his plan wouldn't work inside the jungle, their tiny party would have been under assault from all sides. However here, on open ground with their backs to the cliff, the monsters facing them were in an environment not of their choosing and could advance from only one direction.

The words of a nearly forgotten academy professor trickled across his mind, *Picking your battlefield is half the battle-won.*

The pack instinctively spread out at the edge of the clearing, some instinct holding even these huge predators from emerging into the open. Eventually, the leader cautiously took a few steps forward.

Walters could see tense muscles of the animal ripple in caution as it approached. The human-scent was unnatural, alien in fact, yet the monster could neither see nor hear anything. To an animal that had evolved and matured to a position of dominance in these jungles, this was a most unnerving situation. Their prey typically stood their ground or attempted to flee but not these. She knew they were there and could sense their presence but not the strong scent of fear.

Moving with an abundance of caution, the major withdrew a pocket smoke grenade from his pack, set its target and approach path then carefully launched the device.

Staying low, it skittered to the side passing silently through the brambles, emerging more than a dozen paces off from its launch-point. The target would never guess the true location of the humans. From there it rose, emitting a low buzzing that focused its sound waves to tingle down its objective's spinal nerves. It played deadly warning along the Trex's nerves like an unseen angry bee even as the little grenade measured wind direction and humidity of the target area. The tiny grenade hovered but a moment before zipping off in an arc separating humans and predators, depositing a dense black, foul-smelling smoke screen filled with ear-splitting snaps, squeals, and sparkler flashes.

Before this diversion started, Chief Rendall Gleason saw Major Walters reaching for his weapon's pack and knew what was coming. Moving so as not to attract the predator's attention, he backed off while withdrawing a piton from his knapsack. As the smoke grenade exploded into life, so did the chief. He set the piton into the ground and activated it roughly two paces back from the cliff's edge. It snapped once, sending a spike deep into gravel and rock. Turning his back to the now screaming chaos of the field, he clipped one end of a coil of rope to the piton and threw it over the cliff's edge where it extended until it just met the ground below then thickened to provide a better grip.

Quickly, they threw what they could to the sand below then shimmied down to the edge of the beach, moved out halfway to the water's edge, and turned, setting up their defense behind any boulder or fallen log while hoping the Trex pack members weren't so angry at their mistreatment they would chance a leap from the cliff.

They didn't have long to wait.

Captain Jeremiah Jensen, a North American Union (NAU) marine officer accompanied them and, from the coarse sands below, was the first to spot the animal's emergence. A huge head rose above the cliff top, catching the first rays of Ceti's rising light. Rather than a shout, Jerry's call slithered quietly through their HiveTabs directly into their brain, "Careful, another one just appeared fifty paces south of our position. A head ..."

He fell silent as the second animal looked out over the edge, there was no need to continue. The majesty, sheer size, and deadly-graceful movement of the predator demanded all their attention. No prior description properly prepared them for the size and obvious lethality of this monster. This was a male maliciously gazing at them, its plumage fluttering beneath the star's early morning rays, glowing in brilliance and threat. Keen yellow-slanted eyes scanned the beach below, searching for a sign of these strange intruders.

The intelligence of the predators, as shown by their performing a complex planned encirclement, astounded the NAU captain, "Only way that thing could have traveled that far from the pack would be if they started their envelopment before we even got to the clearing. Thank God we weren't caught in the open jungle or savanna but I bet we wouldn't have been much better off if we'd still be up there on top of the cliff."

As if to confirm his observation, a second monster appeared to the north of their position. Shortly the main body of the pack lifted directly above them, their great heads hovering menacingly over the humans.

Jensen whispered, "Finagle's run amok. They were a quarter step ahead of us all the way. Even the smokescreen didn't hold them for more than a moment's hesitation and ..."

Captain Jankin Decatur's call rode over that of the NAU officer; it came in low, delivered silently by his HiveTab and its tone immediately told them the captain brooked no challenge, "That's enough, Mr. Jensen. Freeze in position. We don't wish to encourage them by revealing our presence. I don't doubt they could easily hop right down and then our only recourse would be to head out to sea and, I venture to say, that is a path even they would not attempt."

The pack waited silently, listening for a small eternity, then three more behemoths appeared off on either side. Decatur whispered,

"Nobody move. Wait undercover. They must have sent pickets out searching for us."

Every predator in the pack could smell their prey; noses flared with an alien scent but the drafts of sea breeze dancing along the cliffs confused them. The hikers crouched inside the brush cover, unmoving until every muscle in their bodies ached. Ignoring even the small Kraken bugs walking across neck, back, and face while experiencing one of the detriments of a planet whose evolution so closely paralleled that of Earth for the tiny monsters thoroughly enjoyed alien, human blood.

The humans knew Trex had eyesight that would catch the slightest movement, recognize the smallest movement.

Then one small female at the edge of the pack barked out a yodel that sounded more like an argument raised by a trod-upon cat than a hunting cry. With it, the big pack leader ratcheted her head round leveling two great eyes directly on them. Eyes located in the universal position of a predator's, forward of its skull to track their quarry in full three-dimensional clarity. Yellow eyes with black cross-shaped pupils seemed to drill-in on its just-discovered prey, the diminutive Margo Stoudt.

Decatur knew the monster would jump. He tensed and prayed that only one came at them for that was about all they could handle even with modern pulsars. Then a thought ran through his mind, even if they killed it, it would most likely land directly on the diminutive journalist accompanying them. He liked Margo but figured her most likely dead already.

The big Trex stared, Decatur saw muscles grow tense. He prayed she didn't run too soon or the entire pack would be upon them and …

Then, they were gone. Five, then ten minutes quietly passed without a single appearance but the humans didn't budge or even let out an easy breath as Decatur silently encouraged them to not move.

Like a storm cloud passing before the sun, the huge male Trex reappeared above them, quickly followed by others lining the clifftop. The pack had been waiting for them to move from cover or make a sound but their prey had not taken the bait. Frustrated, the pack-leader screamed its anger out to the ocean with a piercing cry that threatened to break human eardrums. Its fury was joined by the entire pack, raging on like a hundred huge sets of fingernails scraping down an ancient blackboard. The screams injected chills into human bodies until they thought the noise would never abate.

Then suddenly, it stopped.

The predators went silent, waiting. They held themselves motionless, eyes scanning the beach below for a while before disappearing as suddenly as before.

Chief Rendall Gleason waited several minutes then lifted his great bulk above the brush cover, "Guess dey gave up. Damn critters should be further south dis time of year where it's warmer."

"They must have missed the memo," sarcastically followed the journalist Margo Stoudt as she stood, rubbed her back then began brushing sand from her knees and acting like the whole encounter was nothing. Only Jankin noticed her hands shaking ever so slightly. She tried to hide her reaction and was doing a good job of it. The captain let out a rare smile. Small and brief though it was, Margo saw it and her face flushed beneath dark brunette hair but she accepted the rare reaction as a silent compliment.

Jeremiah retained his obvious awe, "You told me about the 'Trex' but nothing you said compares to their reality."

His gaze never leaving the nearby cliff tops, "From what I've seen so far, you have a beautiful planet but it's no place for a casual walk in the woods."

Captain Jankin Decatur laughed as he started down a game trail, "Oh come on, Jerry. Where's your pioneering spirit? This is a new world, there are always challenges involved. Usually, the Trex don't bother us."

Launching a sly glance over to the chief, "Particularly when they should have migrated south."

"Let's get going, from here we head north and follow the shoreline to a little cove Chief Rendall and I like to call our own."

The morning was a bad start for what Decatur had planned as a pleasant get-away. They all needed a break, a change of environment from the pressures of their failures this early in the conflict. Most of all, they needed to speak of sensitive issues regarding Marine Captain Jeremiah Jensen of the NAU, and for that, they needed isolation from snoopers and probes. So far, the NAU officer was an ally and a friend. In a few months, or weeks, he might be the enemy. It was Decatur's job to convince the NAU officer to continue to support Kraken even if the colony declared independence.

Most of all, Kraken needed a spy.

ABOUT THE AUTHOR

"Philip Nolen" is the pseudonym for

Terrence E. Zavecz,

a retired Engineer, Scientist and Entrepreneur living in Pennsylvania, USA. These days, he writes primarily in Science Fiction but has great interest in history, diving, travel, and all the sciences.

Terrence Edward Zavecz graduated from Lehigh University with a BS in Engineering Physics.

He holds an MS in Metallurgy and an MS in Materials from the Princeton-Lehigh Master's Program of AT&T.

"Quantum Surge" is his first release under this pseudonym. He has other titles published under the name "Terrence Zavecz"

Sign up for my email list and for more information, excerpts, excluded scenes, and technology discussions visit:

http://PhilipNolen.com

www.ingramcontent.com/pod-product-compliance
Lightning Source LLC
Chambersburg PA
CBHW051524250626

47156CB00001B/223